BOOK 1 OF
THE MILLENNIA SERIES

MAYAN
ATLANTIS RETURNS

NEIL ENOCK

Published by:

iTinkr
STUDIOS

www.itinkr.com

Itinkr Inc.
224 - 2nd Avenue N.E.
Calgary, Alberta, Canada, T2E 0E2
www.itinkr.com

Ordering Information:
Quantity sales. Special discounts are available on quantity purchases by corporations, associations, and others. For details, contact the publisher at the address above.
Orders by bookstores and wholesalers. Please contact iTinkr Inc.:
Tel: (877) 578-9771; Fax: (877) 509-1771 or visit www.itinkr.com.

Printed in Canada

Library and Archives Canada Cataloguing in Publication

Enock, Neil, 1957-, author
        Mayan, Atlantis Returns / Neil Enock.

(Book 1 of The Millenia Series)
ISBN 978-1-988108-01-8 (bound)
ISBN 978-1-988108-03-2 (electronic)

        1. Mainstrean--Fiction. I. Title.

PS8609.N667M39 2016   C813'.6   C2016-905624-4

First Edition

14 13 12 11 10 / 10 9 8 7 6 5 4 3 2 1

To my wife and family:
Suzanne, Anika and Brenan,
whose ongoing support
makes these books possible...

To my mother, who
always said I could do anything...

To my Alpha readers who gave such great
encouragement and feedback...
Allan Stickel
Patrick Nichol
Sarah Burrows
Stacey Kondla

To arguably the most supportive writing
community on the planet. There are
too many to mention them all but they
all seem to show up each year at
When Words Collide!
(You know who you are!)

and

To my readers, fans and supporters at
@NeilEnock and everywhere...
for always letting me know that there
is still more to be written!

- Neil Enock

MINOAN
MAYAN
ATLANTEAN

CHAPTER 1

TIME ZONES

"Dad, you're going to be late!" Tara warned, as she hurried down the damp, worn cobblestone path.

"You know, sometimes you sound just like your mother," Bob answered without looking up as he rushed along.

Always doing three things at once, he was trying to keep a sheaf of papers tucked under one arm while simultaneously dialing his phone with one hand and clinging to an overflowing briefcase with the other.

"Fine. You check then," she scolded him.

Still keying numbers into the phone, Bob glanced up at her while he subconsciously flipped his wrist to check the time. The multiple movements contrived to send the phone flying from his grasp. His attempt to catch it served only to release the papers he'd been carrying and scatter them across the dew-covered grass. They fluttered down and settled all around where his phone had just landed.

"Why does this conference have to be in England?" he sighed, as he bent down to retrieve his phone and papers.

"What's wrong with England?" Tara asked.

He paused for a moment, staring at her as he considered his answer. Long dirty-blonde hair framed an angelic face that makeup was helping her to look far older than anyone's 13 year old daughter had a right to. She'd been acting like a

1

complete know-it-all, but he really didn't want to sour her on England. What was it that Jenn had said? Thirteen going on thirty?

He pointed to his now dripping phone and collection of soggy papers.

"When it's not actually raining, it's foggy or damp, the time zone's difficult to get used to, and it's nowhere near where this conference should have been held."

"Well, that last one's true," Tara agreed.

The faint sound of a voice calling from a distance caught their attention. As Bob looked around for the source, Tara grinned and pointed to the phone in his hand.

"Say Hi to Mom for me! And let's go!"

As she ran ahead, he quickly lifted the phone to his ear but was met only with silence.

"Er, Jenn?" he asked, as he hurried to catch up with Tara.

"Bob," she answered, curtly.

"How's Playa?"

"Asleep."

"What?"

"It's 3:30 in the morning here."

"Oh, uh, sorry!" Bob said, sheepishly.

Bob looked at Tara, covered the microphone and shrugged with an I-told-you-so look.

"Time Zone problem," he explained.

Tara shook her head.

"Hi Mom," she yelled loud enough for Jenn to hear. "Dad's late."

He glared sternly at her.

"I'm not late," he said. "We'll be right on time."

"I hope so," Jenn remarked, with a sigh. "You are speaking at the biggest conference on the Maya since the new discoveries. And well... you need to be on time."

"What do you mean by that?" he asked, although he knew exactly what she meant.

"Look Bob, it doesn't matter what I think. Your theories are controversial. Your book is selling well because it's controversial. Right or wrong you need to be on time or..."

"Or what?" he asked, sharply.

Jenn didn't answer right away.

"I don't want to fight, Bob," she said, sounding quite tired. "Why did you call me?"

He shook his head to clear it as he caught up to Tara again.

"I just wanted to confirm our arrival times with you. But I guess it can wait till morning. Your morning, I mean."

Tara had stopped two steps up a wide staircase. *Lady Margaret Hall* was engraved in the faded stones above the doors of the worn brick building at the top.

Tara leaned over and spoke directly into the phone.

"It can wait, Mom, we're here now. We'll call you later. Bye."

She reached over and disconnected the call before either of her parents could say anything else.

"Tara!"

"We're here, Dad, and almost in time," she said, as she climbed the stairs. "So, can we go in now?"

Bob stuffed the phone into his pocket, and climbing the steps after her, muttered under his breath.

"More like your mother every day."

* * *

Jenn hung up the phone and slid out of bed. She walked over to the window and looked out across the dark empty ocean and the faint lights twinkling from the hotels on

3

Cozumel. She wondered if it was as busy there as it was here in Playa del Carmen. Along the shore in front of her, bright lights from the hotel strip lit up the boardwalk and its still-partying crowds. The Mayan Riviera never really slept but the crowds were certainly thinner than they'd been when she'd been part of them earlier that evening.

She turned away from the window and picked up a book from the table beside the window. She flicked on the light and Bob's brown eyes stared back at her from the cover of *The Impossible Mayan*. For the first time she noticed that his unruly dark brown mop had actually been coaxed into submission for the cover shot. She flipped the book over and skimmed the back cover. The blurb ended with... *by Bob Wallace, Avid archeology geek*.

"Good luck, Bob," she said.

She set the book down and slid back into bed.

CHAPTER 2

Lecture Hall

Great care had been taken to ensure that the brick and mortar rotunda of Oxford's Lady Margaret Hall looked exactly as it would have done when the stones were first placed in 1878. Shafts of light filtered equally through original silvered glass or reproduction stained glass inserts in the arched, paned windows, leaving the hallways leading off the rotunda shrouded in pools of shadow. It was all very ancient, dark and mysterious, except for the banner proclaiming, *The New Maya Conference*, the registration tables, and Mavis, the overly helpful, slightly rotund, and very British conference registrar who was at that moment bearing down on Bob and Tara.

"Dr. Wallace," Mavis began in her very proper British accent. "We were beginning to worry..."

"Mister," Bob interrupted her.

"I beg your pardon?" said Mavis, clearly not used to being cut off.

"He's Mr. Wallace," said Tara, smiling. "My mom is Dr. Wallace."

"Thank you, dear," Mavis replied then turned to Bob. "My apologies, Mr. Wallace."

"Doesn't matter to me," Bob said with a smile, followed by a nod toward the door leading into the main lecture hall. "But some of these folks might take offense. Best just call me Bob."

Mavis looked at him as if seeing him for the first time.

"Well, Bob, you can call me Mavis," she smiled warmly. "You may be right about that offense thing, especially with some of this lot. We do need to get you in there though, otherwise that Dr. Masters will just keep on talking."

"Thank you, Mavis, and it's a pleasure to meet you."

Bob offered her his hand, which she shook firmly.

"And you, and your daughter."

"Tara," she added, helpfully. "But didn't we meet you last night at registration?"

"We were introduced last night, dear," said Mavis, winking. "But I think we've only really met just now."

Mavis guided them past the easel in the hall which displayed the day's lecture schedule then quiet pushed open the heavy oak doors into the main lecture hall. As the schedule had predicted, Dr. Evan Masters was giving his keynote address entitled *Refining the Mayan View*. Up next would be Bob's lecture, named after his book *The Impossible Mayan*.

Mavis ushered them into the back of the almost full lecture hall and silently guided Bob and Tara to their seats at the front as Dr. Masters continued his keynote. Mavis seated them, making a point of catching Evan's eye so that he'd know that Bob and Tara had arrived.

"I do love your book," she whispered to Bob, then winked as she headed back out of the room.

Tara pulled a sketchpad, pens, an iPad and headphones from her backpack, while Bob reorganized his notes.

Evan began winding down his talk and thanking everyone for attending the conference. Always trying for the latest style, he'd let his hair grow longer and added a close-cropped goatee to compliment the tailored suits he was so fond of. Before he left the stage, he offered an introduction of sorts to Bob's upcoming lecture.

"As most of you know, renowned archeologist Dr. Jennifer Wallace and her husband, Bob, had the good fortune to actually be on site in Tulum at the very moment the new ruins were discovered. Her work since then has been truly instrumental in expanding our view of the known Maya."

"Unfortunately Dr. Wallace herself couldn't make it to our conference here today, as she's busy preparing for our site visit in Tulum in a few days. Joining us, however, is her husband, Bob Wallace, who will share his views on the Mayan civilization. You may have heard of his work as he has recently captured the attention of the media with a book on his theories, *The Impossible Mayan*. Bob?"

A polite clapping ringed the room and Bob rose from sorting his notes and waved about the room, catching the attention of a few members of the audience as he quickly scanned the room. His gaze paused when he spotted the enthusiastically clapping, striking young lady who stood out from the sea of mostly grey-haired archeologists like a rare gemstone poking out of a rock wall. Evan chose that moment to continue.

"Mr. Wallace's talk will begin in 15 minutes. Please enjoy the coffee and snacks in the rotunda.

Evan came down from the stage and shook a few hands as he made his way over to the young woman who had caught Bob's eye earlier. Evan chatted with her until she headed out to the rotunda and then made his way over to Bob and Tara.

"Bob!" he said, cheerily, as he approached them. "Good to see you again."

"Evan," Bob replied, somewhat coolly. "Thanks for the introduction."

"No problem, my pleasure. So, this must be your daughter?"

"Yes. Tara, this is Evan Masters."

"Nice to meet you," Tara said. "You used to work with my mom, like a long time ago, right?"

"That's right, we each did a thesis on early Mayan civilization. We were at Tikal in Guatemala at the same time, about sixteen years ago."

"Before Mom met Dad," said Tara.

"That's right," Evan replied, smiling, or was it a smirk? "How is Jennifer?"

"She's fine," said Bob.

"Divorced," Tara added, at the same time.

"Tara!" Bob exclaimed.

His sharp tone cautioned her from saying anything further.

"That's alright," Evan said, graciously. "I already knew. I was sorry to hear about that, Bob."

"It's fine," Bob replied, not really wanting to talk about it, especially with Evan Masters. "It was a few years ago and we're on good terms about all that."

"Well, I've got to get ready for my talk," said Bob.

Evan nodded but didn't take the hint.

"Sure," he said, gesturing to Bob's notes and the book on the table. "So, um, how is she about your book and all this?"

Bob paused, taking a deep breath before he answered.

"We have different opinions about my take on it all," he said, looking Evan in the eyes. "Much like yourself, I'm sure."

Evan shrugged with another smile that resembled a smirk.

"I guess we'll see, in time," he said. "Meanwhile, you seem to have captured the public's attention with your... take on it. That's definitely good for archeology."

8

Bob was about to question Evan's use of the word 'take' when the striking young woman poked her head back into the hall and caught Evan's eye.

"Oh, there's my intern," he said. "I've got to meet up with her. You don't mind if we sit in, do you? She's actually a fan of your book."

"Of course. I'll be starting soon."

Bob watched Evan walk away and shook his head.

"Dad?"

"Tara, why did you even go there? I don't get it?"

"I'm sorry. It's just that they used to be friends and you and mom are split now. And he's kinda cute, so I was thinking.."

Bob burst out laughing, which was probably the last thing she was expecting.

"You were thinking that your mom and Evan..."

He laughed again.

"What?" asked Tara, becoming annoyed.

"They dated," he said, still laughing. "Once. Your mom is a lot smarter than Evan Masters. He didn't like that very much. He doesn't like me very much either."

"I can tell that. Why not though?"

"He likes to be in the spotlight. Ever heard of *The World Expert on Mayan Civilization*?"

"Sure," Tara replied. "That's the name of his page on Facebook."

Bob shook his head again as he gathered his papers together.

"There's a surprise! A self-proclaimed title that he started all by himself. Anyway, I've been getting some attention and that's taking away from him and he doesn't like that one bit."

"Your theories are right, Dad," Tara said, with absolute conviction.

9

He looked at her with unabashed pride.

"I'm sure glad you think so. Maybe we'll be able to convince some of these so-called professionals about that. What do you think?"

She smiled and nodded.

'Maybe Mom one day too."

"We'll see. I'm going to go set up. Hug?"

"Dad, I'm almost 14!" she said, indignantly.

He shrugged and began to pick up his papers, before being ambushed by a giant Tara-hug.

"Thanks, pal," he said, then picked up what he'd need on the stage. As he headed for the steps to the podium on the stage he looked back at Tara.

"I needed that," he smiled.

CHAPTER 3

The Impossible Mayan!

"We've all seen this before," said Bob, as he gestured toward the screen behind him on the stage then turned his attention back to the audience. "I think it's worth watching it again."

The amateur video panned across the ruins of Tulum. Taken from a distance, it panned across most of the prominent features of the ancient site and the throngs of tourists wandering amongst them. There was some idle chatter in the background. It seemed that the person filming was taking a break from the crowds with his family. They'd moved off to have a snack in an out-of-the-way area and had settled down on the stone ring of an old well.

"Dad, what are these scratches?" said a young girl's voice from off-camera.

"What scratches?" the person filming asked.

He was focused on the crowds and carefully kept filming them as he backed up towards his daughter.

"These here..."

The crowd in the lecture hall drew a collective breath. They'd all seen this video before. By now most of the world had.

There was a sharp click of stone against stone, then a grinding, sliding noise. The ground rumbled and the picture shook. There were some screams as the camera fell to the ground then all was still, but for the dust settling in the grass.

Bob froze that frame on the screen.

"Our world changed on that day four years ago," he said. "When young Miss Rayne triggered that hidden mechanism, she and her family dropped through what was always thought to be an abandoned well. They ended up in the stairwell to the catacombs beneath Tulum. Fortunately, they weren't seriously injured, but their holiday plans were drastically altered."

He smiled wryly then included everyone in the room in a sweeping gesture. " As explorers of the Mayan past, our plans were forever changed as well."

"Dr. Jennifer Wallace and I had the good fortune to be on site at Tulum when this happened. We were brought over from the pad we were working on while the rescue was still under way. We had no idea what had happened, but with Jenn having the highest on-site rating of archeological accreditation by the Mexican Government, the local authorities immediately put her in charge of exploring the 'hole', just in case there was anything of historical value down there."

He paused and looked around the room. It was about to become more interesting.

"As we're continuing to learn every day, the chambers, the artwork, and the artifacts are now rewriting much of what is known of the Mayan civilization.

Many, including Dr. Wallace, feel that what lies beneath is, and I'm quoting here, 'a collection of artifacts deliberately left for those that would come after, to find and remember a great people by'."

He held up a copy of his book.

"If you've read my book then you already know that I have a slightly different theory."

The people in the room murmured, as he expected.

"Why?" he asked. "Why is the question we must ask ourselves. Why would a civilization that created soaring stone monuments to gods, and equally huge stone monuments to kings, create a completely different kind of monument like this underground chamber? Why are there images and artifacts in there that simply don't exist in any other Mayan ruins that we've found? Why are there answers here to questions that have remained unanswered elsewhere for centuries?"

The crowd was definitely getting uncomfortable now. Bob looked over at Tara and she gave him an encouraging smile. Why couldn't they see things the way she did?

"Let's talk about the beginning."

He flipped up a slide showing one of the carvings.

"This is the first fresco in what I call the 'Hall of the Journey'. One thing about this fresco is quite clear - the date. It's been agreed for years that the Mayan long count calendar started on an arbitrary date. The first day of that calendar is August 13, 3114 BCE, and written here on the first fresco is the date for day one."

He was getting into his groove now and his obvious enthusiasm was settling some of the fidgeting in the audience.

"Above this date is a pictogram showing a ship arriving and a party of Maya greeting it. Yet as far as we know ships like this didn't exist in this part of the world in 3114. Also curious is a man of obvious importance in the center of the group of people standing on shore. He is referenced only by this unique glyph, never before been seen written in Mayan glyphs. He doesn't appear to be a king or a noble of any kind. Most puzzling of all is this other line of characters carved under each of the frescoes. It's a completely unknown language yet it appears under every fresco and also on many of the objects found in the chambers. This event on this date tells us that the start date is anything but arbitrary."

He paused for effect.

"Let's talk about the end. While still controversial, the two most common theories are that the Maya either simply abandoned their cities and went back to a more rural lifestyle, or were wiped out by diseases brought from Spain. Or perhaps both. Fine. Then what is this?"

He flipped to a slide that showed one of the last frescos in the Hall of the Journey and pointed to the date glyphs.

"The date here is in 1220 AD, which is more than four thousand years after the date depicted on the first fresco. Here are lines of Maya people with goods, getting onto ships that look basically the same as the ones from the first fresco. Here is a different figure, tagged with the same unknown glyph as in the first fresco. This time he is leading them onto the ships. The writing below the Mayan is in the same unknown language as that on the first fresco."

He looked over his audience.

"What's going on here?"

He thought he heard someone snicker.

"These frescos are in almost perfect condition. Carbon dating shows they were all made sequentially between 900 and 1200 BC, the same time that the chambers themselves were created. This had to a part of Mayan society. It would have been impossible to build these caverns and all that they contain without everyone knowing. Yet it was all hidden away, with no other records or indications above ground either at this location or in any other Mayan ruin that's been found."

"This is a museum of the Mayan civilization, created by the Mayan people to record their journey from their first meeting with these unknown 'People of the Sea' and then their eventual departure with those very same people, millennia later."

"Poppycock!"

An older man at the back of the room that Bob didn't recognize snorted, stood up and moved towards the door.

"What other explanation is there?" Bob called to him.

The man ignored him and others also stood up to leave as Bob raised his voice.

"By all means, leave if you must. For those who choose to stay, I'll continue to offer scientific proof and corroborating evidence that will allow you to decide for yourselves as to what may have happened."

He stood silently and watched as the bulk of those in the room, led by the 'respected archeologists', pronounced judgment on his theories by their departure.

Evan Masters seemed to be having a hushed argument with his intern, who had obviously decided to stay. Finally Evan got up, turned and shot what might be considered an apologetic look to Bob before he left the room with the rest of the grey-haired brigade.

When the doors closed, just over a dozen people were left in the room, spread throughout the hall. Bob smiled and sighed.

"Well, why don't you all come up to the front?" he asked. "I'll turn off the microphone and we can chat about these things that may have been."

As people moved to the front of the room, Bob looked at Tara. Her smile let him know that he was still winning the day.

Suddenly the lecture hall door burst open and Mavis pushed in. She looked around the room and then at Bob.

"Oh good," she said, slightly out of breath. "Looks like there's a bit of room, after all. A few of our students would like to sit in, if that's alright?"

"Of course!" Bob replied.

Mavis turned and opened the doors and within a few minutes, the room was completely full, with some people even having to stand. Mavis had seated herself right up near the front.

"Thank you!" said Bob, his voice choked with emotion.

"Pish, posh," said Mavis. "Now, let's hear what you have to say... Bob."

"Well then," said Bob, smiling as he examined the sea of new faces. "Perhaps we'd better start at the beginning, once again!"

CHAPTER 4

Lecture is Over

Bob's lecture had ended and all but a few of the audience had filed out of the hall. Those that remained wanted to shake Bob's hand or ask specific questions. He was asked to sign his book a couple of times and just as he thought everyone had left, he heard a lilting British accent behind him.

"Very thought provoking, Mr. Wallace."

Bob turned with his hand extended then froze. It was Evan Masters' young intern. Beautiful, calm, and cool, the redhead was even more striking up close.

"I'm Emma Smythe," she said, shaking his hand. "I'm a student here at the Oxford School of Archeology and currently Dr. Masters' intern."

"Er, hi Emma," he replied, suddenly feeling slightly uncomfortable. "Call me Bob."

"I just wanted you to know who I am and let you know that I thought you were wonderful," she said, breaking into a radiant smile. "It's so nice to hear opinions other than just the usual stuff."

"Thanks, I appreciate that. I'm not sure Evan, I mean, Dr. Masters would agree."

"History has a way of revealing itself, eventually," she said, cryptically. " Evan may never tell anyone, but I think he appreciates your work more than you might know."

Tara noticed her dad talking to Emma and got up from whatever she was working on. Bob spotted her heading over. He didn't want a repeat of the matchmaking effort he'd seen earlier, even if it was on his behalf.

"Lovely to meet you, Emma," he said, a little too quickly. "Perhaps we'll see you at the reception dinner?"

"I expect so. I'll be at the speaker's table with Evan and you, and...?"

Tara had come up beside them.

"My daughter, Tara," he said. "Tara, this is Dr. Master's intern, Emma Smythe.

"Hi Emma," said Tara, politely, then added, "aren't you glad you stayed?"

Appalled once again at his daughter's brashness, Bob was about to scold her when Emma spoke up.

"I am indeed, Tara, very much so!"

Emma smiled again, unaware of how disconcerting Bob found it.

"You must be very proud of your dad!"

Tara nodded.

"Well then," Bob cut in. "We'll see you tonight."

Emma nodded to them both, turned and left.

Tara spun around.

"Tonight?" she asked.

"Yes, we could be sitting at the same table at dinner."

"That's excellent!" she said, happily and Bob could see the wheels turning.

"What's with all this matchmaking stuff?" he asked.

"What stuff?" replied Tara, innocently.

"Really?" Bob countered. "First your mom and Evan and now you're being just a bit too enthusiastic about Emma."

"Well, she's nice."

"Don't change the subject," he said. "What's going on?"

"Nothing, Dad. Really. But we're sitting with her at dinner? That's good, right?"

"Sure," Bob replied, then added, wryly, "You, me, Emma and Dr. Evan Masters."

"Oh!" said Tara. "I see."

Bob had enough of this game.

"What say we get your stuff together and get going? What were you working on so intently? You hardly looked up."

"I was just drawing," she said, offering him her sketchbook.

Her drawing showed a cathedral-like room bounded by massive columns. On the walls between the pillars multiple works of art were interspersed with Mayan symbols and some of the characters in that unknown script that they'd found under Tulum. A tall slender woman was perched on the edge of one of the many benches in the chamber. Her elegant wrap draped over her shoulders and fell low behind her, revealing a complicated design tattooed on the center of her back.

"Wow!" Bob was amazed at the detail. "I see you even managed to get a mandala in there."

"Whatever!" Tara said, changing the subject. "I think it's kind of like a museum, but maybe more than that. It's newer, I think."

"It's very cool," said Bob, in awe. "What's the style of the building? It's not Mayan."

"Nothing specific," she said, shrugging. "I don't think it's finished yet."

"What made you draw it? I've never seen anything quite like it."

"Well," she said, squirming a little. "When those idiots left..."

"Tara!"

"Sorry, Dad. Anyway, when they left I just wanted to

19

sit them down and explain it to them. I thought it'd be great if they could see the whole story and understand. Then the idea of this room just kinda came to me."

"Well, it's just... wow."

"Thanks! Hey, maybe Mom will know what style it is?"

"Maybe," he agreed.

Jenn really was an incredible archeologist. Something about the style did look familiar, but Bob couldn't place it. If anyone could figure out Tara's inspiration it would be her mother.

* * *

The breakfast bar at the hotel had opened moments after Jenn arrived. She desperately needed a good cup of brewed coffee, not that instant stuff they offered up in the room. She'd only been able to nap on and off since Bob had woken her and had never really got back to sleep.

She was surprised how many people were at the breakfast bar so early. There was quite a line. There were a couple of families with yawning kids whose parents were up early to get to the airport on time, a young couple that wanted to go snorkeling at first light, and a group of three mildly intriguing guys, one of whom was politely but obviously trying hard not to stare at Jenn. Those three were busy discussing what they might do later that day when his friends noticed that he was looking in Jenn's direction. Grinning, they immediately tried to draw her into their conversation.

"What do you think?" the fellow in the muscle shirt asked.

"About what?" Jenn countered.

"Cenote-jungle tour, parasailing or Tulum ruins?" asked his friend in the jaunty hat.

She thought for a moment and then looked the polite fellow in the eye.

"What's your preference?"

"I like the idea of the ruins tour," he replied, smiling at her. "But I heard some of it might be closed off for some archeology thing. What would you choose?"

"Doesn't really matter, does it?" she replied. "I'm not the one going. And yes, part of the ruins are closed off. All the new stuff will be closed for another week or so."

"Well, you could come," muscle shirt said. "I'm sure Terry here would be happy to have you along."

Terry was looking at her more intently now.

"How do you know the ruins are closed?" he asked.

"Terry, is it? I think I saw something in the lobby," she replied, smiling at them. "You boys should do the cenote tour. There's a version of that where they take you through the Coba ruins as well. Have a nice breakfast."

With that casual dismissal she turned away and headed over to the coffee machine.

"Who the heck was that?" she overheard jaunty hat asking the others.

Terry answered, but Jenn was already too far away to make out what he'd said.

CHAPTER 5

Conference Dinner

"Yorkshire Pudding!" Tara said quietly to her dad after Mavis had announced the dinner selections. "What's that, Dad?"

Emma overheard her and answered first.

"Oh, it's lovely. You've never had it?"

Tara shook her head. Bob knew that she could be picky when it came to food.

"It's roast beef," he said, trying to keep it simple.

"Oh," Tara said, disappointed.

""You don't like roast beef?" asked Emma.

"Oh sure," Tara said. "Yorkshire Pudding just sounded more interesting."

"Well, it is!" Emma said, proudly. "It's a traditional English baked pudding that is almost always served with roast beef and gravy. Usually with some nice veggies as well. It's very traditional English fare and this is Oxford, so they'll do it up right."

"That does sound better," Tara nodded.

Bob was staring at his daughter as if he didn't know her.

"What?" she asked him.

"You," he said, "don't like to try new foods."

"That was *so* long ago," she chided. "Try and keep up, Dad."

He was still grappling with that when Evan sat down next to Emma.

"Keep up with what?" asked Evan.

Emma answered before Tara could.

"Tara here was just illustrating how sometimes things can go differently than one expects and you must be flexible enough to try new things."

Bob and Tara looked at each other, both wondering if they were discussing dinner anymore.

"Ah," Evan smiled. "I think Emma is still upset that I left your lecture."

"It was quite rude of you," said Emma.

"Kinda," Tara agreed.

"Look, I didn't lead the charge," said Evan, defending himself. "But I do have a position in the community and when the rest of them got up I felt that I should too."

"It's alright," Bob said. "It's done anyway."

"It's not alright," said Emma, pointing at Evan. "He's a hypocrite. He's got your book."

"What?" said Bob, mildly shocked. "Really?"

Evan rolled his eyes.

"Yes, of course. I have to read everything, even if it's not mainstream."

"And?" said Emma, refusing to let him off the hook.

Evan chose his next words carefully.

"You bring up some points that should be looked at more closely. Some of your arguments could make sense."

"Told you, Dad," said Tara, smiling.

"Exactly," Emma added. "So why not stay, listen, and then ask your questions?"

"It's alright, Emma," said Bob. "He did what most people would do. Not everyone will get behind a crazy idea."

"And you do have a talent for crazy ideas," Evan

added, shrugging at Bob.

"So I've been told," Bob acknowledged. Even Tara nodded in agreement to that.

* * *

The conversation shifted to less controversial topics while both the table and the room had filled up. They'd placed their food orders when their waiter came by and inquired as to their wine selection for dinner. Evan took the lead.

"Well, since we're all apparently having the Yorkshire Pudding, it seems a bottle of red would be appropriate."

"Sorry, but I'll have a glass of white please," said Bob, apologetically

"And Ginger Ale for me," Tara added.

"I'll have some white as well please," said Emma.

She looked directly at Evan as she shuffled her chair a little closer to Bob's. Evan didn't appear to like that, but merely shrugged.

"Anyone else?" he asked.

Either the rest of the table didn't care or didn't want to rock the boat. Emma, on the other hand, did. She charged into the middle one of Bob's key theories.

"So Bob," she asked. "Where do you think the Maya might have gone when they left on those ships?"

Bob squirmed a little in his seat. He really didn't want a scene.

"Well, I'm not sure. There were no further records that we found at Tulum and no evidence of a mass arrival anywhere that would coincide with the date. If the Hall of the Journey is a cultural muséum, as I believe it is, then I think that they'd have found a way to come back to make at least one new entry saying where they'd been.

"Maybe they didn't make it," Tara offered. "And couldn't finish the frescos?"

"It's possible that they never made it to where they were going," Bob agreed. "But it doesn't really explain that last panel without a pictogram apart from the weird date and the writing under it."

"So what's with that date?" Evan asked. "It's not just the standard glyphs for the long count, or the civil calendar."

"Well," said Emma. "It does have most of the same date elements, just out of order and with that odd new symbol."

Tara grabbed her napkin and quickly sketched the symbols in question while the others watched.

"You're very good at that," Emma said. "What do you think it means?"

"How would she know?" Evan asked, pompously.

"Excuse me?" said Bob, taking real offense. "Tara can decipher almost any Mayan glyph."

"I blame my mother," Tara added, with a smile.

Emma laughed and diffused any further argument before it started.

"But I don't know what this one is," Tara admitted.

Evan pointed to some of the first group of symbols.

"Well these are standard Long Count form."

"Yes," Bob agreed. "And these are Calendar Round."

"Yes, of course," Evan said, in a condescending tone. "And they're often used together."

"But not in this context," Bob argued. "There's no basis for this mixed up order."

While the discussion between the two men heated up, the other people at the table looked around to see where dinner might be. Emma and Tara ignored them all and studied the drawing together.

"They're out of order," Emma said.

"What if you reverse them?" Tara asked. "The grouping. Maybe that's what this symbol means."

She pointed to the main unknown symbol. Emma considered that for a moment then grabbed her phone and pulled up the calculator app.

"So I suppose you have some theory concerning how your mysterious 'Sea People' changed the Mayan Calendar system?" said Evan.

He was losing his cool and Bob wasn't far behind him.

"Just because it's different to the usual doesn't make it wrong. "Maybe it is a modified date system. This could be a thousand years ago."

"Or a hundred," Evan pointed out. "You're just guessing."

"Well you're both wrong," said Emma, cutting them off sharply and pointing at Tara's glyphs. "This date is just two days from now!"

CHAPTER 6

Transatlantic

Tara stared out the window as the endless ocean un-folded below them. She was deep in thought and had been since they'd left England. She hadn't slept and had hardly watched either of the movies they'd shown during the flight.

"Looking forward to seeing your mom?" Bob asked, trying to break into her reverie.

"Of course," she answered, without thinking. "It's just..."

The PA system interrupted her.

"Good morning ladies and gentlemen. This is your Captain speaking. We hope you're enjoying your flight with us today but all good things must come to an end. Due to some favorable winds we are coming in a bit early and in just a few minutes we'll begin our descent into Cancun. We'll be coming in from the east over the ocean and once we've completed our final turn will be turning on the seat belt signs. Should you be here for work or a holiday, we wish you continued safe travels."

Tara began unbuckling to leave her seat.

"Excuse me, Dad."

"What's up?"

"I'm going to pop up and see Emma for a sec before we land," she replied. "Just want to ask her something."

Bob unfastened his seat belt and stood up to let her out.

"Not too long. We'll be landing soon," he reminded her. "I heard," she said.

Tara made her way forward. There were quite a few people from the conference on the flight. She waved to some of them that she recognized. They were all headed to the practical portion of the Maya conference, the Tulum visit that her mom was leading.

Emma had her head down and was typing furiously into her laptop. Evan was staring out the window, just as Tara had been earlier.

"Emma?" said Tara.

Startled, Emma looked up.

"Oh, hello Tara. I was catching up on some writing."

"Hi, Tara," Evan said, politely.

"Hello," Tara greeted him then turned her attention back to Emma.

"It's been three days," said Tara. "How come nothing happened on the date shown on the fresco?"

"Well there could be lots of reasons," Emma replied, smiling. "It could be that we got the meaning of that new symbol wrong."

"Or you could have the whole thing wrong," Evan smirked.

Emma glared at him.

"That's a possibility too. As is the possibility that we've got the timing of the dates wrong."

"What does that mean?" Tara asked.

"Some of the dates in the Mayan calendar are calculated at dawn and some are made at sunset. We don't know which are which, so the timing could be off a bit."

"Why don't you ask your dad?" Evan asked, rather condescendingly.

30

Tara glared at him.

"Actually, you should," said Emma. "He's got a different take on things and might know why."

Tara nodded.

"Fine, I'll ask him. I guess I'd better get back to my seat then. I'll see you when we land."

"I'm really looking forward to meeting your mother," Emma said, smiling.

"She's pretty cool," said Tara. "Bye!"

Tara headed back to sit with Bob. As she arrived in the aisle beside him, the plane gently banked into its final turn prior to landing. She clambered over her dad, settled into her seat and buckled in.

"How's Emma?"

A brilliant, soundless flash flared brighter than the sun, pouring through the windows as if someone had shone a giant searchlight at the aircraft from below. As the glow faded back to daylight the monitors in the seat backs winked out, the overhead lighting flickered, and screams rang out as the cabin lighting exploded and showered them all with melted plastic, shards of glass and sparks. Arcing waves of what looked like lightning danced along the inside and outside of the aircraft.

As the sparking abated, the plane's engines began to wind down and the plane shuddered and quite obviously began to lose altitude. The plane was suddenly filled with the sound of several hundred very scared people talking to each other.

"Everyone into your seats and buckle up!" one of the flight attendants yelled, as she ran through the cabin heading for the cockpit.

In the seat across the aisle, the two young children screamed and threw their still-sparking iPad on the floor.

"Dad, what's going on?" said Tara, in alarm.

"I don't know, Tara. Let's just do as they say and we'll see what happens."

Bob was equally scared but he couldn't let her know that. Looking towards the front of the plane he saw the flight attendant open the cockpit door and stagger back as a puff of smoke billowed out. Someone near the front of the plane screamed. The smell of burned flesh filled the cabin. Another flight attendant got up to help and they went into the cockpit together.

Moments later they came out of the cockpit, obviously distressed, debating what they should do. The woman who'd run through the cabin took charge and tried the intercom. It was dead. She held up the dead microphone and called for attention as loudly as she could.

"Excuse me!" she yelled, causing the cabin to go silent. "We've lost power and the copilot is injured. The captain is going to try for a water landing off Cancun."

A loud muffled boom rattled and shook the entire plane, momentarily drowning out her voice. She managed to keep her balance and once the plane had smoothed out, she continued.

"We're flying manually and can land safely, but you need to refresh yourselves with water-landing procedures."

A couple of people angrily shouted questions at her but she simply held up her hand.

"People. This is real!"

She was almost yelling but she ticked off the reality on her fingers as she emphasized her points.

"We *are* going to land in the ocean. This aircraft *has* been designed for it. Everyone will be okay *if* you know what you're doing."

Tara reached for the pamphlet in their seat front as the woman continued.

"I'll keep you updated. Please help anybody around you that needs assistance."

The woman talked quickly to her colleagues and they rushed to see who needed help. She ducked back into the cockpit for a moment then quickly came back out and raised her voice again.

"We have about ten minutes glide time. We'll be lowering our altitude and airspeed all the way down to make the water landing work so don't worry. Stay buckled up unless you're helping someone."

She listened to something yelled to her from the open cabin door behind her.

"We'll be heading for the shallows off Cozumel. Now," she sighed before continuing. "Is there a doctor on board?"

CHAPTER 7

Coastal View

It was another early morning for Jenn but this time she didn't mind at all. She hadn't seen Tara for almost two weeks and since her and Bob had taken the red-eye they'd likely be landing soon. They just had to get through the conference tour then she could take a bit of a break from Mayan stuff and spend some time simply being a mother to her daughter. Jenn hoped that Tara had enjoyed the time with her dad but always worried that because both her parents had careers in archeology, Tara would never have a normal life.

Jenn was deep in thought on her way to the breakfast buffet when a familiar voice stopped her.

"Hey, thanks for the tip."

She turned to see the young man she'd seen at breakfast a couple of days earlier, sitting at the bar in the lounge.

"Terry, isn't it?" she asked. "You guys did the Coba trip?"

"The cenote trip, with a side of Coba and a jungle tour besides," Terry replied, smiling. "You steered us in the right direction."

"Happy to help," she said, looking around at the empty lounge. "Where are the other two amigos?"

He smiled.

"Sleeping it off. It was a late night. You headed for breakfast?"

"I am. And coffee."

"Oh, well then you'll have stay here with me," said Terry, smiling as he beckoned the waiter over. "Paulo here makes the best coffee at the resort."

"Si Señorita," said the friendly bartender. "I make you the best coffee, for sure."

Jenn thought she recognized the distinct features of a Maya native and offered him thanks in his own language.

" Dyos bo'otik, I'll try one."

Paulo dipped his head and smiled his appreciation as she sat down beside Terry.

"So what are you..." they both said in unison then paused and broke out laughing.

"Doing today?" Terry finished off. "We're supposed to be on the early ferry to Cozumel for some scuba diving, but I think that ship has sailed, literally. What about you?"

She wasn't sure how much she wanted to share about herself or what she did, but he had a nice face.

"I'm meeting my ex-husband and my daughter at Tulum a bit later for a dig tour."

"I thought Tulum was closed for some archeological thing?" he said before realization dawned. "A dig tour? You're an archeologist, aren't you?"

"Yes, I'm the one giving the tour," she admitted.

"You're Dr. Wallace?"

"You know?" she said, sounding surprised.

"Not for sure, but after our chat the other day I asked around about Tulum," he said, smiling again. "They said some big-shot lady archeologist was staying here for a Tulum tour.

Everybody knew who it was, but I didn't know that it would be you."

"Big-shot, eh?"

"Their words, not mine. I wouldn't worry, I recognize

admiration when I see it. The locals are impressed by you."

"I do my best to be friendly," she said. "They are their ruins after all, not mine!"

"Well, it's working th... What the... "

Jenn had her back to the windows when she saw a golden glow light up Terry's face. She whirled around to see an intensely bright golden flash out at sea and what could only be described as a wall of lightning bearing down on the resort and the city. As they jumped up, the TV in the lounge sputtered and died, light bulbs sparked and burst as sparks engulfed every electronic device they could see. They all ducked to avoid the spray of electrical energy flying around the room.

It passed quickly and Jenn and Terry poked their heads up at the same time as Paulo did. He was closer to the window than they were.

"Dios mio!" he exclaimed, as he looked out the window.

A huge fog bank had appeared in the channel between Playa and Cozumel. Flashes of golden fire randomly illuminated the fog from within, as it rolled toward them at breakneck speed.

"What is that?" said Jenn, pointing out to sea.

An arc of spray raced ahead of the fog, zipping across the water toward them. In seconds it slammed into the resort with a massive boom, instantly shattering every pane of glass that faced the ocean. The flying and falling glass forced them back under cover again.

"Sonic boom," Terry yelled.

The sound had only lasted for a millisecond, but the boom's echoes merged with the continual crashing of flying glass inside the room then continued as the shattered windows from floor after floor fell to the ground outside. As the worst of the noise diminished, Jenn, Terry and Paulo peeked out from behind the table. They moved as close to the window as they dared, until they could see portions of the city below. Every building facing the water had been affected and waves of shattered glass were still falling from some of the taller towers.

Remnants of the lightning still sparked across the streets and vehicles had been wildly affected by the electrical storm. Some had spun out of control, while others had run into buildings or crashed into each other. The luckier vehicles had simply rolled to a stop. Several had burst into flames from the sparks and people were running around in panic, attempting to avoid the vehicles, falling glass, fires, and the noise.

As Jenn and the others took it all in, the wave of fog came ashore and quickly obscured their view, muffling the sounds of mayhem and casting an eerie pall over the area. With no glass to act as a barrier, the fog rolled right into the lounge, bringing with it the odd scent of heated steam mixed with sea spray.

Terry and Jenn looked at each other then out to sea again, but the fog now shrouded everything.

"What on Earth is going on?" Jenn asked.

CHAPTER 8

World View

"Admiral, I have a Priority One from General Aspinal for the Fleet Commander," the *Excelsior's* Com officer handed the headset to the stocky, white-haired gentleman with the five stars on his collar.

The admiral nodded and the General's dark eyes filled the main view screen in the command center of the big ship.

"Cecila, what can the 4th Fleet do for Atlantic Command today?" Admiral Lindquist asked his good friend.

He may have ignored the implied formality but General Aspinal was all business.

"New orders are coming through now, Admiral Lindquist. The Gulf exercises are cancelled. You are to take command of the Carrier *Excelsior* and move it and the entire 4th fleet out of the Gulf and head directly to the Playa del Carmen area, best speed, Condition Red. I repeat, Condition Red."

As she spoke, the Com officer raced over with the printed orders that had just come in. Lindquist glanced at the sheet and turned to the *Excelsior's* captain.

"Captain, signal the fleet. Exercises are over. We've been advanced to active duty. Set course for Playa Del Carmen, best speed, Condition Red. Stand by for further orders."

The captain nodded and turned to pass on his orders. As the bridge lights turned red and the klaxons began blaring their warnings the admiral turned to watch the screens on the bridge as all fourteen ships began a graceful if hurried, starboard turn.

"Alright, General, we're on our way. What's this all about?"

"Get to your briefing room and I'll tell you what we know," she replied. "Jim, what have you got there that's fast, really fast?"

He looked at her sharply in the monitor. She looked worried and her rumpled dark hair made her appear disheveled. He'd never heard her so stressed.

"The *Xavier* can pull five to ten knots better than anything else in the 4th, but it's Littoral Class, not much in a fight."

"Send them on ahead, top speed. We need eyes on that area ASAP."

"Eyes on?" he said. "Lets get a plane in the air and..."

"Nothing airborne, Jim," she insisted. "There's been a massive EMP event off the coast near Playa."

His blood ran cold.

"A nuke?"

"No, or at least they don't think so. Get that ship moving then get yourself to the briefing room."

She signed off.

"Com," he barked. "Get me the Captain of the *Xavier*."

* * *

Fifteen minutes later Lindquist had the captains of the 4th fleet's largest ships in the briefing room, along with the captains of the *Xavier* and most of the smaller ships attending over speakerphone. The monitor feeds were being supplied by Atlantic Command, which was on open audio feed as well.

Lindquist looked around the room and the Com officer gave him the thumbs up. The admiral opened the floor to begin the briefing.

"Ladies and gentlemen, General Aspinal, NORAD / Atlantic Fleet Command, will be briefing you."

"Thank you, Admiral. About 25 minutes ago all contact was lost with Playa del Carmen, Cancun, and the surrounding area. We have a Geosat in that area. This is what it recorded."

The area looked like any other tropical paradise from orbit. White beaches, blue / green waters, a cloudless sky, and long shadows from the early morning sun. Suddenly a bright golden-white flash appeared from nowhere in the middle of the ocean between Cozumel and Playa del Carmen. The flash exploded outward in a circle of golden light from its point of origin. It raced outward and within seconds overloaded the satellite's sensors. The screen became a smudge of white light.

"We'll speed this up for a few minutes," said General Aspinal.

As the sensors slowly auto-corrected for the overload, the golden-white light seemed to diminish in intensity. Once the picture improved further, everyone present could see that a cloud had formed over the initial area and was spreading outward in all directions, just like the circle of light had done, but much slower.

"I'm switching to a live feed now and you can see that the cloud has engulfed an area about 100km across and is continuing to grow," Aspinal explained. "Our people tell me that it's almost certain that some sort of EMP pulse caused this and that it's unlikely to have been a nuclear blast."

"Why do they think that?" said Lindquist.

"The buildings," a voice said over the conference line.

"Pardon me?" asked Lindquist.

"The buildings were still standing before the cloud covered them?" the voice added, hesitantly.

"That's correct," said Aspinal. "Even a small atomic blast at that range would have leveled the city, but there was no apparent damage from an explosion. The fleet's mission is to reconnoiter and report. We need eyes on the area. All communications are down, which would be consistent with an electromagnetic event."

"What about the Mexican government?" asked one of the captains.

"We have been informally asked to assist by the Mexican government," Lindquist explained. "They have two minor naval stations and a ship under that cloud and they can't raise any of them. Everything's down - Internet, radio, wireless. Very little can be shielded from an EMP event of this scale."

The hesitant voice came back on the line.

"We should get hardcopy on the Mexican request for assistance, before we enter the blackout zone."

Admiral Lindquist looked up at that comment.

"Yes we should as soon as it's formalized. Who's speaking?"

"Lieutenant Commander Ryan Johnson, sir, XO on the *Xavier*."

"Where's your captain?" Lindquist asked.

"Asleep sir, I'm in command right now."

"What!" Aspinal cut in,

"Sorry, sir, er ma'am, He was on night maneuvers all night and it's my watch. I was going to wake him but it'll be a few hours until we arrive and he should be rested for whatever we find when we get there."

Admiral Lindquist smiled.

"That'll be fine, Lieutenant Commander. General, what else do you have for us?"

"We have no idea what we're dealing with or what caused it. It's not a nuke and likely not an asteroid or a missile as there was no trajectory track on the satellite feed or on any early warning systems. You're the closest ships to the area so you're going in first. The Mexican government is diverting a ship from a southern patrol and you'll rendezvous with them when they get there. We're reviewing the satellite feeds for more details and will update you with any findings. Just a sec."

She paused as she received new information in her earpiece.

"They're telling me now that the satellite recording shows an aircraft crash landing at the Cancun airport just before the clouds rolled in."

She sighed, grimly.

"Navcon also reports there were four commercial aircraft in the area. That means we're also looking for three other missing airliners as well. Atlantic Command out."

Admiral Lindquist looked around the room.

"You heard the General, we're flying blind, so let's prepare for anything. We're about 150 Nautical Miles, we can push it and be there in about five hours. Get back to your ships, brief your people. Anyone that has any ideas as to what this might be, share 'em! Dismissed!"

"Lieutenant Commander Johnson?"

"Yes, sir?"

"You're going to get there a little bit before us, maybe 10 to 20 minutes sooner."

"Yes, sir?"

"You know what an EMP pulse can do?"

"Yes sir, but it shouldn't affect us, unless it pulses again. Electronics that were off during the initial pulse should be able to be activated if power is available. Replacement parts may be able to fix some of what was damaged.

That's not what worries me, sir."

"You're wondering what caused it?"

"Yes, sir."

"As are we all, Johnson, as are we all. Lindquist out.

CHAPTER 9

In the Drink

"Hello? Sir? Are you with us?" the familiar voice sounded far away.

"Dad!" Tara added from beside him.

"I'm okay, I'm okay," Bob said as he opened his eyes. "Are we...?"

"We're down, sir."

It was the flight attendant that had taken charge. She had been leaning over and trying to roust him. He thought he could make out Slavic features in her bone structure. Some of her blonde hair had fallen out of her ponytail and was dangling in his face.

"Perfect water landing, just a bit bumpy, but we've got to go now. Are you okay?"

"I'm fine," he replied, mumbling slightly.

"He bumped his head," said Tara.

"Can you help him up?" asked the flight attendant.

"Yes, we'll be okay."

"Good girl. What's your name?"

"Tara."

"Okay, Tara, can you get him into the raft?"

Tara nodded and the flight attendant smiled at her.

"I'm Gloria," she said, as she moved off to assist others. "Just give me a yell if you need help."

"What happened?" Bob asked, as Tara pushed him out into the aisle and toward the emergency exit.

"We landed in the water. You bumped your head pretty hard."

That's why he was feeling so groggy! He let Tara ease him towards the emergency exit, where many of the passengers had already evacuated into a collection of inflatable rafts at the bottom of the front and rear exit slides. The sea was calm and a thick fog hung over everything. The raft currently at the bottom of the slide had only a couple of people in it. Tara pushed at Bob to go but just as he was about to jump on the slide he remembered Emma and glanced around. He saw Evan trying to pry part of a collapsed overhead luggage rack off from the seat where Emma had been sitting.

"Emma!" he called, as Tara shoved him down the slide.

"I'll help them," Tara shouted after him as she turned back into the plane.

Bob slid down into the hands of other passengers and then turned to look at the top of the slide. Scarcely a minute later, Tara slid down to join him.

"What? Where's…"

"Help me catch her!"

Bob looked up. Evan was holding Emma at the top of the slide waiting for them. He moved over beside Tara and nodded. Evan let her go and she slid limply down the slide.

They pulled the unconscious Emma off the slide and laid her down in the raft. Blood covered her face but Bob couldn't see an open wound anywhere. Seconds later Evan joined them.

"Is she okay?" he asked, obviously worried. "I couldn't get her out."

Bob was still looking for the source of Emma's bleeding.

"All I can see is a small cut on her forehead," he said.

"I'm not sure where all this blood is coming from."

"That's probably it," Tara said. "Head wounds can bleed a lot."

Bob and Evan both looked at her quizzically.

"Health class," she said, shrugging.

One of the other passengers passed them a first aid kit. Bob nodded thanks, popped the kit open, grabbed some gauze and started cleaning Emma's cut. Evan dabbed the blood from Emma's face with some tissues while Tara stared at the wall of fog surrounding them.

A yell from above signified another arrival, so Evan and Tara moved over to help a few more people complete their slide.

"How long will the plane stay afloat?" Tara asked.

"No idea," Bob replied, absently.

He'd finishing bandaging Emma's cut and was busy packing up the first aid kit when her eyes flicked open.

"Thanks for helping me get her out," Evan said to Tara. "I really needed that extra set of hands."

Emma coughed slightly and they all looked over at her.

"Yes, thanks!" she said softly.

Evan jumped up and crossed the raft to be beside her, while Bob looked up and gave Emma a smile.

"You're back."

"Yes, I think so," Emma said. "Where are we?"

Before anyone could answer, Gloria called down from the aircraft's doorway.

"Tara, could your dad inflate another raft if I sent it down?"

"Bob!" he yelled back to Gloria. "I'm Bob. Send it down."

Gloria sent a package down the slide.

"Pull the yellow cord as you toss it over. It's a small covered raft. Can you lash it to ours?"

Bob nodded, then did as Gloria had asked as soon as the new raft had inflated. Gloria looked down from the top of the slide.

"I'm sorry, but I have to send a couple of bodies down and I'll need help at your end," she said grimly. "Can you set the slide into the small raft for them, then move it back over to our raft?"

Bob looked at Tara and swallowed hard.

"I'll hop over and bring them in," he said, quietly. "Can you help me move the slide back when we're done?"

Tara just nodded. She didn't know what else to say.

* * *

Bob helped get the two unfortunate casualties into the small raft and then zipped up the cover. Tara and Evan pulled the slide back over to receive another injured person into their raft. It was the pilot, who'd been badly burned in the accident. He had somehow managed to land the plane and had even helped Gloria with the evacuation. Gloria was the last person down the slide.

"Well, that part's done," she said, heaving a sigh of relief. "Now we wait."

"Wait?" Tara asked.

"For rescue," said Emma.

The pilot coughed, trying to speak. Gloria offered him some water.

"Sorry," he said, in a raspy Scottish accent. "It could be a while. That was an EMP pulse that hit us."

"What does that mean?" Evan asked.

"Fries active electronics," the pilot replied. "Are the beacons going, Gloria?"

Each of the rafts had a flat panel with a couple of

48

gauges and an orange light sticking up that was most definitely not flashing. Gloria looked around. None of the lights were flashing on any of the rafts.

"No," she said, quietly.

"Hmmm," the pilot gasped, his eyes were glazed. "Cell phones?"

"What?" Evan asked.

The pilot coughed again, so Gloria took a guess.

"If a cell phone was fully turned off, not just in airplane mode, it might still work?"

The pilot nodded. Everyone in the raft took out their cell phones but they were all completely dead, except one that made everyone jump when it beeped as it powered up.

"Sorry," Bob said. "Mine was turned off, but I've got no signal."

Gloria turned to the pilot.

"What should we..."

She trailed off when she noticed that the pilot was no longer conscious.

"Is he?" Tara asked, alarmed. Then smiled as she noticed his chest gently moving up and down. "Never mind."

"So now we wait," said Bob.

CHAPTER 10

Shell Shock·

Sparks flying from the remnants of a couple of light bulbs alerted them to the fact that the hotel's backup generator had been brought on line. Paulo tried in vain to get the large screen TV working again then gave up and moved on to one of the smaller ones that had been powered off before the lightning storm had hit. The power button lit up right away, but although he flicked from one channel to another he found nothing but static.

"Is there a local station?" Terry asked him, then jumped nervously as another sheet of broken glass from an upper floor crashed down on the patio outside.

"That's likely to continue for a while," Jenn said. "Lets stay away from the windows."

Outside, the fog was lifting slightly or maybe just burning off. It had at least thinned enough that they could see shadows of people running with fire extinguishers to put out the flames in one of the burning cars.

"It's so quiet everywhere," Jenn said. "It's eerie."

"I wonder..."

Terry pulled his cell phone out of his pocket but it didn't even power up.

"Nada," Paulo said, pointing at the continuing static on the television screen.

"Figures," said Terry, with a shrug.

Together with Jenn they looked out the window at the parts of the city that were slowly becoming visible. The fog had cleared enough for them to see more people emerging from their vehicles, businesses, and even a few tourists venturing out onto their hotel room balconies. Still the silence and the fog permeated everything, creating a surreal environment that would have caused a Hollywood director to squeal in delight.

Suddenly, the long slow wail of a hand-cranked siren sliced through the silence.

"That's an air raid siren?" asked Jenn.

"No, Señorita," Paulo replied, looking anxiously out toward the ocean "Tsunami!"

"My God!" Terry exclaimed. "What next?".

They all moved around to where they could get a better view of the ocean. The fog was completely blocking anything far out to sea, but they could faintly see the beach and some of the boats moored offshore. As they watched, a large swell lifted the boats, inundating those that were on short anchors and easily picking up the others and carrying them towards the beach.

All the deck chairs lining the beach were empty. Anyone that had been down there earlier had scrambled inside after the sonic boom hit and the fog rolled in. The swell quickly swamped the beach, dropped some of the boats it had picked up, then continued inland, right into the resort's pool area.

People were running and screaming in the hotel lobby below and in the adjoining streets and buildings. There was nothing Jenn and the others could do but watch. People rushed up from the lobby onto the hotel's second floor and many came into the lounge.

"Keep away from the windows," Terry shouted to one family that looked as if they were heading out to the patio.

He pointed to the piles of shattered glass and the parents waved their thanks and pulled their kids back.

Within minutes, the ocean had extended itself to become a solid sheet of water that reached about halfway up the first floor of every building they could see throughout the resort and nearby city. The second floor of the hotel was now packed and Paulo was being run off his feet getting drinks for the crowd of scared and distressed people.

Jenn and Terry decided that they might as well lend a hand.

"What else can go wrong?" Terry said, under his breath.

"Do not say that!" Jenn snapped. "My daughter's due to arrive in Cancun anytime now."

"Sorry!" he apologized, "but I wouldn't worry. Cancun is forty miles away. This stuff shouldn't reach there."

They busied themselves for a while serving drinks to the people in the lounge until some of the hotel staff arrived and took over. When Jenn and Terry returned to the window, water lines could already be seen on the surrounding buildings. It seemed that the flow had crested and might already have reversed.

The static on the TV screen shimmered slightly then cleared to reveal a harried television presenter silently reading from a collection of papers that he held in his hand.

"Paulo!" Terry shouted.

When Paulo looked up from where he was standing behind the bar, Terry pointed to the TV. Paulo nodded and held up the controller to turn up the volume. Everyone in the lounge turned to look at the TV and the room fell silent.

"...activate an old broadcasting system, as all our regular systems have been knocked out. To repeat, Playa Del Carmen has been hit by a series of events that all seem to have been initiated by... something... out at sea. An electrical storm has damaged all electronics that were turned on at the time of the storm. Devices that were not powered up when the storm hit seem to be working normally."

"My phone was off!" Jenn exclaimed.

She quickly powered it up. The familiar startup sound caused a few heads to turn, as the announcer continued.

"...telephone systems, electricity, internet cabling and wireless are all down. Cellular towers are always active and thus far all appear to have been damaged. Hopefully they will have some replacement parts and can get their systems up again with those. We're not in touch with the authorities yet, but will..."

The announcer abruptly stopped talking and listened to someone speaking to him off screen. He came back on with a new sense of urgency.

"The hotel zone has just been hit with a tsunami!" he said when he resumed speaking.

"Tell us something we don't know," Terry muttered.

"... no details but we're working to get a video feed from our rooftop. We have to move the older cameras that weren't in the studio so this is taking longer than usual. Our switching and editing equipment is offline so these will all be raw feeds when we get them."

Someone handed him a sheet of paper, which the announcer quickly scanned.

"Our roof camera is working but we can only see fog."

The TV image switched to show the fog bank enveloping the city but rising as it moved out to sea.

"They tell me that the fog is lifting, so we should be able to get a better picture soon. We'll continue to broadcast with updates as they become available. To recap, a sudden electrical storm has virtually disabled Playa Del Carmen and left us out of touch with just about everywhere, and now it looks like a tsunami has impacted the hotel zone. Electronic equipment..."

"Well, that wasn't very helpful," Terry said, ignoring the repeated information.

"No, but at least someone's talking about it," said Jenn.

She looked at her phone then back at Terry. "No signal. Damn you!"

"What?" Terry asked.

"All I can think of now is, what else can go wrong?" said Jenn.

CHAPTER 11

En Route

Waking to the throb of the *Xavier's* engines laboring at maximum had done nothing to improve Captain Mulholland's disposition, as he seemed to be living up to his 'fighting Irish' heritage and his dark red hair color. This fact was made crystal clear to Lieutenant Commander Johnson as he was being dressed down for not waking his captain right away. Before Johnson could offer an explanation or relay his orders, the captain held up his hand to interrupt as they turned onto the bridge.

"Where the hell are we and what's the hurry?" he demanded.

"En-route to Playa Del Carmen, Mexico sir," replied the Nav.

"Why are we going to Mexico?" asked Mulholland.

"Orders, sir, you need to con-fab with Lieutenant Commander Johnson," the Nav said carefully.

"So that's how it's going to be?" said Mulholland, sternly. "Ops, reduce speed to fleet."

He turned back to Johnson, studying the clean-cut African American as if figuring out what to do with him.

"In my ready room."

"Uh, Captain?" Nav interrupted. "Fleet Command and Atlantic Command have ordered us at top speed to Playa del Carmen."

"They have, have they? Fine. Carry on then."

He turned expectantly to Johnson, who moved as quickly as he could without running.

After the ready room door closed the captain wasted no time.

"You don't like me very much, do you Johnson?" he asked.

"Sir?" Johnson replied, confused. "I don't think that's relevant, sir."

"No?"

"No, sir, we're on red alert heading into a potentially hot situation."

"It's a drill, Lieutenant Commander " Mulholland assured him.

"No sir, Gulf exercises were cancelled. We're on active duty and this is Condition Red. I was trying to tell you.

"Why didn't you wake me?" Mulholland asked.

"With respect sir, protocol is to have the most qualified officer prepped and on deck at destination."

The captain thought for a moment.

"Then it seems I may owe you an apology Lieutenant Commander."

"Not necessary, sir, but we need to get you up to speed, stat."

"Let's have it."

* * *

As they returned to the bridge, Lieutenant Commander Baird was arriving to relieve Johnson.

Johnson?" Mulholland asked. "How long was your watch?"

"Short sir, just three hours."

"Nav, what's our ETA to Playa del Carmen?"

"Just under two hours, sir."

" Lieutenant Commander Baird, I'm keeping Johnson active as XO," said Mulholland. "Stay hot in ops, we may need you there."

"Yes, sir," Baird replied then headed over to ops.

"I trust you can handle XO for a few more hours?" the captain asked Johnson.

"Yes, sir!" he replied, smiling. "Com, can you raise Fleet for an update?"

"Roger that, sir."

'Thank you, sir," said Johnson.

"Well, you started it, so you may as well see what's going on," said Mulholland, with a grim smile.

"Fleet and Atlantic Command on the horn, sir," Com reported.

"Bridge screen," said Johnson.

"Report?" said Admiral Lindquist as his face filled the screen.

"Making best speed to Playa del Carmen, sir," Mulholland replied. "ETA just under two hours."

"Captain Mulholland, we have Atlantic Command on the line," Lindquist announced. "Screens 2 and 3 please."

"Com," said Mulholland.

"Screens 2 and 3, aye sir," he replied, nodding as bridge screens 2 and 3 linked to Atlantic Command's feeds.

"General Aspinal," Mulholland acknowledged.

"Satellite imaging, infrared and our experts all tell us that we're dealing with an EMP event, but some things are not adding up. In the middle of what appears to be a 200-kilometer EMP blast zone we have an inexplicable fog bank that we can't see through. The fog that rolled inland from the initial event is beginning to dissipate and it's dispersed enough so that we can now see there's been localized flooding in Playa Del Carmen. Less so to the south and north, but there's also been some minor flooding in Cancun. It looks to have been a fairly mild and slow moving tsunami, again centered in the very region we can't yet see into. There are no signs of structural damage that would indicate a detonation of any kind. All telecom, wireless, and electrical is dark, although we've detected a few heat signatures that are assumed to be generators coming online."

She turned to the monitor.

"In short, we have no definitive idea what's going on down there yet. The president is looking for answers that we can't give him. So is the Mexican president and the press over most of the planet. Admiral, you have a plan?"

"Yes, General," Lindquist answered. "We need the *Xavier* to proceed directly to the center of the disturbance off Playa del Carmen. You will not be stopping to render aid or assistance or to reconnoiter at Cancun, no matter what you run into. The fleet is sailing at full steam behind you and we'll dispatch aid as needed in your wake. We'll detach one ship from the fleet to the Mexican Navy docks near Cancun and send another into Cancun directly for communication and liaison efforts. The rest of the fleet will back you up."

"We're not to survey Cancun at all, sir?" Mulholland asked.

"Survey all you can, Captain, and report back, but do not stop or slow down. We need to know what's causing all this."

"Yes sir, Johnson passed on that there was to be no aerial surveillance. Is that still in effect? Can we launch the Blackhawks for a closer look?"

"Absolutely not," said Aspinal. "Until we know what's in there, we're not risking any personnel to a further potential

EMP event of this size. If the fog lifts and we get some answers, that could change, so have them on standby."

"Weapons systems?" Lindquist queried.

"Armed and ready, sir," replied Mulholland. "We'll be ready for whatever's there."

The admiral finished up what she had to say.

"We'll continue satellite analysis at this end and pass on updates and anything else we find. I'll have them leave the monitors streaming a live feed so that you can continue preparing. These two hours will pass very quickly, so let's find out everything we can before we get there."

"Yes, General," said Mulholland.

After they'd signed off, Captain Mulholland turned to his bridge crew.

"Ladies and gentlemen, the finest minds in the Navy are working on this, but we're going to be their eyes and ears when we get there."

He looked around at each member in turn.

"Let's get to work. What are we missing here?"

CHAPTER 12

Rescued?

The long low swells of the ocean were rocking some of the survivors to sleep while sending others dashing to the edge of their rafts. Apart from the sound of occasional retching there was no noise at all. No waves smashing into the still-floating fuselage, no foaming whitecaps in the distance, or even the sound of the slap of small waves against the side of the rafts. The water was completely still.

"Evan?" Bob asked. "Have you ever seen waters this calm in the middle of the ocean?"

"I hadn't though about it, Evan replied, looking around. "It is very still. The fog is thinning a little so maybe things will change."

"Shhh!" said Tara, her finger to her lips.

"What?" Bob asked.

"Quiet!" she listening intently. "Did you hear that?"

"No," said Evan.

Bob and Emma both shook their heads. Not even a whisper of the wind stirred the thinning fog. They both listened and held their breath before the faintest sound of a far away horn drifted through the air around them.

"There!" Tara said. "Did you hear it that time?"

"I did," replied Gloria, moving over to the raft's equipment box.

"Me too," Emma added quietly, still a little shaky.

"Maybe," said Bob.

Evan simply shrugged. It was very quiet except for Gloria rummaging around in the equipment box. Then everyone in the rafts heard it. A long low horn that might have been a foghorn if not for the lyrical sub tones.

"Music to my ears!" Bob exclaimed.

Cheers erupted from the whole flotilla and Gloria waved her arms to quiet everyone.

"Cover your ears!" Gloria yelled.

She let loose a short, loud blast on the small air horn she'd pulled from the supply box.

There was an immediate reply from the other horn and this time they could determine which direction it was coming from. Gloria blasted the air horn again before reaching back into the equipment box. She pulled out a flare gun and as the response to her second horn blast faded, she shot a flare high into the air.

Minutes later the horn sounded again through the fog with three short bursts.

"They see us," Gloria said.

She fired off two quick blasts of the air horn then, finally allowing her relief to show, sobbed and sat down as everyone on the rafts broke into cheers again.

"Nicely done," said Bob. "Nicely done."

Everyone in the rafts listened intently for the sounds of engines but they heard nothing. After a few minutes, Gloria tentatively raised the air horn again but before she could sound it, the incoming horn blared a short tone, very near them now. All eyes turned toward the sound as Gloria replied with the air horn.

"Haua!" a lone, strong voice boomed through the fog.

"Haua!" dozens of voices echoed.

64

Gloria stood up and yelled.

"Hello?"

There was no response. Then a shadow appeared through a patch in the fog bank. A long wooden prow pushed through the shadow, quickly followed by the front of a low wooden ship. Water churned on both sides of the vessel as dozens of oars reached down from their pivots and slowed the ship's forward progress.

"Haua!" the voice chanted again.

The oars were raised in unison then plunged into the water to slow the ship further. A cloth canopy above the foredeck came into view as furled sails emerged through the fog, revealing one, two, then three masts. Identical ships were now emerging on either side of the first one, all of them plunging their oars into the water in unison as the boats slowed to avoid colliding with the rafts and the plane.

"What the heck?" said Bob.

As grateful as he was to be rescued, these weren't like any boats that he'd ever seen before.

"Dad?" said Tara, anxiously.

He motioned for her to be quiet but gave her an encouraging smile.

The celebrations on the other rafts ceased as the rest of the survivors looked over the ships that had come to save them.

Bob and Evan were speechless and apparently no one else on their raft could think of anything to say either.

Gloria had remained standing and Evan quickly stood up beside her, followed by Bob. The first ship had slowed down and was gliding to a stop directly in front of them. The other two boats had already stopped, flanking the lead ship with their oars poised in the air. The scene reminded Bob of something he'd read about military strategy long ago.

A tall white robed figure strode onto to the forecastle

of the ship. Insignia in gold on leather strapping had Bob pegging him as a Greek general, if not for the dark blonde locks. Maybe this was a re-creation ship of some sort? The 'general' was shortly flanked by two others, that behaved as if they were two officers flanking their captain, but they were dressed in different attire that anyone would find strange and ancient, unless they happened to be scholars in…

"They're Maya!" Bob whispered urgently to Evan, who ignored him.

"Well, we are off the shores of the Yucatan," Gloria reminded him.

"Ancient Maya," Bob whispered. "What those men are wearing can only be found in a museum. And the boats…"

"Not Mayan," said Evan, flatly. "and look at the big guy."

"No, but they're… well, not from around here!" said Bob struggling to find the right words. "Something isn't right here."

The white robed man that appeared to be the captain raised his hand.

"Kyob'du niekal?" he called down to them.

The language and accent were both completely unintelligible to Bob. When the man received no response other than puzzled looks from the people in the raft, he tried something else.

"Ba'ax ka wa'alik?"

"Aha!" Evan said.

"I told you they were Mayan," added Bob, keeping his voice low.

He turned to Gloria.

"That's as close as they get to saying hello."

"Well, what do we say to them?" she asked.

"Of course it's Mayan," said Evan.

Recognizing an opportunity to be the hero, he turned

to address the captain on the ship.

"Hach ki'imak in wo'ol in kaholtikech," Evan said, haltingly.

Bob translated for Gloria and everyone else on the raft.

"That means *very happy to meet you.*"

The captain overheard Bob translating into English. He wore a curious expression as he looked directly at Bob.

"Bix yanikech?" the captain asked Evan.

"That means *how are you?*" said Bob, translating again.

"Umm," said Evan, unsure of what to say next.

"Tin kaaxtik áantik," Bob whispered urgently to him.

Bob turned to the others in the raft.

"I said that we're *looking for help.*"

"Tin kaaxtik áantik!" Evan repeated to the captain.

The captain nodded then gestured to his officers who left to call the captains of the other ships. While the first ship maneuvered to better allow Bob and his fellow survivors to board, the other two ships moved forward to load people from the other rafts. Hardly another word was spoken as the crews helped the survivors onto their ships and over to the rows of seats under the canopy. There was an awkward moment when the ship's crew members wanted to bring the two casualties on board, but Bob convinced them, with gestures, to hook a line to the back of the ship and tow that raft behind them.

After all the survivors were on board the wooden ships, their rescuers pointed at the listing aircraft. They seemed to be asking about the plane, but neither Bob nor Evan knew enough Mayan to be able to answer them. They both shrugged and shook their heads. That seemed to be enough for the captain. He barked an order, multiple oars hit the water and the ships were underway.

The captain soon joined Bob and the others under the canopy and nodded kindly to them. He seemed content to sit and study them as the ship rowed through the fog in silence. Evan thought he'd try and learn about their destination and asked the captain where they were from.

"Tux a kraal?" Evan asked.

The captain thought for moment then stood and opened his arms wide, encompassing everything in front of them.

"In Kajalé..." the captain started to say.

A shout from the stern interrupted him. Rescuers and survivors all looked behind them and watched as the empty plane slowly and quietly slipped beneath the waves.

CHAPTER 13

Maybe Not

The ships sliced swiftly through the water, moving far faster than seemed possible for boats powered only by oars. Small shudders rocked the hull as they plowed through wavelets that had been stirred into existence by a growing breeze. The ocean seemed to be waking as the fog thinned, becoming less oppressive as brighter patches hinted at the possibility of a sunny day ahead.

A raised voice drew the survivors attention aft. After the plane had disappeared under the water, the captain had retreated to a raised area under the canopy and had since been engrossed in an occasionally animated conversation with several others gathered around a wide table. He obviously didn't agree with what he was hearing. The man that was trying to explain appeared to be the navigator. He held up what looked like a map and shook it at the captain. The captain noticed Evan and Bob looking at him, then shrugged off his navigator and beckoned Evan over.

Evan stood up to join them and Bob decided that he'd better go over as well. Evan glared at him.

"I think he just wanted me," Evan said, arrogantly.

"Then who's going to translate when you run out of Mayan?" Bob asked.

He waited as Evan thought about it for a moment then

grudgingly beckoned for Bob to accompany him.

Bob glanced back to check on Tara. She was sitting beside Emma who was still lying down resting. They were deep in conversation and didn't even notice that Bob and Evan were leaving.

When they arrived at the table, the navigator unfurled the map and placed bronze weights at the corners to hold it down. The outline was clearly a map of the Yucatan, but it was hand drawn and annotated with the same unknown language that Evan and Bob were familiar with from the ruins that had recently been found under Tulum. Maya hieroglyphics accompanied the unknown language. Clearly marked on the map were the locations of what appeared to be every known Mayan archeological site, but even more intriguing to Bob were several other locations that he didn't recognize as ruin sites.

"Tu'ux?" the captain asked them.

"Where?" Bob whispered, under his breath, when Evan looked confused.

"I know he *where*," Evan said, angrily, but I don't know *where* we are!"

Upon hearing them speak, the navigator's eyes widened. A warning look from the captain cautioned him to remain silent.

"You're making them nervous," said Evan.

The captain pointed at the map and lifted his hands with the palms up, asking for an answer.

"Banda?" he asked.

Bob crossed his arms and looked at Evan, who shook his head.

"Fine, that means location. Well, if you know where we are, have at it."

Bob shrugged then moved to the map. Using his hands he illustrated where he thought they might be.

70

"Well, this is Cozumel, and we were coming in from the ocean when the problem happened. The pilot said he was trying to land us in the shallows off Cozumel, so if we made it, we'd be somewhere here."

He indicated a location off the northern shores of Cozumel.

The navigator touched that part of the map and looked at Evan, who nodded in agreement. The navigator then slid his finger over to an X that had been clearly drawn in the channel between Cozumel and the mainland. He tapped it, then looked up at the captain, who smiled and nodded.

A shout from one of the other ships caught the captain's attention. He lowered his head in thanks and indicated that Evan and Bob should go back to where they'd previously been seated.

"What did they want? Tara asked.

"I didn't think you were watching," said Bob.

"Oh, we were," Emma added. "We've been watching everything."

"You're feeling better?" Evan asked, kneeling down beside her.

"Much," she replied, smiling. "Thanks for asking."

"So? What did they want?" Tara asked again.

"I think they wanted to know where we are," said Evan.

"What?" Emma asked. 'Why? They found us."

"Maybe the fog messed them up?" said Evan.

"It was kind of weird," Bob added. "It was more like they wanted to know where they are."

Tara nodded.

"That might make sense."

"Really?" Bob asked. "Why?"

"We've been studying our rescuers," she replied.

"I see," said Bob. "Have you found out anything?"

"Well, your daughter has a theory," Emma said, somewhat tentatively.

Bob looked up at Tara expectantly but was momentarily blinded by a shaft of sunlight reflecting off something poking through the fog bank ahead. The flash of light vanished in an instant, but they all watched Bob as he slowly rose to his feet, his mouth agape.

Directly ahead of them, a solitary golden pillar soared high out of the fog bank, the top narrowing as it gently curved away from them. A horn blared from the direction of the pillar's base, emitting three short blasts.

From the back of their ship an answering horn blew, giving two short blasts. It was quickly followed by another series of three blasts from ahead and to the right. Commands went out and the ships adjusted course. Soon they could make out the outline of a second pillar farther away. Their new course steered them directly between the middle of the two pillars.

"Where are we?" Bob asked.

"He knows," said Tara, nodding toward the captain.

The captain had been watching their reaction to the pillars. When Bob and Evan turned to face him, the captain smiled and opened his arms to encompass the pillars and the area beyond them.

"Otoch," he said, proudly.

"Home," Tara said, before anyone else could translate.

Within moments, they could see that each of the two pillars they were headed between marked the end of points of land and were flanking a channel of some sort. The lifting fog was revealing even more of the pillars off in the distance. Pillar tops thrust through the fog on either side of the first two, all equally spaced and gradually curving away into the distance. Below the golden sentinels, silhouettes and shapes of structures loomed within the swirling fog.

As the ships got closer, Bob and the others could see platforms with railings attached to the back of the pillars. Another horn blast as their ship passed by confirmed that there were people manning the platforms. Following their answering horn, the friendly waves Bob and the others saw from the platforms made them feel welcome to… wherever it was they were going.

"Do you see that?" Evan asked Bob.

The base of each pillar was perpendicular to the sea but from that point the entire pillar curved away from the sea, narrowing and arching back into a point. It was as if the pillars were gracefully and artfully protecting the land they encompassed.

"It's incredible," Bob agreed.

"It's gold!" said Evan.

"What?" said Bob.

"Those pillars are gold," Evan replied. "I'm sure of it."

Whether Evan was correct or not, there was really nothing Bob could say to counter such an absurd claim.

Their ships maneuvered around a small rocky island just inside the entrance pillars, then they veered off to the right. The command went out and the oars dipped to slow the ships. Up ahead a shoreline emerged from its protective shroud of fog. Other ships, similar to the ones on which they were arriving on, lined the docks along the shore.

There was now a steady breeze as they made for a large berth in the center of the docks. There were no ships tethered there but groups of people lined the docks, seemingly awaiting their arrival. Beyond them were several large contingents of what could only be soldiers.

Behind the troops, and presiding over the entire scene, a small group of white-robed people waited patiently halfway up a white stone staircase that led away from the docks and disappeared upwards into the fog. The breeze stiffened and fog blocked Bob's view as it was quickly pushed away from the stairs, right over everyone's head and out toward the ocean. As the fog cleared away, the sun shone brightly on the docks, the staircase, and the massive white, red, and black stone temple that topped the ridge.

CHAPTER 14

Into the Breach

The *Xavier* had been cruising at full speed into the fog for a good ten minutes when the navigator finally stated the obvious.

"Sir, we have zero visibility. Recommend reducing to one quarter."

"Radar?" said Mulholland.

"Sir, radar is able to penetrate the fog but we're getting distorted readings," the Nav replied, nervously. "There's something out there but we can't tell what or where it is."

"Reduce to half," said Mulholland.

"Aye, sir, half."

"NORAD is advising satellite feed updates are available, sir," Johnson reported.

"Put them up, let's have a look," said Mulholland.

Everyone watched as the satellite images flickered onto the main screens. Seconds later they were replaced with a view from the bow of the ship. A massive shape loomed in the mist dead ahead! Alarm klaxons accompanied the automatic video switch.

"Collision alert! Collision alert!" the automated system blared.

"Full reverse, full reverse!" Mulholland called, echoed by the Nav.

A break in the fog dead ahead fully revealed a solid wall directly in front of them. It was worn smooth and curved back as it rose. They were coming to a stop so close to the wall that they couldn't see the top.

"All stop!" the Nav reported.

"Back us away, fifty meters," Mulholland instructed. "Mr. Johnson. Why didn't we see this coming up?"

"Sonar?" Johnson asked the Nav.

As they backed away they could see that the rock wall was irregular in height, and topped out about 40 meters high directly in front of them. Inset in the wall at regular intervals were golden metal pillars that matched the wall in curvature then extended far above the rock face itself.

"Depth is consistent, sir, 345 meters," replied the Nav, sounding perplexed.

"Absolutely no shallows leading to up the shore, sir," said Johnson. "We had no warning. Can you sound ahead under that, Nav?"

"Sonar echo is inconclusive, sir, no clean echo."

"Com, switch us back to NORAD," Mulholland ordered.

"Sir, I have Admiral Lindquist," Com said.

Mulholland nodded and the admiral's face took over a side screen.

"Report!"

"We've encountered a rock formation in the middle of the channel sir," Mulholland reported.

"Encountered? You almost sailed straight into it!" said Lindquist, shaking his head. "We're on a live feed here, captain."

"Sir?" said Johnson. "With respect, sir, we had no warning. The wall is scattering radar and sonar equally."

"Yes, I heard your report, Johnson. The fog is lifting. Have you had a chance to look at the satellite, captain?"

"No, admiral, we were just getting to that," Mulholland

replied.

"Well, we have," said Lindquist. "Turn to starboard and head along that wall and we'll show you what we've got so far."

"Nav, set course westward one quarter and let's keep an eye out as for anything else unusual. Keep us fifty meters off that wall. Visual confirmation and sonar, call the depth, everything recording."

The captain turned back to the Admiral.

"Go ahead, sir."

"The fog is still pretty heavy, but it's thinning as it blows off and we can see through it in patches once in a while. It's difficult to get a sense of what we are seeing, but it looks very much like an island has appeared right there in the middle of the ocean. From what we can see it has shapes that appear to be buildings and an intricate system of waterways."

Satellite pictures flashed by on the screen as the admiral talked. It then changed to a color graph image featuring red dots all over the island and a large yellow blob in the center.

"Our satellite people are learning the limitations of their equipment in a hurry," Lindquist continued, seemingly happy about that. "With the fog so heavy and swirling they're finding that when they're zoomed in they're missing the big picture and when they zoom out we don't get enough detail. We've been able get sporadic readings on infrared, and let's just say that there are lots of people on that island."

"How big is this, sir?" Johnson asked, tentatively.

"We can't tell for sure yet, but it's at least several kilometers in each direction," the admiral answered. "You're headed here."

He ran a mid-range satellite video showing moving fog banks patterned by a stiff breeze. A patch of fog cleared in the middle and a gold and white complex of structures glinted in the bright sunlight. A path led down from the structures to large docks lined with what looked like wooden sailing ships. Three ships were just pulling up to the central docking area. One of them was towing a covered fluorescent orange raft that had some lettering on the side. Lindquist froze the screen at that point.

"I'm told that's the type of raft that one of the airliners we lost in the pulse would have carried. It was probably the flight from London that's unaccounted for. If you look here you can see the entrance to the harbor."

Digital highlights showed the two pillars that framed the harbor where the docks were located. Other digital plots appeared and showed the position of the *Xavier* and the fleet not too far behind them.

"Orders, sir?" Mulholland asked.

"Unchanged. Find out what you can, report back. We're only 15 minutes behind you, but I'd like to let whoever these people are know that we are in fact here. That raft is almost certainly from of one of our planes."

He sighed heavily.

"Damn. I wish we knew more about what this is all about. Maintain Condition Red."

"Aye, admiral," said Mulholland. "*Xavier* out: Nav, set course for that harbor best speed and let's keep an eye out for anything else unexpected. Johnson, how long?"

Johnson looked at the course and their speed.

"About 16 minutes, sir. Nav?"

"Yes sir, 16 minutes is on the nose, sir."

"I want spotters on the forecastle," Mulholland ordered. "Open the deck shutters. All hands on deck. Weapons ready. Guns manned. Issue sidearms."

The captain was taking no chances.

"What are those things?" he asked Johnson, as they

slid past yet another golden pillar that soared high above them and disappeared into the swirls of fog.

* * *

Xavier had sailed passed innumerable golden pillars for almost 15 minutes when the vessel arrived in front of the entrance to the harbor - fortunately without further surprises. The fog over the harbor itself had cleared but the land beyond was still largely obscured.

"Slow to one eighth," Mulholland ordered. "Nav?"

"Sir, sonar reads depth in front of the gates at over 300 meters, but just inside the gate that small island is bringing bottom up to 40 meters. We'll be okay if we stay port center."

Three solid blasts of a horn sounded from the closest pillar.

"40 meters will be plenty, take us in," said Mulholland.

"Sir?" Johnson asked.

"Johnson?"

"That horn sounded like some sort of communication attempt," he replied. "Shouldn't we try and find out?"

"This is a harbor in Mexican waters and we have the Mexican government's authority invested our fleet," the captain said, firmly. "We're going to find out what's going on here, and before the fleet arrives."

Three blasts sounded again, quicker more urgently.

"Ahead one eighth, steady as she goes," Mulholland ordered.

Two horns sounded this time. On the sides of the pillars people emerged and waved flags from the railings. A large beam covered with flags was swung down from the platform behind the pillar. While it didn't actually bar their way, Johnson was convinced that it was a warning for them to keep out.

Everything he could see through his binoculars indicated that they were being warned away.

"Sir, they are definitely warning us off."

"Com, raise Fleet and inform them," said Mulholland, ignoring Johnson. "Ahead one quarter."

The admiral's face appeared on the side screen, while the main one showed Fleet's live satellite feed. Lindquist suddenly looked alarmed, as the screen became interlaced with static. On the main screen the glowing golden area in the center of the image suddenly expanded and suddenly every screen on the ship's bridge filled with static. The last image Johnson saw was the admiral yelling soundlessly into the monitor.

CHAPTER 15

Atlantica

The familiar wail of police sirens broke the silence that held the holiday city in its grip. Obviously the police had found some vehicles that hadn't been running when the pulse hit. Jenn watched as they escorted an ambulance past the hotel, driving through the streets in water that was now less than a foot deep. The remnants of the tsunami were rushing down the streets and back to the sea almost as fast as it had arrived.

A strong gust of wind blasted in through the missing windows of the lounge and knocked loose more glass from the shattered frames in the floors above. Jenn was startled by the sound of the crashing glass, but the breeze felt wonderful. It seemed to signal that the worst was over. The breeze was also pushing the fog out to sea and the returning sunlight left the city looking almost the same as it was before the strange events of the morning.

"What the hell is that?" Terry said, pointing out to sea.

Jenn turned away from the city view. The departing fog was revealing bits and pieces of something in the sea off the coast. Golden spires glinted as they momentarily poked out here and there above the sun splashed fog banks. The spires were quite far away and it was hard to tell what they were, but the outlines of structures at various levels also peeked in and out of the rolling fog. It was becoming obvious there was something absolutely enormous sitting in the water between Playa del Carmen and Cozumel.

"Look at those pylons, they're closer in the front and receding as they get further away," Jenn said. "It must be a ship of some kind,"

"No, Señorita," said Paulo from behind them, awestruck and shaking his head. "I don't think so."

He pointed toward the working television. The station had cleaned up its transmission a little and had once again aimed their long lens out to sea. They were zooming in on a structure that appeared to be floating on the top of the fog. It looked as if someone had wrapped a building around a volcano, then stuck an exhaust pipe down the volcano's throat. That is, if the building was an ancient monolithic stone temple and the exhaust pipe was made of gold.

The view widened and Jenn gasped. The wind was quickly stripping the fog away. There were other structures arranged below and around the main temple situated at the volcano. The structures were made of various types of stone and some had metal-clad roofs. In front of the buildings a huge plaza was inlaid with regular patterns of metal, all pointing towards the center. Everything was large enough to be visible through a telephoto lens from miles away.

Terry put his hand on Jenn's shoulder, turning her to take in the full extent of what fog had been hiding.

In front of the resort and as far as they could see in either direction dozens of curved golden pillars, spaced at regular intervals, were inset into a smooth rounded wall. The height of the wall varied from sea level up to a range of small mountains that eclipsed the view of everything behind them. Although Jenn and Terry were some distance away, hundreds of structures of various sizes could be seen. Sunlight glinted off stone plinths and metal objects that dotted the landscape. Numerous spires of stone rose into the sky, possibly connected by a network of Viaducts and bridges that sprawled across the island.

"Dios Mio," Paulo said.

This time several others in the lounge echoed his words.

"It must be a hybrid between an island and some sort of ship," said Jenn.

"That's a ship?" Terry asked, incredulously.

"Well, it has to be. How else did it get here?" Jenn replied. "It must have come in overnight."

"It can't be a ship," Terry said. "It's miles across. Where would you build it? How could it even exist and nobody know about it?"

"I don't know," Jenn admitted.

On the TV, the camera had pulled back and was now surveying the huge object's individual features. There were several pyramid-like structures that were certainly Mayan in construction and some temples that were built in a far older style, resembling buildings of ancient Greece. Paths of stone and paths made of metal weaved between the structures and over bridges that soared over wide waterways. The spires seemed to be watch towers, each one tipped with a widened end and an open space to see in all directions.

Paulo had grabbed the remote and had turned up the TV's volume.

"...no idea where this might be from or really what it is we're looking at. We still have no communication to the world outside Playa, the Federales say they're working to establish a link by satellite. Wait... our camera has found some people out there."

As the camera's view looked along one of the curving canals, a couple of small rowed boats could be seen moving out into the canal. The prows of dozens of larger wooden ships poked out from beneath the metal-clad canal walls. The camera zoomed out and captured a row of people on a walkway lining the edge of the canal as far as the camera could see. Others strolled among them, dressed in what looked like robes, or shorts and sandals, occasionally stopping to offer a drink or to chat with those in the line. The atmosphere appeared to be very casual and relaxed.

In an instant the tone of the scene changed. The boats in the canal rowed frantically for cover. The people on the wall grabbed at the posts inset into the wall and the others quickly hurried away. Within seconds the line of people was moving, pushing the posts and the wall along with them.

The scene then blurred and the cameraman immediately zoomed out to encompass a much wider view. It seemed that the visual distortion was being produced by some kind of energy field. It had encompassed the entire island in a golden sparkling glow that moments later intensified just before the TV screen filled with static and the picture cut out.

Jenn and the others didn't need the screen any more. Their horizon was filled with a shimmering golden dome, the top half of an ovoid, that seemed to emanate from the central structure, channel down along the golden pillars and extend down right into the sea.

"Okay," Terry said. "I guess maybe it could be a ship."

"But what kind?" asked Jenn.

"Atlantica," Paulo declared, with absolute certainty.

CHAPTER 16

Shield

When the ship docked, the captain invited those that he considered to be the leaders to disembark first. Evan, then Bob, followed by Emma, Tara, and Gloria all made their way down the ramp. At the bottom they stood aside while teams rushed up the ramp and examined the other survivors. At the captain's nod, a man that seemed to be in charge of the teams held back. He took a quick look at the bump on Emma's head then looked closely into her eyes. The man must have given her a clean bill of health because he nodded back to the captain and headed on board the ship.

"They're triage teams," said Gloria, in amazement. "They're checking to see who needs medical attention."

One of the team members signaled as soon he examined the pilot. He shouted a string of commands and a stretcher team and two other medics raced for the ship.

They stripped the pilot of his outer clothes and began applying a type of salve to his burns. The pilot immediately went from grinding his teeth in pain to tears of relief as his discomfort lessened.

"Gloria?" said Evan, with a look of concern.

"I have a first aid ticket," she said. "But they're doing far more than I ever could. I wouldn't worry."

Most of the survivors were in pretty good shape, aside

from a few broken bones, most had only bumps and bruises. Bob and the others turned to see the covered raft containing the casualties being pulled to the dock by its mooring lines. One of the medics peered inside for a moment then looked over at the captain and shook his head.

The captain bowed his head. He sighed then looked up and barked an order and a squad of the troops stepped forward.

"What's going on?" said Tara, in alarm.

"I don't know, honey," Bob replied, nervously. "Let's just wait and see."

The squad marched directly towards them, then spun and angled toward the covered raft. They lined up along the dock, turned and froze, clearly standing guard over the bodies.

Emma sniffed, holding back her tears. Bob watched as a tear rolled down her cheek.

"It's… it's an honor guard," said Emma, choked with emotion. "My dad was in the military. It's a sign of respect."

The captain stepped in front of them and met their gaze. Evan and Bob both lowered their heads in respect.

"Thank you," Evan said.

"Dios bo'otik," Bob echoed in Mayan.

"Mixba'al," said the captain.

Bob noticed something odd in the way the captain answered, as if he were searching for the right word.

"Beya'," said the captain, motioning for them to follow him.

They headed towards the foot of the staircase, the ranks of soldiers parting to let them through. At the bottom of the steps, the captain gestured for Bob and the others to wait. He went to chat with the white-robed group that was waiting. After a brief discussion the robed people turned and proceeded up the steps. The captain then waved Bob and the others over.

When they reached the captain, Bob turned back to look at the docks. The injured survivors were being taken to a low building on one side of the steps. The remainder of the plane's passengers were being directed toward a multi-storey building vaguely resembling a hotel on the other side of the stairwell, the flight attendants helping to keep them moving.

One of the flight attendants waved to Gloria, and gave her a questioning 'What's going on?' shrug. Gloria shook her head but gave a thumbs up sign, which seemed to be what was needed, as she smiled and turned back to help.

Bob turned back to the captain and he and the others began the long climb to the temple above.

They'd nearly reached the top of the pathway when they heard the distinctive throb of engines behind them. Everyone turned to see the frigate *Xavier* slowing as it came into view. As the vessel cleared the last of the fog bank, the guards in the pillars blew three warning horns at the *Xavier*. There was no response and no change in the ship's course. The captain looked at Evan and then Bob, both who could only shrug helplessly back at him. The captain sighed and raised his right arm, then put three fingers in the air.

"Ox!" he shouted.

Within seconds his order was relayed in the form of a second three-horn blast that came from the spire near the temple above. That was then was echoed by nearby spires then relayed repeatedly to encompass the entire island.

The ship didn't change course or speed.

"Ka!" the captain said, as he held up only two fingers.

Two horn blasts rang out and were echoed across the island, fading out while a new sound grew in intensity. Overhead, the humming sound took form, as the sky pulsed with wispy gold and formed an energy field over the entire land. Rising from the golden pillars it seemed to travel along their curved tips then break free and head inland high above them.

Xavier's engine noise increased, the bow wake indicating that it had actually sped up.

"What are they doing?" Bob cried.

The captain looked at him apologetically.

"Hun" he said, holding up a single finger.

One horn sounded and the energy field above them strengthened, assuming a more solid appearance. A hum of raw energy pulsed above and all around them and the world outside the field shimmered and flickered. At the harbor entrance the Xavier's prow had been caught just inside the flickering energy field. The prow, now cleanly severed from the ship by the energy field, continued into the harbor on its own momentum, before beginning to flounder.

CHAPTER 17

Sliced

A final horn had sounded just as the bow of the *Xavier* cleared the pillars protecting the harbor. The shimmering golden light that had flickered into existence like a bubble around the entire island seemed to solidify into a sheet of coherent energy. Where the bubble of energy intersected the vessel's hull, it disintegrated and silently disappeared. The ship's forward momentum was now carrying the *Xavier* at full tilt into oblivion!

"Emergency stop! Full reverse," Mulholland and Johnson both yelled at the top of their lungs.

The engines took a few minutes to respond and both men looked at each other knowing that it would be too late to save the bridge, and themselves.

The energy field flickered then once more became merely a wispy bubble.

"What happened?" the captain asked.

"It stopped," replied Johnson.

"Nav, maintain full reverse," Mulholland said. "Mr. Johnson."

"Sir?"

"Remind me to listen to you more closely. Damage report!"

"Aye sir," Johnson replied "Com, Ops, how are we looking?"

The boat abruptly lurched heavily to starboard. The deck sloped further until it reached an angle where it was able to maintain its starboard tilt. The Ops officer scanned the screens that were still functioning, although a couple of them went dark even as he looked. He tapped at some gauges as if to be sure.

"Uh, sir, the bow is completely gone," Ops said, looking confused. "Sir, what about the spotters that were on the bow?"

"Steady Ops," Johnson said. "Damage report."

"Damage systems are offline," Ops replied. "But from what I saw before they went down the starboard midsection hull is compromised and taking on water."

"Three out of six," Johnson said to the captain. "If the port zone hull is compromised, there's no way we're staying afloat."

Nav was at the window peering through binoculars.

"Sir, the spotters are okay. Looks like they dove off the bow when that thing hit us. They're swimming toward us."

"Wave them off," Mulholland ordered.

"Sir?" said Nav.

"Wave them off!" Mulholland snapped. "There may not be a ship here for them to board. Com, can we seal off the mid sections?"

"Maybe portside sir, but the starboard side mechanism is gone."

The boat slowly began righting its tilt.

"Did you put pumps on that?" Johnson asked.

"No, sir," Com replied. "This could only have happened if the port midsection is flooding."

"Are we out of that harbor yet?" said Mulholland.

"Aye, sir," Nav replied. "Just clear."

"Very well, then. All stop." the captain ordered.

Once all stop had been relayed and confirmed the captain looked around the bridge.

"Mr. Johnson?" Mulholland asked grimly.

"We're done for, sir."

"Right. Com, signal the fleet not to enter the harbor under any circumstances," said Mulholland. "And… sound abandon ship. I want everyone off this boat now."

"All hands, abandon ship!" the klaxons sounded then began continually repeating the order.

Inside the harbor, the sailors that had jumped off the bow section heard the klaxons blaring and started swimming vigorously away.

A monitor on the bridge showed the rear deck where the crew was rapidly launching the *Xavier's* lifeboats and rafts. The stern was now rising, as what was left of the front of the ship filled with water. The first Blackhawk chopper had been rolled out of the hanger and its rotors were spinning up. The crew waiting for the second aircraft stood watching.

"Sir, what about what the admiral said about flying?" Johnson said.

"What do you think?" asked the captain. "What would you do?"

"Well, I wouldn't fly over that," he replied, pointing through the gates. "No matter what happens."

"Well then, you get on that chopper and make sure that nobody does."

"Sir?"

"I'll be along, Johnson. I'm going to clear the boat, but I'll be along."

Johnson grabbed a helmet, fired up the radio and headed to the hanger. The evac was going well. Both lower decks radioed in clear and chopper Tango One was in the air.

"Who's got Tango One?" Johnson queried over the radio.

"Chen here."

91

"Johnson here. Chen, do not approach the harbor or in anyway fly towards or over that island. Do you copy?"

"Sir, we have sailors in the water!"

"Yes, we do, Chen but they're on their own for the moment. Do not approach or fly towards that at all. Maintain station on the *Xavier*. Copy?"

"Aye, sir, copy that," Chen replied. "Maintain on *Xavier*."

"Evac. Con is clear. Weapons bay?" The Evac officer was doing his job of clearing the boat section at a time via the section chiefs.

Johnson had reached the pad and the chopper was on station, waiting for him. He hopped up as the boat lurched again. He hit the side of the chopper door but hung on as the boat listed about five degrees back toward starboard. He was pulled inside the chopper and quickly sat down.

"Can you still take off?" Johnson asked the pilot.

"From this angle? With my eyes closed, sir."

"Well, keep them open and let's get this bird in the air. You heard what I said to Chen?"

"Yes sir, no sight seeing. Roger that."

The pilot grinned and took off. Both birds hovered over the badly listing *Xavier*.

"Weapons bay?" called Evac, requesting a status update again.

"Evac, this is Section Chief Rodriguez," came a voice over the radio. "Weapons is all clear, except for me. I'm stuck in fire control in pod one. That last lurch set me tumbling and I'm stuck in the pod with live rounds pinning my leg."

"I'll get him," Mulholland answered instantly. "Evac, is the boat clear?"

"I believe so, sir."

"Well, make sure while I get Rodriguez."

Mulholland was in the weapons pod in less than two minutes, and quickly freed Rodriguez. There was just one problem.

"Johnson?" the captain called.

"Sir?"

"Rodriguez is free. We've got live ammo piled loose here in the weapons bay and there's water coming in the deck. How long have we got to lash this stuff down?"

Johnson looked down at the ship, which seemed to be visibly sliding forward into the water and rolling to starboard.

"No time, sir! No time! You've got to run now!"

There was no response but seconds later, Johnson saw the two men burst from the access hatch and dash for the rear of the ship. Another starboard lurch knocked them both off their feet as they crossed the chopper pad and set off a series of violent explosions in the weapons bay. The choppers veered off station and headed away as fast as they could as the shells exploded and tore through the ship.

As the explosions continued, both Mulholland and Rodriguez got to their feet, ran and jumped off the side of the pad. Debris flew in all directions, including an unexploded shell that sailed through the air until it encountered the side of one of the two pillars guarding the harbor, where it detonated on impact.

For a moment there was silence. The explosions had stopped and the only noise was the regular thud of the chopper blades. Then the slow grinding of metal wrenching itself apart grew in intensity as the damaged pillar began to collapse into the harbor. Those manning the pillar jumped clear before it hit the water.

Ryan watched from the chopper as both the broken pillar and the remains of the *Xavier* quickly sank out of sight.

CHAPTER 18

Standing Down

After seconds that seemed an eternity, the captain lowered his one raised finger and clenched his fist. A horn sounded and the field overhead shimmered, once more becoming a mere gossamer veil. The people in the harbor towers resumed waving at the *Xavier*, urging it to leave the harbor.

The detached prow of the ship was quickly filling with water and slowing down. A couple of crewmembers clung to the edge of the sinking prow until they knew there was no hope and leapt to safety. The remainder of the ship was visible and still moving forward, although much slower than it had been moments earlier. The churning waters near the *Xavier's* stern were caused by the ship's engines operating at maximum reverse thrust. The vessel finally slowed to a stop and then began backing out of the harbor.

Water streamed into the front of the ship where the prow had been removed. The right side that had been closest to the energy field seemed to be listing heavily. As soon as the ship cleared the harbor, the engines raced to still the ship then stopped. Even far across the harbor, Bob and the other survivors could hear the klaxons.

"They're abandoning ship!" said Emma. "It must be sinking."

The *Xavier* listed further to right. Rafts were tossed

overboard from the flat rear deck and a crane spun and quickly dropped a motor launch into the water. A chopper could be heard taking off and moments later it came into view, launched from the pad on the ship's rear deck. The chopper hovered protectively over the distressed ship.

"Look!" said Emma, pointing further out to sea.

While the drama had unfolded, a large aircraft carrier and several smaller ships had emerged from the fog and were steaming straight for the harbor entrance where the *Xavier* was floundering.

Bob and Evan looked at each other. The captain looked at them both. They were all wondering what would happen next.

"What do you think?" Bob asked.

"I don't know," Evan replied, pointing at the harbor. "That one tried to come in and look what happened."

"I wish we could talk to them," Bob said to himself.

"Dad?" said Tara.

"Yeah, pal?"

"Benefit of the doubt," she said.

"What's that?" asked Gloria.

"It's what I always told her when she was growing up," replied Bob, smiling. "Give people the benefit of the doubt."

Evan turned to the captain and shrugged while Bob smiled hopefully.

The captain had watched their interchange with apparent interest. He actually seemed more interested in their conversation than in the approaching ships. They all continued watching what was happening just outside the harbor.

The cranes had released a few more launches and the crew of the *Xavier* were streaming down the side of the ship and climbing aboard them. The ship seemed as if it were leveling off slightly and looked like it might be okay, but the stern had started to lift up out of the water.

"That's not good," Gloria said.

Another chopper left the tilted flight deck and hovered over the ship. The captain seemed unconcerned about the aircraft. The front of the ship was definitely going down and the stern was rising. There were no more boats or people exiting the ship.

"I hope they got everyone off," Tara said.

The ship creaked and gave a sharp lurch to the right. That was immediately followed by a series of large explosions just in front of the bridge, which spewed debris out of the open front of the ship and through a new hole blown in the side. The choppers quickly backed away from the explosions.

The explosions definitely seemed to make the captain nervous, but still he didn't reactivate the energy field. He seemed to know that something odd was happening and it looked as if he was going to let it play out. There was another huge explosion and the ship lurched and fractured in front of the bridge. Two more people jumped off the ship's back deck into the water as a final barrage of explosions blasted the ship cleanly into two pieces. Debris flew everywhere. A spinning shell exploded as it struck the side of the closest of the harbor's two entrance pillars.

The pillar appeared to hold but the captain was tight lipped now. The front of the *Xavier* was already water heavy and it flipped forward and sank under the water in one smooth motion. The stern crashed down and as the water it had taken on streamed aft, the stern settled deeply into the waves.

A shrieking sound rent the air as the damaged pillar began to tear metal and shred itself. It fractured and began a graceful collapse into the harbor as its crew leapt clear.

The weight of the now water-filled stern of the ship had already quickly dragged it down to deck level, and the rate of tilt wasn't slowing down at all. As the pillar splashed into the harbor and began to follow the first two parts of the ship into the deep, the remainder of the ship reached a near vertical position. Bubbling and frothing furiously, it quickly followed everything else to the bottom of the sea.

The rafts, launches and choppers that were all that remained of the military ship, picked up the last two jumpers from the water then moved themselves further away from the harbor. They then lined up across the entrance and turned to face away from the harbor. They held their position and waited for the rest of the fleet to arrive.

The captain barked out some instructions and three ships in the dock broke their moorings. One rowed for the ship's crewmembers that been on the prow, another headed for the pillar personnel and the third ship sailed towards the harbor entrance.

"Beya'," said the captain, inviting Bob and the others to keep following him up the path.

They climbed the last of the steps slowly, checking back to see what was transpiring out at sea. The two rescue ships picked up their people and headed back for the docks while the third vessel stationed itself in the mouth of the harbor, just inside the pillars.

As they reached the top of the steps, the rest of the fleet had arrived and was stationing itself behind the line of rescue craft. The choppers moved off to the carrier and then all the other ships moved away too. The newly arrived vessels made no move to approach further and angled away slightly so they weren't aimed directly into the harbor.

The harbor echoed with the clanging of metal as the carrier dropped its main anchor into the water. The captain raised his hand again with a clenched fist and then opened his hand, displaying his palm. There were two very quick horn blasts and the wispy shield instantly vanished.

"Quite a show of force," Bob whispered to Emma. "Neither is afraid of..."

His voice trailed off and he stood with his mouth agape as he gazed at the rest of the island. They'd been so busy looking into the harbor and out to sea that they hadn't had time to notice what was behind them. With the fog gone, they could easily see the regular pattern of rings that formed the island. Three rings of water, and three of land. There was a mountain on the central island with a monolithic white structure wrapped around it. The other rings were crowded with hundreds of houses, fields, and temples all connected with stone and metal pathways and bridges and dotted with white stone spires. The inner walls of the canals themselves were covered in metals of various kinds.

The sight jogged a specific memory for Bob.

"The outermost of the walls was coated with brass," he said. "The second with tin, and the third, which was the wall of the citadel, flashed with the red light of orichalcum."

"What's that?" asked Gloria.

Evan and Emma were equally transfixed by the view. While the captain politely but firmly urged them away and led them up the ramp towards the temple, Tara answered for her dad.

"It's Plato's description of Atlantis."

CHAPTER 19

Gone Public

The clearing fog had now fully revealed the shining pillars, gleaming rings, and massive structures to the telephoto lenses trained on the island from Playa del Carmen. The announcer was on screen again. Alternating now between English and Spanish, he talked about the massive shape that had appeared in the ocean.

"A few moments ago, some sort of glowing field briefly enveloped the island. Are we calling it an island?"

A series of loud booms echoed into the lounge from far offshore. Puffs of smoke could be seen rising from one spot on the island. On the TV screen, the image panned frantically around then stopped to show a harbor on the island framed by two of the massive pillars. As they came into focus, one of the towers seemed to buckle and collapse into the ocean. It was followed by what looked like the remnants of a vessel up-ending, then slipping beneath the waves, leaving behind only a small flotilla of ships and a couple of hovering helicopters.

"I'm not sure what just happened, but it looks like some sort of accident on the island may have also claimed a ship."

The announcer was as confused as everyone else.

"We have no idea what ship it was. Wait!"

The camera zoomed out until the view revealed the U.S. flag flying on the deck of an approaching aircraft carrier then zoomed out further to include its accompanying support ships.

"It looks like these ships are from the United States, but we don't know what ship sank earlier."

Papers rustled as the view switched back to the announcer. He continued talking as he glanced down at the new information.

"We have some views from along the coastline you'll want to see. Our crews captured some of the damage that the tsunami left behind."

Shots of overturned boats, chairs piled up along the shore, boats lying in the streets, and piles of floating debris appeared on the screen. One image even showed a diving boat that had been washed up into a hotel's swimming pool. While the video played the announcer delivered some more useful information.

"AT&T has said that they hope to have a cell phone tower operational in the next couple of hours, but that it will be for local calls only, unless they can repair their satellite uplink. TelCel is in contact with their head office by satellite phone and will let us know if they can get things working. Police are advising everyone to stay indoors and wait for systems to come back on line. Do not travel if you don't need to. They're saying that the immediate danger has passed? Perhaps they don't look at the television? Anyway, the Federales have established a communications link to Mexico City. They also say the United States Navy is coming to assist."

The screen switched back to the announcer.

"It would be a good idea to stay put and…"

He was annoyed as someone ran in and handed him yet another note. He read it quickly then straightened his posture and checked his tie.

"Ahem. It seems we've been able to establish our own satellite phone uplink with CNN and that this feed is now going out to the world."

He gestured off screen and the camera quickly switched back to the island in the channel.

"We have a two way feed, and our producer is talking with CNN to get their take on the situation. For our new viewers, we're working with old equipment because of a massive electrical pulse that occurred at the beginning of a very strange day in Playa..."

Paulo muted the TV's audio but the crowd in the lounge protested loudly. He turned the sound back up for them, then he, Jenn and Terry went to a quieter area of the lounge.

"Paulo, you said Atlantica," Jenn asked him. "Do you mean Atlantis?"

"Si," he replied, clearly embarrassed.

"Why do you say that?"

He shook his head. Clearly he didn't want to talk about it. Terry held out some cash, but Paulo pushed him away and turned back to the TV, his eyes wide.

"Turn it up!" Jenn asked loudly.

On the screen was a picture of an airport with a charred streak across one runway that ended at the still burning remains of a crashed plane. The banner on the bottom said *Live from Cancun Mexico*. The image was from CNN through the satellite feed.

"Flight 107 from Toronto lost power and crash-landed at Cancun international airport as it was about to land. Initial reports are that there are no survivors. Three other flights are missing in what authorities are describing as some sort of EMP event that has obliterated all communications over most of the Yucatan peninsula. Satellite communications are being used to bring you this footage and we will continue with this developing story as more information becomes available."

"Is that...?" Terry asked.

"No, said Jenn, tight lipped. "They were coming in from London."

"That's good," Terry said, softly.

"Let's hope so," said Jenn, quickly changing the subject. "Paulo, won't you tell us?"

He didn't immediately answer then glanced out to sea again.

"It is a very old story," he said. "One I never believed, until today."

"What is it?" Terry asked.

"It is said that our ancestors will return to us one day on Atlantica. There are many versions of the tale, Señor, but..."

He hesitated nervously.

"They all say that Atlantica returns to us... with the end of the world."

CHAPTER 20

Bring in the Brass

The carrier had cleared the fog bank and immediately trained all instruments on the truncated frigate which was quickly taking on water as it backed away from the harbor entrance.

"Do not attempt to enter the harbor!" the voice on the radio barked. "*Xavier* is done for. We're abandoning ship!"

The rest of the drama played out while the carrier approached. In keeping with protocol they didn't attempt any communication until the last man had cleared the *Xavier*.

"4th fleet this is Lieutenant Commander Ryan Johnson."

His words could barely be heard above the sound of the helicopter.

"Fleet Admiral Lindquist here. What's your status?"

The question seemed redundant as the last portion of the *Xavier* was just slipping out of view.

"All crew accounted for, sir, but two are in the harbor of this island. Looks like they're being picked up by boats from inside the harbor. I'm on board Tango Two."

"Where's Captain Mulholland?" Lindquist asked.

"He's in one of the launches, sir, he had to jump," Johnson replied. "We're just going to pick him up."

"Belay that," the admiral ordered. "The boats will get to him faster. Get yourself onto this carrier deck stat. I want all your people on the *Excelsior* ASAP."

"Aye, sir."

"Com, Ops, bring them in," said the admiral, rattling off orders. "Nav , line us up on a tangent to the harbor, as non-threatening as possible and drop anchor. Weapons?"

"Sir?" asked Nav.

"From what I just saw, they sliced one of our ships in half in seconds, without firing a shot."

"Yes, sir," he reluctantly agreed.

"I want everything we have ready to bring to bear at a moment's notice, but I want no outer sign that we're doing anything but waiting here. No hatches open, no turrets pointed, not even a single radar or drone scan."

"Sir?"

"We don't know what set them off and I'd rather avoid doing it again. Let's be quietly ready for anything."

"Aye, sir!"

"Com, relay that to the fleet and get Atlantic Command on the horn. I want Johnson in my ready room the second his boots hit the deck."

"Aye, sir!" cried the Ops center crewmembers in unison.

"Sir?" Com shouted after the admiral as he turned to leave the bridge.

The admiral turned back and cocked his head.

"NORAD is already on the line, and sir, so is the president."

"In my ready room."

The admiral turned and strode away.

* * *

Johnson was out of breath when he knocked on the door to the admiral's ready room.

106

"Come!"

Johnson entered. The admiral was examining some of the screens that lined one wall of the room. Some were blanked out, while others showed the harbor and various aerial views of the island.

"Mr. Johnson," said Lindquist. "What happened out there? The condensed version."

"Sir, our orders were to get as much information as we could. We arrived, then entered the harbor when some sort of defensive field cut through our hull and compromised its integrity."

"You're missing one important part there, aren't you?" said the admiral.

"Sir? I don't know. It happened really fast."

"I mean the part where you told the captain you were being warned off."

"Yes sir, but that was the captain's call to make," Johnson added nervously. "It was a very odd situation."

"That's an understatement!" said a familiar sounding voice through a speaker. "Did you feel that you were attacked or were they defending themselves?"

Johnson looked at the Admiral who smiled.

"Go ahead and answer, Mr. Johnson, we all work for him."

Lindquist leaned over and flicked on the monitors that had been blanked out.

Johnson snapped to a salute as the president appeared on one screen, NATO Operations on another, and NORAD Command on a third.

"Mr. President, sir."

"Lieutenant Commander Johnson," said the president. "Pleased to meet you. About my question?"

"I think, sir... I think they didn't want us in their space. They warned us off and we went in anyway. It... it just seemed wrong to me, sir."

"Thank you for your honesty, Mr. Johnson," the Admiral said. "We'll chat about that more later."

"There are a few other questions we need answered," the president added. "With that same level of candor."

"I'll try, sir."

"First off, then," the president began, pointing to the picture of the island. "What is that?"

Johnson hesitated. He'd be the biggest joke in the Navy after this, but he had to answer the president.

"Sir, my first thought was that this is Atlantis."

Nobody laughed, nobody chuckled, and nobody even smiled. Not even the admiral.

"And why did you think that?" the president asked.

"It's a hobby of mine, sir. I got my first degree in archeology so that I could try and find Atlantis. Many of the structures on the island look to be Minoan and many modern archeologists think the Minoan people are from what we think of as Atlantis."

Now that he was talking about his favorite subject, he was on a roll, pointing and gesturing at the screens.

"The shape and size of the island, the circular water-ways, even the metals we can see, they all fit Plato's description of Atlantis. The only thing that doesn't make sense is…"

He hesitated.

"Go on," the admiral prodded.

"Well, sir, there are many structures here that look as if they're Mayan in nature. These temples for instance, are clearly Late Mayan architecture. And it also asks the question - why would it be here?"

He was almost speaking to himself now.

"The most common theory of Atlantis is that is was lo-cated in or just outside the Mediterranean, but now it shows up here, off the Yucatan, with Mayan structures on it.

"Thank you, Mr. Johnson," the president said. "I've heard enough."

"Ladies and Gentlemen?" said the president. "Any problems with this?"

On the monitors nobody dissented, although a few people didn't look very happy about it, whatever it was.

"Well, Mr. Johnson, or rather Ryan, I'm afraid I'm going to have to temporarily relieve you of duty," the President said.

'Yes, sir," said Ryan lowering his eyes.

The president smiled. "I'd like to offer you a position as the front-line member of the Atlantis Command task force."

Ryan's head snapped up.

"Sir?"

"All our experts agree with you. Well, when pressed they do," the president said pointedly into the monitor.

"There's no other conclusion to be drawn here. An emergency international committee has been established and you will be our eyes and ears on the ground, if you accept."

"Yes, sir! Of course I accept, sir."

"Ryan, we need to speak to these people. What do you need to make that happen?"

"I'll have to think about that, sir, but I could definitely use some help on the Mayan side. It's not my area."

The president picked up a clipboard and studied it.

"Do you know anybody?"

"Well, sir, Dr. Evan Masters is well known as the expert on the Mayan, but given the appearance of this you'll also want Bob Wallace, sir. He's been ridiculed for talking about stuff like this, he even wrote a book about it."

The president ticked off a couple of names on the clipboard. Then he reached down and held up a copy of *The Impossible Mayan* and smiled wryly.

"I've very recently become aware of it."

"I think Wallace's wife is also a doctor in the field, sir."

The president shook his head and smiled as he ticked another name off on the clipboard.

"Seems like you're the right man for the job. Jim?" he said to the admiral.

"Sir?"

"You and Ryan are on equal footing here. You've got the ball on navy and military, Ryan's got social, political, and communication. Any problems working together?"

"No, sir!" Ryan and the admiral said together as they saluted the president.

Suddenly, there was a disturbance on the NORAD screen as people pointed and shouted at something out of view.

"Mr. President!" General Aspinal said from NORAD. "You all need to see this."

She gestured off screen and the NORAD feed was replaced with a video of Atlantis from the coast. *Live from Playa del Carmen Mexico* was displayed across the bottom of the screen.

"Atlantis has gone public," she said.

"General," said the president, carefully. "Could you please find out how CNN is able to get a video feed from a city we can't reach?"

"Yes, sir."

"Admiral, your ships will need to be on alert for visitors as well," he added, sighing heavily. "And it seems as if I'll have to address the people sooner that I'd hoped. Ryan?"

"I'm on it, sir. Er, my apologies, Admiral Lindquist. We're on it, sir."

The president smiled, and nodded goodbye before he handed the clipboard with the list to someone off camera.

"Get me all of them."

CHAPTER 21

The Council

The white stone temple slowly revealed itself as Bob and the others walked up the paved slope to the courtyard. The open-sided top of the structure came to a point in what looked like a prow at the center of the building. The roof was supported by oddly styled pillars and the structure itself was open enough to enable them to soon see that what resembled a prow was in fact one corner of a hexagonal structure. Neatly hidden within the pillars, low walls defined a six-sided pillbox inside the pillared hexagon.

After a few more steps up the slope, it became apparent that everything they'd seen thus far was sitting on the top of a large rectangular building, built in a similar architectural style to the top section. A pillar-enclosed top floor sat atop a more traditionally styled main floor with doors and windows set at regular intervals around the building. In the front, a single grand pillar two stories tall divided an impressive entryway that spanned both stories of the main building. Stairs within the entrance seemed to bypass the first floor completely and ended at the second floor of the building. The slope ended at an open courtyard that surrounded the entire building with benches spaced at viewpoints around it. The entire place seemed eerily deserted.

"Do you see those pillars?" Bob asked Evan, keeping

his voice low.

"Tapered from the bottom, wider at the top," Evan said, in his infuriatingly know-it-all voice. "Clearly Minoan."

"Which ties in to the Atlantis theory," said Bob.

Evan just nodded and they both remained silent as they tried to take in all the details of the massive structure.

Gloria overheard their comments and as they crossed the courtyard to the entrance.

"So was this the theory you were taking about before?" she asked Tara.

"Atlantis?" said Tara, looking confused. "Oh no, I was thinking that this might be the ship the Maya left on, like in my dad's book."

"But that was because of the language and the clothing," Emma added, trying to be helpful.

"And if this was your dad's mythical ship, where has it been hiding all this time?" Evan asked.

"Well, if this is Atlantis, where has it been hiding all this time?" Bob shot back, sarcastically.

"Touché!" said Emma.

"Shush!" said the captain.

Everyone immediately stopped talking and he motioned then to a halt just in front of the cavernous entryway where he seemed to be waiting for something.

As Bob and the others stared at the staircase leading up to the darkened roof above, they were able to make out some of the ornate details in the roof of the second storey room. A huge horned shape loomed in the center of the entranceway at the top of the stairs. Emma moved to the side for a better look and then gasped.

"It's a giant bronze bull!" she said. "Beautiful."

They all moved to the side to get a better look, but were startled by a row of guards that stepped from the shadows above and formed a line across the top of the stairs. Bob and the others looked at the captain quizzically, but he smiled warmly and beckoned them to follow him once more.

The captain took them to one of the nondescript doors in the front of the building and through a small room filled with massive ceramic vessels. Other rooms led off to the sides, including one with a staircase that descended to yet another floor. The captain led them down into the dark then along corridors where they were surprised to find light seeping in through strategically placed slots in the floors above them. They followed the captain through twists and turns in corridors and through other rooms until they took another staircase that went up for quite a while before it ended up in what was clearly an antechamber.

A row of guards appeared from around a corner and blocked their progress. They were armed with swords and shields but apparently Bob and the others weren't considered a threat as the guards' swords remained sheathed.

The captain bowed his head to Bob and the others then turned. The guards split ranks to let him through and he proceeded down the hall, turned and disappeared form view. Voices could be heard in the distance but Bob couldn't make out the words or even the language.

"Now what happens?" asked Evan said.

One of the guards spun around and gestured for him to speak more softly. Bob just looked at the guard and shrugged.

A command echoed down the hallway, and the guards opened ranks and invited everyone to step forward. One guard went ahead and, after Bob and the others had all started down the hall, a second guard fell in behind them.

They turned the corner and went up a short flight of stairs that ended on the back of a raised dais at the center of a marble-floored circular room. The lead guard led Bob and the others to stand in a line behind the captain, who stood at the front. Together they faced a raised gallery that was divided into sections by a series of marble benches. Directly in front of them a single empty bench was obviously reserved for someone of great importance. On either side were two longer benches with three people seated at each one.

The twelve people were an even mix of men and women but of widely varying ages. By their appearance, a few of them were Mayan, while the rest could have hailed from anywhere. Although they all wore white, their style of attire varied widely. One of them was Mayan high royalty while others were dressed in more modest clothing, including one man who was clearly a soldier wearing robes similar to the captain's. Rounding out the mixed group of a dozen was a commanding woman with dark brown hair dressed in flowing white robes that draped elegantly off her shoulders.

Standing beside Bob, Tara was the only one that heard him mutter 'princess' under his breath, but she nudged him anyway because he was staring at the woman like a fool.

After a moment, the captain began recounting, in Mayan, the events of that morning to the people they would soon come to know as the council. He spoke far too fast for Bob and Evan to fully understand, but everyone except Gloria could understand at least some of the captain's words. His hand gestures embellished the report so that they could follow along what was being said. As the captain reached to the part about the pillar, Bob could see the council grow tense. Bob decided that he had to say something.

"That was an accident!" he called out in his best Mayan, startling everyone in the room.

One of the guards put his hand on Bob's shoulder, more to caution than to threaten, but a new voice from the

114

back of the room called the guard off, using the strange language Bob and the others kept hearing. Before they could react, the guards began to lead them out of the council chamber, presumably so that the captain could complete his report.

The elderly Mayan who had been watching them from the sidelines came forward as they climbed down the steps from the dais. He edged over to where Bob would have to walk past him then twinkled a friendly smile to Bob as he spoke in near-perfect English.

"Do not worry, you will speak soon."

CHAPTER 22

They're Safe

Paulo would say nothing further about the legends surrounding Atlantica. He obviously regretted saying anything about it in the first place and had gone back to work behind the bar to avoid discussing the matter further. With no new signs of danger and people from the resort coming through to see how everyone was doing, Terry had decided to go upstairs and see if his friends were okay. People were slowly filtering out of the lounge so there was finally room to move around again.

Jenn moved over to where she could look out the window at the city below. Although there was a distinct lack of electrical noise, somebody had grabbed a guitar and was banging away in front of a BBQ restaurant. A coal-fired grill had been dragged out from somewhere and a couple of cooks were already smoking something on the barbecue. One of the shops that hadn't been flooded had sent someone outside who was yelling to anyone that would listen.

"No credit, no debit but we're still taking cash!"

Jenn smiled. Some things never changed! Looking out to sea nothing had changed there either, at least not in the last few minutes. Atlantica filled nearly the entire horizon and the U.S. Navy ships were still camped out in front of the bay. The sound of an outboard motor springing into life drifted up from the shore, followed by the echo of a cheer. A couple of minutes later a large speedboat sped out from a dock that she couldn't see and headed towards the island. There were a bunch of people on the boat, all yelling and screaming. Clearly they'd been drinking all night and were still partying hard.

"That'll end well," she said to herself.

Within a minute the speedboat's engine sputtered and died and the boat slowly drifted to a stop.

"Probably out of gas," said Paulo, as he came up beside her.

"Probably a good thing."

'Could be fate," Paulo said, seriously. "I'm sorry about before, Miss Jenn, but we're not supposed to share about Atlantica with anyone. But maybe now that it's… here, we can talk about it?"

He wasn't really asking her, so Jenn decided to let him work it out for himself.

"Never mind, Paulo," she said. "You can tell me later, if you want to."

She saw Terry entering the lounge. He spotted her and came over. He'd been running and was completely out of breath.

"Are they okay?" she asked.

"They," he said, taking a deep breath. "Left a note… Got up after the boom hit… Left the room and ran into some guy, who had been partying all night. He has a boat and they were going to party more."

Jenn help up her hand.

"Let me guess. They went out to go see what that is?"

Terry nodded, still puffing from running up and down six flights of stairs.

"I think they'll be okay," Jenn laughed.

118

She steered him closer to the window, pointing to the stationary party boat. "They ran out of gas."

Terry shook his head.

"Perfect," he said, rolling his eyes. "Paulo, I'm going to need a beer. Join me?"

Jenn shook her head.

"Any news about your family's flight?" he asked.

She shook her head again. The local station was now showing CNN news interspersed with their own local long range footage of Atlantica. There had been no new reports of plane crashes, which was good. They were actually doing a good job of conveying just how big the effect had been and letting people know that something big had happened.

"Disturbance off the Yucatan Peninsula: U.S. President to Give Worldwide Address at 5:00 pm. Eastern" scrolled across the bottom of the screen.

"Worldwide?" Terry said. "I've never heard of that before?"

"I wonder if he knows anything that we don't," Jenn asked. "We're right in the middle of it."

A strange and familiar sound rang out through the bar. The sound of Jenn's cell phone ringing made everyone look her way briefly, then reach for their own phones.

"I guess the tower's working again," said Terry, turning to Jenn then doing a double take.

She was smiling happily, tears streaming her face as she pointed to the name 'Bob Wallace' on the phone's screen. Terry smiled at her, gave her an encouraging wink and left her in peace.

"Bob?" she asked, tentatively.

"Jenn. Yeah, it's me. We're fine," he replied, his voice barely a whisper.

"I can hardly hear you. Where are you guys?"

119

"Er, that's a bit complicated..." he started to say before she cut him off.

"You wouldn't believe what's happening here."

"Jenn," he whispered, softly.

"Playa has had an electrical storm, an EMP pulse they said, a sonic boom..."

"Jenn," he said, whispering more forcefully.

"Then a small tsunami and this giant island appeared in the ocean off shore, I think a ship sank..."

"Jenn!" he said, loudly. "The island is Atlantis. Tara and I are on it."

"What?"

"Jenn, look I don't have much time. The plane was knocked down by that pulse. We landed in the water and were rescued by ships from Atlantis. Right now we're waiting to go into what I think is the council chambers to speak to them."

There was silence as Jenn tried to figure out what to say.

"Is Tara okay?"

"She's fine. We're fine. I think we're guests, we're being treated well."

"Bob?" she asked. "Atlantis? How could this be?"

"I have no idea, but it is. Just like Plato's description, well mostly. I'll send you a picture of the room we're in."

"How are you going to talk to them? You don't speak Minoan, if that's what they are."

"I think maybe some of them are, but Jenn, there are Mayan here as well and they all seem to speak Mayan."

Her phone's alert sounded and there it was, a text picture of Tara waving and smiling, sitting in a room framed by wide topped pillars and frescoes on the wall reminiscent of things seen only in Minoan museums and more recently the caves under Tulum. A few other people were sitting around, including Evan Masters.

"Evan's with you?" she said, warily.

"Half of the conference was on the plane. Everyone's here."

"But Bob, Atlantis?" she said, incredulously.

"I know, it's unbelievable," he said, "but it seems to be real. I hear someone coming. Don't call us. I'm shutting the phone off to save the battery."

While he talked Jenn was looking out to sea. Another ship was steaming in from the south.

"I'll call back when I can. Bye."

"Wait!" she said, but he was gone.

She must have looked in shock because Terry rushed right over.

"Are you alright?" he asked. "Are they okay?"

She didn't really know how to answer that, but he seemed to be willing to listen.

"Get me a beer and I'll tell you about it."

CHAPTER 23

Interference

"Sir, I have Atlantis Command for Mr. Johnson," the Carrier's Com officer relayed.

"My ready room, if you please," Lindquist replied.

Ryan looked questioningly at the admiral.

"Where else are you going to take it?" he said, smiling.

Once inside, Ryan was greeted on screen by the friendly face of someone he'd heard of but never met before.

"Mr. Baxter," he said to the president's press secretary. "A pleasure to meet you. I didn't know you were on the team."

"Things are evolving rather quickly on this, Mr. Johnson," he drawled in his thick southern accent. "We have been trying to locate these Mayan experts for you, however I'm afraid all I have is bad news."

"What kind of bad news?" Ryan asked.

"It seems that Dr. Masters and Mr. Wallace were on a plane that was scheduled to land in Playa del Carmen right about the time that Atlantis showed up. That plane is one of the ones listed as missing in the event."

"I see. And Jennifer Wallace?"

"Seems she was in Playa waiting to take the other two gentlemen and an entire conference full of Mayan experts on a tour of those ruins under Tulum," Baxter replied. "We have thus far been unable to reach anyone in Playa as all the lines remain down."

Ryan didn't know what to say.

"We have been checking to see who else might be able to help out," Baxter continued. "And I'm sure we'll find somebody, but most of the people we'd like to have on this, were on that plane."

"Well, thanks for trying, Mr. Baxter." Ryan said. "I appreciate your efforts."

"Please call me George, Ryan. You and I will be talking a whole lot more before this is over. Now, I'm currently putting together a speech about this whole mess that the president will deliver to the whole world in just a few hours time. If you discover anything that ought to be added... you will let me know before then?"

"I will, sir, er, George. I most definitely will."

"Excellent! I'm sending over the cell phone numbers for Dr. Evans and the Wallaces and for myself. There's also a list of other possible Mayan experts, so if you see anyone that you can use, please let me know."

"Thanks," said Ryan, as he signed off.

The bridge was abnormally busy when he came out of the ready room. The Com officer was attempting hails on multiple channels and the main screen was filled with the image of another ship arriving. It seemed to be steaming straight for the harbor.

"Ryan," said the admiral, calling him over. "How's your Spanish?"

"Sir?" he asked, then added, "not very good."

"Well, hopefully we won't need it. Com?"

"Nothing sir, no response."

"They're not slowing, sir," Nav added, urgently.

The admiral rattled off orders.

"Weapons, ready a mortar round for a warning shot. Com, get someone on the signal lamp. Ops, let's get a couple of inflatables in the water. Make sure they have a Spanish speaking crew."

"Sir, I'm the only one qualified on Morse signals," Com informed him.

"Mortar round ready!" Weapons reported.

"Nav?" the admiral asked.

"No change in course or speed, sir."

The admiral looked at Ryan and sighed then nodded at Weapons.

"Let's put one in front of him, prep a second. Where are those boats?"

"Ready to launch now, sir," said Ops.

"Make sure they have extra radio equipment," said Ryan.

"Ryan?" Lindquist asked.

"Sir, if that ship was operating in the EMP area their radio could be out."

"Ops, make it so," said the admiral. "Com, get Atlantis Command on the line, tell them we need the secretary of the Mexican Navy, or better, on the line right now."

The dull whoop of the exploding mortar echoed through the ship as the warning round went off. The boat did not appear to slow.

"Another, please," the admiral requested. "Closer."

The seconds ticked by until the sound of the second mortar reached them.

"They're slowing, sir," Nav reported.

"Get those boats in the water," ordered Lindquist. "And let me talk to someone on them."

When he was linked in, the admiral was all business.

"Inform them we're here at their government's request. Ask them nicely to please stand down and wait for orders from their command. Give them a radio if theirs aren't working."

"Yes, Admiral," a nervous voice replied from the inflatable. "Sir, what if they don't comply?"

"Then get out of there quickly, because that boat isn't going into that harbor," the admiral replied. "Com, keep this line open. Weapons, that's a converted U.S. Navy frigate. Figure out what you can do to disable it with the least amount of damage."

"Sir, I have Mexican Naval Command on the line," said Com.

Lindquist nodded and they watched the screen as the rubber craft pulled up alongside the Mexican ship. There was a bull horn exchange followed by a basket being lowered to the craft. As the basket was pulled up, the skipper of the small boat got back on the radio.

"Sir, you were right. They have no working radio gear. They'll be contacting you shortly."

There was a painful silence on the bridge. The ship had slowed but not stopped and they were getting dangerously close to the harbor entrance.

"Sir, I have the Mexican captain on the line," Com announced.

The admiral didn't even wait for introductions.

"Captain, this is Admiral Lindquist of the US 4th Fleet. We're live with your Naval Command right now, but I need you to heave to immediately. The last ship that tried to go into that harbor is at the bottom of the ocean."

A quick report in Spanish followed from Mexican Naval Command and obviously reinforced what the Admiral had said. They heard the Captain bark orders to his crew, after which the ship immediately reversed its engines and came to a full stop.

Everyone on the bridge of the *Excelsior* heaved a collective sigh of relief as the admiral invited the Mexican captain aboard to bring him up to speed on what had transpired so far. The captain's English was good enough to accept the offer. He said that he and some of his officers would board the inflatable to head over to the carrier.

Lindquist turned to Ryan.

"Well, we an tell them what happened so far. Any idea what's going to happen next?"

Ryan shook his head as the Com officer handed him a printout that had come in earlier. It was the list of contacts that Baxter had sent over. As promised, at the top of the list were three names with cell phone numbers beside them.

CHAPTER 24

Language?

Bob and the others were on their way back to the council chamber when Tara whispered to her dad.

"Why didn't you tell Mom that they speak English?" she asked. "Wouldn't she want to know?"

"Tara," Bob replied, "that had to be a trick or something. These people speak Mayan and what I think might be Minoan, except the Minoan culture died out three and a half millennia ago. No, they must have heard us talking, and…"

He stopped speaking as they had reached the stairs to the dais.

At the top, Bob stole a glance at the princess, causing him to bump into Evan. Tara snickered as Bob grunted an apology while they all lined up again. The captain was standing in front but this time he was facing them. When they'd settled, he came over to Evan. Then in a gesture that was completely out of character with everything they'd observed so far, he extended his hand towards Evan.

"In k'aaba'e Cadmael," he said.

The captain spoke slowly for them again, but it took Evan a minute to figure out the meaning even though the captain was pointing at himself. Finally, Evan grabbed the captain's hand and shook it.

"In Evan, Evan Masters," he stuttered, then pointed at

himself. "Jach ki'imak in wóol in wilikech... cha'."

He chanced a smile and the captain smiled back at him.

"What did they say?" Gloria asked.

"The captain's name is Cadmael," Emma replied. "And Evan said 'Pleased to meet you... again'"

"Evan Masters," the captain said, then added tentatively. "In yum tan balun jukubo'ob."

Evan thought for a moment then shot an odd glance at Bob, who nodded his affirmation. Evan gulped.

"What's that?" Tara asked. "It didn't make any sense."

Bob answered without taking his eyes off Cadmael.

"I think our friend Cadmael might be in charge of their navy."

"Why?" Gloria asked.

Tara told her what she thought she'd heard.

"I am boss in front of many boats."

Emma nodded in confirmation.

"Evan," Bob whispered loudly. "Ask him where we are."

"What?" said Evan.

"Tux a lela' tzuk?" Bob said, gesturing to include the island around them. "Ask him."

Evan repeated Bob's question and Cadmael looked up at the council. A nod from a couple of them gave him permission.

"Ajawpeten," Cadmael answered, his arms encircled to include the whole ship around them.

"Island of Kings," Emma said.

"Má tin naátik báaxten jukub okol jol?" Cadmael asked Evan, in halting Mayan.

"I don't understand why ship enter doorway," Emma whispered.

"What?" Evan asked Emma, but Cadmael thought Evan had asked him to repeat his question.

"Má tin naátik báaxten jukub okol jol?" Cadmael said again, sounding somewhat frustrated.

"He doesn't speak Mayan," Bob said, much louder that he'd intended.

The council members stirred at his outburst.

"What do you mean?" Tara asked in a soft whisper, attempting to get her dad to lower his voice.

A discussion rippled through the council seats above them as Bob explained.

"Mayan is not Cadmael's first language. That's why he's been hesitating."

A lilting yet powerful voice emerged from the council. Bob turned to see who was speaking.

"Cadmael!"

The woman that Bob had assumed was a princess had stood up and spoke out again firmly, this time in English.

"Enough!"

An obviously relieved Cadmael exhaled, nodded his thanks to the princess, turned back to face Bob.

"You are right," Cadmael said, in an oddly accented English. "Maya is not my first speech."

He smiled at the effect of his English words and addressed them all inclusively.

"I am Commander Cadmael. I am charged with the security of Atlantis."

He waited for their shock and confusion to subside then asked Evan his question again.

"Do you know why your ship ignored our warnings?"

"I can only guess that they didn't understand them, Cadmael," Evan replied. "I don't know much about naval operations."

"They would have tried to contact you," Gloria added from beside him. "By radio, which I'm guessing you don't have?"

Cadmael regarded her carefully.

"We do not. We put out the warnings."

"I'm sure they didn't understand before, Cadmael," Evan said, quickly trying to take charge again. "But I'm pretty sure they understand now."

Cadmael nodded.

"True, they did not try again. Very well. Questions. How do you speak Maya? It was confusing. We thought it might not survive."

"How is it that you speak English?" Bob asked before Evan could say anything.

Several of the council members rose to their feet at his impertinent question.

"That would be my doing!"

The old man had come up behind them again. He looked up at council and they sat down, deferring to him. Cadmael opened his hand to indicate that the old man should continue.

"I am Aranare, "the old man explained. "You must forgive their caution in speaking with you. We did not expect anyone here for our return. I know your language because I speak for Diachrome Paulin."

Deep breaths from Cadmael and some of the council members hinted to Bob that there was someone that was more important than the council. Maybe this Diachrome was one of their gods?

"He has seen your world many times and recounted to me each time exactly what he saw and what was said," Aranare continued as he paced around them, looked them up and down and smiling. "I have become what you would call a linguist and a teacher. Most of our people have learned your language. What is it called?"

"English," Evan said, quickly. "Our language is English."

132

"English." Aranare said, thoughtfully, as if he was hearing the word for the first time.

He turned and addressed the council.

"Well, my friends. We have come far. Perhaps you should come down here and meet these people and practice your English?"

"I like this guy, Dad," Tara whispered.

"Me too, sweetie," replied Bob, as he caught Aranare's eye and winked at him. "Me too."

The open sided top of the council chamber allowed in sound from every direction. When the first mortar round went off everyone was easily able to hear the noise echoing across the harbor.

"That's a mortar round!" said Gloria, turning to Cadmael. "Is there a place where we can see what's happening?"

He looked up and one of the council members nodded his approval.

"Up," he told Gloria.

He started up the stairs leading towards the seats of the council, with everyone else following along. A second mortar round spurred him and Gloria into a run and they leaped two steps at a time until they reached the top and dashed between the council seats.

The spray was settling from the second round that had landed directly in front of a newly arrived ship that appeared to have been heading directly for the harbor. A large green, white, and red flag hung from a mast on the ship.

"What is happening?" Cadmael asked, politely, while raising his hand over his head in a clenched fist.

"I think it's okay," Gloria said, keeping her eyes on the scene in front of her. "It looks like that Mexican ship was heading for the harbor but they fired a couple of rounds across her bow to get her to heave to."

"The fleet is American, right?" asked Bob.

"I think so," Gloria replied.

"Look, there are a couple of small boats out there as well," Evan said, trying to sound as if he knew what was happening. "They're probably sorting it all out right now."

They looked out at the view from the top of the council chamber. They could see the harbor from their seats but the 360-degree view also gave them full coverage of Atlantis and the ocean surrounding the harbor. It was an excellent strategic command post, yet from the outside no one could tell that there was even an opening in the upper part of the building.

The two small boats collected some people from the new ship and headed off to the carrier. Cadmael lowered his fist as things appeared to agree with Gloria's analysis of the situation.

"Perhaps Aranare is right," he said. "Maybe we can share some English. Can you can tell us what is American and Mexican?"

"And," said the princess, as she pointed to Playa Del Carmen and the strip of hotels lining the shore, "what is that place?"

CHAPTER 25

Pickup

It didn't take Jenn very long to tell Terry everything that Bob had said and she showed him the picture from inside Atlantis. Terry sat with his mouth open for a moment then noticed the beer bottle in his hand. He took a long thoughtful swig.

"So you're telling me that your ex-husband Bob and your daughter are on that island and that it actually is Atlantis?" he said.

She shrugged and took a drink from her own beer. While she was pretty sure that it was true, she didn't think she was ready to confirm it yet.

"I guess it makes sense to me," Terry said.

"Huh?" said Jenn.

"Well, to put it quite simply, what else could it be?"

Terry got up and moved closer to the window for a better view.

Jenn's phone rang again and she answered it instantly.

"Bob!" she said, with relief.

"Uh, no ma'am," an unfamiliar male voice replied.

She glanced quickly at the screen, 'R. Johnson' was displayed.

"Is this Jennifer Wallace?"

"Yes. Who's this?"

"Doctor Jennifer Wallace? Archeologist?"

"Who is this? How did you get this number?"

Jenn was getting irritated now.

"I'm sorry, ma'am, but I'm with the U.S. Navy and I urgently need to know if you are in fact, Doctor Jennifer Wallace, archeologist, and expert on the Mayan Civilization.

"Sure. I mean, yes, that's me."

"Thank goodness. My name's Ryan Johnson and I'm currently with the 4th fleet of the coast of…" he paused. "Sorry, but I need to know where you are right now, Dr. Wallace?"

"If you were going to say the Yucatan or Playa Del Carmen, then I'm looking at your fleet right now, Mr. Johnson."

"So, you're aware of what's happened, what appeared off the coast?"

He was covering his bases for sure.

"We've been experiencing the effects of that apparition in Playa all morning," she said, trying hard not to be sarcastic. "Was there some purpose for your call, Mr. Johnson?"

"Where exactly are you in Playa, Dr. Wallace?"

"I'm staying at the Los Caballeros. I'm in the lounge having a beer with all the others that are stranded here with no power and no clue as to what's going on."

There was silence on the other end of the phone, but she could hear a muted conversation for a moment.

"Dr. Wallace, we're sending a team to extract you by chopper. They will be there in 15 to 20 minutes. A Mexican ground team will be there sooner and will secure you for the flight. Ma'am, do you by any chance know where your husband or Dr. Evan Masters are. We've been unable to locate them."

"Yes, I do".

"Well, if you could tell me that would be a big help."

"Sure. They're both on Atlantis right now, along with my daughter."

There was silence for a moment and she was pretty sure Ryan was going to hang up.

"When you say Atlantis, do you have confirmation of that?"

In the background, she heard a commanding voice yell Ryan's name, followed by a short muffled conversation. Jenn pulled up the picture that Bob had texted her. She smiled and texted it to R. Johnson. She heard his phone alert sound, followed by more silence and then some discussion.

"Sorry, Dr. Wallace," he said, apologetically, "but I have to ask..."

"I just spoke to him, a few minutes ago. Apparently their plane was caught in the pulse and went down in the water. It sounds like everyone's okay. They were rescued by people from the island. He's there right now, with my daughter, Dr. Masters and probably the rest of the plane's passengers as well. He said that it really is Atlantis."

"Dr. Wallace," Ryan said, "We need to talk to you ASAP. Please don't talk to anyone else about this. There are enough rumors already floating around and it could even be unsafe."

"Unsafe?" she said. "Why?"

"People get crazy about ordinary everyday things, ma'am, but this one will give the crazies something to focus on for years to come."

"Well, it's too late. I've already told one person, but he seems fine with it."

From over near the window Terry yelled to her.

"Hey look, the army's arriving. Maybe help is starting to get organized."

"Sounds like the army's here," Jenn said into the phone.

"Yes, they're reporting they're at the hotel," Ryan

confirmed. "I'm going to stay on the line until they have you secured."

"Mr. Johnson," she said, deciding to be polite after all. "Ryan. What do you need me for? I just want to get my daughter back... and Bob, safely."

"Well, Dr. Wallace," Ryan said carefully, "it seems that Atlantis is at least part Mayan, and you're the only expert we can find, at least the only one that apparently isn't on Atlantis right now."

"But what's the U.S. Navy doing here? What's going on? I mean, Atlantis? Who's in charge of this?"

"That, Dr. Wallace, is exactly what my boss is hoping to find out, with your help."

"Well, who's your boss then?"

"He's the same person who appointed me to the International Atlantis Task Force a couple of hours ago and the same guy who gave me your phone number. The President of the United States."

"Hey, what's up?" asked Terry, as he sat down on the couch beside her.

"I'll talk to you shortly, Dr. Wallace," Ryan said.

He hung up as a team of soldiers surged into the lounge, two of them hanging back to secure the door.

"Dr. Jennifer Wallace?" the lead soldier called out.

Jenn slowly raised her hand and the rest of the soldiers moved forward and surrounded her. Terry had no idea what was going on and tried to intervene but the soldiers surrounded them both and faced outward, obviously there to protect them.

" Señorita Wallace?" the captain of the squad asked. "We need to get you two to the roof for helicopter extraction."

"But he's not with me," said Jenn.

"My orders are to put you and anyone you were talking

with on the chopper," he said. 'Did you speak to anyone else?"

* * *

Ten minutes later Jenn, Terry, and Paulo were being handed over and loaded into a U.S. transport helicopter on the roof of the hotel. Two gunships kept station fore and aft as the group set off towards the fleet anchored off Atlantis.

"We're going to see Atlantica?" Paulo asked, his eyes wide with wonder at the prospect.

"Sorry sir," one of the soldiers riding with them apologized, "but they there's said no talking, until you've been debriefed."

"Sorry about this guys," Jenn said, ignoring the soldier's glare.

CHAPTER 26

Drop Off

"Sir, we have confirmation that Dr. Jennifer Wallace has been picked up and is inbound from Playa."

Admiral Lindquist nodded to acknowledge the Com officer then turned back to the meeting at hand.

"Well, Mr. Johnson, I hope your hunch about the EMP pulse is correct or this could be a very short trip for Dr. Wallace."

"What do you mean?"

The captain of the Mexican ship had just arrived on the carrier's bridge with two other officers. He signaled them to hang back then came forward and greeted the admiral.

"Captain" said the admiral, acknowledging with a handshake. "Admiral Lindquist, United States 4th Fleet."

"Captain Ochoa, of the Armada de México ship *Victoria*."

"This is Ryan Johnson. He's part of the special task force that has been set up to handle this."

The admiral pointed to Atlantis.

"Señor Johnson," the Captain offered his hand, and Ryan shook it.

"Captain Ochoa," Ryan said. "To answer your question, the admiral means that if there's another EMP pulse, those choppers will be knocked out of the sky."

"Then why not send a boat?" Ochoa asked the admiral, who nodded to Ryan to answer.

"If I'm right, the Atlantis shield is what generated the pulse that caused all the problems," Ryan explained. "It's not on now so we should be okay."

"Atlantica," Captain Ochoa said thoughtfully, as if something he'd feared had just been confirmed.

His expression became grim and he straightened and turned to the admiral.

"You are right to be cautious. I apologize if my actions caused concern. My only goal was to block you from entering the harbor."

"And why would you do that, captain?" Lindquist asked, carefully.

"There is an old Maya tale of Atlantica returning at the end of the world," Captain Ochoa replied, with a sigh. "It is said that all those who enter Atlantica will vanish forever."

"Why have we never heard of this?" Ryan asked.

"It is Maya 'cuento de hadas' - what you would call a fairy tale," Captain Ochoa replied. "Passed down from generations, never to be written."

"Hmm," said the admiral. "We've already lost a ship to Atlantis, captain. Our goal was also to prevent you from entering the harbor. Mr. Johnson, would you like to bring the captain up to speed?"

"Yes, Admiral," Ryan answered, "but if it's all the same, I'd prefer to wait for Dr. Wallace to arrive and just go through it all once."

"Com, flight ETA?" the admiral asked.

"About five minutes, sir," Com replied.

Lindquist nodded. He wasn't used to being questioned, but Ryan's suggestion made sense.

"Have Dr. Wallace brought to the bridge when they land," the admiral ordered.

"Aye, sir," said Com. "What about the other two?"

142

"Other two?" Ryan asked. "What other two?"

* * *

It took a lot longer than five minutes to sort out who should be involved in the debriefing. In the end, it was Ryan that decided it might as well be all of them, against the admiral's advice. Ryan had a suspicion that the admiral's agreement meant that none of them would be leaving the ship anytime soon, but that didn't seem too important right now.

"Dr. Wallace?" Ryan asked Jenn as she entered the bridge. "I hope you had a good flight? I'm Ryan Johnson."

Jenn studied him. He was around Bob's age, clean cut and in the sort of shape that one might expect of a Navy commander. She found herself liking what she saw.

"You certainly know how to sweep a girl off her feet, Mr. Johnson."

She laughed at the surprise on his face, then rescued him.

"Thank you. The flight was fine and the sight of Atlantis growing larger as we got closer was..."

"Unforgettable," Terry stepped in around her and extended his hand to Ryan.

"I'm Terry," he said then gestured around the bridge. "A helicopter flight, Atlantis and now this! What a holiday!"

"Uh, hi Terry, I'm Ryan. And you must be Paulo?"

He grabbed and shook Paulo's hand as he came in the door. Paulo wasn't even trying to pretend that he wasn't scared.

"Si, señor," he said.

When he saw Captain Ochoa and the two Mexican officers on the bridge, he tried his best to look small.

"I'm Admiral Lindquist. Let's get this started."

143

"Right," Ryan began. "Dr. Wallace, Captain Ochoa, you're to going be briefed on everything we know so far and please contribute anything relevant regarding your experiences since Atlantis appeared. At my request, Terry, Paulo and the captain's officers will attend but we ask you to hang back and don't interrupt unless you have something material to contribute."

The Admiral turned to Terry and Paulo.

"I know you were picked up without a choice. But you need to know that unless you're told otherwise, everything you're going to see and hear is considered top secret. If you can't keep it confidential you must leave now or run the risk of being charged with treason. From either country."

Captain Ochoa explained for his people in Spanish and Paulo looked as if he might leave for a moment then decided that he'd stay after all.

The scope of the meeting was then brought into crystal clarity.

"We'll be on live conference with Atlantis Command at NORAD and both our governments, NATO and other agencies will be on listen only," the admiral said then nodded to Ryan.

Ryan laid out the timetable of events as they'd occurred so far, including the destruction of the *Xavier*. Atlantis Command pitched in with reports of effects that had been felt or seen around the world just as it happened. Jenn, occasionally with Terry's help, described firsthand what had happened in Playa del Carmen and Captain Ochoa explained how his ship had been disabled and what they'd done to become at least partially operational again.

He then explained his approach to block off the harbor at Atlantis and the reason behind it, bringing up the Atlantica story. The captain and Paulo exchanged glances, after which Paulo recounted the stories that had been passed down through his family. He was able to provide a version of the tale that was a little more verbose than the captain's second-hand account.

Jenn took a turn and revealed how Bob and Tara had come to be on Atlantis, showing everyone the picture she'd been sent of the anteroom of the council chamber. After the silence that revelation produced, Ryan thought it a good time to make some plans.

"Obviously we need to talk to these people," he said. "When Mr. Wallace calls back, we have to get him to help us open a dialogue. What else do we have?"

"NORAD is assembling a large amount of data through satellite imagery now that the fog has cleared," General Aspinal, said. "I'll run you through some of the highlights. The island is approximately six kilometers in diameter and is a perfect circle. There are, or were, exactly one hundred of those golden pillars we saw in the video equally spaced around the edge of the island. There are three canals of decreasing width as you move towards the central island. The canal edges appear to house a large number of ships, probably more than a thousand."

Everyone in the room inhaled at the mention of a thousand ships.

"With the new resources that have been placed at our disposal, infrared imaging shows many of these ships are manned and presumably ready to launch."

A ghostly outline of a ship with dozens of heat signatures of people mostly seated in rows, three on each side, filled the screen. As the view zoomed out it revealed another ship holding only a couple of people in the next space, then a manned ship two spaces away, then another until appeared that every second ship in the area of the harbor was fully manned.

"Fortunately, these seem to be the same wooden rowed

ships that you saw in the harbor, but what it does tell us is that there's a high degree of strategy at work here, regardless of the level of technology."

The image continued to zoom out, and while there were random dots everywhere, only one odd row of dots seemed to ring one edge of the canal. As the picture expanded a similar row appeared around each canal.

"What are those rings?" Ryan asked.

"People," replied the general. "We don't know what they're doing, but there are people lining the canal walls. Estimates are between 200,000 and 300,000 people in total on the island. There are fields, plants, dwellings, horses and other animals, birds, buildings of all sizes. We can see store-rooms, temples and even an outdoor theatre here and there. Stone and metal pathways and bridges connect everything. The island is dotted with these white spires which some of our people think is a communication network of some kind."

As the general switched to topography, the picture shifted from infrared to camera view and panned across the surface of the island. There were small pastures, crops divided by stone walls, and one of the theatres she'd mentioned. Then the view shifted to the center of the island. The picture was blurred, as if there was some kind of visual interference, before the camera slowly zoomed out.

"The central island is quite interesting. There appears to be a shield, similar to what you reported before the *Xavier* was sunk, surrounding some of the central buildings of the island."

At a wide angle it was easy to see that there was a round bubble of something surrounding the middle of the central island. Then the picture switched back to infrared and everyone in the room covered their eyes.

"As you can see, whatever's surrounding the center

has a great deal of energy," the general continued, "but even more interesting, the entire island seems to be generating or storing energy! The whole place looked like this on infrared when they first looked."

As she spoke the picture flared into a bright blob of light.

"In everything else you've seen so far, all this has been compensated for."

"Sir, we have activity!" said Com, interrupting the proceedings. "A single ship flying a white flag is headed towards the harbor gates."

CHAPTER 27

Maybe We Should Talk

Bob and the girls remained quiet as Evan did a masterful job of explaining the world in general to Cadmael and the council. Evan's hands traced the positions of the continents and countries in the air, as he reeled off the world's major nations and their approximate populations, paying special attention to Mexico and the United States. Bob had to admit he couldn't have done it as well. Evan had a very quiet and attentive audience until he concluded his talk by informing their hosts that the current population of the planet was approximately seven billion.

Shock and surprise filled the room. Several of the council spoke to each other in their native languages.

"How is this possible?" Bob clearly heard one of the Mayan say to another.

Cadmael cleared his throat for attention and the council's conversations subsided. He turned and looked Evan carefully in the eye.

"What year now?"

"2025."

Once again surprise, and to some extent dismay, seemed to fill the chamber. Evan looked at Bob and shrugged.

"Perhaps," Bob said very loudly, "we should discuss geography?"

He waited for the conversations to die down.

"The city you see off to the west is called Playa del Carmen," he began. "It is located on the coast of what Evan told you is the country of Mexico. The buildings are hotels and people travel from all over the world stay in these hotels on vacation."

"What is vacation?" the princess asked.

"It is a time that people and families take off from work to relax and enjoy," Bob replied. "This is one of the favorite places to vacation for many people because it is so warm and beautiful here."

"Perhaps we can learn more about that later, Itzela?" Cadmael asked her.

Bob was ecstatic. Now he knew her name! Cadmael was waiting for him to continue after Itzela's nod.

"Just south along the coast are the Mayan ruins of Tulum. It is one of the best preserved of all the Mayan cities."

"The Maya are no more?" one of the Mayan councilors asked, gravely.

"No, there are Mayan still," said Bob, relieved to be able to say something positive. "There are about half a million Maya living here, along the coast and down into countries in what was Mesoamerica."

"They do well?" the Mayan councilor asked.

"Well," said Bob, hesitantly, "in truth, not as well as they could. They're a wonderful people, some of whom I have come to call friends, but they prefer to live by themselves and don't pursue the same course that so many in our world do."

He paused but his infernal honesty kept him talking.

"I'm sorry, but because of this, many are not well treated in areas like Playa del Carmen."

The council members grew angry. It was the first time that Bob had seen them like this. The Minoan seemed just as upset and at that moment Bob knew that he wasn't speaking to Mayan or Minoan but simply to Atlantean.

"The Maya here are now part of the Mexican civilization that has been predominant here for about the last 500 years. The last ship that you saw approaching was a Mexican ship and it appeared to be attempting to defend Atlantis, even if there was no threat at the time."

The council members seemed somewhat placated by that, although he could tell that they were definitely going to be asking a lot more questions.

"And what of Keftiu?" Cadmael asked, with sadness in his voice.

"Keftiu?" said Evan.

Bob racked his brains.

"Keftiu," he said then paused. "I remember. Egyptian hieroglyphs depicted the people of Keftiu bringing trade goods of copper, bronze and blue to market."

He looked at the members of the council that were not Mayan.

"Keftiu was thought to be what the Greeks called the island of Crete. The civilization that lived there before the Greeks we call Minoan, after King Minos."

Cadmael's sad expression told Bob that he was at least partly correct.

"Then there were no survivors, as we suspected."

"Well, maybe not on Thera or Crete," Bob said, "but it's believed that the Minoan culture formed the basis for many of the peoples and cultures of modern Europe."

"We were Keftiu," Cadmael said, pointing at himself, Itzela and some others. "Minos was a Giver of Law long ago. I do not know Thera or Crete."

"They are islands in the Mediterranean Sea," Evan added. "On the larger one, Crete, there's a huge palace at a place we call Knossos. It's also just ruins, but it has inspired generations since it's excavation. Nearby on Thera is a Minoan excavation at Akrotiri. We've always wanted to know more about the Minoans."

Bob saw Cadmael wince when Evan said Akrotiri, but he wasn't sure why.

"Well, maybe that's enough about the past for now," Evan said. "There are some pressing matters outside the harbor gates to deal with. Maybe I should go and talk to them."

"You?" said Bob. "Why would you go?"

"To be the liaison for Atlantis," Evan replied, feigning innocence.

"They don't need a liaison," said Bob, growing angry at Evan's self-important attitude. "They need to know that there's no threat here and they'll need to talk to at least Cadmael if they're going to believe us."

"I don't think so," said Evan.

Bob turned to the council.

"Right now they think you're a military threat, but what has happened here was by accident. We all need to calmly go over there and explain what happened."

"You can explain what happened?" Evan asked, sarcastically.

"Of course not," said Bob, rolling his eyes. "That's why Cadmael must come. Cadmael, you need to tell them before they try and do something stupid."

"What do you mean?" Cadmael asked.

"You saw what happened with just one shell going off accidentally? Well, a fleet like that probably has thousands of rounds of ammo like that, as well as guided missiles, lasers…"

"These are other weapons?" Cadmael asked.

"Yes, and very bad," Bob said. "At least we can let them know everything's okay and they don't need to worry."

"The survivors from the plane can go back, the injured can be looked at, and even the bodies can be returned." Evan added.

"A good plan," Itzela said, from her council chair.

Bob looked at her and smiled his agreement.

* * *

About half an hour later, after explaining to Cadmael what a white flag symbolized and then setting it up, Evan, Bob, Cadmael, and Aranare were seated in the canopied area on one of the Minoan flagships as they were rowed out to meet the fleet. As they passed the other Minoan ship that was stationed just inside the harbor gates, Cadmael instructed them to return to port.

"You sure this is a good idea?" Evan asked Bob.

But Bob was thinking about what an idiotic grin he'd had on his face when he'd smiled at Itzela. He just shrugged as they continued forward and quoted something that matched his dismal mood.

"Maybe today is a good day to die."

CHAPTER 28

A Historic Event

"Show me that ship!" Admiral Lindquist ordered. "And patch this through to Atlantis Command."

The main screen flickered to show a telephoto view of one of the rowed ships purposefully making its way toward the harbor entrance. A large white flag hung from the ship's bow. As the camera zoomed in, one of the people in the ship waved the other vessel inside the harbor boundaries off, and it started back towards the docks. Jenn caught sight of the ship's passengers even before the camera finished zooming in.

"That's Bob!" Jenn exclaimed.

"Prepare the captain's launch," the admiral ordered. "Rig a white flag and strip all armament from the boat."

He turned to Jenn. Her face was white.

"Anyone else you know?"

"Just my ex-husband and Evan Masters. I don't see my daughter."

"Well, then I guess you're with us then."

He looked at the others.

"I'll need a Mayan translator as well."

"I can handle that, admiral," said Jenn.

"Very well. Captain Ochoa, Ryan, if you please?" he said, nodding at Com. "Have Captain Mulholland meet us at the launch."

The screens in the carrier followed the wooden ship as it heaved to and held position in the harbor mouth. In a picture that would be later broadcast throughout the world, the captain's launch motored out a respectable speed to meet those aboard the rowed wooden ship from Atlantis.

As they pulled alongside the admiral stood on the deck at the side of the launch. The white robed figure that stood opposite him reflected the same air of easy authority that he himself embodied. As his sailors soundlessly grabbed the ropes tossed from the other boat and pulled the ships together, Lindquist used the phrase that Jenn had taught him on the way over.

"Pahtal taal teelo'?"

The admiral hoped it at least roughly meant 'Permission to come aboard'.

His counterpart looked at him.

"Yes, please come over," he said in English and smiled as he carefully lowered a plank to create a walkway between the ships.

"I am Cadmael, charged with security of Atlantis."

He extended his hand to the surprised admiral as he boarded.

"Admiral Lindquist, Commander of the US 4th Fleet," said the admiral, shaking Cadmael's hand.

"You speak English?"

"We have learned that is what it is called, yes," Cadmael replied.

The admiral glanced back at Jenn as she came across the plank.

She shrugged then saw Bob's shocked face, hopped down and ran over to him. She gave him a quick hug then let go.

"Where's Tara?"

"She wanted to stay on Atlantis for a bit longer," Bob replied. "She's fine. What are you doing here?"

"Ahem!"

Evan cleared his throat as he extended his hand to the admiral.

"I'm Dr. Evan Masters, this is Aranare and Bob Wallace."

Ryan stepped forward and pried Evan away from the admiral.

"This is Captain Ochoa of the Armada de Mexico, Captain Mulholland, U.S. Navy, Dr. Jennifer Wallace, and I'm Ryan Johnson, representing the newly created Atlantis Command."

"Atlantis Command?" said Evan.

"Your presence has caused some attention," the admiral told Cadmael. "Atlantis Command was created to help with coordinating… your arrival."

Cadmael nodded then looked to Aranare.

"I am here as an advisor to the council. We rescued these and others from your airplane. Although some have asked to stay on Atlantis for a bit longer, most would be quite happy to return home?"

"Yes, of course," said Ryan.

Cadmael crossed to the side of the boat facing the dock. He waved his arms in a motion that must have indicated that the other wooden ships should join them. Moments later, two ships departed the docks and headed their way.

The admiral nodded and passed instructions to the crew of his launch.

"Let's get a couple of boats out here to retrieve the survivors from the plane crash."

"There are two casualties and one that was badly burned," Bob added quickly.

"What happened?" Ryan asked.

"We think the pulse that hit the plane burned the copilot

157

and the pilot," Evan explained. "The copilot didn't make it and an elderly lady had a heart attack or maybe a pacemaker failure. The pilot's in pretty bad shape, but he was able to water-land the plane."

"They will meet your boats just outside the harbor?" the admiral asked.

Cadmael nodded and lowered his head in agreement.

"This is a rather unique moment for our people," Lindquist admitted. "We would like permission to record this meeting, if that is okay with you?"

He looked questioningly from Aranare to Cadmael, but they didn't seem to understand.

Jenn brought out her cell phone and flicked it on, searching for a clip of Tara. "Like this," she said.

She showed Aranare and Cadmael a video clip of Tara focused intently, working on a drawing as music blared and her mom sneaked up on her. Just as Jenn was about to move to where she could see the artwork, Tara saw her and covered it up.

"Mom!" Tara said. "Not til it's done!"

Aranare laughed out loud and Cadmael smiled. If there had been any ice in their relationship, Jenn's video had melted it completely. Jenn looked bewildered at the response but Bob explained.

"Tara's been working her charms on Atlantis. This captured her perfectly."

"Yes, you may record," Aranare said. "But if this is what you can do in your hands, I suspect you are already recording from afar?"

The admiral and Ryan looked worried, but Aranare's wink reassured them.

"A precaution," Lindquist said. "Yes, we've been recording since we left the ship."

"As we might do," Aranare said, smiling. "Cadmael?"

Cadmael nodded. "We appreciate that you have asked."

The conversation stopped as the two ships from Atlantis rendezvoused with the boats from the carrier. Navy teams carried the wounded over on stretchers while the rest climbed aboard the boats. The two ratings from the bow of the *Xavier* received some good-natured ribbing as they climbed aboard. Under the watchful eyes of the Atlantean honor guard that had consistently stood with them, the deceased were left in their raft and lifted aboard. Their duty discharged, the honor guards began helping the remaining passengers to transfer.

The admiral and Ryan looked at each other, impressed with what they'd just seen.

"Bob! Evan!" Gloria's voice called from one of the rescue ships. "Bye!"

Bob waved back and yelled a goodbye, while Evan raised a hand and casuallywaved.

"Who's that?" Ryan asked.

"A flight attendant," replied Evan.

Bob snorted at Evans curt response.

"A flight attendant that kept the entire plane organized and calm as we descended then crash-landed in the ocean after the accident. A flight attendant that made sure the plane was fully evacuated, even the casualties, before she got off herself. A flight attendant that knows more about protocol and decorum than you ever will!"

His voice was getting louder as he continued.

"A flight attendant? Really Evan, that's all you can say? Gloria should get a bloody medal!"

Embarrassed at his outburst he sat down quickly and looked away. "Sorry," he murmured.

Aranare stared at Bob thoughtfully for a few moments then broke the silence.

"Maybe we should talk?" he said, with a wry smile.

CHAPTER 29

The Meeting

After they had watched the transfer ships depart, everyone took a seat under the canopy of the wooden ship.

"Why did you enter our harbor?" asked Cadmael. "We warned you to stay out."

"That was my fault," Captain Mulholland replied. "And a mistake, I'm sorry to say."

He took a deep breath.

"I misread the situation and, despite Mr. Johnson's efforts, I ignored your warnings and proceeded ahead. I'm truly sorry for trespassing."

"I don't know 'trespassing'," Aranare said, "but why did you not stop before?"

"It doesn't really matter, sir," Mulholland replied. "It was an error."

"It matters to us," said Cadmael.

Mulholland looked over at the admiral who nodded for the captain to go ahead.

"Your ship's, er, Atlantis's appearance set off a series of events that most closely resemble the effects of a weapon of mass destruction that we know of," said Mulholland, diplomatically avoiding naming the weapon. "With the fleet coming up behind us I didn't want there to be any chance of them running into a weapon like that. I felt the best way to determine what we were up against was to confront it head-on. So, I charged the gates."

"Like a bull," said Cadmael.

"Sure, I guess," Mulholland said, smiling wryly. "Like a bull."

Aranare had been carefully watching the admiral while Mulholland had been speaking.

"An animal to be respected," Aranare remarked. "An interesting combination of grace and power, especially when taunted. I suspect that is why you were picked to come first."

"We were just the fastest ship," said Ryan. "I'm the one that took the orders."

"Perhaps," Aranare said.

He looked at the Admiral and cocked his head.

"There's not many I would have sent ahead without far more detailed orders," the admiral said. "I trusted your judgment in an unknown situation and in spite of the result, I stand behind my decision. I mean no offense, Cadmael."

"None is taken," he said.

"Having said that," said the admiral, addressing Mulholland. "You may want to pay a bit more attention to Mr. Johnson in the future."

"Yes, sir," said Mulholland.

"And we are sorry that your ship was lost," added Cadmael. "Our defenses can take a few moments to activate. Perhaps if we had been quicker…"

"No, this was our entirely our fault," said Lindquist. "We should not have crossed your border without consent. It's just lucky that nobody was killed or hurt."

"Ah, nobody was killed or hurt here, were they?" Ryan asked.

"We were all lucky," agreed Cadmael.

"Good," said the admiral. "Mr. Johnson has come up

with a possible plan to retrieve your pillar that was lost when the ammo exploded on the *Xavier*. If things meet with your approval, then we may be able to help you with that."

Aranare looked at Cadmael with raised eyebrows.

"That could help," Cadmael said.

"Now we must tell you," Aranare said. "That we did not expect anyone to be here when we arrived. Our Diachrome have foreseen the end of your society since millennia past. We came now, to rebuild our society, but they tell us that the end did not come."

He pointed to Bob and Evan.

"Well, where are you from?" Ryan asked.

"I am from near here," said Cadmael, pointing to the coast south of Playa del Carmen, "but I am descended from Akrotiri, as are many of our people."

"We are of those you call Mayan and those you call Minoan," Aranare added.

"Look," said Evan. "I think the important thing here is that there's no need for any fighting. There was some initial misunderstanding but everything is okay."

"Playa is devastated," said Jenn. "And Cancun was hit as well. Things are not really okay. There was a massive electrical pulse, a shock wave followed by a flood. There are lots of casualties and fatalities."

"We intended no harm," said Cadmael. "These are the effects of the drive. It sends lightning through the air. It also can damage those in close proximity to the core."

"That lightning is what knocked their plane out of the sky and what crippled Playa," Jenn said. "Another airliner crashed on the runway in Cancun. Everyone was killed in that. Cars, hospitals, computers, everything got fried."

Cadmael and Aranare were shocked.

"Your ship produces what we would call an EMP

pulse," Ryan added. "Everything electronic within about 200 kilometers of where the pulse hit was affected, if it was turned on."

"Even my ship was disabled," Captain Ochoa added.

"This is like the weapon you said of?" Cadmael asked Mulholland?

"It has very similar effects," he said.

"It has never affected so many, so far away," Aranare said. "We did not know."

They looked at each other silently as they contemplated their next move.

"So," Bob said. "We'll all have to be a bit more careful going forward."

"Aranare," Ryan said. "You said you did not expect us to be here. What will you do now?"

"Nothing has been decided," he said. "Our people will want to know more before we will decide."

"We have the arrival feast today," Cadmael said. "We have prepared for this trip for many centuries and we have arrived."

He looked at those around him apologetically.

"Regardless of who is here, the feast must go on. I mean no offense."

"None taken," said the admiral, smiling.

"We would like to know more about your world, and see this damage we have caused," said Aranare. "I am sure you would like see our Atlantis as well. It is the product of millennia and we are very proud of it."

"It's incredible," Evan said, with awe in his voice.

"We will take this to the council," Aranare said.

"And we will take it to Atlantis Command," the Admiral replied, as he stood up.

"By the way, admiral, our shield must be powered

occasionally to keep it active," Cadmael said. "Do not be worried if you see it flicker momentarily now and again."

"It is a sight to behold at night," Aranare added. "Most beautiful!"

The contingent from the carrier made their way to the plank to head back. To their surprise, Bob and Evan didn't join them.

"You're staying?" Ryan asked.

"You're asking an archeology geek if he's going to stay on Atlantis overnight?" Bob replied.

Ryan smiled and Evan handed him a list.

"These are the ten people that will be staying on Atlantis for a bit longer, at the gracious invitation of our hosts." Evan said, nodding thanks to Cadmael.

"You will learn about us as we learn about you," Aranare said.

"What about Tara?" Jenn asked.

"She really wanted to stay on Atlantis a bit longer," Bob said. "It's truly amazing."

"Well, can I stay with her?" Jenn asked.

Bob looked at Ryan and Admiral Lindquist. He could tell that they didn't want to keep a mother away from her daughter but also that they didn't like the idea of Jenn visiting Atlantis. Not yet anyway.

"I think maybe for today," Bob said, "that we should all return to where we started out from."

"We will talk tomorrow," Cadmael added, reassuringly. "All will be decided."

"Bob?" Jenn pleaded.

"Jenn, I'm supposed to have her for one more day anyway," he said, softly.

Jenn burst out laughing.

"Oh, my God, you would bring that up."

She knew he wouldn't be so flip if there was any danger for Tara. She had tears of relief in her eyes.

"You'll be okay?" Bob asked as he helped her up onto the plank. "We'll both talk to you tomorrow, for sure."

CHAPTER 30

A Celebration Begins

They arrived back at the dock just as the council was arriving at the bottom of the steps from the council chambers. Cadmael told them they should stay on board and he headed down the ramp. At the bottom the male councilors held back and allowed Cadmael to assist the female councilors to board first. They all moved over to make enough space for everyone. To Bob's delight Itzela was the first to come aboard and she came and sat right beside him.

Cadmael made sure they were all safely aboard, nodded to Aranare, then turned, and headed up the stairs to the council temple.

"We go to the plaza," Aranare told them. "It is much quicker by ship and we must prepare for the celebrations."

"How was the meeting?" Itzela asked Aranare.

Bob glanced at her while the other councilors listened attentively. She was striking, and possessed a timeless beauty that made it difficult to determine her age. Still, by the way she carried herself Bob guessed that she must be in her early thirties. He shook his head and tuned in to the conversation.

"It seems Cadmael was correct," Aranare said. "The single ship was one captain's action. It will not happen again."

"And the pillar?" one of the other councilors asked.

"An accident," Aranare said, "and one they may be

able to help us fix."

Startled looks were exchanged among some of the councilors.

"It is too deep here," said the man that had asked the question.

"We have submarines," said Bob. "Ships that travel underwater. They might be some help with that."

Aranare nodded thoughtfully.

"Our arrival has caused much damage," he told them gravely. "Many deaths and injuries."

"What? How?"

The councilors were confused. They wanted to know how they had caused any damage and were truly appalled when they heard about the injured and casualties. They simply didn't know what Atlantis could do to modern technology.

"Our technology is disabled by whatever brought you here," Evan explained. "Everything for 200 miles from here was affected."

"It's why our plane crashed," Bob added.

"We must make atonement," Itzela said.

She looked at Bob as if she were expecting him to be angry with her, or with them. He smiled reassuringly.

"We have agreed that we must both learn more about each other," Aranare said. "But that is a matter for tomorrow."

He looked around to see where they were.

"For now, our guests may enjoy the trip."

The ship had pushed off and headed away from the dock toward the back of the harbor. As they got closer, what had appeared to be the continuous shore at the back of the harbor turned out to be two thin spits of land that concealed a hidden channel between them. As their ship turned into that channel, the continuous brass wall that encircled the inner ring of the canal could be seen at the other end.

As they got closer, Bob could tell that this was what they'd seen from the council chamber above, but from the ship, it appeared to have small bumps regularly spaced along it. When it reached the end of channel, the ship veered starboard into the canal and took a heading roughly parallel to the brass ring. As they drifted closer to the ring, it became apparent that the small bumps they had seen on the brass ring were actually the heads of people standing just behind it. There seemed to be someone stationed about every six feet along the wall.

As the ship passed along, the land rose up on either side of the canal, until there were tall cliffs framing the canal. Just past the point where the harbor could be seen from the canal, a massive stone bridge passed over the canal and connected the cliffs. The brass ring, and the line of people behind it, passed through a special niche carved out of the bridge supports. Although the ring stayed the same, as the ship passed under that bridge the rest of the view changed spectacularly.

The land visible from the harbor mouth and even inside had shown little industrialization, being mostly fields, temples, and a few dwellings. Once past the bridge, the cliffs on either side had been built up and outward, extending out over the canal. An endless row of docks, each berthing a least one ship similar to the one on which they were sailing, curved out of sight as it went around the bend. In some docks the brass wall had been lifted, hinged up on one side to allow the ships to enter and exit. As they passed, a crewed ship that had just disembarked its crew was lowering the brass ring section back into place, after which people moved to take up their assigned spot on the wall.

"That brass ring is floating on buoys," Bob said to Evan.

Evan simply shrugged and didn't say a word, but Bob found the ring fascinating and was trying to understand it.

Every so often there was a station on either side of the canal where there were no ships, merely a space for vessels to load and unload. Each one of these stations was equipped with hoists and platforms to pull supplies up to the top of the canal wall and a staircase where one might ascend to the top. A pair of giant rollers was mounted on pivots attaches to each staircase. It looked like the rollers could be lowered down to ride along the top of the brass ring. As the ship slowed and veered towards one of the stations, Bob just had to ask.

"Does the wall turn?" he asked Aranare.

Out of the corner of his eye Bob saw Itzela smile as Aranare replied.

"That too, is a matter for tomorrow," he said as he got up to disembark.

* * *

There had been symbols designating each of the stations that they'd passed, but they all had the same utilitarian appearance. Bob and the others couldn't imagine that the stairway from any particular station would end up inside a palace.

"This is the guest hall," Itzela explained, as they crested the stairs and looked around.

The vaulted, frescoed ceilings were held up by gilded pillars, the surrounding walls covered in murals. Itzela waved her hand, indicating the massive plaza outside the front pillars. People were milling around setting tables around the edges and food was being prepared at numerous places around the courtyard.

"You will see over the plaza for the celebration."

It took Bob a second to realize she wasn't just speaking to him. Then for some reason she shifted to look directly at him as she continued.

"We will each be in the formal attire of our homelands tonight."

She expanded her gaze to include the rest of the group again.

"You each have a room above here where you may stay during your time here. There is clothing from many lands in each room. I hope you find something that you like."

She waved a young man over and said something to him in what Bob assumed was Minoan. She glanced back and dipped her gaze in Bob's direction. He raised his hand in farewell then realized that she might not even know what the gesture meant. She smiled and turned away. The rest of the councilors and Aranare went with her.

"The councilors must attend to preparations," the young man said. "I will show you to your rooms."

A short journey up a stone flight of stairs led into a hallway containing the doors to their rooms. Evan was directed into the first one and Emma's happy voice from inside as she greeted him, let Bob know that they were together again. Bob was ushered toward the second room and the young man promised that someone would come to collect them before the celebrations began. Bob entered the room and was immediately smothered by a giant Tara-hug.

"Dad!" she yelled. "You're back! I missed you. You've got to see this place."

She let him go and then pulled him into the main room so that he could take it all in.

They were in the middle floor of a long terraced building and had a balcony overlooking the plaza. They faced towards the center of Atlantis but Bob could also see the edge of the harbor with the council building above it. The massive lights of the carrier had been turned toward Atlantis and they glared like angry stars in the gathering dusk.

"This place just gets more impressive all the time," Tara said. "How's mom taking all this?"

"Mom's fine. Except she's really missing you."

"Worried, I suppose?"

"Can you blame her?"

"I guess not," Tara said. "I miss her too. Have you seen what kinds of clothes they have for us? This stuff is crazy."

"Really?" Bob asked.

"What do you think?" she asked and twirled around.

He finally noticed that Tara was all dressed up in a light, flowing, electric-blue gown.

"You look all grown up," he said. "Like a princess."

"I don't think so," Tara said. "You should see what the princesses around here wear! I really wish you could see the detail in this…"

A loud cheer rang out in the distance. Then, as if in response to Tara's wish, the rapidly darkening room became illuminated with the flicker of a golden glow. They looked out the window together. Above them the shield over Atlantis had flickered into wispy existence. It played a small golden light show for them for a few moments then winked out. Cheers echoed from the courtyard as a trough of oil was ignited somewhere below them. The light from the growing ring of fire splashed warmly over their faces as it encircled the plaza. Over on the next ring of Atlantis another fire ring flickered to life and soon, golden flames dotted the island as Atlantis came alive with fire.

"Awesome!" Tara and Bob said in unison.

CHAPTER 31

Atlantis Sunset

Standing on the deck of the carrier, Jenn showed Ryan the video she'd just taken with her phone. The mountains, towers, and temples of Atlantis were silhouetted by the golden glow of the setting sun. Highlights and reflections outlined some of the closer hills and structures and everything faded to black down by the harbor, so the reflections of the silhouette stood out with crystal clarity. It was a spectacular, other-worldly vision that could not have been imagined before today.

"Wow," Ryan said. "You have got to share that."

"I don't think that would be a very good idea," Lindquist said, as he came up behind them.

"Why not?" Ryan asked. "The whole world knows about Atlantis already. What could it hurt?"

Jenn selected the video and typed *Atlantis at Sunset*. She looked at Ryan and the Admiral. Ryan nodded and the admiral simply shrugged. She smiled and pressed 'share'.

Large search and rescue spotlights had been brought onto the deck of the *Excelsior* and were now being activated one by one. The glare was lighting up the entrance to the harbor and the walls on either side of the pillars. The fleets' ships had been redeployed in an arc to better cover the area, and as the sun set, the lights from the ships starkly lit the walls and pillars in a monotone pool of white light.

"Sir?" A rating came up and passed the admiral a handheld monitor.

Lindquist looked at Ryan and Jenn.

"We're keeping an eye on Cadmael."

The screen showed the view from one of the long-range cameras. Cadmael was standing in front of the council temple with his hand raised. The admiral flicked on the audio feed from the command deck at the same time as they heard the echo of a loud cheer from Atlantis.

The audio crackled with a report.

"A few minutes ago, the continuous line of people that was stationed along the wall moved away. It looks like they went to join the celebrations."

Cadmael raised his other arm and signaled something. The shield flickered on above Atlantis and an oval of golden fire danced all around it. The fire seemed to be energized as it touched the pillars and then continued down into the water. Additional sparks and a visible distortion of the oval indicated where the pillar had been lost to the sea. Cadmael lowered his arms and the shield flicked off. He gazed in the direction of the carrier, as if he was looking right at them, and smiled. He then dipped his head in respect, turned and headed toward the stairs.

Across all of Atlantis, lines of fire from oil lamps hidden in the buildings, flared up in rows and patterns. It was yet another awesome sight.

"Take another picture," Ryan suggested to Jenn.

"These people have style," the admiral remarked then spoke into his radio. "Lets kill as many of those searchlights as we can. Lower the others to only hit down by the water. I want Minimal surveillance, but nobody approaches Atlantis."

He turned to Ryan and Jenn.

"If you're done sharing, we need to report in."

* * *

Atlantis Command had taken over the task of linking in NATO, NORAD, and the rest of the world, so they were able to get up and running quite quickly. The report of the meeting with the Atlanteans consisted of viewing the video that had been shot during the meeting.

"So, it's been a very long day for everyone," General Aspinal said. "But while the people on Atlantis are having their celebration, I think we should have a quick recap from each of you. Admiral?"

Lindquist stood then began pacing around the ready room.

"When I woke up this morning, Atlantis was like a fairy tale. Yet I've just come back from a meeting on Atlantis, on a wooden sailing ship that could be a thousand years old with, a man who seems as well versed in military strategy as anyone I've met in the Navy."

"Admiral?" the general asked.

"Cadmael is as shrewd as any commander in our fleet, General. Every thing he does displays knowledge of sound military strategy and exhibits a confidence that he knows he will likely not need to use force. Even that little display of the shield flickering on this evening spoke volumes."

"Even I could see that one, admiral," Ryan said. "He was showing us that they can turn their shield on at any time."

Lindquist nodded.

"Yes, that was part of it, but he was also able to time it to be the opening fireworks for their celebration, which is either elegant or arrogant, and I've seen no arrogance in these people at all. But the most important thing there was that he dismissed the pushers off the walls before he turned the shield on."

"What's that got to do with it?" Jenn asked.

"It's a generator," Mulholland surmised. "The whole of Atlantis is a generator."

"That's what we'd guessed," added Aspinal. "But that was disproven tonight."

"Maybe not," Ryan said, thoughtfully.

"What do you mean?" said the general.

"Well, if Atlantis is a generator, then maybe it's a battery as well."

"How exactly is Atlantis a generator?" Jenn asked.

"A generator needs magnets, rotation, and metal conductors," Ryan explained. "So if the metal walls rotate that takes care of the rotation and the conductors. You'd just need magnets. Lots of magnets."

"Magnetite," Jenn said. "Iron ore. But it didn't come into common use until after the Mayan civilization fell apart."

"Unless it was used much earlier, maybe during the Bronze Age when the Minoans were scouring the planet for copper?" said Ryan. "Is that what you're thinking?"

"Exactly," Jenn replied. "They could have easily found magnetite."

"Okay, enough speculation," the general said. "Ryan?"

"I was focusing on Aranare," he said. "He also has a very self-assured confidence, but I didn't perceive it as military in nature. He spoke of something called a Diachrome and how he'd heard them foretell the end of the world millennia ago. I'm not saying that Aranare is thousands of years old but this Diachrome is the source of his confidence. He simply knows that things are going to turn out alright."

"Okay. Dr. Wallace?" said Aspinal.

"There's one more thing, general," Ryan added, before Jenn could reply. "Much of what we know about the Minoan says they were not a warlike people, that they were always quietly in charge. That's the exact feeling that I got from Aranare and Cadmael today."

"Thank you, Mr. Johnson. Dr. Wallace?"

"I was mostly focused on getting my daughter back," Jenn said. "I really didn't watch anyone."

"Not even your ex-husband?" the general asked.

"Oh, I see what you mean. Well, Bob and Evan are fighting, as always, and Bob is completely unworried about the situation."

"Is that normal?" the admiral asked.

"For him, yes. He's never bothered by anything," Jenn replied. "But if Tara was in any danger at all, there's no way he'd have let her stay. He wouldn't have left her behind even for the meeting. He obviously trusts them with her and I trust his judgment where Tara's concerned."

"And Dr. Masters? Anything thoughts on him?" asked the general, being thorough.

"Evan was trying desperately to be important, just like always. It'll be a good test of Atlantean patience to see if they put up with him for very long."

She stopped speaking and didn't say anything further so Mulholland spoke up.

"I don't have much to add. From an observational viewpoint, I agree with pretty much everything I've heard here. I just wanted to say thank you for giving me the chance to apologize in person."

"Thank you all for your reports," the general said. "Before we go any further, Dr. Wallace, I'm told your *Atlantis at Sunset* video has already been viewed 25 million times since you posted it. They're calling it the fastest growing viral video, ever."

"I'm sorry about that, general," Jenn said.

"I was going to reprimand you, but if 25 million people

from all over the world want to see a video of Atlantis that badly, then perhaps it's not a bad idea. Maybe it'll keep the press at bay."

CHAPTER 32

Millennia Party

With Tara's help, it took Bob five times longer than it might have done to pick out what to wear for the celebration. To her apparent dismay he insisted on wearing something complimentary since they were family, which made it all the harder for her to decide. In the end he wore a simple tunic and what passed for pants. Both were a tan color with a blue design stitched into the edge trim. Since Tara was enjoying the process so much, Bob graciously didn't point out that the clothes they ultimately settled on for him, were the things he'd suggested in the first place.

Once he was dressed, they looked out the window again. Over in the harbor the fleet's lights had been dimmed enough so that they were no longer a blinding distraction. In the plaza below more and more people were arriving and the bustling of preparation was slowly giving way to the revelry of happy camaraderie. As Bob and Tara looked out over the plaza, random passers by happily waved up to them.

"Should we go down?" Tara asked, waving back.

"They said they'd send somebody to get us," Bob replied, as he sat down on a chair overlooking the plaza. "Maybe we should wait."

"Alright," she said, plopping down on the chair beside him.

"It's like a dream, isn't it?" she said, wistfully.

"That's the hardest part," he said, smiling, "A dream would be so much easier to believe."

They sat back and watched the dream play on, until a knock at the door told them it was time to leave.

Bob went over, opened it, and greeted the same young man that had shown him to the room. He turned but Tara hadn't accompanied him.

"Tara!" he called.

He nodded an apology to the young man then went back to the main room. Tara was waiting for him but she was all fidgety and nervous. He'd never seen her like this before.

"What's up, pal?" he asked.

"It's that cute boy again, isn't it, Dad?" Tara said. "I peeked."

"He's not that cute," said Bob, grinning.

"Dad!" she snapped, turning away from him.

This was new, and a side of Tara he'd not seen before. Maybe she'd never seen it before either, since she looked confused as much as anything. Bob took a deep breath and dove in.

"I'm not really qualified to judge a boy's cuteness, honey," he said quietly, gently turning her to face him again. "But I can tell you this."

He wiped away a tear that had sneaked onto her cheek.

"You really do look like a princess tonight. So if this is like a dream, and if that's a boy that you think is cute, then maybe… you should just go with it."

"What?"

"Be the princess, honey," he said, fighting off a tear of his own. "You've always been mine."

"Oh, Dad!"

She hit him, then buried her head in his shoulder. Bob

simply hugged her back. After a moment she straightened up and looked at him.

"You look regal," he smiled. "You ready?"

She smoothed her dress straight and nodded.

"Thanks, Dad."

"That, is what I'm here for, pal."

Tara proceeded to do an excellent job of ignoring the boy as she and Bob came out and joined the rest of the remaining plane passengers in the hallway. They walked over to Evan's door as Emma came out wearing a dress with a similar style to Tara's but with a flaming orange motif. The two girls squealed in delight at their similar tastes. Evan however was a different story. He was puffed up like a peacock in multiple layers of gold-gilded coats and tunics.

"Won't that be a bit warm?" Bob asked, genuinely concerned.

"I'll be fine," Evan said.

Then, as a king would to his page, he waved to the boy to lead on.

* * *

Once on the main floor, everyone was led along the front of the long building, toward the central area where the two channels of fire converged. Tables piled with food were alternated around the edge of the plaza with tables on which ceramic cups were clustered around cisterns. Drumbeats helped to coax the mellow tones of something that sounded similar to a bass flute, into a very danceable tune. Countless friendly faces greeted them as they passed through the crowd, nodding or saying hello in English, Mayan, or languages Bob simply didn't know.

There was a small area in the middle of the plaza for

the councilors but everyone appeared to be welcome as people wandered in and out to congratulate the councilors and in turn to be congratulated on a journey well taken. Aranare was the most mobile of all, wandering freely amongst the throng.

As Bob and the others neared the center a break in the crowd gave them a glimpse of some of the councilors chatting with each other. Itzela stood out spectacularly in a long blue dress that flowed off her shoulders and dipped down so that the middle of her back was bared. Bob stopped sharply when he saw her. Tara was busy staring at the young man who was accompanying them and bumped into her dad when he stopped.

"Tara," said Bob. "Look!"

He pointed at Itzela and Tara's eyes widened. In the middle of Itzela's back was the mandala that Tara had drawn during Bob's lecture in England. The dress was the same, as were the markings on Itzela's back. It was startling. Tara's young man called out to Itzela and then under Bob's watchful eye, guided Tara and the rest of their group forward to greet her.

"Uh, Dad," Tara said, tentatively.

He looked at her, concerned that she was still worried about the boy. But Tara wore an odd smile as she looked up at him.

"Remember when I was talking about the princess dresses around here?" she asked.

"No," he said. "Not really."

Tara snickered and pushed him ahead, gently turning him to face forward to greet Itzela. Her gown was in every way Minoan, the fabric draping off her shoulders in the front as well as the back, allowing her breasts to freely honor her Minoan heritage.

To Bob's credit, he looked directly into Itzela's eyes as he said hello. Once her eyes had warmly returned his smile, he found it much easier to react calmly to… things that did not appear in public that often where he was from. He looked down at Tara and then grinned. She was having more trouble with the situation than he was. As they both politely looked elsewhere, it became apparent that this was a common look for both Minoan and Mayan women of high importance.

Aranare arrived beside them and raised his cup in the air. The plaza quickly became silent as the music stilled.

"The journey began more than five millennia ago. Now… we are here! The Diachrome Paulin!"

Everyone in the crowd echoed Aranare's toast. And that was it. The plaza was filled with the sound of cheering. Someone broke into a song, the music restarted and soon everyone was weaving together in dance. Bob was still standing beside Itzela and she seemed quite happy to look back into his eyes as they too began swaying with the rhythm of the crowd.

Aranare interrupted their dance.

"There will be little quiet this night," he said. "We must all celebrate!"

"Even if we're not supposed to be here?" asked Bob.

"Even so!" Aranare smiled at him, then welcomed Tara as she approached.

"You dress together," he observed.

Itzela's dress was trimmed with some of the same blue that was in Tara's gown and some of the tan from Bob's outfit. Bob and Itzela looked at each other and smiled as the young man that Tara was fond of, joined them.

"Tadeo," Itzela said, happily as she put her arms around him. "These are our friends Bob Wallace and daughter Tara. This is my son, Tadeo."

"Pleased to meet you, Tadeo," Bob said.

"Pleased to meet you, Bob Wallace, Tara," he replied in excellent English. "We chose the same colors."

Tadeo's blue and tan garment was very close in color to the rest of their group. The fact that it closely resembled a skirt didn't bother Bob nearly as much as the fact that he wasn't wearing a shirt and that Tara was staring at Tadeo's muscular chest.

"Tara," he said.

"Oh, I'm sorry. Very nice to meet you, Tadeo."

"I can show you our dances?" Tadeo asked, but he was really only addressing Tara.

She looked tongue-tied so Bob answered for her.

"We'd both be grateful for some lessons."

"Excellent," said Aranare.

He gently pushed Bob toward Itzela and walked away through the crowd, happily greeting those he met.

All of Bob's gentlemanly skills were called into play as he kept an eye on Tara and Tadeo while trying not be distracted by Itzela's unique garment as they learned several energetic dances. He was relieved when the drum beat slowed to a pace that allowed him and Itzela to dance together slowly. Tara and Tadeo remained at arms length and although Bob and Itzela began the same way, she soon pulled him tightly against her.

"This way," she said, smiling at him again.

She demonstrated a much more intimate version of the dance than the one that Tara and Tadeo were doing, one that kept her chest pressed firmly against his. It was an elegant dance and yet the sensation of her bare breasts rubbing again his shirt was making Bob feel far from elegant.

"Normally you would be in the same dress as Tadeo," she said as they moved about the plaza. "It is closer that way."

He didn't know what to say to that, but the truth had always served him well.

"It is something I would like to try," he said then quickly added. "Another time."

She smiled and lingered close to him after the dance had ended. They let go of each other when Tara and Tadeo came over.

"Tadeo says we should try the 'aak' he'," she said, breathless from dancing.

Tadeo nodded emphatically as Bob looked at Itzela.

"A Maya specialty!" she said.

Bob chivalrously stepped aside so that she could go first. "Lead on, Tadeo!" he said.

CHAPTER 33

A Very Long Day

Ryan and Jenn stood directly in front of the main screen of the ready room, studying the highly detailed composite satellite photo of Atlantis as if it was a treasure map. They were each pointing out various features then trying to decide if they were Mayan or Minoan or something else, before establishing the coordinates and writing them down.

They'd been making notes for a while when Admiral Lindquist realized just how long this was going to take. He had one of the off-duty Nav officers join them to record what they were finding, so that they could focus on searching. The Nav also took over switching back and forth from picture to infrared view to coordinate the grid so that Atlantis Command didn't have to constantly stay in the loop. Admiral Lindquist had stayed for a while then dismissed Captain Mulholland and turned to go.

"If it's all the same, admiral," said Mulholland, "I'd like to stay."

"Fine with me," Lindquist replied. "I'm going below to check on the injured from the plane crash."

The admiral stepped out the door but then poked his head back inside the door.

"Have any of you eaten?" he asked.

None had eaten for a while, and Mulholland insisted

on helping. He first found out what the evening's meal had been, then relayed everyone's orders to the mess so that they could keep working. Mulholland got up to answer a knock on the ready room door and was surprised to find the cook himself delivering the three still-steaming roast beef dinners.

"Dinner's here," He said to Jenn and Ryan. "This is the *Excelsior's* head cook, Chief Thompson."

"Thanks, Chief," said Ryan.

"Yes, thanks," Jenn added. "You didn't have to bring it yourself."

"It's no problem, ma'am, sirs," he said, glancing at the monitor. "So that's Atlantis?"

Jenn regarded him curiously.

"You haven't seen it yet?"

"No, ma'am," he replied. "We've been a bit busy with the rush to get here, the extra crew from the *Xavier* - no offense, sir - and then we've had to whip up meals for the plane crash survivors. I did see your video and photos online though. It's amazing and has had almost 200 million views so far."

"What?" said Ryan.

"That's impossible," Jenn added. "There's no way."

The Chief pulled out his phone and checked.

"217 million views," he said, showing them his phone.

"You know that's about $200,000?" said Mulholland.

Jenn looked at him and could see that he was completely serious. Ryan simply shrugged.

"Told you that you should share it," he said.

"I may have to buy you dinner," Jenn replied, smiling.

"I may let you," said Ryan.

"Is this corn?" said Thompson.

He'd moved over to the main screen and was pointing at one of several areas that looked like rows of crops.

"Could be," Jenn said, as she sat down to eat.

188

"See anything else you recognize?" Ryan asked.

"Which one is corn?" asked Mulholland, so that he could make a note of it.

While the rest of them ate, Thompson helped them to catalog and identify many of the crops and some of the livestock that were being raised on the island.

"This series of pens here is different," he said, a little later. "They're too small for herds and there are paths back and forth through the whole area."

"A zoo perhaps?" said the admiral, who had slipped back into the room unnoticed.

The Chief snapped instantly to attention. "Admiral!"

"At ease, Chief Thompson," said Lindquist, giving him an easy smile. "What brings you to my ready room this evening?"

"I did, sir," Mulholland replied. "So that these two could keep on working."

"And he's been a big help," Jenn added.

The admiral looked doubtfully at Ryan who nodded his agreement.

"I'm a farm boy, admiral," Thompson said. "Been around crops and cattle most of my life."

He turned back to the map.

"Now these folks here, they're all set up for a long journey. They have horses, herds of cattle, goats, and sheep, crops of corn and wheat, orchards, why there are even herb gardens spread out here and there all over the place."

The admiral held up his hand and turned to Jenn.

"I see what you mean," he said. "Chief, if you can wait a moment before continuing, I'm going to get us a bottle of red wine or perhaps two out of the captain's stock. Do you think you could have someone else in the mess hall rustle me up one of those roast beef dinners? I'd like to hear more."

They ended up consuming both bottles of wine and would probably have had a third, but everyone was exhausted from the very long day they'd all just lived through. Chief Thompson had given them a completely different perspective of Atlantis as a ship designed to convey a civilization and everything they might need with them. It made everyone in the ready room realize that they needed to shift their thinking from Atlantis as a transport vehicle to Atlantis as more of a gigantic mobile home.

Later, Jenn and Ryan walked together along the deck of the carrier, watching the fires from the celebrations on Atlantis in the distance.

"It's not a major shift in thinking," Ryan said. "But I'm already starting to think of the buildings in terms of what function they provide instead of what ruin is this like and does it do the same job?"

"So more of a civil engineer and less of an archeologist, then?" Jenn asked, with a smile.

"The president asked me to do this job because it was Minoan," Ryan explained. "But first they speak English and now the fact that they're Minoan is almost becoming unimportant. There's probably somebody better for the job."

"Same with the Mayan," Jenn said. "Which also makes my job unimportant."

The looked at each other and laughed.

"Are we trying to talk ourselves out of what's arguably the greatest job ever?" Jenn asked.

"Maybe we should just keep going and see how things turn out?" Ryan suggested.

"Sounds like a plan."

Jenn's phone alert indicated that a text was coming in. She stared at it in disbelief.

"What is it?" Ryan asked.

"My ex-husband," she said slowly, handing him the phone. "He's just sent me a selfie of him and my daughter on what looks like some sort of a risqué double date on Atlantis."

The picture showed Bob and a beautiful bare breasted woman alongside a girl that Ryan assumed was Tara. She was standing beside a bare-chested boy that seemed to be slightly older than her.

"Well, that looks like the attire of a Minoan princess," Ryan said. "And the boy's wearing the right thing for a Minoan youth too."

There was another alert.

Princess Itzela and her son Tadeo with Tara and me.

"Are you sure about the princess thing?" Jenn asked.

"Absolutely," Ryan replied. "There are few surviving frescoes of the Minoan era, but on the two of them that show women, the Minoan princesses or priestesses are always bare-breasted. Her son's clothes seem authentic as well."

"Well, congratulations," Jenn said.

"Uh, what?"

"You just earned your position, well in my eyes anyway."

"Thanks," said Ryan. "Look, maybe we should head in. It's been a long day."

She thought for moment then sent Bob the link to her Atlantis video.

A text came in as she sent the link. She sighed then read the message aloud.

BTW Tara LIKES Tadeo.

"A very long day," she said, in agreement.

CHAPTER 34

Under the Stars

After sampling a wide selection of delicacies from many different cultures, and at least attempting to learn several indigenous dances, Bob suggested a stroll to get away from the crowd. Itzela agreed, but after catching Tara's eye, excused herself for moment, taking Tara with her.

Bob stood with Tadeo in the middle of the milling crowd. Since Bob had no idea what to say to a teenaged Minoan boy that his daughter liked, he elected to keep quiet. A group of boys Tadeo's age came by and asked him to go with them but Tadeo said that he was busy.

"Where are they going?" Bob asked.

"Night swim," Tadeo said. "They want to make first night swim in new world."

"Ah!" said Bob.

They both stood and looked around awkwardly until Itzela and Tara returned.

"Dad!" Tara called, from behind them.

Bob and Tadeo turned to see that the ladies had gone and acquired matching cover-ups, to help keep out the evening's cool breeze. Fortunately for Bob, the poncho-style garments had also covered up the more distracting nuances of Itzela's ceremonial attire.

"What do you think?" Tara asked, spinning around to

show off her flowing cover up.

"It looks great," Bob said. "And now you two match even more."

"We are much warmer," Itzela agreed. "We go?"

They walked toward the harbor area. The plaza only reached to the end of the guest hall and the crowd had more or less thinned out by the time they reached there. Tadeo chose one of the pathways that led off the plaza, which wound through a series of terraced gardens interspersed with places to sit. Many of them were occupied by couples or small groups that had come to admire the view and quite possibly contemplate their future.

Bob held back and whispered to Tara.

"Did you arrange the cover up?"

"That sounds like a line from a movie, Dad."

"Well, if you did, thanks. I'm just not used to that and I couldn't relax."

"That's what I told her," Tara said.

"What!" Bob exclaimed.

"You were being goofy," Tara said, shrugging. "Itzela asked me why you didn't look at her breasts. She thought you maybe didn't like her."

"Tara!"

"Look, Dad. It's weird, but I get it, it's their way. I told her that you like her a lot and explained that we keep them covered up in public. She suggested these shawl things."

"Why did you tell her I like her?"

"Well, I wasn't going to lie," Tara said. "You do like her, right?"

"Um…"

"Let's stop here," said Tadeo.

They had turned a corner and arrived at an unoccupied alcove at the edge of the canal that had good view of the harbor, the fleet, and even Playa Del Carmen. Now that the fleet's lights had been dimmed they could see Playa was slowly coming alive with light as power was gradually restored. Several of the hotel buildings were brilliantly lit.

"So many," said Itzela.

"There are thousands of cities like that and some are much bigger," Bob explained. "Some have many millions of people."

"It is beautiful," Itzela said. "Can we see it?"

"Sure," Bob said. "Probably. I don't see why not."

"You should not go," said Tadeo, then looked at Bob. "We are all that is left of our people."

"It's pretty safe," Tara added. "I've been coming here since I was little."

"That is not what he says," said Itzela. "Tadeo's father is gone now."

She sighed then looked at her son.

"He only wishes me safety," she said, proudly. "But Tadeo, what is our way?"

"There is no safety in fear," he replied, obviously quoting something.

"That's brilliant." said Bob. "And very true."

"Tara says you are also without her mother?" Itzela asked.

"Ah, yes," Bob replied, then added quickly. "But she is not gone."

"Dad says she's over on the carrier," said Tara, pointing. "The big ship."

"You said they split up?" Itzela asked, confused.

"Yes," said Bob. "We were married and now we're not married anymore. We call it divorced."

He wondered if there was such a concept in their culture or if he'd just stumbled onto a taboo.

"Ah, you have both chosen to walk alone?" Itzela asked.

"Yes," said Bob, with a sigh of relief. "It's sometimes best."

"Yes, we have this as well," she said. "And you remain friends?"

"We do," Bob replied. "We still study Mayan history together, which I guess is why she's here."

Itzela contemplated his answer and seemed quite happy with it. Yet Bob remained curious.

"What of your husband?"

"Ián," said Itzela, sadly. "He worked on drive. The shield, as you say. It sometimes changes too quickly. One day it changed and he was killed."

She looked sadly at Tadeo.

"He did not suffer."

"I'm very sorry for your loss," Bob said.

"It was long ago," Tadeo said and tried to change the subject. "No more sad?"

"I'm sorry about your, Dad, Tadeo. And this is getting kind of depressing. Can we do something else?"

Itzela and Tadeo nodded.

"What do you want to do?" Bob asked.

"What I'd really like to do is send Mom a picture," she said. "You told me she was worried, so a selfie should help."

"Ah," said Bob.

He wasn't sure if he should tell Itzela and Tadeo about his cell phone, but remembered that Tadeo had said that there is no safety in fear.

"Okay," he said. "A selfie is a picture of yourself."

"Dad?"

Tara had her hand held out for his phone. Bob handed it over.

"And teenagers are definitely the best at taking selfies,"

he said, with a sigh. "Better explain the flash to them."

Together they explained about the flash, pictures, the camera and then the whole concept of a personal communicator. Tadeo was enthralled by the technology and remained by Tara's side from that moment on. A little later, with Tara's direction, the four of them posed for the perfect selfie, which Tara promptly sent to Jenn.

When Tara handed him his phone after the text had been sent Bob noticed that Itzela had slipped off her cover up for the picture, as had Tara. He sighed. Girls always wanted to look their best, after all He shook his head when he thought about the explaining he'd soon have to do, then noticed the look exchanged between Tara and Tadeo in the picture. He fired off an explanatory text message then quickly slipped the phone back in his pocket.

"That's enough for now. I want to conserve the battery."

He saw a familiar figure rushing along the path towards them.

"Aranare!" he called.

Aranare was out of breath. He'd been moving pretty quickly for someone that was as old as he seemed to be. He took only a second to catch his breath then grabbed Bob's shoulder and pointed up in the sky.

"What," he puffed, "is that?"

A bright shining star moved quickly and steadily through the sky, heading approximately northeast.

"That's the ISS," said Tara.

"The International Space Station," Bob added. "It's a special ship that sails around the planet and looks down on us."

"A satellite?" Aranare asked.

"Yes, but how do you know that word?" said Bob.

Any answer would have to wait as his phone vibrated indicating that a text had arrived. Itzela was startled but Tadeo moved closer to see what was going on.

Bob pulled out his phone while Tadeo muttered an unintelligible word to Itzela, who immediately relaxed and joined them.

"Tadeo, will you explain the phone to Aranare?" Bob asked.

"No need," Aranare said. "I know of this. Your Jenn showed us this at the meeting. A videe-oh she called it. Of you."

He smiled and pointed at Tara.

"Well, she's sent another video," Bob said. "This one is called *Atlantis at Sunset* and so far almost 250 million people have see it."

He played the video depicting the silhouette of Atlantis in front of the setting sun.

"Dad," Tara said, anxiously. "This means everyone will know about Atlantis now."

CHAPTER 35

How to Tell The World

"I'd like to confirm reports that an island has appeared off the coast of Yucatan between Playa del Carmen and Cozumel. We don't know where it's from, why it's here, or even how it got there. We know that the island is inhabited and we're working to establish communications. The appearance of the island did cause several major events, most notably an EMP pulse that knocked out communications and…"

General Aspinal muted the recording.

"That was the president's speech from yesterday at 5:00 pm. By now it's been heard by most of the planet. But this…"

She showed the landing page of Jenn's shared video from the previous night.

"…has now been watched 873 million times and is on target to soon become the most watched video on the planet, ever, within the next few hours."

The General didn't look happy as she continued.

"As a result, we're dispatching further ships to assist you in protecting Atlantis from intruders. Admiral?"

"The danger is two-fold," Lindquist said. "We have the usual problem of treasure hunters and thrill seekers being where they shouldn't be. But if they do manage to get through to Atlantis, it might cause them to turn their shield on again, destroying the trespassers and any chance we have of a discussion with Atlantis."

He looked directly at Ryan.

"We'll have to add to the list of things to discuss with our friends, the additional activity that this will cause."

"List?" Jenn asked. "What list?"

Ryan slid a small stack of papers in front of Jenn. Questions were neatly printed one after the other.

"Atlantis Command," Lindquist said, drolly, "has prepared a few questions that they'd like answered."

"That's crazy!" said Jenn, when she saw the number of questions.

"They mostly fall into the 'who are you and what are you doing here?' category," Ryan said. "But there are a few we should try and ask as soon as we can. Can we expect another massive energy discharge? May we start flying around here again? And now maybe, do you want us to fend off possible intruders for you?"

"I suppose," Jenn said. "It just seems like we should get know them a little first."

"Yes, we should," Aspinal chimed in again. "And we're going to have a few other challenges to deal with as well."

"The press," said Ryan.

"And the politicians," the admiral added.

"So we have to find out who they are, what they want, and ask them some questions," said Jenn, "while fending off possible treasure hunters, then report all that back to the press and the politicians?"

"Not quite," Aspinal replied. "Against my advice and all protocol, the president wants to come to you and bring some of the press corps with him. And the fleet's already stopped more than two dozen boats that tried to make their way to Atlantis last night and this morning."

"This is happening right now," added the admiral. "We need those questions answered before we lose control of the situation or something bad happens."

Jenn stood up abruptly and excused herself. Ryan received a nod from the admiral and went after her. He found her on the carrier deck, looking out over Atlantis.

"You alright?" he asked.

"I think I'm..." she said, searching for the right word, "conflicted."

"Okay," he said, letting her take her time.

"My daughter's over there and that's Atlantis," she said. "And my ex-husband... Well, all that's about enough for me. I don't think I can handle the press or the U.S. president."

She paused and looked at him.

"You do know I'm Canadian?"

"I do," he said.

"Anyway, the president, the press, the Mayan, the Minoan, Atlantis, my family," she sighed. "I can't handle it all."

"You forgot something," Ryan said.

"What?"

"You forgot the world'," he said, making quotation marks with his fingers. "When you shared that video, you sort of became the unofficial spokesman for Atlantis to the entire world."

"This is you helping?" she asked.

"That remains to be seen," said Ryan. "You think you're going to take this whole thing on yourself? Or are you part of a team?"

"I'm part of the team, of course," she said, wondering where he was going with this.

"Then stop taking on the worry of the whole team."

"But that video..." she began.

"Is a focal point at the moment," Ryan said. "But if you

hadn't shared it, someone else on one of these ships would have. This way, an expert released some key data. Believe me, in the long term this will be seen as a very good thing. This is a secret that can't be kept."

"So what should I do?"

"What do you want to do?"

She thought for a couple of minutes, considering the crazy events of the previous 24 hours.

"I need to make sure my family's okay and we need to get a conversation going with Atlantis, which could include getting some of the more important questions answered."

"And?"

"And, nothing. Anything else will follow."

"Exactly," Ryan said, smiling and opening the door for her. "Shall we head back in?"

"Sure. And, thanks."

"For what?" he asked.

"For actually helping."

When they arrived back at the ready room, Admiral Lindquist was discussing press and possible presidential arrangements with Atlantis Command while the Com and Nav officers were working out fleet deployments for the best coverage of Atlantis.

"Ryan?" said the admiral.

"Sir?"

"Assuming we can get confirmation about no further EMP pulses, what would you think about not telling the truth about that for a while?"

"To help keep out the tourists?" Ryan asked.

"Exactly," the admiral replied. "Command has been able to block all the satellites that can image the area. Right now, even Google can't scan for a map update.

"Sounds good, sir."

The admiral nodded then turned to Jenn.

"Dr. Wallace?"

"Yes, admiral?"

"General Aspinal had to sign off, but she asked after your daughter and Mr. Wallace."

"That was good of her," said Jenn.

"She also had a bit of advice for you, which she asked me to pass on."

Jenn raised her eyebrows.

"She said to tell you not to worry, that the press and even the president are pussycats compared to us Navy officers. She also said to remind you that when you posted that video last night, you effectively made the press corps your lackeys."

He smiled at her surprise.

"She suggested that you try and go easy on them."

CHAPTER 36

Tour Atlantis

To Bob it seemed as if dawn arrived earlier on Atlantis. With the sunrise came an awakening call, a soft low horn that was pleasantly unobtrusive. It was a wonderful invitation to start the day, and before very long everyone that had been rescued from the plane was sitting on the stone steps of the plaza, admiring the sunrise and discussing the previous evening's events.

After learning that Evan and Emma had gone off with another of the Mayan councilors the previous evening and talked well into the night, Bob checked with a few of the other passengers. It seemed they had each been spirited away and sequestered for a chat, although no one had been pressured and it had all been friendly conversation as the councilors tried to learn more about us and our world.

"They're trying to learn what they can about us," Emma said. "We'd do the same."

Bob nodded.

"True. We are doing the same. I'll bet they're having a meeting right now to discuss what they learned."

"Not now," Tadeo said, as he came up behind them. "They will meet later in the morning."

Tara got up to greet Tadeo. He said that he was there to take them to eat. They walked along the front of the guest hall until they came to an area where a number of people were eating breakfast, sitting outside on stone slabs. Tadeo guided Bob and the others inside, where a row of tables filled with numerous dishes of food, was attended by cooks working on the other side of the table.

"It's a buffet," Evan said, in amazement.

"It is morning meal," Tadeo said, pointing to the people already eating outside. "These ones worked at night, but all are welcome."

"Maybe it's like a cafeteria?" Tara said.

"Whatever it is, it's breakfast," said Bob, heading over to the tables.

And breakfast it was. Although many items were not familiar, there was a good selection of sliced meats, corn bread, some sort of egg dish, and several flatbreads. Another table served water and a couple of unfamiliar drinks. There was also a table that serving what appeared to be chocolate, prepared in a number of different ways and interspersed with many varieties of fruit, some of which none of them had seen before.

To their credit, and Tadeo's amazement, they each tried a little bit of almost everything. Tadeo was kept hopping explaining what each dish was. There was one meat dish that had the texture of turkey but a taste that was very unusual.

"What's this one?" Tara asked.

"That is Cucu," Tadeo answered. "A special bird for eating. It does not fly."

Evan looked over at Bob with raised eyebrows.

"Do you think?" he asked.

"Maybe," Bob replied. "Tadeo, can we see this bird?"

"Yes! I will take you," he replied, swirling his finger around in a circle, "We go around!"

After breakfast, Tadeo led them down the stairs to a ship anchored at the dock below the Guest Hall. As soon as they were aboard, Tadeo nodded to the captain and they rowed out of the dock. They headed clockwise around the circular canal, following along the brass ring, moving further away from the harbor. The ship slowed when the docks lining the inner side of the canal gave way to a massive cavern that led inward through the rock wall, presumably connecting to the next canal. The ship's path was blocked only by the unbroken brass ring.

Their presence had been noted. Teams on both sides rushed out and pulled ropes to hinge up large sections of the brass ring, one to the left and one to the right, leaving them with just enough space to fit the ship and its extended oars through. The ship's captain shouted and the oarsmen rowed furiously towards the gap. Just as they were about to go through, all oars were put to lie and the ship coasted neatly into the cavern.

The oars were dipped again and the ship rowed through the light cast by the torchlights mounted in the cavern walls. They were occasionally able make out docks and smaller gated caverns leading off the main passage. Their ship slowed as it reached the far end of the cavern, then entered into the next canal with its inner ring made of what appeared to be tin. For a moment they paused and admired the new view. Slightly lower canal walls overhung rows of docks, piers, and dwellings similar to those that were under the built-up eaves of the outer canal's walls.

Tadeo wore a mischievous grin when he joined them under the ship's canopy.

"Short or Long?" he asked.

"What?" said Evan. "What do you mean?"

"Short way round or long way round?" Emma guessed.

Tadeo's smile confirmed her translation.

"Long way," said Tara, who was clearly enjoying the boat ride.

Tadeo bowed his head to Tara then nodded to the captain. The boat was then rowed counterclockwise along the second canal's tin wall. The terrain varied greatly from what they had seen so far on Atlantis. At times the canal wall was low enough for them to see that each field contained a dwelling or other structure that looked more industrial in purpose. When the canal walls were higher, the ship sailed under numerous stone bridges, significantly more than had crossed over the first canal. Strangely, some of the bridges over this canal seemed too narrow to carry even one person.

They'd been traveling for a while when Tadeo called out and pointed. They were approaching a dock located behind the tin ring. Bob guessed that this would put them directly opposite the harbor on the far side of Atlantis. After a section had been lifted for them and the ship had docked, they began climbing a long flight of stairs to reach the top of the canal wall.

"Will Itzela be coming?" Bob asked.

"Council meets now," Tadeo said. "We will go there after."

Tadeo stopped when they'd reached the top of the stairs. Paths led off in several directions and divided enclosures, some of which were surrounded by low stone walls while others had simple wooden fencing. One area had high stone walls with slits at eye level. A low stone fence ran around the perimeter of the taller enclosures set a few feet away from the main walls.

Tadeo held out both his arms and said something. As he spoke, the loud trumpet of an elephant's call could be heard from just beyond him. The sound was followed by a loud trudging noise as an elephant came lumbering round the bend in the path. Tadeo held out his arms again.

"Animals," he said.

Much of the rest of the morning was spent touring the Atlantis zoo. Tadeo explained they didn't know which animals would have survived the end of the world so they brought as many as possible. Much of the collecting was done long ago, but he told stories of the special ships that would bring animals and the challenge of getting them from the ships up into the pens. Tadeo explained that the elephants, which were numerous on Atlantis, were a great help since most of the other animals respected them.

He told a story of the unloading of one special ship millennia ago. The ship had sailed to the farthest reaches of their trading empire. When it finally returned with its cargo of many species, the animals seemed happy and content, leaving the ship side by side as they headed to their pens without so much as a squabble. Tadeo was a great storyteller. Bob could clearly envision the animals leaving the boat two by two, heading up the ramp to their new home on Atlantis.

"You alright, Dad?" Tara asked. "You looked like you were daydreaming."

"Yeah, fine," replied Bob, shaking his head to clear it. "Tadeo, so what about that bird at breakfast?"

"Yes, this way," Tadeo said, leading them along the path that ran beside the canal's edge.

Another path split off and ran straight in the direction of the island's center. A low stone wall bordered the path on both sides, but on the side opposite the zoo the vegetation seemed more natural and wild. They'd only gone a short way when Tadeo stopped them and pointed.

"Cucu," he whispered.

A flock of stubby wingless birds were foraging around

in the jungle undergrowth. Bob and Evan took good a look at the bird's oversize beaks and burst out laughing. The birds were startled, running clumsily away through the undergrowth.

"What's wrong with you?" Tara asked.

"That, Tara," said Bob, as he attempted to calm himself, "Is the almost legendary and very extinct dodo bird."

"The historians got one thing right," Evan snorted. "They sure tasted different."

Evan and Bob started laughing again, while Tara and Emma did their best to explain to a very confused Tadeo.

Eventually they headed back along the path and Bob tried to make sense of what they'd just seen.

"It's beautiful," he said, "Atlantis is an ark. Heck it's *the* ark."

"Tadeo," said Evan, as he looked curiously at the zoo. "Why did your people do all this?"

"That's not fair," Tara said. "That's a question for the council."

Bob was initially surprised at her defense of Tadeo, but not much could startle him after the last 24 hours.

"I am to tell you all that I can," Tadeo said. "It is our way."

"The Diachrome have predicted many things, but none as important as the meeting of the Keftiu and the Maya. The Diachrome said there was to be a meeting with the Keftiu, an earthshake at Keftiu, the destruction of Keftiu and then the destruction of the world. Only the Keftiu could save themselves from the end but they could not do it alone. Only with the help of the Maya. Much of our history is lost, but each thing the Diachrome predicted has happened. And now we are here."

A quick horn blast was heard from the ship below.

"We go to council," said Tadeo.

CHAPTER 37

Spin Control

The faces on the screens and around the room reflected the shock of his suggestion as the admiral continued.

"We have a Chinese fleet, a Russian fleet, and ships on the way from Britain, India and numerous other countries. If we don't declare this a no-fly, no-go zone soon, we won't be able to control it."

"But threatening to shoot down trespassing aircraft, or sink ships!" Jenn said, aghast. "There must be another way."

"We're open to suggestions, Dr. Wallace," General Aspinal said from the viewscreen. "But if we don't soon do something, the people on Atlantis might, and as we've seen they don't seem to take kindly to trespassers."

"Well, this isn't why I came here," she said. "I don't think I can contribute to this discussion."

"But you have, Dr. Wallace, and you must continue to do so," the president said. "It's precisely your viewpoint that we, and the world, needs. You have a historical frame of reference here that most simply don't possess."

"But all this military action..." she began.

"Is something that we're going to have to deal with," the president continued. "Those ships are intent on coming here, and if we're able to start flying again the air traffic in the area will become an even bigger problem."

"If these countries are part of Atlantis Command," Jenn said. "Then why are they sending their own ships?"

"A very good question," replied the president smiling. "General?"

"The Chinese say their mission is scientific. They're curious how something this large has remained hidden so long."

The General flipped a page of her notes.

"The British and many of the other ships are coming to assist. Most worrisome is the Russians, who won't say why they're coming."

"We've shared everything we know freely," said the president. "But some don't believe it, some want to see for themselves and some, well some just want to get their hands on whatever technology this is, or maybe keep us from getting our hands on it."

"Mr. President?" Ryan broke in. "I think we should tell the Atlanteans what's going on and ask them about their shield and the EMP pulse, if it will happen again. See what they say, then decide what to do."

"And until then?" Aspinal asked.

"Let's establish the no-go, no-fly zone for now, but without the threats," said Lindquist. "And even if we can start flying again, we should say we can't, just to keep planes out of the area."

The president nodded.

"That might minimize any conflict, but how do we fly into the area?"

"You don't," Jenn said. "Prove it by living it, don't fly."

"That will inconvenience a whole lot of people," the Admiral added, thoughtfully. "But it could work."

"What about the choppers we've been using?" asked Ryan. "There are pictures everywhere and they can see them from the coast."

Silence filled the room, as a good plan seemed to go up in flames.

"Crash one," said Jenn.

"What?" exclaimed Lindquist.

"Crash a helicopter," Jenn replied. "An empty one. Blame it on the EMP pulse or the Atlantis Effect or something, but crash one and leak it to the press. Let them tell the story."

"Do you know how much an attack helicopter costs, Dr. Wallace?" the general said.

"We don't have to crash an attack helicopter," pointed out the admiral. "Dr. Wallace may be onto something here."

"Can we crash a drone or something else as well?" the president asked.

"Then we can establish the no-go, no-fly zone... for safety," said Aspinal. "Brilliant."

"Still think you can't contribute, Dr. Wallace?" the president asked.

"Maybe," she said. "But I won't be able to lie to the press."

"I think we can make sure that you don't have to," Ryan said. "But you'll have to let the Atlanteans know what we're up to, and why."

"I can do that."

"Then we'll excuse you from the precise details when we get to them, Dr. Wallace," said the admiral.

The lighter mood was interrupted by the buzzing of Jenn's cell phone. She looked worried as she showed the screen to Ryan.

"It's Bob Wallace calling, "Ryan said. "Can we clear the room?"

"Let's clear the room please," the President agreed, perhaps sensing something in Jenn's expression. "Give Dr. Wallace some privacy."

"Mr. President?" Jenn said. "I'm sure Bob will want to talk to you."

He nodded his agreement as Jenn answered her phone. Ryan blanked the Atlantis Command screen and he and the admiral left the room.

"Bob," said Jenn.

"Hi, mom," Tara replied.

"Tara, how are you? Where's your dad?"

"I'm fine, he's right here," Tara replied. "He said you probably needed to hear from me."

"I did," she said, wiping away a tear. "What are you guys doing over there?"

"There was a big party last night, and we went for a boat ride to see the zoo this morning," Tara replied. "We're at the council meeting right now, but something's happening."

"At the meeting?" Jenn asked.

"No, somewhere else. I'll get Dad."

"Tara?"

"Yeah, Mom?"

"I'm on the ship just outside the harbor and I want to put you on speakerphone," she said, as she switched the phone over. "I'm on videoconference with the president and he'd like to say hi."

"The president? I thought boats had captains?"

"They do, Miss Wallace," the president said. "He works for me."

"Uh, hi Mr. President," Tara said, nervously. "I'll get my dad."

There was a brief whispered conversation in the background as Tara spoke to Bob.

"Hello?" said Bob.

"Hello, Mr. Wallace," replied the president.

"Hi, Bob," said Jenn. "You're on speaker."

"Oh, well hi Mr. President. I'm glad you're both there," Bob said. "The council of Atlantis would like to meet with you, I mean us."

"I'm not there yet, Mr. Wallace," said the president. "But if it's alright, I would like to be there for that meeting."

"Call me, Bob."

Jenn shook her head at his lack of decorum.

"I'm sure that would be appreciated," Bob continued. "We've tried to explain the who's who of our world, so they have some idea who you are."

"Where are they from?" Jenn asked. "The ships, the architecture, the language?"

"Do you know?" asked the president.

"Not really," Bob said. "It's like they fell out of the past."

"Well, where do you think they're from?" asked Jenn.

"I think Atlantis is a generation ship," Bob replied. "They have ships, fields, farms, livestock, everything. They even sent out ships to fill a zoo with every kind of animal they could find. We visited it today. Does the phrase 'animals two by two' sound familiar?"

"They said that?" said Jenn.

"Word for word."

"That would agree with what we're seeing by satellite," the president added. "Let me ask you one important question, and answer from your gut please. Is it safe? Are we in any danger from these people?"

Bob took a moment to answer.

"I'd say it's safe. Our only danger would be in not taking the time to understand them."

They chatted for a while longer , discussing the incoming ships and the plans that had been discussed in the ready room earlier. Bob agreed to pass on the information then the president excused himself so Jenn and Bob could chat privately.

"Excuse me, sir?" Bob said. "Before you go I'd like to see if it's possible to get some batteries and a cell phone charger over here. Maybe a couple more phones too."

The president smiled on the screen and winked at Jenn as he answered.

"Actually Bob, you'll need to take that up with Dr. Wallace. I believe that's her department. I expect I'll see you tomorrow."

He signed off. Jenn chatted with Bob for a while, mostly about Tara, then called the team back in. The conversation shifted to making some rough plans for a meeting the next day, and for Bob to sneak over and pick up some supplies. Bob signed off after that and discussions continued. The president came back on, then stayed on the line far longer than anyone had anticipated.

"We've had such useful input from you, Dr. Wallace," the president said. "What would you think about including those other two people that we picked up with you in Playa in these ongoing discussions?"

Lindquist and Aspinal protested, but Jenn agreed.

"That would probably be a good idea, including a couple more non-military voices," she said. "No offense intended."

"None taken, Dr. Wallace," said Ryan. "Let's do that."

"Fine," said the president. "I'll look forward to seeing them at the next meeting."

The president signed off and Lindquist ended the meeting. After everyone had signed off, the admiral headed back to the bridge and left Ryan and Jenn alone in the ready room.

"The Atlantis Effect, I like that," said Ryan, smiling.

"That's what you took from all that?" Jenn said, incredulously.

Ryan shrugged and held the door for her as they left the ready room.

216

CHAPTER 38

A Turn for the Worse

Tadeo had dropped Bob, Evan, and Tara off on the outer side of the canal at a different dock where he assured them the staircase led up to the council chamber. He really wanted to accompany them, but had to honor his promise to Emma and the other archeologists to continue with their tour.

As comfortable as they were beginning to feel around the Atlanteans, they were a little unnerved at the prospect of being left alone to wander around the island. Once they began their ascent, they realized that they weren't really alone. The canal walls became terraced as the hill ascended. Each terrace contained a dwelling and appeared to be cultivated. People along the way seemed happy to see them, smiling and waving at them as if they'd known them their whole lives.

"Why is everyone so friendly?" Tara asked.

"Isolation," Evan replied. "They're used to being alone, and happy to see anybody."

Bob shook his head.

"I don't think that's it. There's no animosity, no fear of the unknown. They seem sure of themselves, comfortable, empowered."

"Well, either way, it's a little unnerving," said Evan.

"It's kind of refreshing, actually," Tara added. "Like there's no hidden agenda. Nobody is trying to sell you stuff."

Bob smiled proudly at his daughter's analysis. They continued to the top of the steps without further discussion where they were greeted by a soldier from the council chamber. He led them directly to the chamber via a much more direct route than the twisting labyrinth of passages they'd traveled through previously.

When they arrived on the dais, Bob noticed that two of the council members had been replaced. One of the new councilors was dressed in the full regalia of a Mayan priest. Bob caught Itzela's eye and smiled. The Mayan priest stood and addressed them in English, which was rather unnerving considering his clothing.

"I am Tzakol," he said. "Also new on council is Aphrodite."

He pointed to the opposite bench where a slim, dark-haired young girl clad in a simple shift stood nervously, politely nodding to them.

"She looks my age," Tara whispered to Bob.

"Shhh!"

"We wish to thank you for joining our celebration and for staying with us," Tzakol began. "We hope that this will continue to allow us to understand each other. In truth, we did not expect to find your people on our return, and it seems also, that you did not expect us."

He paused and looked around at the other council members before continuing.

"We are not yet decided but we are all agreed that we must repair our ship," he said, pointing to the harbor, "and we would very much like to know your peoples."

Evan moved forward to speak as Tzakol sat back down. It quickly became apparent that he hadn't thought about what he'd actually say to the council.

"Yes," he said. "We have many questions ourselves.

We would like to know you more as well. And we..., er, wish to..."

He was floundering so Bob took over.

"There are so many questions it's hard to know where to start. You are the people of Maya and the people of Minos, but we had thought these worlds to be millennia apart. We're curious how this happened. You mentioned this Diachrome and that he foresaw these things happening. What is a Diachrome? How does he fit into this?"

He had clearly touched a nerve as the council members began talking amongst themselves, frequently glancing at the single empty chair in the middle of the council. Bob noticed that Aranare wasn't around. He'd been with them each time they'd been in council before. Bob thought that perhaps he should try and offer more of an olive branch.

"We can contact our people about fixing the pillar," he said. "And I'm sure we can arrange a visit for you to some of our cities to see how we live."

"An exchange program," Tara said, happily. "Like at school."

"What is that?" Itzela asked.

"It's something we do with our youth," said Evan, trying to get back into the conversation. "A student from one school goes to a school in another land while one comes from that land to study at their school. They exchange."

Itzela nodded at Evan's crisscrossing hand motions and the council members seemed to think that the exchange was a good idea.

At that moment a messenger emerged from the center dais stairwell behind them. He gave a worried nod to the council members and they immediately adjourned their meeting and began to file out. Itzela said something to Tzakol who thought for a moment then turned back to the dais.

"We must attend elsewhere," he said to them all, then focused on Bob. "I believe you can contact your people with your phone, I think it is called?"

"Yes," said Bob.

"You will arrange the exchange?"

"Some from yours can tour our Atlantis tomorrow and some of our council can tour your city?"

"We'll make it happen," said Evan.

"We'll try and set it up," Bob corrected him.

Tzakol looked at Evan and then at Bob, sensing their antagonism.

"When you are done, please come?" he said.

Tzakol turned and asked the messenger to bring them once they were finished.

"Can we go up top?" Bob asked the messenger.

He bowed in acknowledgement and they went behind the council seats to where they could see the ships in the harbor.

"Should be a better signal here," he said, as he handed the phone to Tara. "Why don't you call your Mom?"

* * *

They passed the phone back and forth a few times and after what seemed like an endless conversation, Bob finally hung up.

"Took long enough," Evan said. "So we're having our exchange?"

"Definitely," replied Bob.

"Good idea asking for the phones and supplies, then we can document more of this," Evan said. "Who were you talking to?"

"Mom," Tara answered.

"Nobody else?" asked Evan, curiously.

"Oh, you mean the president," Bob said. "Yeah, he'll probably be here tomorrow for the exchange."

"The president?" said Evan.

"Sure," Bob replied, smiling.

"Of the United States?"

"Who else?" said Bob. Shrugging, he turned to face the messenger. "Okay, we can go now."

Tara snickered at Evan's stunned reaction as they left the chamber.

They followed the messenger out behind the Council chamber and along the top of the outer ring of Atlantis, heading away from the harbor. Evan bugged Bob and Tara mercilessly for details about the president. Eventually they told him what had been discussed, but only after making Evan promise that he'd be the one to stay with the president while he was on Atlantis during the exchange. Evan thanked them profusely, then walked on just ahead of them, muttering to himself about protocol, decorum, and who knows what else.

"He is okay?" the messenger asked.

"He will be," said Bob.

Tara snickered again, then looked up as they saw something they hadn't previously seen on Atlantis. A small temple was guarded on all sides by a high wall with guards posted in a tower at each corner of the enclosure. As they came around to the front, a solid line of guards parted to let them pass, then silently formed up again behind them.

Inside the foyer of the building, all of the council members stood chatting among themselves. Several nodded greetings to them as they entered. Aranare had noticed their arrival and came straight over.

"We were called too soon," he said to them. "It is not yet time."

"What?" Bob asked.

221

Aranare's expression became so intense that Bob felt as if he'd been put under a microscope and had every part of his soul evaluated. He must have passed the test because Aranare proceeded to tell him exactly what was happening.

"Our Diachrome Paulin nears his end," he said, sadly.

Aranare then proceeded to tell them the story.

"Many years ago, a Diachrome predicted that one day there would be two, and that it would mean that the time for transition was upon us. Paulin is one of these twin Diachrome. As foretold, his brother stayed behind to carry on the line and Paulin came with Atlantis. What was not foretold was that Paulin should not stay in the shield room. He was exposed to the field of transition. Some are affected much more than others."

All the council members had now joined them.

"I'm sorry to hear that," Bob said. "May I ask what the Diachrome does? I don't understand."

Aranare paused and looked around him, but none of the council members intervened.

"Diachrome may see through the eyes of their children and their children's children," he said. "It is our greatest gift."

"See through the eyes of their children?" Evan asked. "I don't get it."

"They can see the future," said Tara.

Itzela lowered her head in acknowledgment.

"Diachrome have saved our peoples," she explained. "By seeing through the eyes of their own offspring who also grow to become Diachrome when they are older, no matter where or when they are."

"But now they will be no more," Tzakol said, sadly. "Paulin is the last."

"Well, he can't be," said Bob.

As he looked around, he could tell that some of the

council members already knew what he was about to say.

"What do you mean?" asked Aphrodite.

Bob turned to Itzela.

"Tadeo said that the Diachrome foresaw the end of the world in 2012?"

"Yes."

"Well, whether or not the world ended, someone must have been here for a Diachrome to see it."

Bob was stringing his logic together with very few pieces. He hoped he was right.

"It is so," Aranare said. "Paulin was to find the Diachrome in this time. He said he could not see with them until we arrived."

"And now he's dying?" Tara said, holding back tears.

"Yes. We will see him now," Aranare nodded, and opened his arms to include Bob, Evan and Tara.

He led them from the main hall into the adjoining room. A group of people were attending to a man lying on the bed. They moved aside so they could see him.

By his features, Paulin was of Mayan descent and seemed to be no more than 40 years old. He was definitely ill, even his hair seemed to be falling out. His attendants had coated his strangely burned skin with a salve that seemed to be healing it, so the main damage must have been internal. There was very little spark in his eyes when they opened briefly to peer at the visitors.

Aranare beckoned them closer, then positioned them one at a time to allow Paulin see them. He briefly glanced at each of them but when he looked into Bob's eyes Paulin was slightly startled. He attempted to speak and Aranare leaned in closer to hear his words. When Aranare looked up again, Paulin's eyes were closed, his chest rising and falling in a steady rhythm.

Reassured, Aranare ushered Bob and the others from the room.

Once outside they pressed him for more information. Aranare raised his hands for silence.

"Paulin has told me before that we will first find the one that knows of the Diachrome."

He pointed at Bob.

"He says you are the one that knows. Do you know of someone who knows of things that cannot be known?"

"Dad?" said Tara.

"Well," Bob replied. "I don't think so, but, well maybe, I mean, it could be."

"What?" Evan said. "What do you mean, 'maybe'?"

"Well, there's a guy I've worked with on a few digs, even the last one in Guatemala. He always seemed to know where to dig. He's the one that located the underground chambers at Tikal. I guess maybe it could be him."

CHAPTER 39

Supplies

"We've assembled everything you asked for on the launch deck, sir," the Com officer said.

Ryan nodded thanks then looked at Jenn.

"Ready?" he asked.

She smiled and texted Bob.

Your care package is ready.

A moment later Bob replied.

Care package?

She rolled her eyes and quickly responded.

Cell phones, chargers etc...

Oh, cool. Will bring Tara. CU soon.

Jenn looked at Ryan.

"He's completely absentminded."

"We'd better get going," said Ryan.

They made their way down to the stern of the carrier to something Ryan called the 'well deck'. A cavernous area set inside the back of the ship, it was open to the sea. The captain's launch was tied up alongside the dock inside the well deck, beside a stack of waterproof cases that were all ready to be loaded.

"Mr. Johnson, sir!" said, one of the sailors, saluting. "I'll be taking you out to the meeting point."

"Very good, skipper," Ryan said. "Let's get them loaded."

"Do we need to?" said Jenn.

"What do you mean?" Ryan asked.

"Well, we're bringing them here anyway, so let them pick them up. Nothing beats working together."

Ryan looked around the equipment bay. Amphibious assault vehicles were racked alongside various other landing craft that could all be swung into place for rapid launch. The armament on most of them was clearly visible.

"Are you sure that's a good idea?" he said. "I was thinking we'd close up the bay and use the external dock."

She looked around, then shrugged. "This is a military ship. Why hide it? Unless there is something we don't want them to see here?"

"I don't think so," said Ryan, with a shrug he nodded to the skipper. "Let's go get them."

They hopped aboard and the launch backed out of the well then came about and headed towards the harbor gates. They pulled up at the entrance just as the ship from Atlantis was leaving its dock. Ryan radioed Admiral Lindquist and confirmed about using the open well deck.

"No problem," said Ryan when he got off the radio. "So far your intuition's been right on."

She smiled and turned to look at the approaching ship. There was Tara, waving from under the canopy. Jenn waved back and a tear rolled down her cheek.

"Sorry," she said. "I'm never like this."

"Well, these are definitely not normal times," Ryan replied, smiling. "Not to worry. I'm betting she'll be tearing up a bit as well."

The mother and daughter reunion was about as touching as he'd expected. Ryan was also rather happy to see that Bob and Jenn didn't embrace like they had the first time.

"Thanks for bringing her along this time, Bob," said

Jenn. "I was beginning to wonder if you were coming back."

"I will be," said Tara. "Just not yet."

"You remember Aranare and Cadmael?" Bob asked.

Jenn nodded and smiled. Aranare and Cadmael bowed their heads in greeting.

"Yes, of course," Ryan said. "Good to see you again."

He turned to Bob.

"We have the supplies you wanted ready on board the carrier. We'd like to offer you all a quick tour of our ship, sort of a preview for tomorrow's meeting."

"That sounds fun," Tara said.

The two Atlanteans climbed aboard the boat.

"Can we go fast?" Tara asked.

The launch captain glanced at Ryan, who looked at Bob.

"Cadmael, Aranare," Bob said quickly. "Please sit. We would like to show you this boat's capabilities."

Cadmael shouted something to the crew of his ship in his own language and they seemed to relax, at least until the engine roared and the launch took off at full speed.

Tara squealed with joy as twin rooster tails spouted in the launch's wake. The skipper executed a quick precise loop in front of the Minoan ship, showing the crew that they were in no danger. He then turned and zipped across the waves towards the *Excelsior*.

"That was fun," Aranare said, as they sidled up to the dock inside the well deck.

"Very fast," Cadmael added.

"It always feels faster in a small ship closer to the water," Ryan said. "It's all relative."

Admiral Lindquist stepped forwad and offered them a hand climbing aboard. Cadmael and Aranare stepped back and insisted that Jenn and then Tara go first. Aranare then accepted the admiral's proffered hand and the rest of them came aboard.

"Welcome aboard, ladies and gentlemen," said the admiral. "It looks like we share a custom with your people."

"What custom is that?" asked Aranare.

"We say 'ladies first'," the Admiral replied. "At least many of us do. It's a very old custom to honor the ladies."

"It is our way as well," said Cadmael then added. "Unless there is danger."

"Then what happens?" Jenn asked.

"Then," replied Aranare, bowing in the girls' direction. "It is as she chooses."

Everyone smiled as they headed toward the bridge. Cadmael noticed the landing craft stacked in the back of the well deck but said nothing. Jenn and Tara walked behind the others, deep in conversation.

Admiral Lindquist made a special stop at the hanger deck to show everyone an assortment of several dozen aircraft in various stages of deployment and storage. Attack helicopters, several VTOL aircraft, troop transports, and even a Medivac chopper were all lined up in the massive hanger bay.

"We were on military exercises when Atlantis appeared," the admiral explained. "So we have a full compliment of equipment for a variety of situations on board."

"This is for practice?" Cadmael asked.

"Yes," Ryan said. "So we can be ready for anything."

"Do you practice as well?" Bob asked.

"We do," replied Cadmael.

"Lets move on to the bridge," Lindquist said.

If they had been expecting jaw-dropping amazement from the Atlanteans on seeing the bridge's vast array of screens displaying data and video feeds then they were disappointed. Intense curiosity was a far better description. It was as if Aranare and Cadmael had been expecting to see a display of technology and were now experiencing it in person.

However, General Aspinal was clearly astounded when she walked by the main screen at Atlantis Command, glanced over and saw the two Atlanteans standing on the bridge of the *Excelsior*.

"Admiral?" the general asked.

"General Aspinal," said Lindquist. "May I present Commander Cadmael, in charge of Atlantis security and Aranare, advisor to the council."

They each bowed their heads.

"This is General Aspinal of Atlantis Command."

"Gentleman, I'm surprised to see you there today," the general said. "I had understood that this meeting was for tomorrow."

"Yes, general," replied Aranare. "This visit is practice."

"Yes, ma'am," Ryan added. "I thought a dry run might be a good idea."

"Well, I hope your practice goes smoothly," Aspinal said, before bowing her head to the visitors. "I'll talk with you again tomorrow."

The monitor clicked off. After a moment of awkward silence, Bob spoke.

"Did somebody forget to tell the general we were coming?"

The rest of the visit went smoothly. The satellite scans and aerial views of Atlantis were a big hit with Aranare and Cadmael. While they seemed to understand the basics of the technology, the reality was even more impressive than the idea, and they intensely studied the large projection, pointing out the various features of Atlantis.

While they were examining the satellite maps, Paulo and Terry were brought onto the bridge. They were being introduced to the Atlanteans when they were interrupted.

"Excuse me, admiral?" Com called out, wearing a concerned expression.

The admiral excused himself and went over to the Com with Ryan.

"Yes?"

"Sir, Command just flagged a broadcast on Radio Guatemala that might be troublesome."

"Is it to do with our friends here?" Ryan asked.

"Yes, sir."

"Well, let's hear it," said Lindquist.

"Sir, I don't have the original material," Com replied. "But Command says the announcer was quoting a press release in which the Guatemalan President was disallowing any prior land claims by returning Maya peoples. He directly referenced Atlantis."

"Land claims? said the admiral. "Well that'll stir up a hornet's nest. What do you think, Ryan."

"I think that we may have to add another question or two to that urgent list."

They rejoined their guests and finished the bridge tour, then walked outside and around the flight deck where Aranare and Cadmael were able to closely examine some of the aircraft. Eventually they decided that it was time to head back.

Tara must have had a quick discussion with her mother, because Jenn didn't argue about Tara going back to Atlantis. As they loaded the cases into the launch, Ryan read off the checklist, which included laptops, cell phones, radios, flashlights, generator, chargers, and more. Bob figured they'd need less than half of it, but they loaded everything anyway.

Cadmael stood at the front during the launch's slightly more sedate journey back to the meeting point. After a nod from Aranare, Cadmael directed the boat captain only to slow down as they came by their ship. Cadmael yelled a simple order to the crew and at his word they dipped the oars to turn and begin their journey home. Cadmael then asked the skipper to take them in, past the gates of Atlantis and into the harbor, all they way to their home dock.

CHAPTER 40

People Power

The group that had visited the carrier arrived back at the council chamber in the middle of a somewhat animated discussion. Emma and Evan sat listening on wooden chairs that had been added to the dais. Bob set the two cases he was carrying behind the chairs then came around and sat down beside them. He tried to catch Itzela's eye, but she seemed to be avoiding his gaze.

"What's going on?" he whispered.

"I'm not sure," replied Emma. "They were asking about the world again, how things are arranged, politics, even about how people live their lives now. Then they switched to a mix of Mayan and Minoan and lost me, and from there it seemed to become this."

She gestured toward the discussion being carried on above them.

"I think they're trying to decide what to do with us," Evan added.

"That is close," said Aranare as he took a seat beside Bob and listened to the council members for a moment longer before continuing.

"They talk about what are we to do now that we have arrived and your peoples are here."

Tara set down her cases then saw Tadeo in the wings

of the chamber. She smiled and waved him over as she quietly popped open a case and slid out a laptop. She glanced up at Bob and he shrugged, then nodded his approval. Tadeo and Tara sat at the other end of the row of chairs and, in whispers, she began to explain to him what the laptop was used for.

Cadmael had placed the cases that he'd been carrying beside Bob's and Aranare's. Several members of the ship's crew arrived one by one from beneath the dais and quietly placed the rest of the crates behind the row of seats. Cadmael glanced at Aranare and rolled his eyes as he strode to the front of the dais and listened. Finally, Tzakol made a pointed remark that drew only silence from the other council members. Cadmael choose that moment to speak.

"We know we cannot go back," he said authoritatively, in English. "So perhaps we should include our friends in this discussion. These are the only ones who can tell us of how things are and how they have been since we left."

No one responded.

"It is true that we did not expect to find them here, but our purpose has not changed."

There were murmurs of agreement from the council and Aranare got to his feet.

"We seek.a home for our people," he said. "And with their help we will find the Diachrome in this world to help guide the way. Paulin has seen this."

"But why did the world not end?" asked Aphrodite. "It is the only thing that has not happened as foretold."

There were more murmurs of agreement from above and even Cadmael's expression revealed the depth of their concern.

"What was the vision?" Emma asked. "What was seen that was so bad?"

"It was the end of the world," Aranare said, solemnly.

234

"Each Diachrome has seen the same vision, it is very strong. There are many details that are taught to all. It is said that the Sun lashed out and heated the center of the world and made it as liquid. Great chasms opened up under large cities and buildings fell as the cities broke apart, their pieces sliding into the sea. A great volcano arose and exploded in the big land and the expulsion from that burnt or covered all the land. It was possible for a very few to flee in an airplane, and even as they left, ships as great as your carrier were picked up by a great wave then smashed down as great waves washed over the land."

He paused and looked at the council members before continuing.

"Islands became filled with fire and then even larger waves washed over the whole world, sweeping away all of the people. The Diachrome have always told us to hope that a very few people might have survived, hiding in three great ships of metal that rivaled our Atlantis."

"This did not happen?" Cadmael asked.

"Trust me," replied Evan. "It never happened."

"Definitely not," Emma added, trying to reassure them.

"As you have said," Cadmael said. "But now many of our people fear it is yet to come."

There was silence until Bob cleared his throat and stood up.

"Um," he began, addressing them carefully, "I think Cadmael, Aranare, and everybody, that you can tell them it's going to be alright."

"What?" said Evan. "Are you talking about?"

Bob looked at Tara, who smiled and nodded. She knew exactly what he was thinking and started searching the internet.

"This is going to be… difficult to explain," said Bob.

"Found it, Dad," Tara told him.

"If the council would like to come down here and gather around," said Bob. "I have something that I think will explain a great deal."

"Bob?" Evan asked.

Bob held his finger to his lips as the council members came down to the dais. Tara turned the laptop around and Bob gathered everyone in front of it.

"As Cadmael and Aranare saw today, and Itzela and Tadeo saw on the phone, we have the ability to project images on a device."

He turned to Tara.

"Can you skip ahead to the parts they mentioned?"

She nodded and he turned back to the council members.

"Tell me if this is what your Diachrome have described to you," he said, "and please don't be worried."

Tara played the video, skipping ahead to show scenes of the ground splitting open, of buildings collapsing, cities sliding into the ocean, then the volcano, everything Aranare had described. Even the three giant metal ships surviving in the final scene. Tara paused the video.

"But you said that it did not happen," Aranare said, struggling to understand.

"It didn't," replied Bob. "But is this what Diachrome have described?"

Aranare nodded slowly as he sat on one of the chairs.

"But..." Itzela began.

"It's a movie," said Evan.

"It is, in fact, the movie called 2012," Bob explained. "A movie about the end of the world, as predicted by the Mayan calendar."

"But what is a movie?" Cadmael asked slowly.

"I do not understand?" said Tadeo.

"It's pretend," Tara replied. "It's not real."

Tadeo still looked confused, along with everyone else but Tara had an idea.

"It's like this," she said.

She spun the laptop around and used the camera to video herself for a minute.

"I'm talking to you from here on Atlantis," she recorded.

She then popped open the photo app and turned the computer back around.

"Here's what I recorded."

She played back the video.

"And here it is, with a little movie magic."

She showed the same clip, but this time the background was replaced with the image of a careening roller coaster sliding down the track. She was rewarded with looks of amazement and wonder.

"This is a simple computer," she said, pointing at the laptop. "And even I can do that. There are people that specialize in making movies that can create almost anything, including everything you saw in that movie.

"Everything your Diachrome have seen could have been from this movie," Bob added. "The Diachrome that's here now must have seen it!"

He saw many emotions flicker across the faces council members as they processed this new information. He couldn't imagine what was going through their minds right now. Their future had just been altered by a past they had no control over. Would they be angry and frustrated that they'd made their journey for no reason? Or perhaps feel despair and hopelessness because their future had been sabotaged? Bob scanned the council members until he found Itzela's eyes. She returned his concerned look with one of appreciation then gave him a nod to let him know that she understood. It seemed as if she'd already found a way to rationalize what she'd just heard.

Aranare stood and walked around the dais. He looked several of the councilors directly in the eye, as if he were taking a reading from them. He then returned to the computer and contemplated it thoughtfully.

"I have little doubt this is what our Diachrome have seen," he said, choosing his words carefully. "I would like to see this entire movie to be sure, but I think that perhaps this is the way it is supposed to be."

"What?" said Evan. "You just travelled through time to escape the end of the world that didn't happen! Why are you not upset?"

Bob smiled.

"Don't you remember, Evan? It's always been their way."

He quoted something that he'd heard about the Mayan that he had never understood, until now.

"The future is behind you, the past is just ahead."

"It is true," said Itzela. "The Diachrome always see for a reason. They saved our people, so we could save their people."

"By bringing them here?" Emma asked. "How did that help?"

"To find the Diachrome in this time," said Bob. "That has to be it."

"I believe so," said Aranare, nodding.

"And what then?" Tzakol asked. "What next?"

Everyone looked at Aranare, who looked directly at Bob.

"With your help, we will find this new Diachrome and ask him."

CHAPTER 41

Criss Cross

In the early light of dawn, the wing of helicopters could easily have been mistaken for a flock of birds. As they drew closer to the *Excelsior*, the smaller shapes forming the outer 'V' resolved into Apache attack helicopters, while the inner reverse 'V' took on the distinct outline of Osprey VTOL craft. The combined roar of the engines and propeller wash was deafening as the craft slowed and landed in formation on the carrier deck. Ryan wondered what the Atlanteans were making of all the racket. As the last craft settled and blades and engines began to wind down, Admiral Lindquist caught his eye.

"They must trust us," he said. "If they didn't fire up the shield for that racket."

"Isn't there usually a bunch of fanfare and ceremony?" Jenn asked. "I mean, he is the president."

"He is," The admiral smiled. "But the general is furious about him even being here. She's locked down everything, and has come along to personally keep an eye on him."

"Why furious?" Jenn asked the Admiral.

"Under normal circumstances, there is no way any head of state would tour somewhere that hasn't been fully secured," Lindquist shook his head. "The president is taking a big risk in the military's eyes."

"Since there has never been a circumstance like this,"

239

added Ryan. "The President is ignoring all protocol, travelling incognito while supposedly keeping his existing schedule. He wants to keep it low key," said Ryan. "But the general is still furious about it."

"Then why so many helicopters?" Jenn asked.

"Two Apache for escort and a shell game of three Osprey for the president, his security, and the press contingent," replied the admiral.

"What's the other Apache for?" said Jenn, counting three of each.

"Oh, that's yours," the admiral replied.

"Mine?" said Jenn, startled.

"Well, your idea anyway. That's your sacrificial lamb."

"You said that we should show them how dangerous it is," Ryan explained, pointing at the members of the press that were just exiting one of the Ospreys. "So we'll show them with that."

He pointed at the last Apache, noting the look of horror on Jenn's face.

"Don't worry, we're not going to crash a manned ship."

"I should hope not," Jenn said.

"Well, not exactly," the admiral added. "Let's go."

They moved forward and met the president and some of his security detail halfway. There were still quite a few formal military greetings to be done, especially as General Aspinal had accompanied the President in person. The press contingent was alternating between gawking and taking pictures of Atlantis and trying to capture the moment of the president's arrival. Jenn held back and watched the press mill around, worried that they'd soon be all over her.

"Dr. Wallace?"

Jenn turned to face the president.

"Mr. President!"

"A great pleasure to meet you," he said, casually gesturing to Atlantis. "We appreciate your help with this."

"You're welcome. I haven't really done much yet."

General Aspinal had made it through the greeting gauntlet and overheard her comment.

"You've basically been our first contact and have since become the de facto expert on Atlantis by sharing that video," she said, looking Jenn directly in the eye. "You've even out-strategized some darn fine U.S. military minds about how to keep unwanted guests away."

The General smiled warmly.

"Nice to meet you Dr. Wallace."

"General Aspinal," said Jenn, a little flustered. "Sorry if I overstepped."

"Nonsense," the president said. "We're all on the same team here. Admiral Lindquist tells me there have been some interesting developments."

"Yes, sir," said Ryan. "Perhaps we can discuss that in Command?"

He glanced pointedly at the members of the press that were starting to converge on them.

The president nodded.

"That sounds like a good idea, Mr. Johnson. Lead on."

He turned to the press and raised his hands for silence.

"Ladies and gentlemen, we'll have a briefing shortly. Until then, settle in and enjoy the view."

He waved out across the Atlantis-filled horizon.

"To the briefing room," the admiral ordered.

"It's as we feared," Aspinal reported. "Talking about the 200 kilometer EMP blast radius has effectively created an artificial border. People are booking flights to get as close to here as they can without crossing that 200 kilometer limit.

Ships of all kinds are setting sail for Playa del Carmen and Cancun. If they find out it's actually safe here, they'll be all over Atlantis as fast as they can get here. Some aren't waiting. We flew over this beauty cruising past Cancun, sailing south."

The monitor showed a massive multi-story luxury yacht. A few people swam in the swimming pool and played volleyball on the helipad. The back of the ship seemed to be open to the water, much like the *Excelsior*.

"Is that a well deck?" Jenn asked.

"Complete with a mini-sub from what we can tell," Aspinal replied. "They'll be in Playa within the hour."

"If these people and others get too close..." said the President, leaving the sentence unfinished.

"There are also ships from pretty much every Navy that can float a boat on the way here," the general added. "Unless something changes, it's about to get very busy around here."

"We'll have to move up the timetable," said the admiral, grimly. "Ryan?"

"I'm afraid so sir."

Only one of the pilots that had accompanied the president's detail was present at the briefing. The general called on him now.

"Commander Lawson," Aspinal asked "How soon can you be ready?"

"Uh, what's going on?" Jenn interrupted.

"Dr. Wallace," said the president. "This is Commander Brett Lawson. He's been training pilots on the Apache since they were brought onto service. He's going to be flying the helicopter that will 'fall victim' to the Atlantis shield."

"I thought it would be unmanned?" said Jenn.

"Dr. Wallace," Commander Lawson replied, "I'm the one who insisted it had to be manned. We won't fool anybody if it doesn't look real."

"But you'll be injured or even killed."

"With respect ma'am," he said, smiling, "I have no intention of letting that happen."

"Commander Lawson," the President added, "is also a Hollywood stunt pilot. In just about every scene where an Apache helicopter has been filmed doing anything crazy at all, he was probably at the controls."

"This won't be my first water landing," Lawson said.

"Perhaps we can bring everyone up to speed at the same time?" said Lindquist. "In case of problems, the submarine *John Warner* is now on station beneath us. We'll also have our own submersible rescue teams in the water. The well deck is cleared and ready to receive casualties in secrecy, if necessary. Commander Lawson has brought along some equipment that will, I'm told, give the press an impressive show of the effects of an EMP pulse. The Apache is designed to be completely shielded against an EMP blast. The plan is to show our best defense being taken out by a mere shield test of Atlantis. The chopper will spark out, immediately lose power, and spin into an uncontrolled descent into the ocean. Brett will eject before it hits the water. If anything goes wrong, submersibles will move in and retrieve him underwater."

"Our biggest challenge will be making this look like an accident," Ryan added. "We also have to make sure the press has cameras rolling before and during the crash."

He paused and thought for a moment.

"We were originally going to do this on the way back from the tour, but it looks like we need to do it before."

He turned to Jenn.

"Dr. Wallace, we were hoping to ask them in person on the visit, but can you to get hold of Atlantis and tell them what we want to do and why."

She nodded.

"Why may be difficult to explain but I'll try. What about the reporters though? Won't they know something is up when only one thing's affected?"

"We'll fire a portable EMP device across the press gang," the admiral said. "It's invisible and we'll go high enough to cause interference but not actually disable their cameras. Ryan, have someone check that there's no pacemakers in the crowd. It wouldn't do to have a member of the press drop dead."

"I brought enough equipment to rig a second chopper to look like it's disabled," added Lawson. "We could spin up another chopper, or maybe an Osprey on the deck, and just kill the spin at the right moment."

"That'd be a triple indicator," the President said. "Two different craft and the cameras."

"I'll need a bit more time to rig the Osprey," said Lawson. "Give me a couple of hours. You'll need to keep the press away while we're working as well."

"Feed them," the president suggested, "and I'll give them their press conference. That's an easy two hours. Dr. Wallace, would you like to sit in on that?"

She really wanted to refuse but nodded in agreement.

"We'll need her on and off to help coordinate the press movements just before we fire," Ryan said.

'Yes, but you'll have to be somewhere away from the press to coordinate with Atlantis to set off the test pulse," the president added. "Or they might guess something's up. Well, sit in when you can. You're a celebrity in their eyes."

"I can figure something out," Jenn said, then turned to Lawson. "Are you sure this will work?"

"It has to," he replied, with a wink. "There'll be no second take on this one."

CHAPTER 42

Across

The buzzing of his cell phone woke Bob from a sound sleep. Usually an early riser, he was surprised to see that he'd missed the dawn and that morning was well underway.

"Hello?" he answered, sleepily.

"You slept in?" said Jenn.

"Mmm," he mumbled, rubbing his eyes. "Must be the ocean air."

"Well, wake up. We have some stuff to deal with."

He rolled out of bed and looked out over the courtyard. People were already up and about.

"I'm good," he said, yawning. "What's up?"

"Short or long version?"

"Start with short."

"We need you to get the Atlanteans to flick their shield on for a moment, to run a shield test, at a particular moment."

She took a deep breath.

"We want to crash a helicopter and make it look as if the shield disabled it."

Bob sat down on the edge of the bed.

"Okay. Guess I'll need the long version then."

* * *

"Tara, get up!" said Bob, rustling her sheets.

"Five minutes," she mumbled from under the covers.

"Sorry, pal. I need you to stop being a teenager for a minute. We have to go talk to the council right away.

Tara sat bolt upright.

"Atlantis. Right," she looked at him. "Okay, I'm up. Get out."

"Good morning to you too."

Bob smiled and left Tara to get herself organized.

She came out less than five minutes later.

"So what's up?"

"I'll tell you when I tell the council," he replied "Because this is going to be rather difficult to explain."

"Well, you can practice on me while we get breakfast," Tara said, moving towards the door. "Shall we go?"

They headed out into the hallway, retracing their steps to the cafeteria that they'd attended the day before. Along the way, Bob tried to explain.

"Mom says there are ships and people from all over the world headed here right now. The president is worried that it'll turn into a gong show or that it might escalate into something bad happening, or worse, that it'll upset our hosts and they'll do something bad."

"Dad, they wouldn't," said Tara, sounding offended.

"I know, sweetie, but they have a point. People, our people, can do very stupid things and we don't know how our new friends will react. Anyway, they have a crazy plan to keep people away for a while longer. They just need Atlantis's help to pull it off."

She looked expectantly at him.

"They want to use a little Hollywood magic to show the world that it's unpredictable and therefore unsafe to be anywhere near here."

* * *

"...by having you activate your shield in one of those quick tests that you've been doing from time to time," said Bob, as he continued addressing the council. "During the test they'll broadcast live how your shield 'accidentally' disables one of our most advanced flying ships. It will lose power and crash into the sea."

"Your people will think us monsters," said Itzela.

She was clearly upset, as were many of the other council members.

"They'll just think it was an accident," Tara assured her. "It should actually work pretty well. In our world people usually don't believe something unless they see it happen."

"Right," Bob added. "And the reporters that are now on the carrier will be broadcasting live to the world. The incident will happen without warning and they'll report the accident as it happens."

"And the goal of all this is to keep the, what did you call them, riffraff, away?" Aphrodite asked.

"Yes," replied Bob.

"Evan Masters," Tzakol said. "You have said little. What do you think?"

Evan looked up, then got to his feet.

"I think it's probably a very good idea, both the plan and the goal of keeping people out. I'll be happy to help."

Bob spent some time explaining the stunt and how everyone would be safe, then together they determined who would go to the *Excelsior*, who would guide the president's tour, and who would be going to Playa. It was decided that Itzela, Tadeo, Aranare, and Cadmael would go to the carrier with Bob and Tara for the initial meeting. Evan agreed to stay behind and work with the Atlanteans to coordinate the test pulse, as long as he was the one to be assigned to chaperone the president on his tour.

Bob and the others readied themselves to head down to the dock, but Itzela pulled him aside and whispered something in his ear. He smiled.

"Cadmael, Aranare," Bob said. "Before we put on this show, would you like a ride in one of the flying ships?"

Ten minutes later Commander Lawson was landing an Osprey on the plaza in front of the council chambers. Ryan and Jenn came down the back ramp and helped everyone get on board and secure themselves for the flight.

"Wish we had time for a proper flyover," Lawson said over the headset to everyone. "But we shouldn't keep the President waiting."

He made the trip to the *Excelsior* in a series of wide sweeping turns that allowed the first time flyers to see as much as possible of their land, the harbor, and the fleet from the air. In a wide sweeping turn he approached the far side of the fleet where he pointed out the huge luxury yacht.

"That's Spielberg's yacht," he said. "Just arriving in Playa as the general expected."

He swooped around, lined up along the deck then came in slowly, landing not too far away from a makeshift podium that had been set up where it would have Atlantis as a backdrop. Once they were down, Ryan and Jenn escorted everyone to the podium for introductions. With the cameras clicking, the president welcomed the people of Atlantis, on behalf of Atlantis Command and a very curious planet.

Jenn excused herself as soon as she'd been introduced so that she could be in position for the call. The president started talking about the tour scheduled for that afternoon and how much he was looking forward to it. That was Jenn's signal, so she called Evan on Atlantis and got him on the line.

"Stand by."

"Okay," Evan replied.

"On an occasion such as this it is traditional to offer a ceremonial fly-by in respect of our new friendship."

The President turned as an Apache helicopter came into view off the stern of the ship and moved along parallel to the vessel with Atlantis as the background. The Osprey they'd arrived in began spinning up to join in the flyby, and Atlantis's golden shield flickered into existence behind them.

As the crowd gasped at the sudden appearance of the shield, sparks flew along the control surfaces of the Apache. Something on board exploded into flames and plumes of smoke. The Osprey on the deck behind them also threw sparks and flared out as the engine noise from both craft instantly went silent.

The Apache pilot seemed to be trying to recover but with no power there was little that he could do. The aircraft started rotating faster and faster, tilting as the tail rotor failed and the Apache quickly fell. It hit the water with a loud splash and titled over sideways. Seconds later there was a loud bang as the blades blew off and the cockpit decoupled from the helicopter as its escape rockets fired underneath it. Normally they'd have propelled it upwards, but since the helicopter was already partly submerged, the rockets pushed it down further into the water until it popped up and skipped across the surface, careening wildly until the rockets cut out.

As the gasping crowd watched and recorded, the shield over Atlantis flicked off as the battered cockpit came to a halt then slowly slipped under the waves.

"Oh, my god!" Jenn exclaimed.

"What happened?" Evan asked. "What happened?"

"Call you back!"

Jenn hung up and raced with everyone else to the edge of the ship to see what was going on. The admiral was ordering the rescue boats out to the scene when a load cheer went up. The helicopter cockpit's flotation devices had activated and popped it up to the surface. A bloodied hand slowly slid open the cockpit's hatch and then gave a thumbs up.

"Pick him up," Lindquist ordered and a couple of small boats quickly converged on the cockpit.

* * *

When later they reconvened on the podium, Cadmael offered a heartfelt apology for the near tragedy that Atlantis's power cycling requirement had caused. The president glossed over the incident, happy that nobody had been killed and admitting that they'd been warned but had thought it was now safe. He agreed to keep flights in the area suspended until it was deemed safe and Cadmael said that they'd see if there were a way to properly schedule the field tests. When the president asked if they could continue with the planned tour Aranare suggested that perhaps they should travel by boat.

CHAPTER 43

Undercover

The three launches that carried the president and the contingent that was to tour Atlantis backed slowly out of the well deck then accelerated forward, quickly disappearing around the side of the *Excelsior*. Admiral Lindquist asked that the remaining reporters accompany him to the command deck, where they'd be able to watch the tour's progress from the ships monitors. Apparently an invite to the command deck of a carrier was almost as welcome as a trip to Atlantis. The reporters fell over themselves to accept and followed the admiral away. Once they'd left the bay seemed oddly deserted.

"Now," Ryan said. "We just have to figure out how to get you all into Playa without attracting too much attention."

"We will tour in secret?" Itzela asked.

"That might be best," said Bob. "You won't see the normal way of life if you're being mobbed because you're from Atlantis."

Aranare nodded his agreement.

"So how are we going to do this?" Bob asked Ryan.

"I might have an idea about that."

Commander Lawson emerged from the shadows at the back of the bay. He smiled as he wiped blood from his arm and dabbed at his face.

"You are hurt?" Itzela asked, concerned.

"A little bruised up," he admitted. "But the blood is fake. I couldn't jettison the blades and blow the cockpit without risking hitting the carrier so I had to wait. I've never been a skipping stone before."

"And your injuries?" Bob asked. "All makeup?"

"You bet. I told you it needed to look good. Did we fool them?"

"Hook, line and sinker," Ryan said. "You sure you're okay, Commander Lawson?"

"Completely fine," he replied, then added. "And I left the Navy five years ago. Call me Brett."

"So what's your idea for Playa," Bob asked.

Lawson grinned from ear to ear.

"You're going to love it!"

* * *

The incessant ringing of the phone finally broke through his jetlag induced slumber.

"Stephen!"

The voice on the phone was familiar, but he couldn't place it over the roar of the background noise.

"Who's this?" he asked, still half asleep.

"It's Brett, Brett Lawson. Can you spare a minute to chat?"

"Oh, hi," he said. "Sure, but I can hardly hear you. Can you call me back?"

"Uh, actually not really," Brett replied. "Could you maybe go to your window?"

Stephen shrugged and pressed the button to retract the shades as he rolled out of bed. He slid on his slippers then came round the end of bed. Looking up, he stopped cold. Hanging in midair, hovering directly outside his stateroom window, was the windshield of a U.S. Navy CV-22 Osprey with a smiling Brett Lawson waving to him from the pilot's seat.

"What the hell are you doing here?" Stephen asked him calmly, over the phone.

"Permission to come aboard?" Brett asked. "And I'll tell you all about it."

Stephen threw up his arms and laughed.

"Do I have a choice?"

A short while later they were all sipping coffee and being offered snacks on one of the yacht's upper decks.

Brett had introduced Bob, Itzela, Aranare, Paulo, and the two reporters that he'd brought along to meet director Stephen Spielberg. Brett then pulled his friend over to the railing overlooking the helipad.

"I can't believe you landed that thing on my helipad," Stephen said. "How did you know I'd even be here?"

"Just a guess," Brett admitted, "There's no way you'd miss seeing the real Atlantis. When we flew over earlier and I saw the *Seven Seas*. I knew it had to be you."

"You know, I no longer own this boat?"

"Sure, your new trinket is floating in the Mediterranean, right?" said Brett. "So you probably flew to Fort Lauderdale, rented your old boat back for a week or so, then sailed down here to have a look."

Stephen's silence told Brett that he'd guessed correctly.

"So, when did the Navy stop you?" Brett asked, pointing at the two patrol boats that lay between them and Atlantis.

"The captain said as soon as we turned towards Atlantis. I was still sleeping."

He turned towards the other guests.

"Those two are really from Atlantis? And they want to tour Playa Del Carmen?"

"Yes, but under cover," Brett replied. "Too many crazies to let them just walk around."

"What do you want me to do?"

"I thought you might like to be their tour guide," said Brett. "You have enough pull to get wherever you want without being questioned. You also have the connections and resources to keep them safe, and you won't sell them out to the press for a buck."

"You sure about that?" said Stephen.

"I'll chance it," Brett replied, smiling. "Besides, you'll get to know them a little and maybe get a tour of Atlantis at some point. They seem like good people."

"They do," Stephen said, then pointed at Paulo. "Who's he?"

"Bartender from Playa. Says he can get them in to see some Mayan elders."

Stephen thought about that for a minute or so, then turned to address everybody.

"We're going to pose as wealthy tourists in our travels," he announced. "So we can move about with relatively little interference. Princess Itzela? Edwina is the ship's purser and she'll help you find some clothes so that you can blend in. The rest of you can have a talk with Harry, the ship's butler."

"That includes you, Brett," Stephen said loudly, as Brett tried to sneak away. "You started this, so you're coming too."

It seemed that once Stephen Spielberg committed to something, things happened quickly. Before long they were outfitted with the latest summer fashions and climbing aboard the *Seven Seas* launch that had been dropped into the sea from its internal garage.

Throughout their journey to shore, Stephen conferred with everyone then relayed instructions to people in Playa via Edwina. After finding out what types of things Itzela and Aranare wanted to see, he discussed the best way to do things with Paulo, from a native Mayan standpoint, with Bob from an archeological standpoint, and with Brett, who somehow seemed to be an expert on Playa's nightlife.

They all had very different ideas of what should be done and how, but somehow Stephen pulled it all together into a plan. The press that had come along kept true to their word and asked no questions at all. They were more than busy just taking pictures and video clips as the day's events unfolded.

Upon their arrival at the dock in Playa, they were greeted by a fleet of three shiny black Hummers and attended to by security personnel befitting the president himself. They were loading up to start their tour when Brett cornered Stephen.

"This is awesome, and I appreciate all the help, but you've gone gangbusters with this. What gives?"

"Nothing," Stephen smiled. "I'm just happy to help."

Brett shook his head.

"You never do anything without a reason."

"Well," said Stephen, winking at him. "It has absolutely nothing to do with the fact that James Cameron is going to be pissed."

"What? Why?"

"Remember the series that he headed up for *National Geographic*? It was called *Finding Atlantis*."

He smiled as he climbed into the nearest Hummer.

"Well, he may have been finding it, but now maybe I can get there first."

CHAPTER 44

Welcome to Atlantis

Whether the pace had been set to accommodate the camera operators or to entertain the newcomers, the slow cruise from the *Excelsior's* dock through the harbor entrance and up to the main dock allowed the scale of Atlantis to unfold majestically for everyone. Hardly a word was spoken during the entire trip.

When they arrived at the main dock and disembarked, Evan Masters and Tzakol welcomed them, flanked by the same impressive guard that had been assembled when Evan and the other survivors had first arrived after their rescue.

"Mr. President!" said Evan, extending his hand. "Dr. Evan Masters. A great pleasure to meet you."

"Dr. Masters," replied the President, shaking Evan's hand.

"I am Tzakol."

The impressive Mayan offered his hand before Evan could introduce him. He then offered a perfunctory bow to the rest of the group.

"We will first attend council," he announced.

"As you wish," the President said.

"The view from the top is a great place to start the tour," Evan added, as they followed Tzakol to the stairs and began their ascent.

When they reached the courtyard at the top they were met by the rest of the council, as well as Emma, Tara, and Tadeo. After introductions had taken place, Tadeo asked the president if he preferred to meet at the indoor or outdoor council chamber. He waved his arm and indicated a grove of trees just off the courtyard on the inner side of the ring.

"It's a beautiful day," said the president. "Let's stay outside."

Tadeo bowed slightly and headed towards the trees.

"Tadeo is on council today," Tara whispered excitedly to Jenn as they walked along. "He says it's his first time."

"How old is he?" Jenn asked.

"He's fifteen, but he says that age isn't a consideration for council. That girl Aphrodite is only fourteen."

'That's interesting," the President said, as he came up beside them. "My apologies, but did I overhear you say that two of the council are minors?"

"Yes," Tara answered. "But it's not based on age."

"And you said it's Tadeo's first day?"

"He's standing in for his mother," Tara explained. "She'll be back later."

"How do they get voted in?" the president asked.

"You'll have to ask," replied Tara. "But I don't think they do things like we do."

Tadeo stopped at a gap in the trees and they looked down at a replica of the council chamber carved into the stone of the mountainside overlooking Atlantis. The trees framing the outdoor council chamber shaded the entire area, and like the pillars in the indoor chamber, the trees allowed the council to view the majority of Atlantis and the inner harbor without obstruction.

"This way," Tadeo said, as he led everyone, including the council, down the slope to a viewing area just below the seating.

Once they'd gathered, Tzakol swept his hand across the view behind him and addressed the group.

"This is our home," he said, pointing to the ground beneath him. "Now we stand on Delta."

He moved his arm to point at the next two land rings. "Gamma, Beta."

He then gestured toward the higher structures on the central island.

"Today, we may see all but Alpha."

"Thank you, Tzakol," the president said, then asked. "You're in charge of council then? Will you also be our guide?"

"Tadeo will be your guide," Tzakol replied. "No one is in charge of council."

The president thought Tzakol had misunderstood and wasn't wasn't quite sure how to explain what he meant. He tried to offer an explanation.

"I speak for the people of my land," he explained. "They elected me to represent them, so I'm in charge for them."

"Ah!" Tzakol nodded. "Evan Masters has spoken of this. You are one who speaks for many."

"Yes," the President said. "Exactly."

"We do not have this," Tzakol said.

He turned to Tadeo and gave him a nod to start the tour.

"Follow me," Tadeo said.

They headed along on a path below the viewing area that led them across and then down towards the canal inside of the Delta ring. Evan thought the route looked familiar and Tara shortly confirmed it.

"This is the way we came up after our tour," she told Jenn.

As they descended the paths and stairways to the

canal, Tadeo pointed out some of the small farms and their crops along the way. Finally, he stopped at one of the farms and asked Tara and Jenn to come to the front of the group. He showed them the tiny strip of land with a small hut on the edge of the terrace that overlooked the canal.

"I will work here for my time on council," he told them, proudly.

"You mean you'll live here while you are on council?" Tara asked.

He shook his head.

"I live on Alpha, with my mother Itzela. Here I will work to atone for my time on council."

He looked over a Tzakol who gave him a proud smile then looked pointedly down the trail. Tadeo took one last look at the farm and then set off again. Before too long they were at the dock and climbing aboard one of the Minoan ships. After they cast off, the president sat down with Jenn and Tara.

"Tara, I'm beginning to think that I'm going to have to stay close to you to figure this place out. Evan has no idea. Did either of you understand what Tadeo meant back there on the hill?"

Tara shook her head.

"No," Jenn said. "It sounded like he had to work to be on council."

"That is so," Tadeo confirmed, as he joined them. "All on council must take the greater responsibility."

"I don't understand," Tara said. "Our council members get paid for their work on council."

"And one speaks for many?" Tadeo asked.

"Yes," the president answered. "As I do."

"We are taught of this in our history," Tadeo said carefully.

He obviously wanted to explain but didn't want to offend the President.

"But we are taught it ends… in failure."

"Can you explain?" Jenn asked.

"It is from our beginnings," Tadeo began. "Long ago, our home supplied all that our people could want and all were happy. Then strangers from a far land came by ship, to trade for our metals, tools and swords. They traded many wonderful things to he who was the keeper of our stores. They told him grand tales of their king, he who had sent them to trade. They were bold tales of one who commanded his ways over them."

Tadeo's disgust flashed in his eyes.

"The stores keeper had made none of what he traded and much was not his to trade, but swayed by the many riches offered, he traded them anyway. He received some rare goods indeed with his trade, and they were coveted by some of our people who decided to overlook his wrongdoing that they might receive a share of these rare goods.

For a long time, these ships returned regularly, and each time the stores keeper took more and more goods from our people and each time gave back less and less of what he received in trade. Soon with the lessons learned from these visitors, he declared himself our king and convinced those who had helped him to take what he wanted from the rest of our people. It was a time of great sadness for our people, and it continued on, even after the stranger's visits ceased.

After a long absence, the strangers' ships came to trade once again. They had fought many battles with a great enemy at much cost to their people, but had achieved victory with our swords. They were able to offer little in trade, but needed our swords to continue their quests. When he who called himself our king refused, he was quickly offered a demonstration of how they had achieved their glory. He his supporters were killed and the strangers took all they could carry from the storehouses and left.

Tzakol had seen the enthralled group listening to the story and came over to join them. He picked up the story.

"It is said that the people saw the result of these ways and with the guidance of Minos, Giver of Laws, came together and decided that no single voice must ever again be allowed to speak for all. The stocks of swords and tools were rebuilt and when next the strangers' ships returned, they were met with solid lines of swords, as all prepared to defend the new ways.

Those ships never landed, they never traded and they left empty handed. Before too long word arrived that they were consumed by their own greed and had themselves been conquered."

Tzakol paused before continuing.

"It became the greatest strength and from that day, only respect was shown to the people. For millennia they watched as countless peoples conquered or enslaved their neighbors in the name of some man or some god then raised up their armies, only to fall victim to the next king or famine or fate. But with no desire for conquest, the people's ships traded freely across the known waters, always welcomed without fear. Maya learned of this from the people millennia before the great cities, the memories fading as time passed, to be reminded again only upon the arrival of Atlantis on our shores. All of this because now, as it was then, only many speak for many."

Tadeo repeated to sum up the tale.

"Only many may speak for many and to keep balance, there must be a price to those who speak for many. The greater the deeds of a council member, the greater the price to restore the balance. I will till the land for a season for my service."

"But why would anyone want to be on council then," Tara asked, confused.

"It is the greatest honor," Tzakol replied. "All await their turn at council, that they might serve."

The president had listened closely, as they all had. Evan spoke first.

"But how do you…"

The sound of a loud horn very nearby cut him short. Shouting ensued as the rowers pulled heavily on the oars, veering the ship to one side of the canal to avoid a flotilla of ships that had been lashed together into what looked like an immense barge.

Tadeo jumped up, red-faced. He shouted something unintelligible at the captain and Tzakol calmly and pointedly said something back to Tadeo. Mortified, Tadeo bowed his head to the captain apologetically.

"I have missed my duty as guide," he said to everyone as he steadied himself.

He pointed to the barge, the flat deck being assembled across it and what looked like overhead cranes being assembled from the top of the canal wall.

"Here we begin a new pillar for the harbor."

CHAPTER 45

Welcome to Mexico

Paulo had been insistent that they park the cars and walk into the neighborhood where his parents lived. It was a nice district, as he'd said, but the neighbors would have been very suspicious of a fleet of shiny black Hummers pulling up in front of a house in the working district of Playa. He had them park at the cemetery, saying it was the only way that they would not seem too out of place.

Paulo's parents were a little overwhelmed when he showed up with seven acquaintances and no notice. Still, as was their way, they carefully greeted each of the visitors one at a time, including the press and the two security people that had come along for the walk. When they got to Stephen though, their decorum fell apart.

"Stephen Spielberg?" Paulo's father repeated with a questioning smile, still holding the handshake. "Indiana Jones?"

"Yes," Stephen nodded.

His father pumped and pumped Stephen's hand. "Indiana Jones! Mama, Indiana Jones!"

Paulo's mother smiled at the special guest and Paulo intervened to free Stephen from his father's grip.

"Yes, Papa, yes," he said. "Papa, these people are from Atlantica. Aranare, Itzela."

As they lightly bowed and said hello in English, Paulo's father looked at his son as if he were playing a joke on him.

"Atlantica?"

Paulo's mother fired off a stream of Spanish at her husband that no one but Paulo understood. She then threw up her hands and flicked on the TV. The local channel was still showing footage of Atlantis and the surrounding fleet.

"Atlantica!"

She declared, pointing both hands at the screen.

"He no watch TV," she told the others in halting English. "Welcome to our home."

Paulo spent the next few minutes speaking Spanish, explaining to his father what had happened, while his mother offered everyone coffee then got locked in a conversation with Aranare in Mayan. The others sat around somewhat uncomfortably until Paulo had finished. His father pretty much looked about as shocked as you'd expect, if someone had just convinced them that a fairytale was real.

"He's okay," Paulo smiled. "I'll get some clothes then we go and see the village mi mama says."

"We should see the village near Coba," Stephen said. "It was highly recommended."

Bob shook his head and smiled at Itzela. Before he could say anything, Paulo explained.

"We can go but Coba has old Maya village for tourista," he said, smiling. "To see elders, we will need a different place. It is near Tulum."

* * *

At Aranare's request, they'd called the driver of the Hummer carrying the press team, and asked him to get them lost for a couple of hours. As a result only two Hummers had made the sharp turn off the dusty road. The third had to stop to let the dust clear but when it did there was no trace of the other two vehicles, which for some reason they couldn't reach by phone either.

The village wasn't on the map or on Google, but it was just west of Tulum, right where Paulo's mother had said it would be. A mixture of old and new buildings in various styles, there was nothing especially Mayan about the village. In addition to not being on the map, and almost completely shrouded by a canopy of trees, it could have been anywhere in Mexico. They parked the cars and walked into what seemed to be a central courtyard, looking around for someone to talk to. Paulo looked worried, while Brett looked perplexed.

"Expecting huts?" Stephen asked him.

"Well, no" he said. "But something at least. Where is everybody?"

A young boy wandered out of one of the buildings.

"Hola," he said.

"Hola," Bob replied. "We're here to see the elders."

The boy cocked his head, as if he didn't understand.

"We bring visitors..." Bob started to add, until Aranare tapped him on the shoulder.

He crouched down and smiled at the boy. He rattled off a string of Mayan so fast that the only words that Bob caught were Diachrome and Atlantica.

The boy smiled and bowed his head.

"You are expected," he said then turned.

Stephen told the security people to wait by the cars. The boy took them to a nondescript door leading off the courtyard and ushered them into a cantina. A dozen tables were served by a small wooden bar with a handful of assorted stools lined up in from of it. The back wall of the bar opened onto a spectacular vista. A patio area overlooked a terraced garden that dipped down to a large open cenote, in which a few people were enjoying a leisurely dip.

An assortment of Mayan men and women of various ages occupied a few of the stools and some of the tables. All of them had turned or looked up to see who had entered. The man behind the bar looked angrily at the boy.

"Nico!" he barked.

Nico bowed slightly. "These are the ones," he said.

The bartender came around to look at the new arrivals. He stopped when he reached the Atlanteans and looked closely first at Aranare then Itzela.

"Itzela," she said.

He said nothing but bowed deeply in respect.

"Aranare?" the bartender asked, as he turned to face the old Mayan.

Aranare bowed in confirmation.

"Then our past stands before us, as was foretold."

The bartender smiled and bowed again then gestured to the seating area in the patio.

"There is much to know."

As Itzela and Aranare stepped out onto the patio, everyone in the bar got up to join them.

"Nico," the bartender called. "Look after our guests."

The boy smiled, scooted behind the bar, and hopped up onto a small stool.

"Cerveza?" he asked smiling.

"Guess we're not invited," Brett said, then turned to Nico. "Dos, por favor."

"Makes sense," Stephen said, as he nodded yes to Nico for a beer.

They took a seat at one of the tables with Paulo and Bob as Nico brought them all a round of beer.

"So, Bob," Stephen said. "Tell me about Atlantis."

268

* * *

Stephen and Brett listened attentively while Bob related his tale of the plane crash and rescue, and told them what he could of Atlantis. Paulo contributed details about what had happened in Playa, but only if prompted. He was preoccupied observing the meeting in progress on the patio.

"Señor!" Paulo said to Bob, nodding his head in the direction of the patio.

Itzela had left the meeting and was headed back inside. They all stood as she came in, and Stephen offered her a chair. Before she sat Itzela smiled at Paulo.

"Can you go there?" she asked him, pointing to the meeting.

"Me?" he asked, looking worried. "Why?"

"They asked. They would like to meet you."

Paulo hesitated but her smile reassured him and he stepped outside. Aranare introduced him to the elders. Nico brought a cold beer over and set it in front of Itzela as she sat down.

"What is this?" she asked.

"Beer," replied Brett. "You don't have beer?"

He took a healthy swig of his own bottle.

She lifted her bottle to her lips and Bob was worried that she was in for a shock.

"It's like wine," he said. "But tastes very different."

She took a sip then smiled and had a bigger taste. It obviously agreed with her. Mimicking Brett, she chugged a third of the cool brew.

"Very good," she said setting the bottle down on the table.

"Don't go too fast," Stephen said. "It really is like wine."

269

She nodded her understanding.

"How was your meeting?" asked Bob, changing the subject.

"It is for Aranare," she replied. "It is good."

She had a more sedate sip of her beer and looked out at the cenote.

"I have come here before."

"What?" Bob asked. "How? When?"

"Before we left," she said, looking Bob in the eyes. "Some has changed, some has not. It is a special place."

She unexpectedly grabbed Bob's hand and stood up.

"I can show you?"

Bob got to his feet.

"Of course," he said, glancing looked at Stephen and Brett to see if they were coming too.

"You two go have a look," Stephen said. "Brett and I have some catching up to do."

Bob nodded. Brett just gave him a wink and turned back to talk to Stephen.

As they walked among the dense trees, Itzela told him that this was the place where they'd once come to meet with the elders who had chosen to remain behind.

"So they know where the Diachrome is?" Bob asked.

"They say they do not. But Aranare will ask. This is also a beautiful place with many cenote. This way, come."

She led him along a side path into an area of denser jungle and after a few turns arrived at the edge of a secluded cenote. Sunlight filtered through the trees and into a blue-green pool about 15 feet below them. A vine-covered trail clinging to the sidewall led down to a spot where you could walk into the cenote. A rope dangling from a tree on a nearby ledge looked like a much more interesting way to enter the water.

Bob was wishing that they'd brought swimsuits when

a splash and a shout from below drew their attention to a couple swimming casually out from under the ledge.

"There are caves below," said Itzela.

The couple heard her and waved. Itzela waved back, as did Bob until he noticed that this was obviously a swimsuit-optional cenote. He turned away to offer the couple some privacy. Itzela however, had already pulled off her top and was smiling at him invitingly.

"You will come?" she asked, as she kicked of her shoes and wriggled out of her skirt.

"Uh," Bob said. "Of course."

He tugged off his shirt and unbuckled his belt, pausing to watch Itzela run to the edge and leap for the rope. She caught it, swung out even further then let go, splashing happily into the water.

He joined her rather unceremoniously moments later. She'd been watching him while he finished stripping down, which further exasperated the condition he was in after seeing her disrobe. He leapt to grab the rope but missed it entirely, splashing down head first in the water beside her.

She was laughing when he came the surface and once he'd got his bearings, they swam together to the back of the cenote under the overhang. The water was colder in the shade, which helped diminish some of the effect he'd been trying to hide. They looked around the cave in wonder as they swam. Several small caves led off the main cenote, stalagmites and stalactites framing the entrances.

He was so preoccupied looking around that he swam right into her. Itzela spun around and let his momentum carry him forward until his arms were around her and her bare wet chest brushed against his. He pulled her close, utterly enjoying the feeling of her bare breasts against his skin. She looked up at him and smiled.

"This is how it should be," she said, reminding him of the night they'd danced.

"Well, this is a little wetter than the dance but it's..."

He stopped talking as she covered his lips with hers, and then forgot about everything except kissing her, which continued in earnest until they heard Nico calling for them.

CHAPTER 46

More Atlantis

"How long will it take to make a new pillar?" General Aspinal asked.

She was looking around the barge and seeing how hard they were working to get the replacement pillar ready.

"Many months," Cadmael replied. "But it has been centuries since one was made, so it is hard to know."

"Did Ryan tell you that he has a plan where we may be able to retrieve the broken one for you?" the general asked.

"Yes," Cadmael said. "But only as a possibility. We must put things in order as we can, so we will begin a new pillar. Would you not do the same?"

"Yes I would."

"But what of the cost?" the President asked. "Won't it cost more to make another one?"

"What is cost?" Tzakol asked, curiously.

Nobody answered right away. It was a question that none of them had expected.

"He means money," Evan said, trying to be helpful. "How much money to make a new pillar?"

Tzakol shook his head.

"What is money?"

"Gold," Evan said. "Do you trade with gold?"

"We have the gold," Tzakol said, pointing out some of

the shiny parts already laid out for the pillar construction. "Some was traded for."

"In many cultures, including ours," said Jenn attempting a different explanation, "people have traded goods for gold, then traded that gold for other goods. Gold used like that is what we call money."

"The amount of money," the president continued, "or gold that is needed to make something like the pillar, is what is called the cost of the pillar."

Cadmael and the Atlanteans simply did not understand.

"There only is the gold and those that make the pillar," Cadmael said. "We do not know this cost."

"We will continue the tour?" Tadeo asked politely, perhaps sensing that the conversation was going nowhere.

They left the barge and climbed down to the deck of their ship. The rowers began propelling them on to their next destination. Jenn was chatting quietly with the president so Tara moved over to sit beside Emma.

"How can they not have money?" Tara asked her.

Emma smiled.

"I think everyone is wondering the same thing. Look around."

It was true. All the people from outside Atlantis were busy talking or whispering to each other in small groups, even the press had stopped their incessant recording to talk amongst themselves. The puzzled expressions were reflected by their hosts, as the Atlanteans pondered what had caused such a change.

"They're wondering what's wrong," said Tara.

"Well, that will never do," declared Emma. "You know, I'm usually the chatty one, but I've been just sitting back taking it all in."

She winked to Tara as she stood up.

"Tadeo!" she said, loud enough to interrupt everyone's conversation. "Where are you taking us next?"

"We go to market," Tadeo smiled. "Many people, many foods, many things from Atlantis are there."

"That sounds lovely," said Emma. "Is there only one market?"

"There are many," he replied. "Each district produces its own goods and crops, and each district has a market where they are brought. All are very busy."

"Our ships start at each market each day," Cadmael added. "They pick up goods and spend the day distributing them to the other markets. Along the way they pick anything that is needed for their home market district."

"You have roads and bridges," Tara pointed out, as they passed under one. "Why do you send things by ship?"

"Not everything is by ship," Tadeo said. "Smaller goods are passed by horse above. Heavy goods must go by ship."

Their ship's captain shouted to Tadeo, who nodded back, then pointed ahead to the dock they were veering towards. It was anchored by a staircase in the side of the canal wall like the others that some of them had seen. A large ship with no sailing masts was tied up at the front of the dock and a rope on a pulley was slowly lifting a small bundle of timbers out of the ship's hold.

"Now you can see," said Tadeo.

After the brass wall section was pivoted out of the way, they pulled up to the dock on the far side of the stairwell. Tadeo hopped onto the dock, ran over and had a quick chat with the captain of the cargo ship. He returned as the rest of those on the tour were disembarking. Tadeo smiled broadly and headed straight for Evan and Emma. He waved to Tara to come over as well. When everyone was gathered on the dock Tadeo raised his hands for silence.

"This ship comes from a market on Beta," he said, pointing to the timbers being hoisted above them. "The wood is an extra cargo for a special work. The ship's main cargo today from Beta is Cucu."

He looked at Evan and smiled.

"Cucu?" Evan said, then realization dawned and he turned to the president. "Dodo! They are carrying dodos."

That caused a flurry of excitement among the press and completely dissipated any remnants of the discussion they'd all been engaged in about money. The reporters filmed the scene and they all watched closely as a wooden cage of dodos was extracted from the ship and hauled upwards. They quickly climbed the stairs to follow the cage as it went to market.

The new dodo arrivals were kept in their own pen, next to a few birds that remained from a prior batch in the livestock area of the market. They were fed and watered while they were there. Tadeo explained that some people kept them for the eggs and others cooked them for the meat. The next container to be brought up contained several crates of dodo eggs. Everyone followed the crates through the market's crowds to a different section of the market, walking along while Tadeo explained how everything worked together.

Each district market received an equal amount of whatever was available. There were live animals, an enclosed meat market, a covered perishables section and open areas for dry goods, hardware, pottery and much more. There was a row of special bins where expired produce seemed to be kept, and a good-sized cafeteria style restaurant completed the market area. Tara asked about the special bins.

"At days end, any produce that will not last is put here," Tadeo explained. "The ships take these back for feed for the animals."

"What about the meat?" Evan asked. "What happens to the old meat?"

"Each day, only what is needed is killed, Tzakol replied. "There is always some extra, which will come here for the evening meal or the next day. Some is also sent for the animals that need meat to survive."

"Almost all ships call at our zoo, as you have called it," Cadmael added. "With food from the markets. If they have enough produce we sail to another place where the extra is used for the land."

"We call that recycling. How do you keep track of everything?" Aspinal asked.

This was a fair question since a majority of the market's stalls and tables were unattended.

"Each market has overseers," Tadeo replied. "These ones make sure that things are run well and that anything extra is made ready."

"So they own the market?" Evan asked.

Tadeo looked at him blankly. It was obviously another word he didn't understand in this context.

"They run the market, they are the bosses?" said Evan, attempting to help Tadeo understand.

"Ah! Yes, they are much like council." Tadeo smiled. "Markets serve the many, the overseers run the market. They too pay a price in service for their actions for the many."

"No," Evan said. "That's not what I meant."

"Evan," said Emma, sharply. "I think Tadeo explained it very well. Any task that affects the many carries a price for the one, for the honor of the task."

Tadeo nodded agreement.

"How do you make sure that too much isn't taken?" Emma asked. "And that there is enough?"

"All take only what they need," Tadeo replied. "If

there is not enough for all then the overseer must decide."

"Is there ever a problem?" asked Jenn.

"At times," Tadeo smiled mischievously as he led them toward the cafeteria. "On those days the food here is very good. We will eat now?"

They were all hungry and lined up to sample some of the dishes at the buffet. As they sat down to eat the president spoke with Tadeo.

"I'm still trying to understand how this all works," he asked. "May I ask you some more questions about it?"

"Of course," replied Tadeo.

"So you don't use money, and we haven't traded with you yet. So how do we trade for our meals?"

"You are guest of council," Tadeo said, shrugging. "Guest of all the people. Council has traded for you by approval."

The president nodded.

"I understand. Another question then. How do you pick an overseer? Or how does one become an overseer."

"This is more hard," said Cadmael. "Overseers must have many skills. If these skills are seen by others, they may suggest someone to be an overseer."

"Or desire," Tadeo said. "Desire alone can succeed."

Cadmael smiled at him.

"Perhaps, Tadeo, but skill must be seen or one is not appointed."

"So when I asked for council?" Tadeo asked him.

"Your skill has always been there," replied Cadmael.

"Well, anyone can see that!" Tara added, then blushed as everyone looked at her.

Cadmael burst out laughing, followed by the rest of the group as Tadeo's cheeks also quickly filled with color.

CHAPTER 47

More Mexico

As Itzela and Bob climbed up the path along the side of the cenote, half a dozen young local boys and girls arrived at the top and stripped down, then yelling and screaming, swung or cannonballed into the water.

"I haven't gone skinny dipping since I was their age," Bob said.

"What is skinny dipping?" Itzela asked.

"This is," he replied, laughing. "Swimming without clothes."

"Why would you swim with clothes?" she asked as they reached the top.

Nico interrupted as he handed them each a towel, then smiled, turned, stripped off his clothes and followed the others into the cenote with a loud yell. Bob pulled Itzela close to him and kissed her again.

"At this moment I can't think of a reason."

Their hair was almost dry when they arrived back at the cantina. Aranare had rejoined the group, although Paulo was still sitting with the elders.

Aranare looked up and saw Bob and Itzela holding hands as they walked out of the jungle. Smiling, he continued his discussion. The others looked up as Bob and Itzela sat down at the table.

"Have a nice swim?" Brett asked.

"Nico said there's a great cenote back there," added Stephen.

"It is pretty nice," Bob agreed.

A tap on the shoulder caused him to spin around. He found himself looking into the face of the bartender, or rather the elder that had been behind the bar.

"You are Bob Wallace?" he asked, leaning in for a closer inspection.

"Uh, I am," he said, nervously, trying not to back away.

"You will find the Diachrome," said the bartender.

He then moved over to Stephen, who stood and extended his hand.

"You are the director for *Jurassic Park*?"

The bartender shook Stephen's hand.

"Yes," Stephen replied.

"Good movie," the bartender said, then turned to Aranare, Itzela and Bob once again, bowing deeply to each. Paulo and the other elders came back inside as well.

"Good journey," he wished them, then opened the door so that they could leave.

The bartender gave them each another respectful bow as he ushered them out of the cantina. He paused when got to Paulo.

"We will see you soon?"

Paulo nodded and headed out the door.

"We're kicked out?" Brett asked, as the cantina door closed behind them.

"No," Aranare said. "But there is much to do. We go to Tulum now."

* * *

On the drive to Tulum, Aranare explained to Bob and Stephen that the Spanish, the Aztecs, the Mexican government and others had tried to disband the elders many times over the centuries. No matter what, some always returned, but at some point the Diachrome's descendants had not. They had tried to keep the memories alive as best they could.

"They were most worried when the chambers under Tulum were discovered," Aranare told Bob. "And even more worried when your book appeared, telling of strange ships that carried the Mayan away."

"Very few believed me," said Bob.

"It is no matter," Aranare said. "We will see what you have found at Tulum."

He looked at Itzela then back to Bob.

"You are as one?"

Bob had no idea what he'd just been asked so he just stuttered in response. Itzela was far more composed.

"Perhaps," she said, smiling at Bob.

Their driver had called the missing Hummer carrying the press team shortly after leaving the hidden village. When they arrived at the tourist area outside the walls of Tulum, the press team's Hummer was there and they had already arranged to get everyone around the gauntlet of tourist hawkers and state security. The private security detail and honored guest Stephen Spielberg allowed them access through the south gate exit turnstiles. However, when they reached the cordoned off area around the catacombs their unfettered access was blocked.

"They're not going to let us in," Stephen said, as he returned with his guards to where the others were waiting. "Neither these guys nor my name is enough."

"Let me have a try," said Bob.

He headed around the corner was back in less than thirty seconds.

Come on," he told everyone.

They walked around the corner and the guards that had previously denied Stephen access were now holding the gate open and inviting them forward.

"How did you do that?" Stephen asked. "I have to say, I'm kinda used to being the one they do that for."

Bob pointed at the sign across the top of the entrance, which read *Welcome New Maya Conference Attendees.* There were also banners on either side of the door. They had Jenn's picture at the top and a picture of Bob, holding a copy of *The Impossible Mayan,* on the bottom half.

"Well, this time, you can be the one who knows a guy who can get you in," Bob said, smiling.

Stephen shook his head and Brett chuckled as they nodded thanks to the guards. They were each handed a flashlight as they passed through the doorway.

The stairwell had been completely cleared and restored to some of its former glory. LED lighting had been hidden inside the oil-fired sconces that had originally lit the chambers.

They wandered around the Hall of the Journey and Aranare took them on a tour of the other chambers that he remembered.

"Much has been taken," he said.

'It is in various museums," Bob replied. "For study.'"

"Hmm," said Aranare.

He peered into a small room that contained what looked like a broken fountain. The bottom of the fountain was filled with water but there was no spray or even a trickle of water. He reemerged and continued on, but Bob, who was bringing up the rear with Itzela, noticed Aranare give a quick nod to Itzela. She grabbed Bob's arm to get him to hang back. Once the others were out of sight she pulled him into the room.

"Shhh," she whispered. "You will not say?"

"Of course not," said Bob, wondering what was about to happen.

She shocked him yet again by dropping her clothes on the ground once more and stepping into the fountain.

"You do that a lot," he said.

She smiled at him then reached into the water, into the drain hole at the fountain's center, grasped something inside and pulled. The bottom of the fountain split down the middle and each side slid back partway into the floor.

In the dim lighting of the room, the pool under the fountain was pitch black. Itzela looked as if she were ready to jump in.

"Wait," Bob said.

He flicked on his flashlight and leaned over to hand it to her. He slipped and almost fell into the fountain.

"Well, if there is light…" she smiled, and beckoned him to join her.

For the second time that day, Bob stripped down. He grabbed the flashlight that she'd been given and flicked it on so that they would both have one. Itzela smiled and carefully slid into the inky black water. Bob climbed into the fountain and saw her light moving below. He took a deep breath and dove down to join her.

The dark salty water yielded no secrets until they neared the bottom of the pool. She carefully fanned the silt and pushed her flashlight into the sand. A translucent blue reflected back some of the light, transmitting the rest through the entire floor of the pool. As the silt settled, Bob could make out rows of large crystals stacked on top of each other lining the bottom of the pool.

She grabbed his hand and headed upward.

"What are those things?" Bob sputtered, as he broke

the surface. "They're beautiful!"

"We must be fast," she said. "Tell you after?"

She reached down and again pulled the lever near the drain hole and the bottom started to slide closed. They dried themselves with their clothes then wrung them out. They were still getting dressed when Brett appeared around the corner and shone his flashlight at them.

"Hey!" Bob yelled, not having to fake embarrassment at all.

"Sorry, guys."

Brett turned away and clicked off his light.

"Wanted to make sure you were okay. Didn't know you'd snuck off. Should I come back?"

"It's not like that," Bob said, as he came round the corner tucking in his shirt. "I slipped in the fountain. We both got wet and were just wringing our clothes out to dry them when you showed up.

Brett looked them both up and down.

"Sure, if you say so."

He smiled and led them back to the others.

They all climbed into one Hummer for the ride from Tulum back to Playa Del Carmen. The security guys and press hopped into the other cars. The trip back was uneventful until Itzela fell asleep on Bob's shoulder. A huge amount of ribbing and an endless stream of 'get a room' jokes occupied the rest of their journey, until Itzela woke up at the first traffic light they stopped at.

"What will we see here?" Itzela asked, once she was more awake.

"We talked about vacations before," Bob said. "Well, you can see what some of our people do when they are on vacation."

The sun was sinking when they got out of the vehicles

at the southern end of the tourist zone and began walking towards the north. The security detail doubled as they began their walk and Stephen assured everyone that the Hummers would swoop in for pickup if they ran into any trouble. Stephen was taking no chances with his part of this adventure.

With their press detail snapping pics and shooting video, everyone except Paulo looked in shops and stores along the way. Itzela found a light shawl that she liked, which led into a discussion about money, which Bob was able to illustrate by purchasing the shawl for her. They ended up seeing the same shawl a little further along the street for about half the price, and the sales girl asked how much they wanted to pay. This confused the discussion even more, until Bob noticed the *Made in China* tag and things quickly became too complicated to explain.

"Tell you after?" he asked Itzela.

She smiled and thanked him for the shawl.

They stopped at the beach by the *Mayan Gateway* sculpture so that Itzela could see people swimming in clothes, or at least in swimwear. The sculpture itself was most moving for Aranare, especially after Paulo told him that it was erected in honor of the end of the Mayan Calendar.

It seemed that with Atlantis framing the background, the sculpture's name had taken on a whole new meaning for everyone. The press were going nuts with pictures, but Bob made sure that he got a picture of Itzela and Aranare by the sculpture. Aranare insisted that there should also be one of just Bob and Itzela. Then Stephen took a beautiful shot of Atlantis glowing in the sunset's golden light as seen through the darkened sculpture, Bob and Itzela holding up each side of the Mayan Gateway.

With Stephen Spielberg as their guide, the group was able to access anywhere that they wanted to go. He showed them into a couple of exclusive dance clubs and an upscale dining establishment. One place he'd hoped to take them was still without power. The doorman told them that power hadn't yet been fully restored in the city. Indeed, the town behind the strip was illuminated only by random pools of light, where people had access to generators.

They stopped at one of the hotels and went down to the beach. Itzela and Aranare gazed at the firelight lighting up Atlantis then Aranare pointed up. A bright light tracked through the sky just as it had done a couple of nights earlier.

"ISS?" he asked.

"Yes, I think so," Bob replied.

"Can we tour there?" said Itzela.

Bob smiled.

"I don't think even Stephen Spielberg could pull that off for you."

Stephen shouted from the walkway above them.

"Hey! You guys have to hear this!"

They came up the path and around the pool. Stephen was standing beside a display of paintings set up around a man who was painting with cans of spray paint.

"What's up?" Bob asked.

"This is Porfirio Jiminez," Stephen said. "He's been painting spray paint art for years. Tell him what you told me?"

"Pleasure to meet you, Señor Wallace," Porfirio offered his hand, which Bob shook.

"A few years ago I met a man who told me a story about the Mayan ship Atlantica coming back to us," Porfirio began. "My parents had told me stories about Atlantica when I was a child, but this man had many details about the city made of gold. I painted a picture for him from what he said, and never painted it again until I read your book."

He paused and thought carefully.

"I have never showed it to anyone before, but now that Atlantica is here…"

He pulled out an old worn portfolio. Stuck between two other works, and partially stuck to them, was a magnificent painting showing Atlantis hovering in mid-air off the coast of the Yucatan. The most interesting aspect was the graphic that represented a single person who was watching the ship leave.

"He told me this man was the last Diachrome," Porfirio said.

CHAPTER 48

Hello World

"It's almost ten o'clock! Where are you Brett?" Ryan whispered into his phone.

"I'm in position," he replied. "Start the show."

"Roger that," said Ryan, nodding to the Ops crew.

On the *Excelsior's* flight deck, near the center of the ship, bright searchlights flicked on and lit up the exterior of the Operations Center. The lights swung outwards, playing across the Ospreys, Apaches and other helicopters arranged along the length of the deck then finally focusing on the makeshift stage, behind which shone the lights of Atlantis.

"Ladies and gentlemen of the press," Ryan barked through the ship-wide Com system. "Please join us as we wish Atlantis a warm return."

Searchlights played across the waves in front of the carrier. The roar of dozens of jet turbines filled the air, growing steadily louder as a dozen land-assault hovercraft crisscrossed each other in the pools of light the searchlights had created. The ear-splitting roar of their turbines became deafening as fireworks were launched from two of the craft, while the rest maneuvered in patterns around each other.

They continued to complicate the crisscrossing patterns and set off more and more fireworks to the delight of the cheering crowd assembled in front of the stage.

Ryan picked up some night-vision binoculars and looked across to the end of the row of helicopters. An Osprey with no running lights on, was just settling in to the spot they'd cleared for it at the back of the row of helicopters.

"*Excelsior*, the Osprey has landed," Brett said over his phone.

"Nice flying," Ryan said. "I think you made it without being seen."

"Of course," Brett replied, cockily. "By the way, we're coming in one heavy."

"What?" Ryan said. "This isn't a shuttle service."

"Oh, you'll want this one," Brett told him. "Trust me."

The president walked out to the podium at the center of the stage. The president squinted as the giant searchlights were turned back towards the stage. He plucked the microphone from its holder then turned to look at Atlantis.

"Can we kill these lights?" he asked.

The big lights were immediately extinguished and most of the deck lights were dimmed or turned off within a couple of minutes.

"I toured Atlantis today," the president began, slowly. "Not a holiday resort or a retired space shuttle, but the actual city of Atlantis."

He gestured toward the city then turned around, moving back into the light so that he could be seen.

"I can't tell you exactly how this happened," he said, smiling. "And the list of things we don't know is only growing. So let's talk about what we do know. I represent the United States here today, as just one member of a multi-national panel that has been formed to work with the people of Atlantis to learn what we can discover about each other. This panel will be operating under the name Atlantis Command, and will also be taking a position in a protective role of the city-ship."

He paused for a moment before continuing.

"Now as some of you may have seen from the events of this morning, Atlantis is protected by some sort of shield. Apparently that shield must be discharged from time to time. If you watched it, you already know that a small flicker of this shield can, even by accident, take out our most EM-shielded attack helicopter. What you don't know is that two days ago, when Atlantis first appeared, the Navy cruiser *Xavier* was, also accidentally, sliced in half by the shield when it inadvertently trespassed across the Atlantis harbor."

The press in front of him clamored at that revelation and he raised his hand for silence.

"It's a miracle that in both of these accidents there was no loss of life. So, in order to prevent even the possibility of a more serious accident, Atlantis Command has declared an international no-Fly, no-go zone in the area."

There were murmurs from the people in front of him.

"General Aspinal will shortly fill you in on the details of that zone, and you'll hear from several experts, some of who have been on Atlantis since shortly after its arrival. After that, we'll be granting the press who travelled with us today on a cultural exchange tour of Atlantis, permission to release all of the footage and stories that they obtained while on the tour."

The president opened his hand toward where the people from Atlantis were standing and one of the spotlights swung to illuminate them.

"Before that, just two more things. I would like you to meet some of the people we've met from Atlantis."

He called them out by name.

"Council members Itzela and her son Tadeo, Aphrodite and Tzakol, Admiral Cadmael and Advisor Aranare."

Each of them smiled and bowed as their name was called. However, the president had to conceal his surprise when he saw Stephen standing next to Itzela.

"Lastly, because the shield of Atlantis is as beautiful as it is powerful, Admiral Cadmael has arranged a demonstration to counterpoint our fireworks."

The president stepped back and Cadmael came to the podium and turned to face Atlantis. He raised his hand and the glowing gold field shimmered into existence over Atlantis. He held his hand high for a couple of minutes, then the shield vanished as he lowered his hand. He bowed and headed back to rejoin his group.

The president returned to the podium.

"I have just now been told that we had a little assistance today with the land-based side of our cultural exchange tour from someone who is no doubt better-known throughout the world than I will ever be. Director Stephen Spielberg!"

Stephen waved from the sideline as the president ended by introducing General Aspinal.

After the press had been satisfied and left to file their stories, the others decided that they should quickly meet and recap the day. They ended up commandeering the officer's lounge, since there were now twenty of them in the group, not including the president's bodyguards, who were eventually ordered to wait outside. Those that hadn't previously met introduced themselves and a dozen conversations erupted at once.

With so many people and so much going on, the conversation spun rather aimlessly until Aranare suggested that each person should say what was on their mind. When the president stood up to speak, Aranare held up his hand.

"We say, as you do, ladies first."

The president smiled understanding and sat down again.

"Itzela?" said Aranare.

She stood and thought for a moment.

"We are surprised to find you here on our return but I am most happy that we did. I wish to understand how your world works. Today I saw people with many nice things next to people with nothing. I asked and they said that this thing money is the problem. I would like to know more about how that works. Perhaps we can help with the problem?"

She looked at Bob, smiled and sat down.

General Aspinal stood next.

"I'm very worried about security. Our little show today probably bought us some time, but sooner or later there's going to be a problem."

She paused and looked towards Aranare, who smiled, encouraging her to go on.

"I'd also like to see if we can make sure that EMP pulse doesn't happen again, at least without notice. With so much equipment and people close by, it could get very messy if it goes off again."

Tara was next.

"You may want to know about us, but I want to know more about your culture, Itzela. I want to know how Atlantis works so well with its very different cultures and how your council can work with young people on it. Oh, and I'd really like to know how you came here, to our time."

"I'm interested in your history," Emma said as she got to her feet. "Of course from the Mayan times but also from before, from the Minoan times. We know almost nothing about that period and what we do know is from stories and stories about stories of those times. To have you here to talk to, well, science tells us some things, but you're a living history of that era."

Aphrodite stood next and began by answering Emma's question.

"There may not be so much to discover as you hope, Emma. Much of our history has been passed on by stories as well. It is difficult to keep records for thousands of years."

She lowered her eyes.

"Most of all I wish, to find the Diachrome in this time, so we might know why this has happened and what will become of us."

That reminded Jenn of something she hadn't done.

"Oh, my god!" she exclaimed. "Bob, I fell right asleep after you called and totally forgot to tell everybody about 2012!"

Off To Guatemala

The explanation about the vision of 2012, the ensuing discussion about the nature of the Diachrome, how Atlantis's five millennia journey seemed to have been prompted by a movie, raged on into the wee hours. Eventually, everyone decided to approach things after a good night's sleep. With the president and Aranare's approval, Stephen decided that he'd stay on the *Excelsior* until an Atlantis tour could be arranged for him too. Then Brett slipped the President and General Aspinal quietly away on the same Osprey they had come in, with Captain Mulholland catching a ride back with them. Everyone that had started the day on Atlantis, including Bob, Tara, Evan, and Emma, were returned there in launches.

The next morning Ryan and Admiral Lindquist were discussing the Guatemala incursion with Captain Ochoa on the view screen when Jenn arrived.

"Gentlemen," she said, then noticed the concern on their faces. "What's up?"

Ryan looked at her thoughtfully.

"Just how important is it that they find this Diachrome person right now?"

"To them, I'd say it's everything," she said. "You were there last night."

"It seems the Guatemalan President may be a bit worried about all this Mayan attention," captain Ochoa said. "After the speech last night and the videos from the tour, he closed the country's borders."

"What?" Jenn asked, puzzled. "Why? It's got nothing to do with Guatemala."

The admiral took a deep breath.

"It is said previous Guatemalan governments may have conducted mass genocide on their Mayan population several times over the last century. The current president was elected on a platform that promised to look into and prosecute those that had perpetrated these crimes. To be blunt, he hasn't done what he said he'd do and he's worried that the worldwide attention the Mayan are getting could have serious political repercussions for him."

"So he's what, hiding out?" said Jenn, shaking her head.

"Well, hiding anyway," Ryan replied.

'The Mexican government had good relations there before," Captain Ochoa said. "But I don't think it will go so well now."

"U.S. relations were already strained," the admiral added. "The border closure hasn't helped us any. The State Department is busy trying to track down all our people."

"Damn," said Jenn.

"I'm sure they'll find a way to get them through as soon as they can," Ryan assured her.

"That's not what I'm worried about."

"We'll just go in as ourselves," Bob said, when they reached him by phone. "We've never really gone in with a government on a dig before anyway."

"But things could be a lot more dangerous there now,"

Ryan said. "Borders closed means borders closed!"

"Well, then we'll go in to get him out," Bob said. "We can do that, right?"

"Wait a minute," Ryan said. "That might work. We can send someone in to extract a U.S. citizen."

"He's not from the States," said Bob. "He's Australian."

"You're talking about Guy?" Jenn asked.

"Sure. Who did you think I meant?"

"That's why we can't reach him," Jenn told Ryan and the admiral. "The man's a recluse. Bob, do you really think Guy might be their Diachrome?"

"He was always coming up with these crazy hunches," Bob replied. "And he was always right, or darn close. Look, let me worry about Guy. I've talked Cadmael out of sending a team of soldiers with us to protect the Diachrome, but he insists on himself and Tadeo coming, at a minimum. Can you line up some fake archeologist ID's for Tadeo and Cadmael, and maybe Paulo, if he can come?"

"Anything else?" Jenn asked, sarcastically.

"Yes actually," Bob said. "A couple of things. Evan wants to come to Guatemala and he's driving me nuts about it. Is there something he can do here that will make him want to stay here?"

Jenn looked over at Ryan, who shrugged.

"Also," Bob continued. "I need you to look after Tara while I'm gone and she kinda likes it here. How would you like to spend a couple of days on Atlantis while I'm down south? I've already asked the council."

"Bob? This is Ryan Johnson. Do you think Evan would mind staying and giving Jenn, Stephen Spielberg, and me a tour? I also have some ideas about fixing that harbor pillar that I'd like to bounce off the council?"

"That's almost like giving him real work to do, Ryan. It's perfect," Bob said. "I'll get him to set it up, as well as that meeting with council."

"Thanks, Bob," Ryan said.

"Evan should thank you," Bob replied, laughing. "Now I won't have to strand him in Guatemala."

"Are you sure you can handle this Guatemala trip?" Ryan asked.

"We'll be fine, but can we call the cavalry if we get stuck?" Bob asked.

"You can call," Ryan replied. "But we can't promise you anything."

"Understood," said Bob. "We'll call for a ride over there in a bit."

A little over an hour later, Bob, Cadmael, Tadeo and Tara were climbing out of a boat in *Excelsior's* well deck. Ryan and Jenn greeted them and briefed everyone on the way to the flight deck.

"Paulo is waiting up top and your identification is there as well," Ryan said. "It seems you were all part of the archeological conference on the New Maya in England and were booked on a flight to Belize to the Philip S.W. Goldson International Airport via Miami. Your flight was booked three months ago and you were scheduled to fly five days ago. It was delayed until it could be properly routed around the new 200 kilometer limit around Playa."

"This will hopefully help with your cover story," Jenn added. "Since you should have been in Guatemala before the borders were closed, your trip will hopefully be perceived as having nothing to do with the current Mayan situation."

"We've tried everything to reach Guy at Tikal," Ryan explained. "We burned up the phone lines from the ship and Atlantis Command asked some local contacts to look around, but nobody's seen him in weeks."

"Did they see him before that?" Bob asked.

"Yes, I think so."

"Getting supplies no doubt. The bugger is at Uaxactún," said Bob, shaking his head. "Twelve miles north of Tikal. That's why we can't reach him. There's no cell phone service there."

"Does that change anything?" Ryan asked.

"No, he's just chasing a different dream, is all," Bob replied, with a sigh. "Were you able to rent us a car?"

"Better," Ryan smiled. "Between Mexico and the CIA, we have assets in Belize and in Guatemala that will be assisting you. You're not actually going to land at the international airport since we can't get you on that plane in Miami. Your international flight will be met by a small light plane that will pick you up and take you to the municipal airstrip in Belize City. Since it's rarely used and can be approached from the sea, we'll land the Osprey instead of the light plane and you'll be met by a car there. Your driver is with Mexican Intelligence."

Tara snickered.

"Tara?" asked Jenn.

"Nothing."

"What's up, pal," Bob asked.

Tara sighed.

"Well, he said the CIA, then Mexican Intelligence, and you're going to look for someone who is MIA."

Bob winked at her and Jenn just shook her head.

"I told you it was nothing," Tara protested.

As Ryan helped them onto the Osprey he continued the informal briefing.

"Your Belize contact will have some local money for you, as well as U.S. dollars. He'll get you to the border, but getting through into Guatemala is all up to you. Once you're through, the CIA contact in Guatemala will meet you on the other side of the border."

"Contact names, places, it's all written down in the dossiers," Jenn added. "Bob, I also hand wrote all the pertinent stuff in Mayan in this notebook you can carry with you. Come back safe."

"Sure will," he said, pocketing the notebook.

"Careful, Dad!" Tara yelled to him.

"Any questions?" Ryan asked, as he prepared to shut the ramp door.

"Too late to change my mind, right?" Bob asked.

He smiled and gave Ryan a thumbs up.

"You guys okay?" Bob asked Tadeo, Cadmael and Paulo.

They nodded somewhat uncertainly.

"Good hunting!" said Ryan and hit the button to close the ramp door.

CHAPTER 50

Need A Lift

The waves outside the harbor were kicking the spray high enough that their skipper politely slowed the launch down so that everyone wouldn't get soaked.

"Looks like we're going to council first," Ryan said, as he hung up from talking to Evan. "Apparently they want to ask us about something."

"That's great," Tara said to Stephen and Terry. "It's the best view from there."

She seemed excited to return and show them Atlantis. Ryan moved across the launch to sit with Jenn.

"She doesn't seem worried about her dad at all," he said. "Come to think of it, neither do you. Not any more. What changed?"

"You're going to think I'm crazy," she said "But it was Tara's silly joke."

Ryan looked confused.

"Bob has a tendency to find himself in bad or difficult situations," Jenn explained. "But every time Tara's cracked a joke just before he left, everything has turned out fine. It's silly, but it seems to work."

"Well," Ryan said. "Let's hope she's right this time too."

Itzela and Tzakol met them at the dock and escorted them up to the council chamber, where Evan and Emma were trying to answer questions about how our modern society functioned.

"So everything people do in your world is to get more of this money?" Aphrodite asked.

"Not everything," Emma said. "People try to make enough money to live on, and some are content with that, while others want to do more."

"You have said that some do not have enough money for food, for medical services, or even for school," Aphrodite asked. "So those that do more assist these people?"

"Some do," Emma replied. "But more often it's those that are simply content that assist the less fortunate."

Aphrodite shook her head.

"I do not understand."

Ryan cleared his throat and Tzakol glanced his way.

"Aphrodite?" he said, nodding towards Ryan and the others arriving.

She looked at Ryan then nodded at Tzakol to continue.

"Ryan Johnson," Tzakol greeted him. "You have said there is a way to return the pillar lost in the accident?"

"There may be," Ryan confirmed. "It's not certain, but I think it's worth a try."

"Can you explain?" Tzakol asked.

Ryan nodded.

"The Navy has a salvage ship, the USS Grasp, that we can use to recover the top of the pillar from the ocean floor."

He pulled a pen from his pocket and pantomimed the process.

"Once it's raised the pillar can be placed on a barge, where your people can prepare it for reconnection. The pillars are very high but there are crane barges that can lift it and hold the pillar in place while it's reattached."

They seemed to understand.

"This will be faster than our way?" Itzela asked.

"I've seen the pictures of your assembly barge," Ryan said. "It's very good but I think we can be done long before you even finish building the new pillar. We'll need to work with some of your people to make sure and we'll need to make sure we can grab the pillar with the crane."

He paused to let that information sink in.

"If you'd like to try, I ordered the *Grasp* to the area two days ago. It's standing by with a barge that should be able to accommodate the pillar. There are crane and lift specialists from the Corps of Engineers onboard and ready to get to work. We'll only have to move a crane barge here from the private sector for the installation."

The council members looked at each other and there was no dissent. Tzakol bowed deeply to Ryan.

"You may send your ships," he said. "We will inform those at the pillar that you will be joining them. Perhaps after your tour?"

"I would like to have look around."

Ryan bowed to Tzakol as Itzela stood up.

"Aphrodite and I will be your guides," she said.

Because everyone except Stephen and Ryan had already been around Atlantis once, this tour took a slightly different route. On the stairs down to the dock, Itzela asked if there was anything special that they'd like to see. Jenn asked if they could see some of the Atlantean homes, Tara wanted to look at schools and museums, and Ryan was interested in anything that was old Minoan. Emma, Stephen, and Terry were happy with all those but Evan had one more request, one that he was being very cautious about.

"I don't wish to offend you or your people Itzela," he said.

"What is it you wish to see?" she asked.

"I'd be honored if you'd consider showing us the real council chamber."

Evan bowed respectfully.

There was silence while Itzela pondered for a moment.

"Then we shall begin the tour on Alpha," she said, as she smiled at Evan. "I believe Tzakol may want to be there as well."

"There are two council chambers?" Ryan asked. "But why?"

"Evan Masters?" said Itzela. "You have found a truth, can you say the reason?"

"It's a decoy?" Evan replied, but he wasn't completely sure. "To confuse those that might try and attack the council?"

"It is from our beginnings," said Aphrodite. "The visitors said one thing, then did another. It is not our way. So a way was built to show the truth, without telling all."

Itzela looked up the hill.

"This is the council chamber," she said. "But there is another."

They used the *Excelsior's* launch for the expanded tour, which attracted a great deal of attention on the inner canals of Atlantis. The launch scooted through the tunnel under Gamma and landed at a dock behind the tin ring of Beta. As they climbed the stairs to get to the surface of Beta, Itzela told them that it was the quickest way to get to council, and that they would also see more of what they wanted.

They walked along paths between houses, temples, and other structures. Stone aqueducts carried water to each of Atlantis's rings. Bridges and viaducts took people over the canals and across the streams that crisscrossed the land rings of Atlantis. Trestle-like bridges held strips of shiny brass aloft while strips of tin pressed into channels were etched into the surface of Gamma like rivers. Above or below, all these strips of metal seemed to head directly towards the center island of Alpha.

Many of the structures on Beta seemed newer and more were decidedly Mayan in their construction style and appearance than they had seen elsewhere. Itzela explained.

"Before Atlantis came to Maya, Beta was very open, so when Maya came, they could build here more easily. Now we will go across."

They reached the inner edge of Beta and stopped at a short bridge. Across it, the edge of Alpha was packed with houses, temples, and numerous other buildings, increasing in height and size closer the center. The massive central citadel wrapped around the small mountain at the center of Atlantis. Even in daylight the flicker of a shield around a small area above the citadel could be seen.

After they crossed onto Alpha, Itzela pointed out schools and other important structures as they climbed closer to the citadel. She stopped in front of a small stone dwelling that looked the same as many of the others they'd passed along the way.

"This is my home," Itzela said, proudly. "You would like to see?"

"We'd be honored," Jenn replied.

Itzela's home was about the size of a small bungalow. It was neat and tidy and the walls reflected her love of art. The furniture seemed almost modern in its design, but the wood itself was completely unknown to the visitors. The house looked onto a green space that had a garden and a central gazebo, with another dozen or so other houses also opening out onto it.

Tara looked around as Itzela told them about the dwellings different features. Tara was clearly disappointed by something.

"What's up, Tara?" Jenn asked her, quietly.

"I just thought a princess would live in a castle."

"Look at her proudly showing off," Jenn whispered. "This *is* her castle."

They left Itzela's home and moved inward and upward until they reached a courtyard. At its center stood a rough duplicate of the council chamber building that they'd left on Delta. This one however, seemed to project an indefinable air of maturity. It was constructed in an alternate combination of the black, red, and white volcanic stone that seemed to define Atlantis, and while the exterior shape was very similar to the building on Delta, there were subtle differences.

They walked through the main entrance and ascended the stairs directly into the main chamber. On Delta the council chamber had been in the octagonal cupola of the second floor. Here it occupied the entire main floor, which allowed room for hundreds to attend meetings. In this version, the cupola seemed to be used only as a viewing gallery.

Nearly every vertical surface was adorned with frescoes or trimmed with gold accents. The walls were a treasure trove of art in many styles and each support pillar was flanked by a statue of some kind. The council chamber managed to state elegance, without seeming opulent. Itzela let them take it all in for a moment.

"This is the main council chamber," she said. "It is used in quieter times."

"It's magnificent," Stephen said. "Truly magnificent."

"You must see here," Aphrodite said.

For the first time since they'd met her, she actually

seemed like a child as she dashed up the stairs to the viewing gallery with Tara close behind. The rest of them followed at a more leisurely pace.

They stood along the railing and looked down on the chamber from above. Inlaid patterns in the floor resolved themselves into familiar constellations with gold and silver stars and planets contrasting the ebony darkness of the marble floor.

"It's Beautiful!" Tara said.

"Yes," Aphrodite smiled, then turned and pointed out behind them.

They turned together and looked out of the cupola windows. From here, almost two thirds of Atlantis was visible and because they were so close to the center, everything they saw appeared to be overlaid by a sparkling spider's web. The viaducts and channels of metals they'd passed over or under on their journey all seemed to be converging on a point just above and to the left of their position.

"Where does that all lead?" Terry asked.

Aphrodite looked anxiously at Itzela, who nodded approval.

"Come," she said, as she walked to the very front tip of the cupola.

She pointed up and to the left. Slightly higher and closer to the center of Atlantis, they could make out the edge of a dome of a glowing golden shield.

"Shield control," Itzela said, with a sad expression. "We do not go there."

They descended from the viewing area and left the main council chamber without further discussion. They headed directly away from the shield control area towards another large temple where Itzela said they could see things of the past.

"A museum!" Tara declared, excitedly.

The excitement was short lived as Ryan received a text that the *Grasp* had arrived at the harbor entrance. Ryan needed to go and Terry wanted to accompany him. Itzela said that they could see the museum another day, but could also continue the rest of the tour after they dropped off Ryan and Terry.

Aphrodite whispered something to Itzela that made her smile. She looked mischievously at the group.

"Aphrodite would like to take show you our fast way," Itzela said. "Is it okay?"

Aphrodite led them back to an area just off the courtyard, beside the council building. Two concave half tubes set into the ground descended at a steep angle towards the canal.

"It's a water slide!" Tara exclaimed.

"No water," Aphrodite replied, pointing at a large stack of woven mats.

"Show them," said Itzela.

Aphrodite picked up a mat, showed everyone the smooth side and then set it down half draped over the edge of the first tube. She sat on the mat then shimmied over. She and the mat slid into the middle of the tube and then downward, picking up speed quickly and vanishing from sight down the curving path.

"No way!" Jenn said, incredulously.

"Way!" Tara said, grabbing a mat and heading for the far slide.

"Not there," instructed Itzela, tapping the closer slide. "Here."

Tara smiled and in seconds was screaming joyfully as she slid out of sight.

"Where does this go?" Stephen asked.

"Beside the bridge," replied Itzela.

"I'm definitely too old for this," Stephen said as he

dropped down a mat and hopped on.

Itzela came down last, her smile as wide as any of the visitors' as she clambered off the flat area by the bridge and stacked her mat. They all chatted and laughed as they walked across Beta. The visitors were surprised when they were shown another slide from the surface down to the dock.

"These are incredible," Emma said, as she climbed out of the slide onto the dock.

"And very useful," Ryan added.

"Yes," agreed Itzela. "For if there is trouble."

"You are well prepared," Ryan said.

On the launch, Aphrodite explained that the slide system had been started long ago to move products, but had been quickly adapted to move people. She said there were a lot of slides that went to different places, so you had to be careful which one you took.

Ryan got a call before they reached the pillar. He listened carefully then gave a few suggestions before hanging up.

"The *Grasp* is in position but they have a couple of problems," he said. "They can't seem to grab the pillar and aren't sure they can lift it anyway. It may be too heavy for them."

"What did you tell them?" Terry asked.

"The *John Warner* is going to see if they can secure the lift cable from below," replied Ryan. "They're putting divers in the water and the *Grasp* is launching its submersible to assist."

Itzela dropped Ryan and Terry on the *Grasp*, where Tzakol and some of Atlantis' pillar experts had joined them. However, many hours and many attempts later, it became apparent that they simply didn't have ability to lift the pillar.

"There's nothing that can go that deep and has enough lifting power," Ryan told Admiral Lindquist over the phone.

"Command tells me there's a lifting barge stationed in New York Harbor that can hoist it aloft once it's on the surface, but we just can't get it that far."

"Excuse me," said Terry. "There is something that might do it, but we'll have to have a chat with the president first."

CHAPTER 51

Trouble in Paradise

They'd arrived at the airport in Belize as planned. Well, technically speaking, they didn't land *at* the airport. Their pilot had approached the group of low hills at the end of the runway by coming in a few feet over the ocean. He'd hovered over the scrub in a small depression between two of the hills, dropped the ramp so that they could hop out, then turned and headed straight back out to sea. Cadmael said that the chance of anyone having seen them land were very small.

Their approach was so stealthy that they shocked their contact, a big ex-Jamaican named Jefferson, when they walked up behind him in the airport parking lot and tapped him on the shoulder. He told them that he thought he'd heard something, but hadn't seen anything. Jefferson ushered them into the beat up Nissan Pathfinder that he'd equipped with shovels and stakes in the roof rack and a toolbox full of surveying tools in the back.

"It's just over two hours to the border," he said as he pulled out of the small airport's gravel lot. "But the border is closed. Only residents are being allowed through. What will you say when you get there?"

"I was just planning on talking our way through," Bob replied.

"You'll need to do better than that, my friend," said

Jefferson. 'They're not just going to let you in."

"How come you're working for Mexican Intelligence?" Bob asked. "No offense, but you don't seem the type."

"And you don't seem to be much of an archeologist," Jefferson replied, smiling. "According to some, anyway. But here you are with people from Atlantis."

"Touché," Bob said.

"I was on the Belize police force and we were able to stop several large shipments of drugs from passing into Mexico, or help arrange to have them stopped when they arrived. The pay is better than the police force, and I can do a lot more good this way."

They kicked around border crossing ideas throughout their journey, but came up with nothing except perhaps crossing the border illegally. Jefferson said that would be a bad idea, since border tensions with Belize were high even before the crossings were closed. He suggested that they might have better luck if they walked across and hired a car on the other side. When they stopped he handed Bob a wad of Guatemalan money and another containing U.S. currency.

"This should help with bribes," Jefferson said. "Or car rental, if you make it."

"Thanks," said Bob. "Appreciate your help."

"I'll let them know you're at the border," Jefferson said, wishing everyone good luck before he drove away.

Jefferson had been right. They got nowhere at the border, and the fuss that Bob made about it did nothing except get them detained. They waited quietly to be interviewed by a border agent.

"What is your plan?" Paulo asked.

"I'm going to tell the truth," Bob said. "It's always the best plan, even if it hurts a bit."

Tadeo looked at Cadmael, then back to Bob.

"That is our way as well," Tadeo said.

They waited over an hour until the door opened and a dark-skinned, uniformed officer came in and sat across from them. He appeared to be of Mayan descent and his rank bars looked to be those of a captain. His name tag read *F. Balam*. He slid their passports from an envelope onto the table in front of him.

"The border is closed," he said firmly in English. "Why do you try to cross?"

"We search for a fellow archeologist," Bob said. "A friend. He was at Tikal but we've been unable to reach him since Atlantis appeared. We're worried about him."

"It is of no concern," the captain said. "The border is closed."

"It is a concern because of why the border is closed," Bob said.

The captain raised his eyebrows so Bob elaborated.

"If the border is closed to hide some Mayan-Guatemalan past, and he's discovered something worth hiding for, then those above you, will want to know."

The captain studied Bob for a moment, then smiled and turned to Tadeo and Cadmael. He slid a picture from the envelope. It clearly showed Bob, Tadeo, and Cadmael with the president and all the others standing together on the deck of the *Excelsior*.

"Then these two will be able to tell me if there's anything worth hiding for at Tikal," he said, smugly.

"There is nothing at Tikal, but Tikal," Cadmael said. "It is very old."

"We seek only this man," Tadeo said. "For what he may know."

"Then it is of no concern," the captain said. "And you

will not pass."

He stood up to leave, but Paulo spoke up loudly.

"Will you let a cousin pass?" he asked. "On the family's honor?"

The captain reached for their passports and examined Paulo's again.

"You are Paulo Balam?"

Paulo nodded.

"You are with…"

"Cadmael and Tadeo, from the Council of Atlantis," Paulo said. "This is Bob Wallace, as he said."

"Fredrick Balam," the captain said as he sat back down, regarding them cautiously. "Tell me Paulo, how did you come to be here with these people?"

A couple of hours later, as darkness was falling, they were unceremoniously kicked out of the border crossing building by a guard who told them loudly and in no uncertain terms that the border was closed and they would not be allowed to pass. They walked past throngs of people who were also trying to get across the border.

They hadn't walked far when a vehicle pulled along-side them. "Dr. Wallace?" a woman's voice called through the open window.

"Actually, it's just Bob," he said. "Christina?"

"Si."

She stopped the car and he opened the door so they coould get in.

"Welcome to Guatemala."

Christina had the dark skin, long dark hair and smol-dering black eyes of a Mayan. Her hair was tied back in a sim-ple ponytail. After they'd been driving for a while and had all introduced themselves, Christina turned to Bob.

314

"How did you get through the border? They're not known to be accommodating, under any circumstances."

"It seems we had a friend inside, and one with us."

He smiled at Paulo.

"They said they could not let us pass then sent us away. Fortunately they sent us out the wrong side."

"You *do* have a friend inside!" said Christina, admiring the strategy.

"Oh, by the way," said Bob. "The captain said they'd have to put a tail on us."

"They did," Christina said, glancing in the rear view mirror. "Where are we going exactly? I'd prefer to lose them in the wrong direction."

"We are heading for Uaxactún, just north of Tikal," Bob replied.

He saw the look on her face.

"I'm guessing you know where that is."

"Hang on," she said.

She swung the car south onto the road that bore the sign pointing to El Naranjo. She made a few more sudden turns and the tail appeared to be lost. She pulled into a side road, backed down it slightly and killed the engine.

"We'll just wait here for them to finish their search," she said. "So, tell me all about Atlantis."

They talked until the two cars that had been tailing them sped by a few minutes later.

"This is the main road to Flores," said Christina. "We turn off before to go to Tikal. They'll go and look ahead, then come back and work their way along the side roads to find us. That's when we can go."

Sure enough one of the cars zipped back down the road about ten minutes later, followed a few minutes later by the second vehicle.

"Now we can go," said Christina, with a smile.

CHAPTER 52

The Phoenix Project

Terry said nothing further while the *Grasp's* engineers continued to look for a way to hoist the pillar from the depths. Eventually Jenn returned with the others from their tour.

"How did it go?" she asked Ryan, as they boarded the launch.

"Not very well," he admitted. "Terry says he has an idea, but that he can't tell us, yet."

"Soon," Terry said. "I promise, if it can be made to work I'll tell you."

"Tell us what?" Tara asked, as they sat down.

"I really don't know," replied Ryan. "I know you're staying on Atlantis tonight, but we need to get back to the *Excelsior* to report on our lack of progress."

"No problem," Jenn said, smiling. "Itzela has arranged a room for you as well, so you may want to grab a few things."

"Uh, okay," he said. 'I will, if I can."

"Excuse me," Tara said. "Have you even met my mother? You're staying on Atlantis tonight, trust me."

"Tara!" Jenn protested.

Tara just smiled and walked away.

"Sorry, she's more like her father every day," said Jenn, with a sigh.

They went straight into the ready room on arrival. They quickly learned that Bob and his group had landed in Belize, made it to the border, and were trying to get across.

"That was about 15 minutes ago," said General Aspinal, from the monitor. "Border crossings there aren't usually quick and with the closure, well, it could be a while until we hear anything."

"Understood," said Jenn.

"So what happened with raising the pillar?" Aspinal asked.

"We were less than successful, sir," Ryan replied. "We were finally able to get a cable onto it with the team from the sub, but the *Grasp* is simply not designed to lift anything that heavy."

"Why is it so heavy?" the admiral asked.

"Well, sir," said Ryan. "It seems Dr. Masters initial assumption was correct. Their people tell us that the pillars are primarily made of solid gold."

"I see," said Aspinal. "That fact will not leave this room. Dr. Wallace, did your group find out anything new on the tour?"

"Nothing important," she replied. "They showed us their main council chamber, let us use some very cool slides that they can use to get to the canals quickly, and we saw the power grid that Ryan was talking about. It seems to end up at their control center, that part that has that shield around it."

"Nothing important?" said Aspinal. "That's all pretty important."

"I'm sorry," Jenn said, looking questioningly at Ryan and Terry. "I thought you might have heard about that stuff already."

"We were busy with the pillar," said Ryan.

"There was one other thing that happened after you

left," Jenn added. "When we toured the museum it seemed pretty obvious that they've made at least one other time jump. There was a fresco of Atlantis over the ruins of Thera and then the next one was off the shore of Tulum with buildings already started. The dates weren't that far apart."

"And their Diachrome can see into the future?"

The president had joined the conversation from another monitor.

"Yes, sir," Jenn replied. "I believe so."

There was silence in the room.

"These people have a city of gold, a time machine, and they can see the future?" the president asked. "What do they need us for?"

Terry cleared his throat.

"Alright," said the president. "I'll need the room on a secure line. Terry, Ryan, Jenn, and Admiral Lindquist only."

After the line had been secured and Atlantis Command and General Aspinal had signed off, the president spoke.

"Terry, I assume this meeting has been requested?"

"Yes sir, Mr. President."

"Immunity for all present?" he asked.

"On their word," Terry said.

"Then you may proceed."

"What I need to tell you is probably the most closely guarded secret on the planet," Terry began. "I'll need your agreement not to disclose any of this. But before you do, I also have to tell you that the penalty for breaking the agreement is definitely illegal and often fatal."

"What the hell?" asked Ryan.

"It's okay to bow out, Ryan," the President said. "Many have."

"This can't be right," said Ryan.

"It's not a government thing," the President continued.

"But I can tell you that I, personally, am bound under the same agreement."

"Well, then I guess I'm in," said Ryan.

"Sure," added Jenn.

"If it's Phoenix, I'm in as well," said Admiral Lindquist. "But your secret lives in rumors."

"It is Phoenix, admiral, and thank you all," Terry replied, sounding relieved. "The Phoenix project was started a long time ago by some of the wealthiest people on the planet. They wanted to ensure they had an out, a place to go and an escape route if anything bad or cataclysmic happened. Since the nuclear bomb, the has project evolved into a series of generation ships that are always on standby and ready to go. They're staffed with a crew that have been trained and are prepared at any moment to leave for a new life."

"That's kind of sad," Jenn said. "I mean, I understand how it could happen, but it's really kind of sad. Why are you telling us this?"

"Because I work on P34," Terry said. "It's the latest of the Phoenix ships. It's ultra high tech and has capabilities far beyond anything else in or on the sea, including the ability to quickly get that pillar up to the surface."

"But I met you at Playa before any of this happened," Jenn said, confused. "Why? Did you know something was going to happen?"

"No, definitely not," Terry replied. "I was on holidays. I met a couple of my old school pals there for a vacation. I never know if I'll be called away forever and…"

He trailed off in thought for a moment.

"Anyway, P34 is here. There were a couple of clients in Playa so it was sent in on alert as soon as the anomaly was detected. I was located, notified and asked to investigate."

"When I found out he'd been brought to the *Excelsior*

anyway, I asked for Terry to be included," the president said.

"Paulo too?" Jenn asked, recalling that conversation.

"He doesn't know about any of this," the President said. "He was just caught up in it."

"So where is this P34?" the admiral asked. "We've seen nothing in the area."

Terry smiled.

"You won't. It's fully cloaked, undetectable in the water or on the surface. You have to understand, admiral, this is a consortium of the wealthiest people on the planet. They created and own the companies that develop the technologies that you use for detection. They'd never allow a technology out in the world that could beat a Phoenix's cloaking system. We've looked into the problem and can definitely pick up the pillar and get it to the surface."

He looked at Ryan.

"You'll still need that crane barge you mentioned to lift the pillar high enough to install it."

"Phoenix is ultra secret, it's pretty much a cult," the President said to Terry. "So I have to ask, why risk even a chance of being seen? Why are you offering this?"

Terry was almost embarrassed.

"Phoenix wants the Atlantis shield technology. They see it as the ultimate defense. There's nothing else like it."

"What makes you think they'll give it up?" Ryan asked.

"I don't know if they'll even consider it," Terry said. "But I've been instructed to offer and to ask."

CHAPTER 53

Pass the Beer Nuts

After as they pulled out of their hiding spot, Christina had Bob open the glove box and told each of them that they needed to carry a pistol. Bob objected while Cadmael and Tadeo looked on, wondering what they were talking about. Paulo said nothing.

"I've been to Guatemala many times," said Bob. "And I've never had to carry a gun."

"I'm guessing you weren't being hunted for violating a closed border at the time?" Christina said. "Anyway, I'm less worried about them than the road bandits. Things aren't too safe in Guatemala right now."

"What is a pistol?" Cadmael asked.

Christina held hers up and Bob shook his head.

"It's a personal weapon," he said, struggling to explain it for them. "You know how the pillar collapsed when it was stuck by the shell from the ship?"

Cadmael and Tadeo both nodded.

"A pistol also has a small shell and a firing mechanism that will send the shell out of the barrel very quickly."

Bob wasn't happy to see they how interested they were in the explanation.

"What is it used for?" Tadeo asked.

"Around here?" Christina asked, but Bob shushed her

before she could say any more.

"It is a defensive weapon," Bob said. "But it can easily be used to kill someone."

Tadeo had been reaching for the gun, but pulled back his hand when Bob said the word kill.

"This small thing?" Cadmael asked. "Surely not."

"They really don't know?" said Christina.

"Not where they're from," Bob replied.

They drove in silence for a while until they came to a side road that looked as if it had been abandoned for a while. Christina veered off and zoomed down the road to a rotting outbuilding that might have been a garage in a previous life. She drove around back, parked the car, and hopped out with her pistol held behind her back.

"Hello?" she called. "Anybody here?"

No one answered.

"Grab a pistol, Bob. Paulo, and all of you come on out here," she ordered.

"I don't think so," said Bob.

"It's just target practice," she said.

She walked over to a fence and set up a few rocks on top of it.

"Do you want these guys to see what a pistol can do or not?"

"No," Bob insisted.

"Suppose we run into trouble?" she said. "Shouldn't they know what they're up against?"

Bob looked at Cadmael, who nodded. He obviously understood enough to agree with what Christina was saying.

"Let's go then."

Bob sighed, shook his head and grabbed a pistol. Christina backed off from the rocks she'd set up.

"It's very loud," she said over her shoulder, opening fire.

She nailed four out of six shots, with one bullet missing and one blowing a hole in the top board of the fence. Cadmael looked shocked and Tadeo was scared and covering his ears. She looked at Bob. He shrugged then took his turn and nailed five of his six.

"Not bad," she said. "You can shoot. Paulo?"

"It's okay," Paulo said. "I can shoot."

"I can shoot targets all day long," Bob added. "But nothing else."

"Too bad you missed one," said Christina.

"I didn't," Bob said, as he checked the chamber to be sure it was clear.

"Come have a look," he said, waving Cadmael and Tadeo over.

The six inch fence post had a single hole shot clean through it, dead center. Bob pointed out the back of the splintered post where the bullet had exited the wood.

"Guns are very dangerous," he said. "Those holding them can do a lot of damage."

Tadeo nodded.

"I understand."

"Than you for showing us this," Cadmael said to Christina. "It is good to know."

"Then let's get going," she said. "We have a long way to go."

Cadmael talked with Christina for much of the rest of the journey, asking about guns, how they were controlled, who could carry them, and why such a dangerous thing was even allowed.

To her credit, she answered him levelly and honestly. Even as a CIA agent, she didn't condone the open use of firearms and said that she wished there were better ways to control things like guns. She talked about her role in the country and the daily war on crime and drugs that was waged in Guatemala. Paulo broke his silence to add a couple of stories about gang violence in Mexico.

Their conversation was briefly interrupted by having to carefully skirt around a road block at El Remate. Christina wasn't sure if it was police, the army or criminals, but she didn't want to take a chance, whoever it was.

They saw little traffic after that and before long were taking the fork from the paved road that led them down the rutted gravel path that would bring them to Uaxactún.

* * *

There was a fire-pit burning in the village next to the Uaxactún site when they arrived. There were still a couple of locals throwing wood on the fire between swigs of Gallo. When they pulled up and asked about Guy, they were met with cheers and bottles were raised in Guy's name. When that simple motion threw one of them off the bench, the other one struggled to his feet and staggered over to Guy's tent as Bob and the others followed.

Guy was passed out on a cot, but after a few splashes of ice water, he achieved consciousness.

"Bob?" he slurred in a drunken fog. "Izzzat you?"

"Yes, it's me," Bob said.

"Heeyyy! You're 'ere."

He tried to throw his arm around Bob and missed.

"How long have you been drinking?" Bob asked.

"I'll 'ave you know, mate," said Guy, his slurred Australian accent making him even more difficult to understand than usual. "I didn't have a bloody sip, until Atlantis showed up."

"That was three days ago," said Christina.

"It is?"

He wavered, then looked at Bob and steeled himself.

"You said not to hang about at Tikal, so I took myself to Siaan K'aan."

He smiled.

"And you bloody well found me!"

His eyes rolled back and he collapsed, mostly missing his bunk and falling to the ground.

Bob looked at the collapsed heap.

"I think we'll be staying tonight," he said. "He's toast."

"You think?" said Christina.

Bob looked at the half dozen cots in the tent, all covered with gear. He pulled out his phone. No signal.

"We can stay in here, but we should check in."

"I'll grab the sat phone" said Christina. "But I'll be staying in my car tonight, thank you very much."

"This is Siaan K'aan?" Tadeo asked.

"We call it Uaxactún now," Bob replied. "It was called Siaan K'aan. You know it?"

"It is spoken of," said Tadeo.

Christina ran back in, the sat phone in her hand.

"We have a problem."

"So after you'd been inside the border station for a few hours," Jenn recounted on the speaker phone, "Jefferson got worried and called in. Then Stephen used his contacts to get hold of the Guatemalan president, who apparently used to be in show business or something. Anyway Stephen used his name and was actually able to get hold of him and since the UN have now offered all Atlantean's diplomatic immunity, the Guatemalans agreed to offer you safe passage."

"So that's good, right?" Bob asked.

"Well, then you up and disappeared and nobody was able to find you," Jenn continued. "So now they've issued an alert and mobilized the police and the army to find you."

"That might not be good," Christina said, slowly.

"Why not?" Bob asked.

"The army, the police, and the government are all different factions," she explained. "If somebody wants to make a statement, they try might and grab you and hide you for a while."

"That's what they're worried about here," Jenn said. "Did you find Guy?"

"Drunk as a skunk," Bob said. "He'll be unconscious 'til morning."

"We'll come and get you in the morning," Ryan said, over the speaker. "Is the line secure?"

"It's CIA secure," replied Christina.

"Okay then, where are you?" Ryan asked.

"Where we planned," said Bob. "Uaxactún."

"Why are they searching for you in central Guatemala?" Ryan asked. "They said you headed south from the border."

Christina smiled.

"Guess we had some pretty good help down here," Bob said.

"We've been cleared to pick you up once they locate you," said Ryan. "Can you stay hidden until mid morning?"

"Unless they send someone looking," Christina replied. "Nobody knows we're here."

"Well, don't tell anyone," Ryan said. "We'll have satellites keeping an eye on you from above and will let you know if anything's headed your way. Keep the sat phone handy."

"Damn!" Christina said, annoyed.

"What?" asked Ryan. "What's up?"

"That means I'll have to stay in the stupid tent as well," said Christina as she winked at Bob and the others.

CHAPTER 54

It Was just a Dream

'C'mon, mate, rise and shine."

The sounds of the rainforest just a few feet away washed over the tent. The smell of coffee filled the air. Beside the tent flap, the small two-burner stove was busily percolating coffee on one side and boiling some eggs on the other. The sun looked as if it had been up for a while. Bob looked at his phone. It was 6:30.

"How long have you been up?" he asked Guy.

"About an hour," he replied. "Since sunrise. Coffee?"

"Si," said Christina, smiling as she sat up on the cot. "Good morning."

"Good morning, sunshine. I'm Guy. Who might you be?"

"Christina, and thirsty."

"Bob, make yourself useful and pour the lady a coffee, would you?"

"Black," Christina added.

"Black coffee coming up," said Bob, rolling off the cot.

"What is black coffee? Tadeo asked, rubbing his eyes.

Paulo raised his hand for a coffee and Cadmael was stirring as well.

"A couple more then," Guy said. "Good morning, all."

He threw the front flap of the tent to one side and the sunlight streamed in.

"Another beautiful day in Guatemala," Guy said. "There's eggs and buns if anybody wants brekkie. I'm short on bacon."

"You seem okay this morning," said Christina. "You were pretty out of it when we got here."

"Nonsense, love," he said. "I was probably just resting my peepers."

"You were smashed," added Bob. "Well and truly gone."

Guy seemed offended at the suggestion.

"Drinking Gallo?" he said. "That'd never happen."

"It's not the type of beer, my friend," said Bob. "It's the quantity."

"Bah!" Guy scoffed. "How do Cadmael and Tadeo take their coffee?"

"I don't think they even know what it…" Bob started to say. "Hey, how do you know their names?"

"You must've told me," said Guy, looking slightly evasive. "Last night."

"You were unconscious," Bob said.

Everyone was up now.

"What else do you remember?" Tadeo asked.

"Nothing," Guy replied. "You said you were looking for some Diachrome guy with these two. Something about the other guy dying?"

With that statement Cadmael got up and came over to stare intensely into Guy's eyes.

"What is his name?" Cadmael asked. "The Diachrome that's dying."

Guy looked at Bob.

"Your friend is getting kind of intense here, mate. Maybe you should ask him to back off."

"It's kind of important, Guy," Bob said, seriously. "A matter of life and death."

Guy turned back to Cadmael and looked directly at him. "Paulin," he said. "His name is Paulin."

"Thank you," said Cadmael.

He turned and exchanged glances with Tadeo. Bob saw them both briefly shake their heads and Cadmael went to sit on the edge of his cot.

"That's it?" Bob asked Cadmael. "Nothing more?"

"He is not who we seek, Bob Wallace," said Tadeo.

"But isn't he the one we came to get" Paulo asked.

"He was," Cadmael replied. "But he is not the one."

"What do you mean, came to get?" asked Guy.

"Then how did he know their names?" said Christina.

"He knows the names," Cadmael replied. "But he did not see them."

"What the hell are you guys talking about?" said Guy. "What is all this? What's a Diachrome anyway?"

Bob looked at Cadmael and received a nod to go ahead.

"A Diachrome can see the future," said Bob. "And the people of Atlantis rely on him to help guide their... well, their whole civilization."

"I see," Guy said as he turned away to pour himself a coffee. "And you thought I was him?"

"I thought maybe," Bob admitted.

"Why?"

"Because you always have these crazy hunches and know stuff. Just like you knew their names," Bob replied. "You've done it since I've known you."

Guy thought for a while. He offered Tadeo, Cadmael, and Paulo each a coffee and then sat down with them.

"Look, I don't know who you're looking for, but it's not me."

"But..." Bob started to say.

"I'll tell you a secret, though," said Guy, lowering his

voice. "The reason I knew all that stuff from before and their names and everything this morning."

"What's the secret?" Bob asked.

Guy smiled then chuckled.

"You talk in your sleep, mate. Everything I've ever passed on came right out of your mouth. That Diachrome thing... Paulin. You were yammering on about all that stuff early on this morning. It woke me up like always, so I listened."

"No way!" Bob exclaimed.

"Sorry, mate, but you've been listening to yourself talk." Guy said and turned to serve himself an egg.

Bob thought about all the things he'd heard Guy say over the years. It might be true. They'd always been on digs together when Guy had his crazy ideas. But if that was true then...

"Steady," Paulo grabbed Bob as he staggered. "Are you okay?"

The inside of the tent seemed to be spinning slightly. Paulo helped him to sit on a cot, but the dizziness was getting worse. Bob shook his head as he heard Guy from far away.

"So when did this Paulin fellow die?"

...a deeply saddened Aranare peered kindly into his eyes. His own heart was light. He knew now, that it was time to leave. He smiled a warm goodbye to Aranare and let his eyes flutter closed...

"Bob, wake up!"

Tadeo spoke loudly to get him to respond. Bob shook his head and sat up quickly then felt dizzy again.

"What happened?" he asked.

"You fainted," Guy replied. "Nice going."

"Thanks for the catch, Paulo," said Bob .

"Maybe that's why I never told you before," Guy said, smiling at him. "You're a big wuss."

"Shut up and give him some water," said Christina. "Fainting can be a sign of all kinds of things. Give him some space."

"I'm okay," Bob assured her. "Sorry, it's just been a very busy few days. I think things may have caught up with me."

"Perhaps," Tadeo mused. "You are feeling better?"

"Much better," Bob replied, surprised at how good he suddenly felt. "I'm going to get some fresh air. Save me an egg?"

He walked outside and felt the sun on his face and the gentle morning breeze. Everything was fine again. Except that dream he'd had with Aranare in it. Something was very wrong there. Something had changed. He walked back into the tent.

"We should probably check in," he said.

He looked around and saw the sat phone on the table.

"May I?" he asked Christina.

She nodded and he reached for the phone. Just before his fingers touched it, the phone rang with an incoming call.

CHAPTER 55

A New Diachrome

"Hello?"

"Thanks goodness it's you!" said Jenn. "Tara has wandered off."

'What do you mean wandered off?"

"I don't know," Jenn said, sounding very worried. "When I woke up she was gone. I don't know what to do."

"She's probably just gone for breakfast," said Bob. "Go out the front door, turn left and walk along until you see the tables where people are eating."

"Okay," Jenn replied. "We'll check there right away."

"Who's we?"

"Ryan. Johnson. From the carrier? He's the one that gave me the sat phone. You cell's not working."

"Oh yeah, no service here."

A long woeful horn sounded across the courtyard. People called out. Jenn looked out the window and saw there were people running around in different directions.

"Something's happening," said Jenn.

Seconds later there was a loud knock on her door.

"The Diachrome is gone." Bob said.

"What? What makes you say that?"

"I'm not sure," Bob admitted. "But I know."

The knocking became more insistent.

"I gotta go," said Jenn. "Talk to you later."

She opened the door to let Ryan in.

"Has she turned up?" he asked. "Are you ready to go?"

"Bob said she might have gone for breakfast," Jenn replied. "He told me where to look."

"Alright. Let's go."

He opened the door to find Aphrodite standing there, about to knock. Her eyes were heavy with sadness.

"The horn tells that our Diachrome Paulin has moved on," she said then sighed "And your Tara has been found where she should not be."

"Come in," said Jenn. "Tell me please."

"We must go to council," Aphrodite replied. "I am sent to bring you to Alpha."

They hurried to the top of the stairs in the back of the guest hall that led down to the docks below. Aphrodite stopped them before they started down.

"Here," she said. "This is faster."

She led them around a couple of corners into a small room with a half-round tube and a stack of mats. They smiled, hopped on and reached the dock in moments.

"Shall we take ours?" Ryan asked, pointing at the launch. 'It'll be quicker."

Aphrodite bowed her agreement and they hopped aboard. The motion woke the skipper, who was snoozing on one of the seats opposite his relief, who didn't wake up.

"Need to go to the same place as yesterday, skipper," Ryan said then looked at Aphrodite for confirmation.

She nodded and they backed out of the dock as soon as the brass ring had been raised. The skipper was about to get underway when a loud horn sounded. One of the Minoan ships was making double time as it came up behind them. The skipper moved to get out of the way when the horn blared again.

"Wait!" Jenn called out. "It's Aranare!"

She waved to the figure standing in the bow and he waved back. The oars hit the water in unison and began slowing the ship's forward progress. The ship managed to glide to a stop right beside the launch and Aranare hopped aboard.

"You go to council?" he asked.

Aphrodite nodded.

"I may come with you?"

"Of course," Ryan answered. "Skipper?"

When they arrived, there were hundreds of people at council and things were in an uproar. Not only was the Diachrome dead, but Tara had been found in the main Hall of the Journey on Alpha. Aranare and Aphrodite stayed with them on the dais as Jenn and Ryan joined a frightened Tara.

Aranare raised his hand and the room fell silent.

"It is true," Aranare confirmed. "Our Diachrome Paulin has left us."

There were sobs and cries as the people in attendance realized that worst fears had come to pass.

"He was at peace," Aranare said. "And we will say our goodbye in time. But first."

He looked at Tara and smiled reassuringly.

"That hall is only for those on council, the Diachrome and his aide. It is hidden, but you knew its location. What do you say, child?"

"I'm sorry," said Tara. "I meant no disrespect. I was dreaming of the hall. It's the same room that I drew at my Dad's conference. In my dream I went to find it."

She sobbed a little.

"I'm so sorry. I must have sleepwalked. When I woke up I was in there."

Aranare looked carefully at her as murmurs rippled

around the room.

"What's happening?" Jenn whispered to Aranare.

He looked at her and winked. His eyes shone with pride and happiness as he turned back to Tara.

"You cannot have seen this," he said, smiling at her. "It was just a dream. But you drew a picture of this room before?"

"Yes, a few days ago." Tara replied, still confused.

"And today you awaken in that same hidden room, a special room that requires a key. Do you know the key?"

The room fell completely silent.

"What key?" said Tara. "No, I don't remember any key?"

"It is a special key of words," Aranare replied. "Without the key, the words within the hall are of no meaning."

He looked at her closely.

"Can you dream it?" Aranare asked, encouragingly.

"I... I don't know," she said with a shrug. "I can try."

Tara closed her eyes and concentrated.

"Remember the hall," Aranare said, quietly.

She thought of the hall... and then she could see it!

"I'm in the hall," she said out loud.

"Now think of the key," said Aranare.

"I see..." Tara trailed off then added, "Paper, I need paper."

Jenn grabbed a notebook and a pen from her pocket and thrust them into Tara's hands.

She started to write a series of symbols in a strange language.

"I don't know what it means," she said, her eyes still closed.

Aranare smiled at her while the council members and many of those present stared, some of them turning pale as Tara finished and opened her eyes.

"Is that it?" she asked.

"Yes, Tara," said Aranare, "it is. May I ask where did you see it?"

She sighed and closed her eyes again. She was back in the hall and there was a shiny black granite surface on one wall. Her vision wavered and shifted. Suddenly instead of the wall, she could Bob looking at his reflection in a grimy mirror. He waved to her as if he knew that she was observing at him.

"I see…"

She started to explain, but then Bob shook his head and mouthed the word no. He grabbed the paper on which he'd written the symbols of the key and flipped the page. Tara watched as if she were looking over his shoulder as he wrote her a note.

'Hey, pal, please don't tell them it was me, not yet. Love you!'

He held the note up to the mirror but the wording was reversed in the reflection. Bob looked at her in the mirror again, smiled and winked. Tara gulped and opened her eyes.

"Uh, sorry. I'm not sure where it came from."

Aranare regarded her curiously. He was sure she'd seen something more, but he held his tongue. He turned to the room and lifted the note Tara had written high above his head. Heads bowed all around them, including the council members.

"As it is written," Aranare said loudly, with pride in his voice. "So shall it be."

The council members looked up and even Aphrodite was beaming at Tara now.

"As it is written," the council members said in unison. "So shall it be."

The entire room followed suit then they all broke into loud and happy cheering, some of them with tears of joy streaming down their cheeks.

"Aranare, what is this?" Jenn asked, confused.

"Your daughter," replied Aranare, his voice choked with emotion, "is Diachrome!"

CHAPTER 56

Extraction

Bob returned to the tent and walked over to the coffee pot. He was still feeling slightly dizzy and spilled and some coffee, which he carefully began to wipe up.

"You still feeling off, mate?" Guy asked.

"Not a hundred percent," replied Bob. "That's for sure."

"You were saying some odd stuff there before your little walkabout," Guy said. "Did you find the john?"

Bob nodded.

"You sure you're okay?" Christina asked.

"It's nothing. I'll be fine,"

He was saved from further questioning by the ringing of the sat phone.

"Yes?" said Christina, as she answered it. "Sure. Bob, it's for you."

"Hello?"

"Hi, Bob," said Jenn, sounding worried. "Are you alone? Can you talk?"

"No," he said, carefully. "Not really."

"Then, just listen. Somehow, they think that our Tara is their new Diachrome."

"Okay," he said as calmly as he could. "That's very interesting. What does Aranare think?"

"He is the one who said it," Jenn said. "They're all

treating her like she's a princess or something. I really don't know what to do."

"Well, remember what I always say? When you don't know what to do? Do nothing."

"I know, but it's hard when everyone else is doing something. He says there has never been a female Diachrome before, or one so young. This all started because she snuck into some hidden room and knew their secret password."

"I see," Bob said.

He couldn't really add anything else.

"I forgot," Jenn said. "You can't talk, sorry."

"Yes," said Bob. "That's true."

"Did you find Guy?"

"Yes, but it's not what we thought."

"Right," she said. "Of course not. Well, Ryan wants to talk to you."

"Okay," said Bob. "Put him on and I'll see you soon."

"Bob," Ryan began, there's some pretty crazy stuff going on around here."

"Sounds like it," Bob said. "What's up?"

"Command has picked up a couple of jets headed your way. Probably to confirm you're there."

"Should we leave or hide?" Bob asked, genuinely concerned.

Ryan laughed.

"Neither, just the opposite. Since we have permission to extract once you're located, when the jets fly over, make sure they see you and get Christina to report that she's located you."

"What?" said Bob, confused.

"We've already got an extraction team inbound," Ryan explained. "The Guatemalan jets will confirm that you're there and direct the troops that are already on their way to hurry up and get there. We've timed everything out and we'll have your exit strategy sitting on the ground there before anyone else arrives. Since your location will have been reported, we can come in and extract you under our agreement."

"Sounds doable," said Bob. "What about the old airstrip that's here? Can't the jets just land?"

"Actually, no. They tell me that they can't land even a light plane there because it hasn't been maintained for decades. Just stick to the plan. It allows us to keep our commitment to the Guatemalans and get you back here quickly and safely. Jenn wants another word with you."

"Thanks, Ryan."

"You were right, you know," Jenn said, when she came back on the line.

"What?"

"About their Diachrome Paulin. He died this morning. How did you know?"

"Just a hunch. You know, everyone gets them."

"True," she said. "Well maybe you can tell Cadmael and Tadeo? They should know."

"Uh, shouldn't it come from their own people?"

"Aranare asked if you could tell them," Jenn said. "He also asked that we keep Tara a secret for now, from our people."

"Alright," Bob reluctantly agreed. "I'll tell them, then we'll deal with that when we get back."

He said goodbye and hung up. Cadmael and Tadeo looked at him expectantly. They seemed to know that he had news for them.

Bob was pondering how exactly he'd tell them about Paulin when he heard the distant roar of jet engines growing louder.

"Everybody outside," he said. "We have to let them see us here."

"What? Why?" Christina asked.

"Ryan said so," said Bob answered as hurried outside. Two jets screamed overhead and banked into a wide turn.

"They'll be back," he said. "Christina, you need to call in and report that you've found us."

While they waited for the jets to return, Bob did his best to explain Ryan's strategy. Christina said it was a good plan, since it would be a win for everybody and nobody would lose face.

After waving at the jets as they passed by in what Christina told them was a slow fly by they all went back inside the tent.

"You need to get packed up, Guy," said Bob. "You're coming with us."

"Why?" he asked. "I'm not the one they're looking for."

"You want to be here when the army arrives?" asked Christina.

Guy stared at her for a second.

"Right!" he said. "I'll get my kit together."

"What about you?" Bob asked Christina. "You coming too?"

"That, would cause problems," she laughed. "I'm from here. But thank you."

Bob pulled Cadmael and Tadeo aside.

"I am sorry to tell you that Paulin has died."

"We know," said Cadmael.

"How could you know?"

"You told Jenn on the phone that he was gone," Tadeo replied. "And you spoke with the certainty of he who knows. Your friend who knew things before they happened and says he knew them from you. You are the one we seek."

Bob sat down on the nearest cot.

"Excuse me? What just happened here?"

Tadeo smiled.

"I am Aranare's student," he said. "I am with you for this reason. You are Diachrome. My job is to help Diachrome."

Cadmael shook his head.

"And you have been among us since we met."

"Excuse me," said Bob. "I'm not Diachrome. I can't see the future."

"Then how did you know Paulin had died?" Cadmael asked.

"It was just a feeling," said Bob. "And it wasn't the future. You said Diachrome could see the future."

"Aranare also says Diachrome do not tell everything," Tadeo said. "He says they keep many secrets. I think you have secrets now."

Bob rolled his eyes.

"I'm not going to get anywhere with you, am I? Guy!" said Bob as he got to his feet. "Do you need help packing up?"

It didn't take them long to reach the abandoned airstrip at the center of the village of Uaxactún. The only problem was that the airstrip was far from abandoned. They put in a call to let Ryan know.

"From what I can see," Christina explained, "it looks like the airstrip was paved recently then painted over to look like it was still wrecked and covered with scruff from the air. Probably the work of drug runners."

"Well, that might explain the three aircraft now headed your way," said Ryan. "Troop transports from what we can tell. I've let our team's pilots know. Get everyone to the north end of the runway, and the second the Osprey's ramp begins to open tell everyone to run for it. It's going to be close."

It wasn't long until their extraction team was in sight.

It comprised of a single Osprey flanked by a pair of Apache attack helicopters. The Osprey came in with its rotors tilted full forward. The pilot angled them quickly to vertical and brought the craft in hot, spinning it around and dropping the ramp as it came close to a stop at the end of the runway. The pilot never touched the ground and once everyone was aboard, the Apaches flanked the Osprey as the aircraft all moved quickly northward. Just before the ramp closed, Bob and the others could see the three planes coming in from the south, one of them already on landing approach.

The Osprey gained altitude quickly and within minutes they were at full forward thrust. The crewmen on board handed out earpieces and the pilot came on the radio.

"Have a seat and relax folks. We'll be out of Guatemalan airspace in less than ten minutes. In case you're interested in statistics, the fastest aircraft in the Guatemalan Air Force are the ones that overflew you earlier. Those have a top speed of just over 500 km/h, just the same as this CV-22 Osprey that you're in now."

"Since they headed back to Guatemala City, that means that there's no way anything they have can catch up with us. We'll back on board the *Excelsior* in approximately an hour. Oh, and your pal Christina relayed a message. Said to tell you she got out of there in plenty of time. So, just sit back, relax, and enjoy the flight."

CHAPTER 57

Hidden Asset

"Okay, they're safely inbound from Guatemala," Ryan said, hanging up the sat phone.

Jean and Tara both breathed a sigh of relief. They'd all been listening over the launch's radio as the extraction unfolded. Admiral Lindquist had been supplying Command data through one of the monitors on the launch's dash.

"Command will monitor them all the way in," he said. "Terry and I will meet you at the council chambers on Delta."

"On our way," Ryan said, as he clicked off the monitor.

"All is good?" Aranare yelled from the back of the boat.

Ryan gave him a thumbs up signal, then realizing that he might not know what that meant, nodded and yelled over the roar of the launch's engine.

"All is good!"

Aranare told Itzela and the three other council members that had accompanied them in the launch and they broke into smiles.

"Are you sure you don't want to be dropped off at the guest hall," Jenn asked Tara. "You should have a nap. You must have been up all night."

"No way, Mom. "I'm fine. Besides," Tara said, her voice dropping to whisper, "they look at me differently now."

Jenn held her hand and tried to reassure her.

They arrived at the dock at the same time as the admiral's launch. They were about to send the launches back to meet the ship that was ferrying the rest of the council when it came into view at the back of the harbor.

"Those guys are flying!" said Ryan.

"I didn't know a rowed ship could move that fast," Terry added.

"Our ships can be quick," Aranare agreed.

Ryan and Jenn pulled Aranare and Itzela aside and gave them a quick rundown of the swap that Terry had proposed. They said they'd see if council would consider hearing him.

Once the ship had arrived, the council and Aranare had a quick meeting right on the dock, borrowing a sat phone so that Tadeo and Cadmael could also be included. Tzakol and Itzela came over to Terry afterwards.

"The council has been told of your trade request," Itzela said. "It has agreed to hear you."

Tzakol bowed in agreement and waved in the direction of the staircase leading up to the chamber above.

"We'll be right there," Terry said, he turned to the Lindquist.

"Admiral," he said, once the Atlanteans were out of earshot. "If this goes ahead, we'd like to move quickly. Can you back the fleet off the harbor by about a kilometer and make sure there are no submarines in the area?"

"How big is this thing?" Lindquist asked.

"It's not that big," replied Terry. "But we need room to maneuver and to be honest, the cloak isn't as effective close up."

"Alright," said Lindquist.

"Oh, and admiral? The *Grasp* and the launches will have to be pulled back as well."

"Not the barge?" Ryan said, try to be sarcastic.

Terry didn't bite.

"We'll need that to put the pillar on. Which reminds me, Ryan, you should probably get that high-lift crane you mentioned on the way here. We'll have the pillar up and on the barge shortly."

As they climbed up the steps, the fleet pulled up anchors and began to move further away. By the time the group arrived at the top, all ships had pulled back and were starting to regroup.

"The fleet's clear, Terry" Lindquist said, after received a confirming call. "Holding station, one kilometer off."

Terry slid back his sleeve and keyed something into a wrist-rack mounted device. There was a reply seconds later.

"There's still a sub down there, admiral," said Terry. "Just a sec."

He fiddled with the device some more.

"It's Chinese," he said. "Stealth class. You may not be able to detect it."

He keyed something into the wrist device.

"We've relayed the position to your Command."

Terry moved over so he could show the admiral the sub's position beneath them in real time. Lindquist spoke into his phone and ordered the *John Warner* to intercept the Chinese vessel and escort it from the area. Everyone watched Terry's wrist monitor as the American submarine turned and headed toward the Chinese vessel's position. As the *John Warner* came closer, the Chinese submarine turned and headed out to sea, with the *John Warner* in pursuit. Another submarine joined the pursuit from the east just before they all ranged off the screen.

"Insurance sub," the admiral said, winking.

"P34 in position."

They were all startled by the voice that came over Terry's wrist-rack.

"Commence retrieval," Terry said.

"But you haven't made a deal yet, have you?" asked Jenn.

"It's a good will gesture," said Ryan.

"Exactly," Terry added.

"That doesn't sound like the Phoenix I've heard about," said Lindquist.

"Even Phoenix is run by people, admiral," Terry said.

"So you made the call?" Ryan asked.

Terry grunted noncommittally as they climbed the steps to the council chamber.

The pitch was very simple. Phoenix wanted to see the shield generator and would be happy with anything that could be shared about its method of operation. In return they'd pick up the pillar and bring it to the surface. The council didn't need too much time for deliberation and quickly agreed, which surprised everyone. However, the one change that they requested was even more surprising.

"We are agreed to share this with you, so long as it is also shared with the Atlantis Command," Tzakol said.

"That's interesting," Terry said, thoughtfully. "And unexpected."

His train of thought was interrupted by a short audio message from his wrist device.

"P34. Pillar is secure, ready to surface, confirm visual."

Terry hesitated for a few seconds. He flicked a button on the wrist device before addressing the council.

"On behalf of the Phoenix Project," he said. "I accept and agree, including that the shield technology be shared with Atlantis Command."

"Received and understood," his wrist device replied. "Confirm visual."

"I need to be in line of sight for visual confirmation," Terry said to Tzakol. "Is there somewhere I can see the harbor?"

"Yes," Tzakol said.

He stood and beckoned them to come up to the council's level, where Jenn had looked out over the harbor earlier.

Once everyone had assembled, Terry confirmed that he had line of sight and the surface of the water just in front of the harbor began to bubble and steam. It looked as if it were boiling but Terry explained that the ship was simply creating a foggy mist that would be delivered over the next fifteen or twenty minutes. Its purpose was to further obscure the Phoenix craft.

"You make fog?" Aranare asked.

"Yes," Terry said. "It's the way we work, under the fog, in secret."

Aranare looked at Tzakol who smiled.

"Your ship is outside the harbor?" Aranare asked.

Terry flipped through a couple of screens on his wrist device.

"Yes, well clear. Why?"

"Our shield makes fog," Aranare said.

Tzakol moved to the edge of the window where he could be seen by those in the nearest tower.

The admiral pushed a button on his sat phone.

"Lindquist here. Stand by for a possible shield test on Atlantis. There will be a shield activation and likely a fog. This is just a drill."

Tzakol raised his hand and made a gesture they couldn't see clearly. The full shield flickered into existence around them, solidifying into the same opaqueness that had sliced through the *Xavier*, and then seemed to become even more solid. Still semi-translucent, the shield allowed them to see the fog shooting up outside the shield, presumably boiling up from where the shield contacted the water.

After two minutes, Tzakol brought his hand down and

the shield flicked off. Fog continued to roll upward and outward from the edges of Atlantis and the quickly growing fog
bank that was still being created had obscured the entire fleet
and blocked any view from Playa del Carmen.

"Surface cover established," said Terry.

"Say again?" came the reply from his wrist device.

"Full surface cover established," Terry repeated.
"Bring her up."

Just outside the harbor, the surface of the water
swelled up, then flowed away from a long flat area wider than
the mouth of the harbor itself. It soon became obvious that
something was emerging. It just happened to be an invisible
something. It looked as if a long wide hole in the ocean had
just opened up. Water streamed off the flat invisible top surface
suspended over the hole.

"Once it's reached surface depth," Terry explained,
"the camouflage optics will adjust and it will look less weird."

Moments later the whole area flickered and the hole in
the ocean simply disappeared. It was as if the ocean continued
right through the hole's previous location. Only water lapping
and waves breaking against the camouflaged hull gave it away.

At the end of the Phoenix closest to the downed pillar,
a section of the ocean appeared to lift up out of the water. The
massive door pivoted upwards, lifting its camouflage with it.
A couple of sleek launches zipped out of the bay while the
door was still opening and headed for the barge that the *Grasp*
had left behind.

"Three aircraft approaching due south." Terry's wrist-
rack barked again. "Targeted. Suspending EVA. Advise disposition."

"Admiral?" Terry asked.

"That's got to be Bob and the extraction team," Jenn
said.

The admiral grabbed his sat phone.

"Lindquist here. Advise Apaches on incoming flight to hold, have the Osprey…"

He looked at Tzakol and Aranare questioningly. Aranare pointed to the courtyard in front of them and Tzakol nodded his approval.

"Have the Osprey land in front of the council chamber on Delta. Absolute radio silence and warn them of a Hard Debrief about anything they observe during the landing."

Terry nodded his agreement and spoke into his wrist device again.

"A single Osprey is cleared to enter visual range. Disengage targeting. Continue EVA," he said.

"Confirm," came the terse response.

"P34. Confirmed."

CHAPTER 58

Cloaked

"You heard me right," the radio squawked. "Warbirds are to hold position until bingo fuel and then make for *Excelsior*. Keep it on the deck. Extraction One, you are cleared to land in front of the council chambers on Delta Ring. Hard Debrief on arrival. Acknowledge."

"Wardbird One, copy, Warbird Two, copy."

"Extraction One, copy," their pilot added.

"Radio silence now. *Excelsior* out."

'That's weird," said the pilot.

"What is?" Bob asked.

"There will be a Hard Debrief on arrival at the council."

"What's a Hard Debrief?" said Bob.

"I could tell you, but then I'd have to kill you," the pilot replied.

"Ha, ha," said Bob. "Really, what is it?"

"That's a Hard Debrief," said the pilot, turning to him. "Whatever it is, you are not allowed to talk about it... Ever."

They flew through some of the fog that was still drifting over Atlantis and the fleet. As they reached the harbor, the pilot flew over and headed directly toward the council chamber. The fleet seemed farther away than it had been earlier but everything else looked the same, well, except for the half barge sitting just outside the harbor.

"Was that a half a barge?" Bob asked.

"Since we're already in line for a hard debrief, I think I can say yes," the pilot replied.

They looped tightly and he threw the Osprey's rotors into full vertical before they landed gracefully on the stone courtyard outside the council chambers.

Only a few of their people were there to greet them, but the entire Atlantis council was present, standing off to one side watching and discussing what was happening. Terry quickly explained the required level of discretion to the new arrivals. Once everyone had committed, he brought them around the Osprey to the top edge of the stairs where they could watch what was happening.

After opening like a portal to another world, the huge well deck of the Phoenix had swallowed the entire barge. Inside, something glinted gold as it was lowered onto the barge. A few minutes later, the two launches pulled the barge, complete with its new cargo of the retrieved pillar, out of the well deck toward the shore. The barge was secured then the launches headed back inside the well deck.

As soon as they'd cleared the edge, the door started closing. There was some extra swirling around the door after it closed, then a section of the ocean's surface, approximately half as wide and twice as long as the harbor entrance, began to depress. It was very hard to tell how tall the Phoenix was, but the depression seemed well over forty meters deep when the waves started lapping over it. Soon water foamed over the top and the invisible vessel was completely submerged.

"P34. Clear," Terry's wrist rack barked one last time then was silent.

'Does that mean we can get things back to normal?" Admiral Lindquist asked.

"Yes, admiral," he replied. "Thank you."

Lindquist looked at the pillar sitting on the barge out in the harbor.

"Thank you for that," he said as he grabbed his sat phone. "End radio silence. Warbirds, head home. Extraction One will be on the way shortly."

"What about the fleet?" Ryan asked him as the admiral hung up. "Leave them back there?"

"When is that crane arriving?" the admiral asked.

"It'll be a couple of days," Ryan said. "But they'll need time to get things fixed and prepared anyway."

"I wouldn't underestimate them," the admiral replied.

He pointed toward the inner canal. A fleet of ships was already rowing out and heading for the barge and the pillar.

"They seem to be getting right on it."

The admiral's sat phone buzzed and he turned away to answer.

Ryan turned to Bob and the others to welcome them, but was interrupted by the arrival of Evan and Emma, breathless from climbing the stairs from the canal.

"You're back," Evan said to Bob.

"Yes, where have you two been?" Bob asked.

"Er, we slept in," said Emma.

"What's going on," Evan asked, looking at the Osprey. "Are we flying here now?"

Ryan counted on his fingers.

"Let's see. The Diachrome Paulin has died, Bob and his team have escaped from Guatemala, the pillar's been raised from the bottom of the ocean. And…"

He looked at Jenn but decided not to mention Tara's new status.

"Yeah, I guess that's it."

They were all watching Evan digest everything when

Guy, who'd been admiring the view of Atlantis, turned around and broke the silence.

"This place is great," he said. "Exciting!"

"It might be getting even more exciting," said Lindquist as he rejoined the group. "Bob, did you find what you were looking for?"

"Not really, mate," said Guy. "They just found me."

The admiral raised an eyebrow.

"It was quicker to bring him back than explain," Bob said. "What's about to get more exciting?"

"After today's display," the admiral replied, with a sigh. "Atlantis Command would like us to ask if there is any way that Atlantis can be moved. To a less visible location."

Bob turned to look at the members of the council, but they'd finished talking and had moved closer to Bob's group to hear what was being said. He saw Itzela trying to catch his eye, but he wasn't sure if he was ready to deal with that yet. Instead he found Cadmael, who had an answer.

"What you ask may be possible," Cadmael said.

Just then, Aranare politely pushed through the council members with Jenn and Tara in tow. Tara ran ahead to Bob and hugged him hard. She had to be scared following the morning's events. He certainly was. He finally allowed himself to look at Itzela. He wasn't sure what he'd expected, but all he saw in her eyes was compassion. He smiled and held out his arm.

Itzela came forward and Bob pulled her into the hug as well, surprising Tara who was then comforted by them both. Bob looked up to see that Jenn had moved beside Ryan and was holding his hand for reassurance. She smiled at Bob, and somehow he instantly knew that everything was going to be alright for her.

Tadeo stood resolutely beside Aranare and both stayed

aloof from what had become an emotional moment. Finally Aranare broke the silence.

"Admiral," he said. "It is early, but already the day has been full. Perhaps we can allow those that need some time…"

"Agreed," said Lindquist. "This fog will blow off soon and I'd like to get the Osprey out of here. Too hard to explain to the press. Ryan, Terry, Paulo, you're with me."

"Admiral," Jenn asked. "May we borrow Ryan for a bit longer?"

"Certainly, Dr. Wallace," he replied. "Anyone else coming back to the ship?"

Guy winked at Bob.

"I'd like to have a look, Admiral," said Guy. "And my stuff's stowed on your bird already."

Lindquist nodded so Guy continued.

"Dr. Masters, maybe you can come along and tell me what this is all about over a pint? You do have beer on that ship, don't you, admiral?"

"Dr. Masters?" said Lindquist. "We could use your expertise if you're up for a quick jaunt. You can head back afterwards if you like."

"Why yes, admiral, Emma and I would be happy to assist," said Evan, after receiving a nod from Emma.

"Excellent. Everybody aboard. Let's go," said Lindquist, then noticed that Guy wasn't actually moving yet.

"We may even be able to find a pint somewhere."

"Marvelous!" Guy exclaimed.

He strode over to Bob to say goodbye and while he was shaking his hand, Guy muttered under his breath.

"She's bloody lovely, and you owe me one for Evan."

Bob smiled.

"Come back and have a look around later," he said.

They watched the Osprey take off, then dip low and

skim through the fog as it headed off to the carrier. When they turned around most of council members had already started heading back into chambers. Bob moved to head that way, but Aranare stopped him.

"Not for you," he said, smiling at those that remained. "There are the outdoor council chambers with the pools below, or the guest hall, or there is a ship below to take you anywhere you wish. Your family should speak."

Bob looked around. Itzela, Tara, Jenn, Ryan, Tadeo, and himself were all that remained. He looked anxiously at Aranare.

"I don't know what to say about anything. I'm not even sure what's going on."

The old man shrugged.

"No one knows!" he said, then smiled. "But still we find a way."

CHAPTER 59

Newfound Ability

"The pools below the outdoor council are nice," Itzela said. She glanced at Bob who seemed a little worried about that.

"There are many places to sit and talk among them," she added.

"That sounds nice," said Bob. "But I could use some lunch. Maybe the guest hall would be better?"

"We are hungry as well," Tadeo said. "Food can be brought."

Bob sighed.

"The outdoor council it is then."

He headed quickly in that general direction and Tara quickly ran to catch up with him. The others stayed tactfully behind.

"What the heck is going on, Dad?" she asked. "I could see you!"

"And I could see you too, pal," he said. "Well, I couldn't see you, but I saw where you were, and I knew you were in trouble."

"But Dad?" she said. "Diachrome?"

"I know, but I don't see what else it can be," he said, smiling. "We'll get through this."

She struggled with her thoughts for a moment.

"Why didn't you want me to tell them it was you?"

"I don't know. I didn't want to confuse things or…"

He glanced at her sideways.

"Or what?" she said.

"Or maybe I was scared," he admitted, sheepishly.

"Dad," she said, punching his arm.

He pretended to be really hurt, then pretended to try and punch her back. She took off ahead and he chased after her. When he caught up he lifted her off the ground so she couldn't run and she squealed. He set her down and they laughed together.

"You two!" said Jenn, shaking her head as the rest of them caught up. "Like father, like daughter."

"In many ways, it seems," Aranare said, in a deep serious voice.

Bob looked at him and he was rewarded with a wink.

"I see," Bob said, with a smirk. "Alright then, oh Wise One. How does this all work?"

Aranare studied Tara and then Bob thoughtfully.

"I can tell you many stories of Diachrome from thousands of years past," he began. "But the story of a Diachrome so young or a female Diachrome are not among them."

"Oh, great!" Tara said, exasperated.

"From all we know, it is very rare that two Diachrome are ever together at one time."

"What do you mean two Diachrome?" Jenn asked.

"Bob is also Diachrome," Tadeo replied, as if it were common knowledge.

"Oh, great!" said Bob.

He and Tara looked at each other and both burst out laughing.

When their hilarity had subsided, Bob and Tara deflected all further questions until they were all seated in the treed glade, beside the series of hot pools that started just below the lookout at the outdoor council area.

"So how can Bob be Diachrome?" Jenn asked.

"He knew when Paulin passed," Tadeo replied.

"Actually," Bob began, then realized what he was about to say. "I, well, I guessed."

"Diachrome may not share all their secrets," said Aranare. "But they are usually much better at hiding them than that."

Bob realized that he couldn't hide this from Aranare.

"I saw through Paulin's eyes," he said, gently. "As you said goodbye to him. He was at peace and happy when he let go. I could feel it."

Aranare bowed his head in silent thanks.

"You are Diachrome," said Itzela, smiling at Bob, a tear of happiness in her eye. "You have the honor."

After a moment, Aranare composed himself.

"Much has changed," he said. "There are no stories of a Diachrome seeing through the eyes of a predecessor. Always forward, never back."

Bob could sense that Tara was about to tell them more about his help with the key.

"Not now Tara," he thought to himself.

Okay Dad.

They looked at each other in shock. Their lips had not moved. Fortunately Aranare held everyone else's attention as he continued.

"There are more stories that have been forgotten that can be remembered," he said. "It is possible that all this has happened before."

"Don't you keep records?" Ryan asked.

"There is much to record over hundreds of years and many millennia," replied Tadeo. "Do your people keep such records as this?"

"No," Ryan admitted. "I guess not."

"Diachrome have existed from millennia past," said Aranare, moving into story mode. "Since before the long count was begun. They have many visions through the eyes of their descendants. Some are small, like a crop growing well or the crop doing poorly, some are big, like meetings of the Keftiu and the Maya."

"Sorry," asked Jenn. "Keftiu?"

"It's the old Egyptian name for the Minoan people," Ryan explained.

"We are Keftiu," Itzela confirmed.

"The visions of the Keftiu," Aranare continued, "were many, but the day of the first meeting was set as the first day of the long count, and the end of the long count was set as the end of the world. Diachrome said that only the Keftiu could save themselves from the end but they could not do it alone. Only with the help of the Maya."

"So your peoples have been working together for over five thousand years?" Ryan asked.

"Yes," Aranare confirmed. "There are gaps, but there have always been Diachrome to see the way."

"And no Diachrome has ever seen past the end of the world," Tadeo added.

"Past 2012?" said Bob . "Perhaps they were afraid to look beyond that date?"

"But we haven't really seen the future," Tara said. "At least I haven't."

Everyone looked at Bob.

"Nor have I."

"That is why we must train you," said Tadeo. "We can help you learn to see."

Their conversation was interrupted by people bringing trays of food, and pitchers of beverages. As they munched on cheeses and sipped a drink that was somewhere between juice and wine, Jenn tried to pick up the conversation.

"Does the council train the Diachrome as well?" she asked Itzela.

"No," Itzela said. "Council listens to Diachrome, then guides the people."

"So you..." Jenn began.

"I am not here for council," said Itzela, smiling at her. "I am here for Bob. As Ryan is here for you."

"What?" asked Tara.

Itzela thought she didn't understand.

"I came to be with the father of the Diachrome, to support," Itzela said. "Ryan is with you for support. For the mother of the Diachrome, is he not?"

"Mom?" Tara asked.

She smiled at Ryan, who was actually blushing. Jenn tried to change the subject.

"Don't tell me Tadeo is here for Tara?"

"I am here because I am trained to be aide to Diachrome," said Tadeo.

Ryan and Bob diplomatically said nothing while Aranare, who could see where the conversation might be leading, decided to get them back on track.

"It is fortunate," he said loudly, "that we have two aides for two Diachrome. We shall begin training as soon as possible."

"So what does that mean?" Bob asked. "How will you train us?"

"You have had visions," Aranare replied. "You of Paulin and Tara of the words of the key. We must find how these came to you. Knowing how you were when they beset you, may help us learn what will bring them again."

"Like our state of mind?" Tara asked.

Tadeo nodded.

"That is a good way to say it."

"Well, I was kinda terrified," replied Tara. "When council was upset with me."

"So you reached out for an answer," Aranare said. "And one was given."

Tara looked at Bob.

He's going to figure it out.

Bob smiled at her.

I think maybe this thought talking is one of those Diachrome secrets, and I'm not worried.

"I was confused when I saw Paulin," he said out loud. "Sort of dizzy."

"You almost fainted," Tadeo reminded him.

"You really don't need to tell everybody that," said Bob.

"All is good," Aranare said. "Many Diachrome could only see in dreams, some needed the smoke to see."

"I don't even know what that is," Jenn said. "But there will be no 'smoke' for Tara."

"These are both Diachrome without the smoke," Aranare reassured her. "There is no need."

"You must stay on Atlantis," said Tadeo. "So we may teach you."

"What do you mean must?" Ryan asked.

"He is young," Aranare said, chiding Tadeo. "But we of course hope that you both will stay so we can teach you what we can. Diachrome will do as they do, as they always have."

"Well, it's probably the best idea," Ryan said.

"Why?" Jenn asked, surprised that he'd agree.

"Right now nobody with the fleet, except maybe Guy, knows anything about these two being Diachrome. "If they're here, there's less chance of others from our world finding out."

He turned to Aranare.

"In the past, some our peoples have reacted badly to things they don't understand. But with the Phoenix group involved, let's just say it might be best if they didn't know."

"Why?" asked Aranare.

"Like the people in Tadeo's tale the other day," Ryan replied. "There always some that will try and take what they want. I have no knowledge that Phoenix is like that, but I'd rather not risk people I care about, or, well, anybody."

They talked for several more hours. Aranare and Tadeo told many stories of things Diachrome had seen and how things had been done because of the visions. It was well past sunset and after the lights of Atlantis had been lit when servers brought lanterns and hot drinks to repel the evening's chill. As they chatted more, it became obvious that Itzela had been correct about Ryan having feelings for Jenn.

The fires of Atlantis helped all things to seem balanced. Tara watched as her mother and father, each sat with their new people around a fire, and calmly chatted about how being able to see the future shouldn't have to change... her.

Dad, this is kind of weird.

He smiled.

Yeah, it is. Let's call it a night.

CHAPTER 60

Relocate?

Except for Tara, who'd stayed with Jenn, everyone had retired to their own quarters in the guest hall. It had been late when they'd arrived and if it wasn't for the prospect of a nice hot cup of coffee on the *Excelsior*, Bob would have preferred to stay in bed.

He found himself with Cadmael, Aranare, and Ryan on an early morning launch heading to the carrier to discuss the moving of Atlantis.

"It's Guy's fault," Bob said. "I wasn't missing coffee until he made it in Guatemala."

"What is coffee?" Cadmael asked. "You spoke of this on the trip before."

"It is like the fruit of the cacao bean," Ryan explained. "It's dried, ground up, and made into a hot drink. It's very popular just about everywhere."

"May I try?" Cadmael asked.

"I think that can be arranged," said Bob, smiling.

Cadmael quite liked coffee, and was still talking about it when they arrived on the bridge of the *Excelsior*. Admiral Lindquist, Terry, Emma, and Evan were all waiting for in the ready room.

"It is like the old Mayan Ka'kau' drink I had once,"

Cadmael said. "Do others drink it here?"

Five coffee cups were raised, while Emma countered in true British style.

"I prefer tea."

"You're up early," said Bob, needling Evan.

"No more sleeping in," Evan replied. "We missed way too much yesterday."

"Now that we've covered all that," Admiral Lindquist said, "Can we talk about the possibility of moving Atlantis?"

Cadmael and Aranare acknowledged with a small bow.

"My first question is rather basic," said the admiral. "How does Atlantis move?"

"Small movements can be done in the water," Cadmael replied. "But much undersea can be lost. For larger trips it is best to move above the waters."

"That thing can fly?" Guy said as he entered, pointing to the huge city in the monitor.

"If I know how your helicopters work, like feathers in the air?" said Cadmael, making a rotating motion with his hand. "Then no, it does not fly. But it can be made to move through the air."

Ryan nodded.

"Okay, let's take that as read for now. Where should it move to?"

"We should like to move by Tulum," Aranare replied.

"Why do you want to be by Tulum?" the admiral asked. "And if that's the case, why did you land here by Playa instead of there?"

"Coming here was so that was no damage to Tulum," said Cadmael. "You have seen that our main drive can be a problem. We did not wish to destroy those that we hoped might be there."

"So all that stuff will happen again when you move to

370

Tulum?" Terry asked. "Because it was pretty devastating."

"No," said Aranare.

"We will use shields to move by Tulum," Cadmael said. "Unless you cross the shield, it makes no problems."

"The shields can move you through the air?" Terry asked.

"It is a way to use them," replied Aranare.

"Okay, let's say it's safe," Ryan said. "Where will you put down?"

He flicked a few keys and a satellite image of the coastline appeared on the main monitor. He moved a laser pointer and clicked a circle graphic that was on top of the current location of Atlantis. He slid it southward to just in front of Tulum.

Aranare nodded.

"That seems simple enough," said Lindquist. "What happens to anything that's under Atlantis as it passes over?"

Aranare glanced at Cadmael, who shrugged.

"We do not know."

"Okay," Ryan said. "We need to look into that, just in case. Any other major details?"

"When will you move it?" Emma asked.

"I don't think that's a major detail," Lindquist replied.

"I'm sorry, admiral," Emma said. "But seeing a six kilometer wide island pick up and fly through the air will be somewhat unnerving. As will seeing it disappear one night only to reappear elsewhere else in the morning."

"When you put it that way," said Ryan.

"It's the way I see it too," added Evan. "It's important."

Bob's eyes narrowed slightly. Was Evan actually trying to be helpful?

"I think we'll get Atlantis Command in on that decision," said the admiral.

"And Jenn please," Ryan added. "Her thoughts have been pretty darn helpful so far."

Lindquist nodded.

"I think the general will agree with you on that. So, can we do a walk through?"

Cadmael looked at him, furrowing his brow.

"Now?" he said. "You wish to move now?"

The admiral chuckled.

"No, definitely not. I just wanted to walk through, or rather talk through, what will happen on the day."

"Ah," said Cadmael. "Good."

Cadmael described how the ship would engage its shields and then slowly increase the power. There would come a point where the shield power would overcome the Earth's power and the ship would begin to rise. Terry interrupted to try and figure out if that meant overcoming gravity, and they worked out that this was precisely what it meant.

Cadmael explained that Atlantis had to rise slowly or the seas would flood with huge waves. Ryan mentioned the recent tsunami before the admiral asked everyone to allow Cadmael to finish before interrupting him again. Cadmael explained that there would be a small moment when the water would release them.

Once clear of the water, they would raise the ship higher and increase the power. Then those stationed on the pillars would use the levers mounted in the pillars to change the shape of the shield, which would either let them turn Atlantis or provide power for starting and stopping lateral movement.

Once they arrived at Tulum they would reverse the take off sequence and land gently in the waters off the coast. Where, Cadmael reminded everyone, this part of their journey had started.

"I don't get it," Bob said. "It seems too simple."

Ryan shook his head.

"It's anything but. Their shield overcomes gravity until Atlantis lifts clear of the water. There's a pop when the surface tension of the water releases the ship. They raise and lower slowly to eliminate tsunami waves during the takeoff and landing. It sounds like there are levers that disrupt the field without being cut off by it. The disruption causes forces that turn or power horizontal flight. Cadmael, do you have to cancel out the force of the turn and the flight?"

Cadmael was puzzled.

"When you moved forward," said Ryan, moving his hands to elaborate. "Then you take away the power. Does the ship continue to move forward or does it stop by itself."

"It continues on," Cadmael replied.

"So you have to apply a force in the opposite direction to stop it?" Ryan asked.

Cadmael nodded.

"It is so."

Ryan's face was lit up like a kid with the keys to the candy store as he turned to Terry and the admiral.

"This means that Atlantis is functioning as a perpetual motion, antigravity machine," said Ryan. "It's so... impossible!"

"It may be," Aranare added.

"Er, what?" said Ryan.

"This is done with all pillars," Cadmael said. "With one down, it may not be possible."

"We will need a test," Aranare said.

"How big a test?" asked Lindquist.

Dad, where are you?

"Damn!" Bob said aloud, by accident.

Just a sec.

"Uh, we'll have to test everything," he said. "The lift,

the spin, the drive. Heck we should do it in daylight and show everybody that Atlantis isn't dangerous."

He was rambling now and Tara could tell. He could hear her snickering inside his head.

"We can even stick something under there to see what happens."

That snickering isn't very ladylike.

You're funny when you're flustered. I can see where you are. You're on the carrier.

Yeah, and in a meeting.

"Bob?" Ryan said. "Did you hear me?"

"Sorry, I was daydreaming."

"I said we'd have to clear everything with, well everyone," said Ryan.

"But you're right," the admiral agreed. "Cadmael?"

"It must be a full test," said Cadmael as he stood. "We will make ready."

On the way back to the mess hall to pick up some more coffee to take to Atlantis, Bob experienced seeing through Tara's eyes. There was Jenn, getting dressed. Tara must have been helping her mom pick out clothes. He directed a quick thought to Tara.

Tell her the blue top looks great.

Dad! That's rude.

So is snickering in someone's ear when they're in a meeting. We're going to need to come up with some rules.

True. Otherwise this could get to be very confusing.

Why?

Cause you were just looking at Mom, but thinking about Itzela.

Bob shook his head and smiled. He could tell that Tara was holding back another snicker.

CHAPTER 61

Test Flight

Almost soon as Cadmael returned to Atlantis, a general warning horn had begun blaring repeatedly. Any ships in transit on the canals had been rushed into docks. The barge where the pillars were being assembled, along with the boats and barge in the harbor by the recovered pillar, were doubly and triply lashed down.

Within minutes of an apparent all-clear signal, the metal rings on the sides of all the three canals were manned and being pushed into motion. The big wheels attached to the stair columns were lowered down to contact the top plates of the metal rings and periodically, as a new connection was completed, sparks flew as a result of the contact.

Itzela, Jenn, and Guy watched the wheels turn from the viewing gallery at the top of the council chamber on Delta.

"Looks like you were right about the whole generator thing," Jenn radioed to Ryan. "All the wheels are turning now."

"I wonder how much power they can generate?" said Ryan.

"So you are a bit of a geek," Bob smiled, as he walked up to them.

"I guess," said Ryan. "Do you know how much power they can generate or how they connect it to the shield?"

"Hey, wait a minute," Bob protested. "Just because I'm

supposed to be this Diachrome thing doesn't mean I magically know how this stuff all works."

"What's the view like on Alpha?" Jenn asked.

From where they stood, Bob and Ryan looked around the uppermost courtyard that surrounded the central temple of Alpha. As they'd guessed when they'd been inside the council chambers below, the webs of metal that lay across Atlantis terminated at, or in some cases under, the courtyard on which they stood. Hundreds of workers filled the massive courtyard, yet it was so large that their view still remained largely unobstructed.

The rivers of brass carried by aqueduct from Gamma rose from the land below them to reach the level of the courtyard then dove under its surface. Strips of tin inlaid in the surface of the courtyard twisted and turned to touch each of the golden sculptures that dotted the stone. They then flowed off the edges of the courtyard in tin waterfalls that became the rivers of metal that flowed in power from the tin ring of Beta.

Far off in the center of the courtyard, a raised platform of orichalcum held a massive cluster of blue crystals. Tucked under the intake end of the golden chimney that rose above all of Atlantis, the cluster was at least three stores tall and was flanked by half a dozen singe crystals of the same color. Each of the large surrounding crystals was taller than a horse.

Four or five attendants stood beside each of the many smaller sculptures that were laid out in a ring around the center. Most of the attendants were in the process of mounting small blue crystals into receptacles in the sculptures. Others aligned brass and tin rods to contact with the rivers of tin above or through holes to connect to the brass conduits below.

"Guys?" said Jenn. "What's up?"

"It looks a lot like the cover of a science fiction novel," Bob replied, yelling as power hummed all around them.

376

"Or standing on a giant printed circuit board," Ryan added.

"Yeah," Bob nodded. "That too."

A shout from Cadmael alerted them. He was standing beside one of the larger sculptures explaining something to Tadeo and Terry. He shouted and backed them away from the group operating the sculpture. The operators took hold of wooden handles and turned the entire sculpture so that the section that resembled an outstretched hand pointed towards the center crystal.

As soon as it pointed to the center, a shower of sparks arced around its base as the connection was completed. An affirmative shout echoed from one of the nearby teams beside a smaller sculpture. They slid their crystal into a different position then dropped the brass rod into a hole, allowing it to connect with the brass below. More sparks flew and as the operators cowered, a bright blue beam emanated from the small crystal, shooting forward to terminate on a single face of one the six large crystals nears the center.

The orichalcum below the crystal glowed fiery red and a bright white beam shot from the top of the crystal into the bottom of the golden chimney. The beam emerged from the top as a golden shimmering glow that instantly covered Atlantis with the gossamer shield that Cadmael had first told them was some sort of standby mode.

"Jenn, can you see this?" Ryan yelled into the radio, but only heard static.

Following another shout, the sculpture was turned away from the center and the beams terminated. The shield disappeared as instantly as it had appeared.

'Say again?" Jenn said on the radio.

"I think they're testing the crystals," Ryan shouted. "We'll call you back."

Cadmael soon called Bob and Ryan over and confirmed that they would run tests on all the shield crystals before a lift attempt. During the next crystal's test, Bob reached out to Tara. He easily connected with her without trouble and asked what was happening where she was.

The fleet has backed off and we're watching the test on the monitors. Playa is on a monitor too. Tsunami warning sirens have been going off for a while. They already cleared the beaches and streets. How long will this take?

A little while. Don't rush them, they want to get this right.

I know. Let's talk during the test, okay?

If we can.

K, now watch the test. It looks cool and I want to see!

He smiled and told her to her to go ahead and watch until she got bored.

It was an hour or so later, after the every crystal had been tested and the all clear had been given, when she reached out again.

Dad, I just got a text from Stephen. He's live-casting the test by satellite from his yacht!

Well, it should be good quality video, at least. Here we go!

A horn sounded and groups of people rushed to the edge across the courtyard. Flagged signals were relayed across the spires of Atlantis. As Cadmael had explained, each pillar would receive instructions relayed through the spires by flags. Each flag bearer was flanked by a team. One communicated to the person on each side and one communicated with the pilot.

A nod from Cadmael saw three sculptures turned and the beam of light from each touching a large crystal. This seemed to establish the shield strength that had cut the *Xavier* in two. Next, three more beams lit up the other three large crystals. The shield was now more opaque than they had seen yet. An additional beam was added to one crystal and Bob sensed that something had changed. It appeared that way to Tara as well.

Something's happening, Dad! The shield is bowing in where the pillar's missing. Wait. There are things coming out from the pillars on either side of the missing one. They're stretching the field!

Show me?

Bob looked through Tara's eyes and saw the golden tabs being swung out from their recesses in the pillars. Another beam was added and he could partly sense and partly see that Atlantis was trying to slide towards the bowing of the shield and the island was beginning to rise out of the water. The pilot barked some instructions and the sliding feeling diminished. Another beam was added, and this time the lift was felt by everyone.

It's kinda moving forward, Dad.

He saw it on the monitor, but it diminished and the water became still. Bob looked at the pilot, who was studying some sort of instrument floating in a pool. The pilot nodded and a second beam touched a third crystal.

Atlantis was rising! The close-range cameras that Tara was watching could see the lift, but Stephen's feed hadn't picked it up yet. As the last three crystals were gradually doubled up with beams, the lift became a smooth ascent. In around ten minutes the bottom of the shield of Atlantis was at least 200 meters above the surface of the water and it had stopped rising.

"All is good," said Cadmael, smiling. "We are able to move with the damaged pillar."

"You're compensating with the tabs on the pillars?" Bob asked.

Cadmael looked at him curiously.

"How?"

He then seemed to recall that he was talking to a Diachrome and nodded.

"What did you just see?" Ryan asked.

"There are these tabs that stick out and distort the field at the pillars," Bob replied.

"That makes perfect sense," said Ryan. "If the bubble's distorted it'd move to or away from the distortion. Then you could use tabs on the opposite pillars to compensate."

Cadmael look at him, nodded then smiled.

"Nailed it," Bob said to Ryan. "You really are a geek!"

Tara spent the remainder of test watching Stephen's feed, with Bob tagging along, as Atlantis rotated back and forth, moved forward then moved back and shuffled from side to side. Cadmael was about to declare the test a complete success when a shudder ran through Atlantis.

Dad, one of the tabs looks like it's melting. Atlantis is sliding forward again.

"Cadmael, you've lost a control tab!" Bob shouted.

Cadmael relayed the information to the pilot, who compensated to control the slide then quickly lowered the ship.

"Please, not too quickly," said Ryan, and that instruction was relayed to the pilot as well.

There was one more shudder, which Tara confirmed was a second tab coming apart, but it happened just before they powered down and didn't seem to affect anything.

As the shield was powered down, Bob felt dizzy. His eyes blurred and he grabbed onto Ryan for support.

"You okay?" Ryan asked.

"I saw something," Bob replied, his face ashen. "Fire! Raining down from the sky."

CHAPTER 62

Rebuilding

The test had proved that Atlantis couldn't safely move without first repairing the downed pillar. A quick survey by the launch confirmed that they also now had two other pillars to repair. The tabs on the pillars on either side of the downed pillar had given way. After talking with Cadmael, Ryan had promised that those would be easy to fix with the crane that would be arriving soon.

Bob's fiery vision wasn't so easily dealt with. Ryan had grudgingly agreed to keep the details within their group for the moment. They met at the outdoor council area without Jenn or Itzela, who seemed to be getting along far too well for Bob's liking.

"I reserve the right to change my mind," Ryan said. "If I think any of you are in danger."

"There's no context," Bob said. "We don't even know if it was real. If it was, there's no way to know where or when it will be."

He threw up his hands, exasperated.

"Argh! I can't believe I just said that."

"It is good," said Tadeo. "You speak like a Diachrome."

"Yeah?" Bob said. "Well, a Diachrome might have known that keeping the pillar tabs extended for so long would tax them to failure. It was probably just a daydream or something."

You don't believe that, Dad," Tara said. "Or you wouldn't be so worried."

"Sorry, pal. I was startled, that's all. Why don't we all go see if there's anything we can do to help get this tub moved?"

As they got up to leave, Tadeo asked Ryan.

"What is a tub?"

The tub in question was also the subject of a discussion that Terry was having with his superiors at the Phoenix Project. While they'd been pleased to receive the video that he'd shot from the courtyard during the test, the Phoenix people needed more details if they were to discern the true nature of the shield.

Terry offered to try and get samples of the crystals and when that was deemed to be acceptable, he asked if he might offer the Atlanteans a little more non-classified assistance. Armed with their approval, Terry set out to find Cadmael.

Terry caught up with Bob, Ryan, and Guy on the main dock at the harbor. They were looking for Cadmael too and had been directed to the ships rebuilding the pillar. They all took the launch across the harbor in the first light rain that they'd encountered since Atlantis had arrived.

Cadmael wasn't in charge of the reconstruction. Bob and the others only had to hear a couple of crusty utterances to guess that Cadmael's father was the crew boss. They smiled as the previously inscrutable Cadmael bowed to one of his father's requests.

"I guess we should we rescue him?" Bob said to the others, who all shrugged.

"Cadmael!" Bob called, from the launch. "Do you have a minute?"

Cadmael must have understood the underlying intent

as he immediately brought his father over to greet the new Diachrome. This encouraged Cadmael's father to be nice to him but Bob and the others were unable to get rid of the old man for the rest of the visit.

In the end it worked out for the best. The five of them poured over the plans for the pillar and its internal mechanisms then compared it with the pillar top on the barge. They were learning a great deal, specifically how long it would take to complete the task, when Terry decided to offer some Phoenix-style assistance.

"I have access to a machine that could help with the removal and trimming of these pieces a couple of hours," he said. "We can also configure them to rejoin the pieces without the need to recast."

"We already suggested a welder," Ryan said. "But the engineers said it would remove too much material."

"I'm thinking of a sub-molecular laser," said Terry. "It should be especially effective at rejoining the cast gold slabs without overheating the joint, which would mean as-cast stability."

"That's a great idea," Ryan agreed. "Too bad it's still theoretical."

Terry shrugged.

"Not really. There's one plant in Jiangsu in China that has a production model in service."

"And that helps, how?" Bob asked.

He was following the conversation about as well as Cadmael and his father, whose reactions resembled two people watching a tennis match. Both of them were waiting for even a snippet of information that they could understand.

"If a type of technology is in public use," Terry said. "Then it's declassified by Phoenix and becomes something I can use to offer assistance."

"So do you just happen to have a sub molecular laser with you?" asked Ryan, a little sarcastically.

"No," Terry replied. "It's on the P34. I can have it here in the morning. I'll need to bring a few technicians along as well though, people that are trained on it."

"Just say yes," Ryan said to Cadmael, shaking his head. "This will save you days or weeks."

Cadmael agreed and Terry radioed in the request. They all clambered ashore to see how the repairs were proceeding on the base of the pillar. They'd nearly reached the top of the scaffold near the break when an almost silent launch whispered into the harbor and pulled up beside the pillar barge.

"I distinctly said tomorrow," Terry said into his wrist-rack.

"We weren't busy," came the terse response.

"Are all you Phoenix boys so chatty?" Bob asked.

"We don't get out much," Terry admitted, then raised his wrist.

"We're checking the break on the land side," Terry said. "We'll be down shortly."

"I'll come up," the voice replied.

Terry rolled his eyes.

"What?" said Ryan.

Terry pointed to the Phoenix launch just as someone sporting a jetpack launched from the deck and zoomed over to join them. For the first time since Bob and the others met him, Cadmael was stunned, his mouth open, speechless.

"No way!" Bob exclaimed. "Can I try that?"

"Sorry," replied Terry. "That one *is* classified."

"You guys really do have all the toys," said Ryan.

Within an hour the Phoenix team had assessed what support they'd be able to provide, after a scathing lecture about revealing classified technology from Terry, had begun work immediately. They worked alongside the Atlantean crew and deployed several of their portable laser units at both sites.

Since there was nothing they themselves could really do, Bob, Ryan, Terry, and Cadmael took the launch back to the guest hall for dinner as dusk arrived. Guy offered to stay and help, declaring that it would be like a working tour of Atlantis. In the boat Cadmael studied Terry carefully.

"You have helped us greatly once again," Cadmael said. "What will you now seek in trade?"

"Nothing," Terry answered. "I'm happy to help. But I do have a question about our first trade."

Cadmael nodded.

"The demonstration was incredible," Terry began. "But is there any way we could have a look at a one of the crystals? We have not seen their kind before."

Cadmael smiled and reached into the bag that had been slung over his shoulder all day. He extracted two leather wrapped pouches and passed one to Terry and one to Ryan.

"Aranare said you might want these," said Cadmael. "Here are small crystals of the same kind and pieces of our metals that bring power to the shield. The crystals are rare indeed, as is our orichalcum. We hope you can find what you need with this."

"Thank you, Cadmael," Terry and Ryan said in unison.

"Jinx!" said Bob.

Terry and Ryan laughed and then explained the joke to Cadmael.

Really, Dad?

Tara's sarcasm echoed in Bob's head.

Hey, pal. What are you up to?

Tadeo and I have been busy. Have a look.

She was seated at one of the quiet areas bedside the

guest hall. Tadeo, Itzela, Jenn, Aphrodite and a couple of the other members of the council all sat with them. Aranare and Tzakol were looking over their shoulders. Bob could see that they were preoccupied with the laptops.

What's going on?

When we got back, Mom and Itzela were surfing the web. So we grabbed the case of laptops and a few who said they were interested from the council and brought them over here out of the way and showed them how to look stuff up. Tadeo's especially good at it!

I hope you're giving them some context, pal. There's a lot of crap on the web.

Oh yeah, Mom and I have been trying to do that. It's been a busy afternoon. What are you up to?

Almost there. Have you guys had dinner?

No. That will be good timing. Something else on your mind?

I was just wondering, do you know what's up with Mom and Itzela?

Nothing bad, Dad. They're friends now, I think.

He sighed and thought to himself.

No good will come of this.

Hey, I heard that!

CHAPTER 63

Revelations

Bob and the others joined Tara's internet surfing group for dinner. Itzela had saved a seat for Bob and Jenn had saved one for Ryan. Terry and Cadmael sat at the long table too. They talked about the day's events and the work going on to restore the pillar. Bob thought that there'd be many questions as a result of everyone exploring the online world, but there was no conversation at all about that. Something seemed strange.

"Itzela," he said. "You went on the internet today. Did you find what you were looking for?"

Itzela looked at Jenn, but seemed a little uneasy.

"Jenn showed me some things, yes."

"Aphrodite," Bob asked. "What did you search for? Did you find it?"

"I looked for Atlantis on the maps to see how we fit here with the land," she replied. "But I found no Atlantis. Jenn said it must have to update?"

"That could be," said Bob. "Tadeo, you were looking for something?"

"I searched for Keftiu and then Minoan," Tadeo replied.

"Did you find anything?"

"For Keftiu I found only pictures from another country.

For Minoan there are many things, but most are of the old palace on Keftiu."

"Well, that's good, isn't it?" said Bob.

"But the pictures of the palace you call Knossos are wrong," Tadeo added. "The construction and design are not of our people and Jenn told me this was made up by the man who discovered the ruins. This seems wrong."

"Everywhere we looked in the internet," Itzela began, "there were truths beside lies, or lies beside lies said as truth. It was interesting but we have no need for such as this. Your Google must be broken to allow such lies."

Bob was stumped. Terry was smiling, clearly trying to stop laughing.

"Something funny about that, Terry?" Bob asked.

"Actually, yes," said Terry.

He smiled and looked around to see who was listening.

"There's a story in the Phoenix group about when the internet first became popular. They were going to either shut it down or try and control it, but they realized that if they got everybody busy arguing about which lies were actually true and which weren't, that would help prevent people from searching for any real truths. In the end it added a whole new level of distraction, away from them. What Itzela said just now sounded pretty much the same to me."

"So Phoenix owns the internet?" Itzela asked.

"Nobody owns the internet," said Ryan answered, then saw Terry's expression. "You're kidding me?"

"Sorry," Terry said. 'They own all the infrastructure and own or control all the software."

"They can't own it all," Ryan said. "Someone would know."

Terry thought for moment.

"Well, I'll try and explain. Do you own land?"

"I have a small house," Ryan said, proudly.

"Is it paid for?"

"That's personal," Ryan replied.

"Humor me?" Terry asked.

"Well, okay, about half.

"The bank owns the other half?"

"No, I own it, the bank holds the mortgage."

"In legal terms, the banks owns your house until it's paid for," Terry said.

"I think he's right," said Jenn.

"Who do you think owns the banks?" Terry asked.

"Your people?" said Ryan.

"Well, Phoenix membership doesn't work together on everything, but the membership is pretty big," Terry replied. "Together, they own or control 100% of the banks and over 90% of the land on the planet."

"They can't," Bob argued. "What about credit unions? Government banks? Private banks? Plus, almost of them all trade on the stock market."

"Since the gold standard was removed, all government banks are underwritten by international institutions, as are credit unions and private banks," Terry explained. "These people own the international institutions. Banks float a percentage of their shares on the stock market so that they can use up as much of other people's money that's in circulation as they can, but never enough to give up actual control. They've been doing this since money existed and they are very good at it."

"That," Bob said, slowly. "Really sucks."

Dad, look around!

At Tara's suggestion, Bob saw that the Atlanteans had carefully been listening to every word. While they might have misunderstood parts of what was said, they seemed horrified at what they'd just heard.

Thanks, pal.

"Cadmael," said Bob. "Perhaps it's time to introduce more of your people to coffee?"

Coffee as a distraction worked quite well, but came with the side effect of stretching the rest of the evening a few hours beyond when it could have ended. Bob and Tara guided the conversation away from the more sensitive topics a few more times over the course of the evening.

At the end of the night they were sitting outside at the same spot where Tara had been conducting the internet session earlier. Most of their hosts slowly trickled away until only Itzela and Tadeo remained with Terry, Tara, Ryan, Jenn, and Bob. Terry pulled Bob off to one side for a chat.

"These people seem to have really taken a shine to you," Terry said. "I'm sorry if I upset anything with my discussion about Phoenix activities."

"It's a different view into a different world," Bob replied. "And I don't understand their reaction, but I'm going to try and figure it out. How is it that you know so much about Phoenix?"

"Most of us are raised into this job," Terry said. "We're given statistics like that and encouraged to explore them. I think it's so that we know we're playing for the winning team, should we ever get called to active duty."

"Active duty? Like some sort of catastrophic event?"

"Exactly. Anything that would force a generation ship to go active would have to be pretty catastrophic."

"But the uber-rich would survive," said Bob then asked, "How do they get to be this way?"

"They're just people like us," Terry replied. "Most were dealt their lot from their parents and don't know any other way."

"Do they really control so much?"

"From what I know," said Terry, "Phoenix membership controls or influences pretty much everything."

"Does that not make all others chattel?" Itzela asked, as she joined them.

"We're not chattel," Bob told her, defensively. "We're free. We vote for our government."

Terry raised his eyebrows.

"Maybe we've said enough about this for now," Bob said, before Terry could answer.

Terry got the message.

"It's been a long day," he said. "I should be getting back to the carrier."

They moved back to the group and Terry said his goodbyes. Ryan stood as well, and said he also had to get back to report on the day's events.

"You will return for Paulin's ceremony tomorrow midday?" Itzela asked them. "We send him on."

"We will," Ryan said, as Terry bowed in agreement.

They left and used the tubes to slide down to the dock where the launch was tied up. As they backed out of the slip, Terry looked thoughtfully up to the top of the tubes.

"Something on your mind," Ryan asked.

"These are interesting people," Terry replied.

"That's an understatement," said Ryan.

"These tubes," Terry said. "We have them on the Phoenix. A brand new innovation to speed deployment."

"And now you know the idea is thousands of years old."

"Exactly!"

"Hmmm. You shared a lot tonight," Ryan said. "You going to get in trouble for that?"

Terry shook his head.

"Probably not. They'll be too busy with them."

They looked across the harbor at the crews repairing the pillar. Flashes of laser light occasionally overpowered the floodlights that had been brought in to light the area. Someone flew from the barge over to the base of the pillar using one of the jetpacks.

"Lots to think about," Ryan said.

Terry's silence seemed to indicate that he agreed.

Itzela and Bob watched as the launch travelled out towards the *Excelsior*. She turned and looked into his eyes.

"Our way is that no person may own land. We do not have money. We do not give control."

He looked deep into her eyes and saw that she was worried.

"We think we are free," he said, "but it seems that we may all be slaves."

"So much is different here," she said, shaking her head.

He smiled reassuringly and reached for her hand. Bringing it to his lips he gently kissed the back of her hand. He let go and she placed it over his heart.

"True, but we have a saying," he said, as he pulled her closer. "Opposites attract."

CHAPTER 64

Miracle Cure

A little too much introspective silence on the trip back to the *Excelsior* had led to discussions of the shield and the flight demonstration. That had prompted Terry and Ryan to open the pouches that Cadmael had given them. They examined the contents, which were as he'd described, without learning anything new. As the launch turned to line up to enter the well deck, a small wave had bumped the boat and caused some of their samples to scatter. Terry cut himself slightly while retrieving his orichalcum sample from under the seat. The skipper provided a band-aid for Terry's cut and they headed off for bed.

Terry's hand felt as if it were on fire when he woke up. The cut was still bleedingd and an angry red rash surrounding the cut actually looked like a burn. Terry went to the Com at the arranged time to meet Ryan, but the admiral took one look at Terry's hand and sent him down to the infirmary. The doctor seemed quite happy to see him.

"Just call me Doc," he said, smiling, as he dabbed on an antibiotic from the cabinet. "We don't get many customers when we're just floating here as support. I've only got one victim left from the plane crash."

"I heard that!"

A distinctly Scottish voice came from somewhere behind the curtained off area in the back of the sick bay.

"Hush up or I'll have to put you under again," Doc said.

"You're welcome to try!" came the voice over the curtain.

"What's his problem?" Terry asked.

"That's the pilot from the plane crash," Doc replied, then raised his voice. "A difficult patient."

"I heard be was badly burned," Terry whispered. "How's he doing?

"Burned?" Doc murmured. "That gives me an idea. I'll be right back. You can go talk to him if you like."

Doc slipped out the hatch and left Terry and the pilot alone.

"How are you doing back there?" Terry called over the curtain.

"Bored out of my mind. How are you doing?"

"I'm good. Mind some company?"

"Anyone but Doc. He gets on your nerves after a while."

Terry slid the curtain aside enough to enter. A blonde man in his mid forties lay on a bed. He seemed perfectly fine except for a missing eyebrow. When he turned to look at Terry, it seemed that most of the hair on the left side of his head was also missing and there was only stubble. Terry looked around for the burn victim.

"Expecting someone else?"

"The pilot from that plane," said Terry.

"That would be me," he said. "Duncan Mulligan, at your service. Who might you be?"

"I'm Terry. No offense, but I'd heard you were badly burned."

"I was," Duncan replied. "Whatever those people treated me with fixed the burns up straight away."

He showed Terry his left arm. There were a couple of

dark patches of skin but the rest was a healthy pink.

"Looks pretty good," Terry said. "Except for those dark parts."

"Excuse me," Duncan declared, loudly. "That's all that's left of me tan."

"I told you he was a difficult patient," said Doc as he swept the curtain open.

Duncan shook his head at the Doc, crossed his arms and said no more. Doc opened a plastic case he'd brought with him and took a foul smelling clay pot out from within.

"Let's see how this does for you," he said.

"What is it?" asked Terry.

"I'm not sure," Doc replied, "But it completely cured his burns."

He nodded at Duncan who looked away, but slipped Terry a wink.

"They gave me more than enough for his treatment." Doc held Terry's wrist.

"I don't..."

Terry winced as a blob of the paste was spread on his wound. He shuddered as the pain was instantly numbed by the cool paste.

"How's that?" Doc asked.

"The pain's gone," said Terry, surprised.

"Well, if Duncan's experience is any indication," Doc said. "You'll be completely healed in a couple of hours."

"You're welcome," Duncan said, then he turned to Doc. "But you're not."

Doc ignored him.

"I've got to get this stuff back under lock and key. You boys play nice."

"He's a nutcase," Duncan said after Doc had left.

"Really?" asked Terry.

"No, not really. I'm just really bored. I've been good to go for a couple of days, but he's keeping me for what he calls observation."

"Well, it does seem like a miracle cure," Terry said. "I can see why he might want to be cautious."

"He's nuts," Duncan scoffed. "He tells me I'm in perfect health, which is impossible."

He looked as if he needed to talk, so Terry just listened.

"This was to be my last round trip flight," Duncan explained. "I was diagnosed with colon cancer a few months ago. Treatments are supposed to start next week."

"I'm sorry to hear that," Terry said.

"I'm not. Not any more. Doc says my blood work is perfect, x-rays, trace markers, the works. I told him I was worried about cancer so he's checked three times using everything he can here."

"And?" Terry asked.

"No trace," said Duncan. "Nothing."

He nodded at the paste on Terry's hand.

"That stuff's got rid of it."

Duncan's theory was pretty hard to accept yet when he walked onto the bridge a little over an hour later, Terry's hand was completely healed. All that remained was a slight pink line where the skin had been perforated.

"Your hand looks better," said Ryan.

"The Doc's miracle cure?" Lindquist asked.

He caught Terry's eye. He appeared to be serious and Terry took that as a warning not to discuss it.

"Some magic salve," he replied, nonchalantly. "Probably uses it on horses or something."

The admiral laughed.

"That sounds like Doc."

"Glad you're here," Ryan said. "We'll need to get going soon."

On the monitor, dozens of ships were rowing out of the entrance and taking up positions in a huge semicircular arc that centered on the harbor. Evan and Emma rushed in.

"Are we too late?" Emma asked.

"We were just getting ready to go," Ryan replied.

They all climbed aboard a launch and headed out to a gap that had been left in the row of ships. Admiral Lindquist had the boat stop and hold position in the gap. A shout rang down from the boat next to them and bumpers were lowered down to them so that they could lash the launch into the arc of ships. One of the largest of the Atlantean ships they'd seen soon emerged from the canal under full sail, heading swiftly for the harbor entrance. Bunting flew from its masts and along the railings. Everyone assumed that it was the funeral ship. Ryan's phone rang with a call from Jenn.

"We're all on the big ship," she told him quickly. "Let the admiral know there'll be full a shield activation as part of the service."

"Alright," Ryan said. "See you after?"

"Of course," Jenn replied and hung up.

Terry quickly radioed the Phoenix maintenance crew to stand down while the admiral put the fleet on alert.

Lindquist then called out to the adjacent ship and they tied off with them as well, completing the semicircle. The big ship furled its sails as it neared the entrance and glided through the harbor entrance. The rowers stayed the ship's forward motion and turned it to face Atlantis before the oars were shipped.

Long wooden runners were extended out from the front of the ship forward, forming a 'V' half a ship's length in front of the boat. A bundle that must have continued Paulin's body slid down the runners and stopped at the wedge of the 'V' just before it touched the water.

On the big ship and all the vessels around them, people lined the railings to pay their respects. A hand was raised and the shield flickered into life, strengthening quickly to comprise what Ryan now knew was six beams. A loud chant rang out then Paulin's name was repeated over and over again. Rowers pushed the big ship slowly forward until the bundle touched the shield and disintegrated. They continued forward until the bundle had been fully consumed by the shield of Atlantis.

The shield flicked off and the big ship continued smoothly into the harbor. The chanting of Paulin's name had ceased as the shield was extinguished. A shout from the ship next to them and a tug on the lines to the bumpers, let them know the ceremony was over.

As they waited for their turn in the queue of rowed ships to clear the gates of Atlantis, Ryan talked to Evan and Emma and Terry used time to have a short discussion with Admiral Lindquist.

"That cream's a miracle," Terry said. "Look at my hand."

"It certainly is," the Admiral replied. "You've seen Duncan's burns?"

"You mean the lack of them?"

"I'm trying to keep it low key," said Lindquist. "A burn cure that effective will make medical history."

"I'd like our medical people to do a CT scan on him and maybe an ultrasound."

"We don't have that kind of equipment here," said the Admiral.

"We have a big unit on the *Phoenix*," Terry said. "But

we have people and portable scanners that are nearly as effi-
cient. I could have them brought over."

"You have a portable CT machine?" the Admiral asked.

Terry hesitated for a moment, then nodded.

"When is that coming out in public?"

"I think they said in another three years," Terry replied.

"So why are you telling me now?"

"Because as you said, admiral, this could make medical
history."

'If they even want to share it," the Admiral reminded
him. "We haven't asked."

"So let's find out exactly how real it is before we ask,"
Terry suggested. "At least we'll know what we're negotiating
for."

Admiral Lindquist thought for a moment.

"I'll make a deal with you. If I allow your tests, and the
cream is what we hope it is, and we can make a deal for it,
then I want you to get those portable scanners out on the market
in the next year."

"What do scanners have to do with a burn cure?" Terry
asked.

"Nothing," the admiral replied. "But I almost lost a
friend of mine a few years ago, largely because they couldn't
get him a CT scan soon enough."

"I'm sorry," Terry said. "But, your friend, he's okay
now?"

"Only because I pulled every string I had to get him
the scan."

Terry nodded.

"I'll do what I can."

CHAPTER 65

Time Out

They abandoned their position in the procession of ships so that they could rendezvous with the big ship, which had sidled up to the main dock below Delta's council chamber. Ryan's cell phone rang as their launch pulled up to the dock. He took the call as the others climbed out onto the dock.

When he hung up, Jenn and Tara were waiting at the side of the launch for him.

"Big news?" Jenn asked him, jokingly.

"Kinda," he said, glancing over his shoulder.

Steaming around the side of Atlantis headed for the harbor was another ship that looked like just like the *Grasp*. It was towing something very large. All that was initially visible was the tip of a crane that towered over the golden pillar with the broken tab.

"That's the *Grapple*," said Ryan. "Towing the crane barge that should be able to help fix these pillars up."

The crane's arrival meant that there was even more work to be done. After a quick conference on the dock, Terry and Cadmael decided that they should try and fix the tabs first, since that would test both the lifting power of the crane and their overall plan.

Cadmael and Terry would go on site and coordinate,

while the council on Delta would organize material movements. Evan and Emma offered to stay with the council and liaise with the fleet in case there was anything needed from them.

"We should to report in to Atlantis Command," the admiral told Ryan. "But we can drop them at the pillar site on the way."

Tara cleared her throat. The Admiral glanced her way and she pointed at her cell phone and nodded.

"And then it seems that the rest of you have the rest of the day off," he said. "Tara?"

"I hope you don't mind, but I texted Stephen," she said. "I told him that if he was still near and if it was okay, that we could all use a break."

Jenn and Bob started at their daughter in astonishment.

"I may have called it a time out," she said, with a smile. "Either way, with the admiral's help the *Seven Seas* will be here shortly to take us all on a cruise for the evening. Aranare, Itzela, Tadeo, this is for you as well."

"Ryan," Lindquist added. "You'll be good to as soon as we report in."

Tara, what are you up to?

Nothing. You guys have been busy and with everything that's happened… well, we all need a break and you know it.

Bob thought there was probably more being schemed here than just a break, but he had to admit that a time out for them all might be a good thing.

Terry had the *Phoenix's* launch collect Cadmael and himself, while the admiral's launch stopped at the guest hall to let everyone going ashore grab a few thing, before retuning to the *Excelsior*. By the time they'd reported the day's events to Atlantis Command and got themselves organized to leave, the *Seven Seas* had already pulled alongside the carrier.

Stephen welcomed everyone aboard and when Tara thanked him, he gave her a big hug and said he should be thanking her for keeping things interesting. Itzela offered him a gift of a tray of flowers, explaining that it was their custom when visiting someone.

"You are my guests," said Stephen. "You've each been appointed a stateroom and the ship's staff is at your disposal. They will show you to your rooms."

He smiled at them all before continuing.

"Now, Tara says that you all need a break, so I've had the captain set a course for Cancun. Once we clear the blockade, we'll be sailing for about an hour."

"What blockade?" Bob asked.

"Dozens of ships have sailed into the no-go zone," said Ryan. "All hoping for a glimpse of Atlantis. Some paparazzi, some just curious, some thrill seekers. We have patrol boats keeping them all at a distance. They've been nicknamed The Blockade."

"Why didn't you tell us?" Jenn asked. "This means that whole demonstration didn't work?"

"It worked fine," said Stephen. "But there are always those that'll come have a look anyway, just like me!"

Bob opened his mouth to reply but Stephen held up his hand.

"Enough! Your time-out starts now. Relax, Explore, Enjoy. High tea will be served on the upper deck in an hour. Attendance is *not* mandatory."

As it turned out, everyone did show up for tea, all far more relaxed than they'd been an hour or so earlier. Tara had found the games room and shown Tadeo how to play pool, mini-basketball and some electronic games. Ryan and Jenn had never had time alone with each other since the day they'd met, so they spent the whole time sitting and talking. Aranare spent all his time with Stephen, getting a very unique viewpoint from the wealthy, self-made filmmaker that balanced some of the negative dialogue that the Phoenix group appeared to have generated.

Bob's room was adjacent to Itzela's and they were connected by a patio with a hot tub. As they'd been told, each of their rooms had been outfitted with a wardrobe of clothes that had been hand picked for them, including swimsuits. Nothing had been organized, but when they both came out of their staterooms at the same time wearing swimsuits, they took that as a sign that they should try the hot tub. They were still wearing them, under towels, when they arrived for tea.

"Who does your shopping?" Tara asked. "Must be someone with great taste!"

"The purser and others on the crew," Stephen replied. "Did they find something you like?"

"Lots!" Tara said. "I don't know what to choose."

"Is that Cancun already?" Jenn asked, as lights of the hotels began appearing on the horizon.

"Should be," Stephen said. "Which means we should discuss possibilities."

"Like what?" Bob asked.

"Well, Cancun has great food and great clubs, both for adults and teens. There're some pretty good shows at the resorts and on the strip, and there are lots of great beaches for just walking and talking. The launch can take you for a cruise along the coastline or you can stay on board and enjoy the chef's creations. We'll get under way somewhere around midnight, so whatever you decide to do should be finished by then. I've arranged undercover security for you wherever you go, but I'll not be coming ashore with you."

"Why not?" Ryan asked.

"The yacht is to well known here, and so am I," Stephen replied. "If I stay on board, the paparazzi will have something to focus on and will most likely leave you alone."

"That does not seem fair," said Itzela.

"It's fine," Stephen said. "I've been here many times."

Bob was pondering what he should do when Tara came up with a great suggestion.

Why don't you take her on a date?

That's a great idea. I wonder where I should take her?

Just ask Stephen. He'll know somewhere.

"I know just the place," Stephen replied when Bob asked for suggestions. "Have you asked her yet?"

"Well, no," said bob. "I just thought..."

"Women do like to be asked," Stephen said, raising an eyebrow.

Bob couldn't argue about that. He found himself nervously standing in front of Itzela's door a short time later.

"Just a minute!" he was relieved to hear, after he'd knocked.

Itzela was wearing only a towel when she opened the door a crack and she didn't invite him in. He asked if she'd like to go on a dinner date and, after looking back into her room for a moment, she said yes and asked if he could pick her up in half an hour. There was something odd about the conversation, but he couldn't put his finger on it.

He showered, shaved, and put on some khaki dress slacks and a black short-sleeved dress shirt. He checked himself in the mirror several times and found that he was getting nervous. He arrived early and waited for Itzela to answer. When she opened her door, he almost fell over.

"Do you like it?" she asked him anxiously, twirling for him.

Her elegant black dress was slit below the waist, showcasing her beautiful bare legs. Shiny black leather sandals trimmed with gold accents wrapped around her toes and sent tiny straps winding around her feet and above, to buckle just above her ankles.

Her natural complexion and beautiful eyes needed no makeup, but her hair had been swirled into a more modern style than before. Her flowing tresses covered the dress' single gold clasp at the back of her neck, and brushed across the open back of her dress that showed off her mandala tattoo.

"Wow!" he said, stunned. "Wow!"

She saw how her look had affected him and flowed herself into his arms. They kissed passionately and his hand gently touched her back. As the kiss intensified, she arched into him, and his hand slowly slid up her back towards the clasp of her dress.

Don't you dare!

Tara's thought startled him, but Bob pulled away as smoothly as he could and looked into Itzela's eyes.

"We should probably go," he said, smiling, then spoke to Tara.

I'll deal with you later! And you'd better not be in my head any more tonight.

Eww! Gross. But the dress is awesome right?

Bob watched Itzela walk along just in front of him.

You helped?

A little. After she looked online she knew what she wanted. I just helped her pull it together.

I'll see you at the boat.

It took Bob a little longer than he'd planned to actually reach the boat. He wasn't the only person who'd had a kiss cut short and Itzela apparently wanted to finish that kiss before they left. Jenn and Ryan had elected to stay and sample the onboard cuisine and get to know each other a little better, so Tara, Tadeo, and Aranare accompanied them to shore.

The skipper of the launch helped them ashore and sorted them and their security into three separate vehicles as they all had different destinations in mind. After the first two had pulled away, Aranare turned to the skipper.

"You will be joining me then, Stephen?"

"How'd you know?" said Stephen, laughing as he pulled off the skipper's cap and glasses.

"You do not seem the type to let others control your actions," Aranare replied. "Shall we go?"

It was a perfect time out for them all. As great as their evening had begun, when they stepped out of their car at a quaint oceanside pub called *The Impossible Mayan*, Bob knew that they'd been steered in the right direction. Tara and Tadeo managed to find a McDonalds, several arcades, catch a show, and still have time for a walk along the beach. Ryan and Jenn indulged in the sumptuous delights of the *Seven Seas* chef's creations and talked for hours under the stars.

When Nico found Aranare and Stephen in the lounge of the Casa Maya Hotel, he apologized for taking so long to get there. In a special room that overlooked the ocean, Stephen sat quietly while Aranare recounted the events of the previous few days to the elders that had made the journey to Cancun.

On the drive back to the launch, Stephen asked how the elders known where he would be.

"They have always watched for us," said Aranare. "And it would always be a place with Maya in the name."

Stephen nodded, but Aranare had more to tell him.

"They also told me a phone number on my visit," he said, looking at Stephen apologetically.

They broke into laughter together.

Laughter seemed to be the best medicine on the way
home. In the launch and on board the yacht, all the way back
to Atlantis, they swapped stories of Aranare's clandestine
activities, along with Tadeo and Tara's record setting gaming
sessions. Jenn and Tara spoke of the fantastic food and
desserts they'd sampled, which naturally then had to be
brought out again, to be sampled by the rest of them.

As they approached Atlantis, Bob had them in stitches
with his version of *Fly Me To The Moon*. He'd tried karaoke for
the first time earlier that evening and adjusted the words of
the song for Itzela. His new lyrics were *Fly Me To Tulum*, in
honor of their impending trip.

They took the launch to the guest hall and all said
goodnight. Bob said goodnight to an exhausted Tara and then
headed for bed. When he reached his room, he reached out for
Tara's thoughts and felt only the calmness of sleep. He smiled
and came over to Itzela, who seemed to have found her way
into his room.

With the fire-lights of Atlantis lending a golden tinge
to their inner glow, their lips met tenderly at first, then with
more urgency until Bob finally reached up and undid the
clasp, removing all that lay between them.

CHAPTER 66

Trouble in Paradise

Fueled with coffee and napping in shifts, Terry and Cadmael had worked with their teams alongside the Navy personnel all night. By daybreak, both the pillars with the broken tabs had been repaired. The crane barge had nearly been moved into position for the main pillar lift. The barge lash-up with the two melted and misshapen solid gold tabs was tied up at the shore just beside the barge containing the rebuilt pillar top.

While the others had been away on their time out the day before, Terry had the *Phoenix's* doctors drop by and scan Duncan. While they were watching the crane being jockeyed into its final position, Terry got the call with the results. There was no trace of cancer and the medicine showed no side effects that they could detect. To be sure they'd compared their scans to Duncan's personal doctor's scans, which clearly showed a growing cancerous mass.

Terry knew that this information would be earth shaking and he dutifully reported it to Phoenix. He was told to carry on and tell nobody. His people could easily handle the mechanical problem of putting the rebuilt top back on the pillar, so Terry hopped a launch for the *Excelsior*. He closed his eyes to grab a little sleep on the way over.

Tara woke up to the sun slightly higher in the sky than she was used to. Then she remembered how late it had been when they'd got in. She poked her head round the corner but Jenn was still asleep. She checked Bob but all she saw was the mandala that she'd drawn at the conference. It took her a second to realize that she was actually looking at Itzela's back through Bob's eyes and that he was lying beside her, just watching her sleep. She quickly stopped looking and smiled to herself.

Dad, you up?

Just waking up.

She could sense him pulling covers over Itzela.

The time-out was a great idea. Thanks!

It was nice. It's pretty late though. I think we slept in.

We can fix that. You get your mom up and head for breakfast and I'll meet you there in a bit.

They all arrived for breakfast around the same time, Itzela just a little later than the others. Tara knew that she'd had to go to her room and change. Everyone thanked Tara for instigating such a relaxing evening. Both her parents and their new people didn't seem ready to showcase their affection in public yet and somehow that made Tara smile.

During breakfast, Ryan took a call from Admiral Lindquist. Apparently Terry had a question that he wanted to ask the council and he felt they should all be present.

Tadeo looked at the watch towers and said that council was on Delta. They quickly finished their breakfast and hopped the launch over there.

Terry and the admiral introduced Duncan to everyone at council. It was hard to believe this was the badly burned man that had saved their lives only a week ago. Terry explained that the salve that had cured the burns was unknown to his people. Doc added that Duncan would have needed many surgeries and still might have died from his burns.

"This is Imogren?" Itzela leaned over and asked Cadmael, who nodded confirmation.

"It is a common enough flower," Tzakol said. "I see no reason not to offer it to our friends."

He swung his hand wide to include everyone, but Terry looked very uncomfortable.

"I'm tasked with asking that you offer this only to Phoenix."

Everyone looked puzzled.

"Why would you seek this?" Tzakol asked.

Terry didn't answer the question.

"I'm instructed to offer you whatever you need," he said. "Anything. In trade."

Tzakol narrowed his eyes, as did most of the others present.

"Anything? For a salve that cures burns?" said Lindquist. "Anything?"

Terry was frustrated that he'd been put in such a difficult position.

"It's not just a cancer cure," he said. "It's..."

"Cancer?" said the admiral. "Well, now that would make sense."

"Duncan!" Doc said. "You said you were *worried* about cancer?"

"I had cancer, Doc" he admitted, then pointed at Terry "You told me it's gone and his people confirmed it."

"Admiral!" Tzakol raised his voice. "Why would this make sense?"

Once the commotion had subsided, Admiral Lindquist explained.

"Cancer is one of the leading causes of unnatural death

these days," he said. "It's an uncontrolled growth in or on the body. It strikes at any age but mostly in older people. It's virtually incurable and the treatments we have can take a lot away from the person that has it. If this Imogren can cure cancer, then there are millions who would give all that they have for it, pay anything."

"This is why your Phoenix seeks Imogren?" Itzela asked Terry.

"I think so," Terry said, clearly embarrassed. "Many of the Phoenix members are older. I'm sure some have cancer. This would cure them."

"But why only for themselves?" Itzela asked.

Terry lowered his eyes and shook his head sadly.

"Money," he said. "It's about money."

Tzakol got his feet and looked around the council. There was no dissent.

"We will search this cancer on your internets," he said. "If it is what you say and the Imogren can help, then it will be for all. You may tell the Phoenix we do not trade without honor."

He looked down at Terry with disgust in his eyes.

Aranare cleared his throat. Tzakol turned and saw Aranare standing between Bob and Tara. Tzakol was horrified. To not include the Diachrome was a grievous error. He bowed in their direction.

"Bob, Tara," Tzakol called on them. "What say you?"

You're on, Dad.

Thanks a bunch.

"Cancer is exactly what the admiral said it is," he began. "If Imogren can help, and it grows freely, then it should be given freely."

He turned to Terry.

"Phoenix can't have this one, Terry. You'll pass that on?"

Terry nodded, unsure and unaware of why they were including Bob and Tara in this. He was clearly happy to have some help though and nodded his thanks to Bob.

Bob turned back to the council members.

"Don't judge Terry too harshly," he said. "We have a saying here 'Don't shoot the messenger'."

Tzakol looked at Tara, who shyly nodded her agreement.

"As it is written," Tzakol said.

"So shall it be," echoed the others in the room.

That's going to get old, pal. I think we just did our first official duty.

I think I'm going to be sick.

Maybe try not to?

Tara glared at him and he smiled back at her. Everyone surged around them, wanting to know what had just happened. They went outside to discuss matters. Terry skirted the crowd, still embarrassed, but Tara called him over.

He should know what's going on, Dad.

That's my girl.

"What was that about?" the Admiral asked. "Why did they turn to you?"

"Okay, before we say anything," Bob began. "We need this kept strictly among those of us here. We're still figuring it out ourselves and need some time. Terry, can we trust you not to pass this on to Phoenix?"

"After what they just asked me to do?" he said. "No problem."

Bob and Tara endeavored to explain, but talking about themselves was not in their nature. Tadeo and Aranare took over and explained as best they could that Bob and Tara were Diachrome. Bob was surprised to see Evan looking at him with sympathy and understanding and Emma almost cried with joy for Tara. Terry however, was visibly shaken.

"You okay?" Bob asked him.

"What's it like?" he asked. "To be in charge of your own destiny?"

"Hmm," Bob said, smiling. "I'm no more in control of my own destiny than I was before this. The real secret, I suppose, is that I'm no less in control either. We each do the best we can."

"You don't work for Phoenix," said Terry.

"Perhaps I did," Bob said thoughtfully. "Maybe too many of us still do."

Terry shook his head.

"You'd better let them know their answer," said Bob. "Good luck."

Terry walked to the edge of the courtyard and made the call. He walked back slowly and joined Bob, Cadmael, Aranare, and Admiral Lindquist.

"How did it go?" Bob asked.

"They're not happy," Terry replied. "I've been ordered to stand down on assisting Atlantis. The bottom line is that they want the cure, but they can't get over their own greediness enough to let everyone have it."

"So when will you be pulling your people out?" the Admiral asked, looking at the pillar.

"There's still a code of ethics," Terry replied, with a thin smile. "I'll honor the agreement I made, as will the crew. We won't be able to assist with anything new though."

"I so want to say honor amongst thieves," said Bob, slapping him on the back. "But I told you he was a good guy!"

The crews worked on throughout the day. Just before dusk, the top of the pillar was lowered back into place. Terry's team swarmed over it, seamlessly welding solid gold to solid gold with their portable laser units.

Terry stayed at the courtyard while the work continued, fielding calls almost continuously from Phoenix. He steadfastly refused to dishonor the agreement he had made. His people finished by testing the tab motion, then gathered their gear and left in the launch on which they'd arrived. Terry came over to talk to Bob.

"I'm headed back to the carrier," he said. "I think Phoenix is conflicted."

Bob said nothing.

"Why are you still here?" he asked Bob. "You stayed all day.

"You said Phoenix is conflicted?" said Bob.

"Yes, internally. This hasn't ever happened. Well, except for Hitler of course."

Bob raised his eyebrows.

"Of course."

"They're up to something," Terry said. "I'm not sure what."

"What do you mean?"

Terry had to break some vows to do what he did next. He lifted up his wrist-rack and showed Bob an augmented satellite feed of the area they were in. About 5 kilometers south of Atlantis was a large rectangular object labeled P34. More disturbing was the much larger rectangular object 15 kilometers north of Atlantis labeled P35.

"It arrived about 20 minutes ago," said Terry. "I didn't even know that there was a P35, but we're kept in the dark about lots of things. They told me they were sending something, but didn't say what or why."

"What does your gut say?"

"Watch it like a hawk," Terry replied. "It's easier to avoid detection if they stay put, so they probably will. I'll do my best to let you know if they move."

"So, what does your gut say?" Bob repeated.

Terry looked him in the eyes.

"This is trouble," he said. "Real trouble."

"That's what my guy was telling me," Bob said. "And now you know why I stayed."

CHAPTER 67

Fly Me to Tulum

Signs reading *Atlantis Go Home*, and chants of the same, scrolled across the main screen as they scanned over one news report after another. Scores of newspaper headlines and blog titles had the same or similar messages about Atlantis bringing doom and destruction. *Pressure to Disband Atlantis Command* was the last one that stayed on the screen for a moment, before being replaced by the president on a monitor, directly from the White House.

"This all started overnight," he said. "That last one is true by the way."

"This is Phoenix," Terry said. "Sowing distrust. Their members own the media."

"They own more than the media," the president added. "I have emails from more than half the Senate requesting that we withdraw the United States from Atlantis Command and offer no further support. The same is happening in other countries."

"Orders, sir?" Lindquist asked.

"No change," the president replied, grimly. "You're on loan to Atlantis Command. Should that change, you'll remain on station on behalf of the United States, and Mexico, unless we hear otherwise from Mexico."

"Yes, sir," said the admiral and saluted.

"Keep your eyes open, admiral," said the President, as he signed off.

Admiral Lindquist turned to face the room.

"Suggestions?"

"We should move Atlantis today," Jenn said. "To Tulum."

"Out of sight out of mind. Good idea," Ryan agreed.

"It can be done," Cadmael said.

"You'll need to clear the airspace, admiral," Bob added. "And I'd like to move Tara and Jenn off Atlantis for the trip."

"What?" said Jenn.

"I'm worried about the repair, that's all" Bob said. "I don't want you guys there if something fails."

That's not why, Dad.

Shhh.

"Perhaps Tadeo and some helpers as well?" Aranare suggested.

"Admiral?" said Bob.

"Let us know what you need," the Admiral replied.

"I'll return to my ship," said Terry. "I can keep a closer eye on P35 from there."

Bob nodded.

"Good idea. I'll walk you down to the launch bay."

That seemed to end the meeting. Bob had a quick chat with Terry on the way down to the launch bay and when he left for P34, Ryan went with him, after promising Jenn that he'd be right back.

On their own launch, Cadmael and Aranare discussed what they should send along for Tara's contingent. Bob watched as the *Grapple* exited the harbor with the crane barge in tow. He then moved over to sit with Jenn.

"Sorry about kicking you off Atlantis," he said. "But you, Tara, and Ryan all need to be on the bridge of the *Excelsior* when Atlantis flies.

"What," she said. "Why?"

He said nothing and let her figure it out.

"You had a vision?"

He smiled.

"Sort of. Enough to know a few things."

"So," she said, slowly. "You really are Diachrome?"

"Maybe," he said. "I guess so, yeah."

"And Tara?"

"The same," he replied, smiling "But it's going to be okay."

"Damn you."

She pretended to hit him and he drew her into a hug.

"It's going be okay," he said. "I promise."

He held her for moment until she regained her composure and pushed away.

Nicely done, Dad.

You gotta stop eavesdropping! But while I've got you, can you text Stephen? Tell him we're moving Atlantis to Tulum this afternoon and that the lift-off would look great shot on an old film camera.

Really?

Just text him.

He felt her sniff and grab her phone. He smiled.

"Where did you go just then?" Jenn asked. "You were somewhere else."

"I was talking with Tara," he admitted.

"Like telepathy?"

"Hmmm? Never thought of it like that. I guess so."

"I can see that being a problem," she said.

Mom!

"You have no idea," Bob said. "We're here."

He ignored Tara and pointed to the docks up ahead.

A dozen sections of Gamma's brass ring were pivoted up and there was more activity that they'd previously seen at the docks. Ships were being loaded with people and supplies.

"What is all this?" Jenn asked.

"Insurance," Bob replied.

Not long after, eighteen ships rowed out of the harbor and headed for the *Excelsior*. There were nineteen if you counted the launch that carried Tara, Ryan, and Jenn that had gone ahead. They watched from the monitor as the stately wooden ships rowed to beside the big carrier and then encircled it, taking up a protective stance around the huge ship.

Bob watched the monitor through Tara's eyes.

That had to be Cadmael's idea.

Likely. We're nearly ready here. Do you have Terry online?

"Dad wants to confirm that you're online, Terry," Tara said out loud.

"I'm here," came the reply from the wrist-rack that Ryan was wearing. "Standing by."

Now they all know we can talk telepathically.

It'll save time.

"He says they're nearly ready," Tara said.

"Doesn't that get confusing?" asked Jenn.

"Yes," Tara said, as Bob said the same word simultaneously.

Atlantis' shields flickered into existence and shimmered as they ran through their crystal tests. Soon the shields hardened and the island slowly began to rise.

Tell Terry to look sharp.

As she passed that on, Bob gave her an odd request.

I want you to tell P34 and the entire fleet to be ready to shut down all power when I tell you.

Dad?

No questions, just tell them it's life or death. And yes, text Stephen, he should shut down now, just not the camera.

They're asking all kinds of questions.
Just ignore the questions. They'll do it.

On the monitor, Atlantis had lifted clear of the water and was rising higher. It was so huge that even 200 meters above the surface it looked as if it were merely skimming the waves. They looked up and could see the outline of bottom of the harbor, light shining through the waters contained by the shield.

"It's so beautiful," said Tara.

"We have a launch!" Terry barked over the wrist-rack. "Six missiles out of P35. They are... Looks like they're targeting the central courtyard on Atlantis."

"We see nothing!" said Lindquist. "Give us a location!"

"No time!" said Terry. "Counter-measures!"

Far to the south there were six geysers as P34's counter-measures left the water. They heard the sounds of rockets ripping overhead then six massive explosions erupted in the air over the northern side of Atlantis.

Bob connected with Tara.

That was round one.

"What!" she yelled aloud, terrified.

As everyone looked at her, she appeared to be listening elsewhere.

"Dad says to cut all power now!" she cried.

"Oh God, I can see it!" she screamed. "Terry! Admiral! You have to cut all the power to everything. Now!"

She collapsed sobbing into her mother arms as Lindquist gave the order to shut everything down.

"Admiral!" Com said.

His face was white as he looked at the north facing screen as it faded out. Hundreds of missiles trails were leaving the water and arcing towards them.

"We should go outside," Tara sobbed, regaining her composure enough to talk. "It's going to be okay."

They ran outside. People screamed and sobbed. The monitor hadn't lied. Hundreds of missiles were still rising into the sky. As they looked up they saw there were even more missles raining straight down on them from above.

"An orbital launch," the Admiral said, sadly. "We have no chance."

"We do," said Tara, pointing toward Atlantis.

The shield seemed to be solidifying. Translucence was being replaced by what looked like solid gold. A golden oval hung in the sky. It glowed red, then yellow, then white.

Tara? Is it time?

She waited just a few seconds, then said aloud and in her head simultaneously.

"Now!"

Atlantis simply vanished.

Air rushed in faster than the speed of sound to occupy the space where Atlantis had just been. The wind knocked some of them off their feet, while the sonic boom that immediately followed toppled more people.

Tara clung to a sanction on the tower.

"Wait for it!" she yelled.

With an even louder explosion of sound, the glowing white-hot ovoid containing Atlantis reappeared exactly where it had vanished. A spray of water accompanied the air that it had kicked up and anyone still standing was knocked off their feet. They were all showered with sparks as the massive EMP pulse of Atlantis's arrival spread out from the center.

The EMP wave raced through the fleet, sparking over anything metal and occasionally popping or exploding something that had been left on. Above the carrier, the incoming missiles exploded one after another as the pulse wave engulfed them. The sky was filled with fire raining down as the fuel and explosives from the hundreds of missiles was consumed by their own demise.

"He said he saw the sky raining fire!" Jenn said, as she held Tara tight.

"He didn't see it, Mom," Tara said, through her tears. "I am!"

Most of the falling debris from the missiles was being vaporized as it struck the Atlantis shield. It was cooling quickly, yellow fading into gold as it slowly descended. Looking underneath it they could see far to the north where a huge rounded rectangular shape had popped up to the surface. The pulse had stripped P35 of its shield and was playing havoc with the vessel's internal systems. Massive explosions and fires ripped through the hull in multiple locations. The view from the *Excelsior* was slowly cut off as the bottom of Atlantis gently touched the surface of the water in front of them. Steam shot out from the touch of the surface and steam and fog quickly enveloped everything.

"Look!" Ryan shouted.

They spun to see P34 sitting on the surface just a few kilometers south of them, it's cobalt blue surface fully exposed and uncloaked. The fog covered it up within moments and as it also enveloped the carrier they were pelted with debris from the exploded missiles. The P35 apparently hadn't only been targeting Atlantis.

The hail of debris ended quickly and soon the only thing that was visible was a small patch of blue sky high above them. Tara looked up and pointed. A bright star pulsed once, twice, and then brighter than the day in the sky directly overhead, then it winked out. Before the fog closed completely over their heads, they saw trails in the sky as shards from the exploding star burned up in the atmosphere.

"Probably their orbital missile platform," said Lindquist. "A low orbit for accuracy would put them right in the range of the EMP pulse."

Everyone okay?

I don't know, Dad. We can't see much.

Ah, the fog. I forgot. Tell the admiral he should be able to power everything up again and there are some people that will need rescuing from that big bad ship.

I'll tell him. See you soon?

We'll be right there. Tell the admiral to send the press and camera crews over with the P35 teams. This all needs to be on record. Phoenix won't cover this one up.

CHAPTER 68

Leave the Future Behind

Phoenix naturally did far more than just attempt to cover things up and that proved to be far more than just their unmasking.

When the fog lifted, P34 was gone. Terry, however, had shown up on the *Excelsior* before the ship left. He explained that each Phoenix ship had a self/auto destruct that could be triggered remotely. When the EMP pulse had hit, that equipment, which they couldn't before access or power down, had been destroyed. It was also the only reason that there were still survivors on P35 to pick up.

Terry had sent his ship on to rendezvous with some of the other ships that Phoenix had summoned to the area, presumably for another attempted cleansing mission. His people told the other vessels how they could destroy the self/auto destruct mechanisms on board their ships. They then explained what had occurred at Atlantis and waited to see what happened.

Later that evening there were three ex-Phoenix vessels patrolling the area around Atlantis. Their crews had asked for asylum and offered their ships to Atlantis Command. By the next morning, every ship that the Phoenix controllers were aware of had joined them, save one. P32 had been too worried to allow the self-destruct mechanism to be disabled. While

Terry and the others had pleaded with them, Phoenix Command had activated the mechanism remotely and destroyed the ship.

The video of that senseless event, and Stephen's footage of the Atlantis attack, were posted online the next day, which somehow resulted in all the major nodes of the internet going down simultaneously. Military forces around the world stormed the controlling technology centers, took them over, and simply turned the internet back on. Major newspapers and chains around the world refused to carry the story, so it was given to small, independent publishers, who made it their mission to ensure that the story was seen or heard everywhere they could reach.

After that, Phoenix activities seemed to drop off the radar. Terry and P34 rejoined the *Excelsior* for a meeting called by the president. Bob and several others attended on the bridge of the carrier.

"We think we've taken all the ships," the president said over the view screen. "We're working on tracking down the rest of the organization but would like your help, Terry, in completely shutting Phoenix down."

"I'd be honored, Mr. President," said Terry.

"I'm sorry, guys," Bob said. "But that's just not how it happened."

"What do you mean?" Terry said.

"Chrysalis!" said Tara.

"That's how it happened," Bob smiled and pointed at her. "I knew it had to be you that came up with the name."

"What's Chrysalis?" the President asked.

"Where the Phoenix rises from its own ashes," Tara explained. "The Chrysalis transforms one life into another."

Tara turned to Bob, shocked.

"Atlantis is leaving?" she said, in alarm.

He smiled at her.

426

"It is council's decision that Atlantis must leave. And I know, that you know, that it's the right thing to do."

He turned and nodded at the president.

"Right after your speech tomorrow."

"What speech?"

While the president explained to the world what the Phoenix Project was, what it had become, and what had transpired with Atlantis, Bob met with council one more time.

"I can tell you that we go today," he said. "But it will be me that travels forward with you and not Tara."

"Are you sure?" Aranare asked. "Should not the youngest move forward?"

"I thought so," Bob said. "But that's not what happened."

He looked at Itzela but his smile encompassed them all, his new family, his new world.

"Once again, we must leave the future behind."

Later on the deck of the *Excelsior*, Bob said his goodbyes.

"Nice speech!" he said to the president. "Calling them global terrorists was a nice touch."

"I guess you could have saved me the trouble of writing it?" he said, with a smile, glancing over at Atlantis. "It has to be this way?"

"You have nearly the entire Phoenix membership in custody," Bob said. "The world's economic slavery system has been ended, and with it, a way of life that was always, well, unsupportable at best. The world has been altered and I can promise you for the better. But where you go now, how you get there, must be up to you."

Bob got a little emotional.

"I'm leaving you, with the very best thing that I can, to

help with the changes that are coming."

He wiped his eyes.

"Help her with Chrysalis?"

"I promise I will do my best," the president said, shaking Bob's hand and stepping back.

Jenn came over next, while Ryan hung back.

"So, you and Itzela?" Jenn said.

"Yeah," he replied, smiling. "And Ryan?"

It was her turn to smile.

"Maybe. He seems nice."

"I see good things for you two."

"Is that you or the Diachrome talking?"

"Both," said Bob, smiling.

"I'm not sure Tara can live without you," Jenn said. "You are two peas in a pod, after all."

"Yes, but we still get to talk to each other every day."

Bob tapped his forehead and hugged her goodbye.

"Oh, I almost forgot!" he said. "Those are for Tara and you guys."

He pointed at the barge with the thousands of tons of ruined solid gold tabs on them.

"Should keep you going for a while and help with Chrysalis."

"What?"

"Currencies will very soon be based on real things like gold again," he said. "Put it to good use."

Terry came over next.

"Why are you here?" Bob asked.

"Uh, To say goodbye?" said Terry.

"Goodbye?" Bob said. "I was hoping your crew might be ready for active duty?"

"What?" said Terry, caught completely by surprise.

"Well," Bob began. "Atlantis has a Minoan population

from 3000 years ago and a Mayan population from about 1500 years ago. Do you know anyone else who's prepared for a generation journey from our time that could help round that out?"

"Are you serious?" Terry asked. "People have been asking what's going to happen next?"

"Figure it out quickly," Bob said. "Ryan says P34 will fit in the harbor, but just barely."

"The ship too?" Terry said, incredulous.

"It's your home, isn't it?"

"I'll ask," said terry, hesitantly and hurried away.

Since you already know they're coming, why didn't you just tell him?

Tara was walking up beside him as she spoke in his head.

"There are always choices," he said.

"I don't get a choice," Tara said, as her tears came and she hugged him tightly.

After all the other goodbyes had been said, Bob and Itzela held hands and joined the others that were leaving, standing on the top deck of P34. They waved goodbye as it sailed past the *Excelsior* and into Atlantis's harbor.

Ryan and Jenn waved back from the carrier, along with the president, Stephen, and the entire ship's crew. The rest of the world waved goodbye to them as well, over TV and computer screens. Tara stood apart from them all, with Tadeo watching over her.

Eventually Atlantis rose slowly from the water, glowed as it had done before and disappeared from their lives forever.

"They're okay," Tara said, after a few minutes.

And cheers erupted across the deck behind her and around the world...

Hey, pal. You going to be okay?
I don't know. Where, or when, are you?
We made it. We are when we're supposed to be.

I miss you, Dad.
I miss you too.

I'm going to miss my Tara-hugs the most!